Praise for Lulu Taylor

'Utterly compelling. A really excellent winter's story'
Lucy Diamond

'This is such great escapism it could
work as well as any holiday'
Daily Mail

'[This] engrossing romantic saga is
a hugely enjoyable, escapist treat'
Sunday Mirror

'Pure indulgence and perfect reading
for a dull January evening'
The Sun

'Wonderfully written . . .
this indulgent read is totally irresistible'
Closer

'The book is full of mystery and intrigue, successfully
keeping me guessing until the very end . . . An evocative
read, full of dramatic secrets that will make the reader gasp'
www.novelicious.com

'A poignant, sophisticated and romantic love story'
www.handwrittengirl.com

THE
WINTER
CHILDREN

Lulu Taylor moved around the world as a child before her family settled in the Oxfordshire countryside. She studied English at Oxford University and had a successful career in publishing before she became a writer. Her first novel, *Heiresses*, was nominated for the RNA Readers' Choice award. It was followed by *Midnight Girls*, *Beautiful Creatures* and *Outrageous Fortune*, all set against the backdrop of glamorous high society. She is married and lives in London.

THE
WINTER
CHILDREN

Lulu Taylor

PAN BOOKS

First published 2015 by Macmillan

This edition first published 2022 by Pan Books
an imprint of Pan Macmillan
The Smithson, 6 Briset Street, London EC1M 5NR
EU representative: Macmillan Publishers Ireland Ltd, 1st Floor,
The Liffey Trust Centre, 117–126 Sheriff Street Upper,
Dublin 1, D01 YC43
Associated companies throughout the world
www.panmacmillan.com

ISBN 978-1-0350-0931-2

1 3 5 7 9 8 6 4 2

A CIP catalogue record for this book is available from the British Library.

Typeset by Ellipsis Digital Limited, Glasgow
Printed and bound by CPI Group (UK) Ltd, Croydon, CR0 4YY

Visit www.panmacmillan.com to read more about all our books
and to buy them. You will also find features, author interviews and
news of any author events, and you can sign up for e-newsletters
so that you're always first to hear about our new releases.

To Gill, with love

Prologue

Francesca leans across the table and puts her hand over his.

'Oh, Dan, I'm so sorry.'

Dan looks up at her, his eyes full of pain. 'It's okay. It's fine. It's just . . . she suffers. You know. It's a kind of madness and she can't let it go.'

'Of course.' She smiles at him, hoping she is projecting all her sympathy. She truly is sorry because she hates to see him unhappy, but deep down in a place she hardly dares look, there is a secret desire that this should be one part of his charmed life that fails to go smoothly. 'Have you thought any more about adoption?'

Dan sighs. She rubs her thumb gently over the top of his hand, relishing its smooth warmth. She still likes contact with him when she can get it. It has a slight thrill of the forbidden about it but there's also a tiny element of ownership. *I've known you so long*, it seems to say. *We can do this. We have permission to touch in this intimate way, usually reserved for lovers.* At a recent party in his flat, she put her arm round his waist and slipped her hand into the back pocket of his jeans, letting her palm settle over the curve of his buttock. She kept it there for several minutes before he slid gently out of her reach and went to get more wine. Olivia, of course, had gone to bed.

'She talked about adopting a Chinese girl,' Dan says, 'after she read something in a magazine. But I'm not that keen. It would be an absolute last resort. I mean, it's such a risk. You just have no idea what child you're going to get.'

Francesca blinks at him. *You never know what you're going to get even with your own children.* But Dan has always liked to work in certainties, or as certain as he can make things. He likes plans and strategies, and clear cause and effect. She can tell that he is finding the frustration and unanswered questions of infertility a miserable experience. *I wish I could take it all away. Make it easy for you.*

He sighs again. 'Adoption is not a serious option yet. She won't give up while there's a chance she might be able to get pregnant. The thing is, the expense . . . the money . . . we've done four rounds of IVF. We can't afford any more.' He slides his gaze away from hers. Despite the candour between them, he's still proud. 'And besides, things are dodgy at work. There's another round of redundancy coming. I've already survived two. I might not be so lucky next time. We can't spend everything we have on something that might never come off. Money down the literal bloody drain.'

She tightens her grip around his hand and says eagerly, 'Let me help.'

'What can you do?' he asks with a small laugh that's not scornful but hopeless.

'I can spare some money. You know that.'

He tenses and pulls back a little. 'No. I can't do that.'

'You can. Why not? You know how things are – we've got more than we can possibly need. If it's just a matter of money standing between you and the thing you and Olivia want more than anything else in the world . . . It's ridiculous when that's something I can easily help with.'

He stares at her now, as though seeing her for the first time in a long while, real surprise in his eyes. 'You'd do that?'

'I'd do anything for you,' she says fervently.

He frowns slightly.

I've gone too far. He's wary now. She hurries on. 'Because I want you and Olivia to share in what I've got. The children are the world to me. There's nothing else like it. If I can help you guys experience the incredible adventure of parenthood, then I want to. It's amazing to know you're leaving a part of yourself behind, and it's endlessly fascinating seeing the people you and your partner can create between you. Every day I see bits of myself or Walt in the children, or I wonder how we managed to mix ourselves up to make something so fresh and interesting. You and Olivia will make beautiful, talented children. I want to meet them.' *That should do it.*

Her words seem to have the desired effect. Dan looks less wary but now there's a different expression on his face, one she can't read. This surprises her. She's always been able to intuit what he's thinking. It's what makes him rely on her the way he does. When he tells her that no one knows him as well as she does, she is certain it's true. *Only I know the real Dan. And I still love him.*

'What is it?' She leans back in to him again, taking every opportunity to be close. 'Something's wrong.'

'Well . . .'

'What? You can tell me. You know that.'

'There's a problem. One that money can't solve, I'm afraid. You see, Olivia's eggs are no longer viable. They've found out that her ovaries are prematurely aged. More IVF is pointless. She's never going to have a child of her own.'

'Oh! God, that's awful. I'm so sorry.' Deep inside there's a tiny swell of triumphant glee. *I've won. She's never going to have his children after all.* 'Poor Olivia. Poor you.' She squeezes his hand and he gives her a grateful look.

'Thanks, Cheska. It was a blow when we found out. Olivia's devastated. I think we have to face the fact that this is the end of the line for us. We're just not going to have children. The thing to do now is accept it and move on. Olivia can't, of course. Not yet. She still thinks that she can get pregnant. She wants us to use an egg donor but I've told her that's out of the question.'

'Really? Why?'

He looks intense suddenly. 'It's what you said. About how you can see you and Walt in the children, and how you're fascinated by the people you've created. I can't bear the thought that one half of our children's genetic inheritance will be that of a complete stranger. A whole family history we don't know about. I hate that idea. Maybe it's wrong of me – it probably really is wrong of me – but I don't want us

4

bringing up the children of an anonymous donor from God knows what background. Even if they're half mine. Does that make sense?'

She stares at him. The lines of his face are softening as he enters the next phase of his life. The sharp-boned look he had in his twenties, with the hollows in his cheeks and the lustre of his dark hair, turned in his thirties into something a little pudgier and paler as he sat behind a desk and worked long hours. Then, with the usual shock of seeing forty approach, he began to get into shape, losing weight and getting fit again, but now his dark hair has streaks of silver in it and the stubble speckling his jaw is grey. It doesn't stop her thinking he is still the most beautiful man she knows. 'Yes,' she says slowly. 'Of course it makes sense.'

'Olivia doesn't understand. She thinks I'll love them. She says she'll love them even though she's not related to them at all. She can't see it. The way I feel, I mean.'

'I know how you feel. It's completely understandable.' She's conscious of a swirl of inspiration rising inside her. She's just seen the way to make her own triumph complete. *If . . . But how? Could I . . . Could it work?* 'It's only natural to want to know your children's heritage. How will you understand them otherwise? But . . . you know . . . there is a way that you and Olivia could both get what you want.'

She stares at him, and waits for the realisation to dawn on him, but there's nothing. He frowns again and says, 'What do you mean?'

There's no point in waiting, she sees that. He'll never think of it himself. 'I could donate eggs to you and Olivia. I know I'm a little older than egg donors generally are but I'm not forty yet. There'd be no harm in trying, would there?'

He gapes at her, astonished. Then says in a tone of wonder, 'You?'

She nods, smiling, her eyes shining. 'Yes! It's a perfect idea. You know me. You'll always be able to ask me anything about the genetic inheritance. You know that I'm intelligent and sane.'

'But . . .' He looks baffled, bewildered as the idea takes root in his mind. 'You'd do that for us?'

'Of course!' She laughs merrily. 'I'm not offering to actually have a baby for you! Olivia can do that bit. It just seems a very neat way around the issue.'

The spark of interest in his eyes goes out. 'Olivia would never agree,' he says briefly.

'Why not?'

'Think about it. She never would.'

Francesca pretends to find this odd, but of course she can easily guess why Olivia would never contemplate accepting her eggs, not for an instant. 'I suppose it's hard, because we're friends . . .' she says slowly, nodding. 'She might feel the baby was not entirely hers.'

There's more to it than that of course. They both know it, though it's one of the few things they've never discussed. *The secret things. The unspoken things. And what exactly does Olivia know?* She's always assumed that Dan has told her very little. He's good at self-preservation after all.

Francesca knows when to make a tactical retreat. 'Of

course. You're right. It's a silly idea. There are so many obstacles, I'm sure it would be practically impossible anyway. And, as you say, Olivia simply wouldn't want to accept the eggs of someone as close to you both as I am.' She leans back in her chair and laughs again. 'I mean, you could hardly sort things out so that she didn't know whose eggs they were! Well, if you really wanted to, you probably could; I'm sure a clinic might be persuaded to do it. Not here, maybe. But abroad. I don't suppose it's *impossible*, not if you really wanted it. But as good as.'

She lets her words hang in the air, wondering if they'll have the desired effect. He ought to be laughing and saying straight out that he'd never deceive Olivia in that way. But he's not. He's looking at her with the kind of gaze that tells her his brain is whirling over the possibilities, imagining a future where Olivia gets her dearest wish and he does not have to compromise. *He's actually thinking about it.* A strange happiness grips her. Suddenly she wants this more than anything in the world. And she can see that in his mind, Dan has already made the leap over the barrier that ought to be insurmountable. *He's thinking about lying to her.*

She should be shocked but she's always known that he's capable of being ruthless. And if it means that the two of them are bound even closer, then she doesn't mind. *After all, love is seeing someone's faults and loving them anyway.*

She can't imagine a life in which her existence isn't governed by her passion for Dan. It's been a part of her for so long that she never questions it.

She watches as he ponders her outrageous, audacious

suggestion. All these years she's quietly hoped that none of the fertility treatments would work. But this . . . this would be best of all.

PART ONE

Chapter One

Six months later

Olivia wakes with a start and turns to the clock. It's five thirty in the morning. Gardening hours. But she's not gardening this morning. She wants more than anything to do a wee.

She slips quietly out of bed, taking care not to wake Dan, who's breathing in the heavy pattern of sleep, picks up her phone from the bedside table and tiptoes down the hall to the bathroom. There they are, waiting where she left them: a clean water glass and a foil-wrapped stick.

This is the earliest possible date she can know whether or not this round has been successful.

Don't get too excited, she tells herself strictly as she slides down her pyjama bottoms and picks up the glass. She's been here too many times before, with the test registering negative. And a few times, it's been positive and she's been through all the elation and hope, only to have it dashed a week or two later when everything ground to a halt.

But this time it's lovely fresh eggs, not my tired old things. This time we have a chance.

She holds the glass in position and carefully does her wee. She knows that morning urine is best because it has the highest concentration of the human pregnancy hormone in it. She puts the full glass down and unwraps the pregnancy test. She could do it blindfold now but she reads the instructions just in case, sets her phone to the stopwatch function, dips the end of the stick in the glass of warm urine, holds it for five seconds, then replaces the cap and sets it down. The patch of damp passes through the control window and shows the pink line that confirms the test is working. Now she must wait two minutes. She presses the button on the stopwatch and tries to think of something else.

I'll clean my teeth. That will waste some time.

At the basin, she watches her reflection clean its teeth slowly, her blue-grey eyes observing herself.

Are you pregnant or not?

There certainly isn't any sign of it on her face. She felt no different on the return journey from Spain, after the eggs had been implanted, but there's a strange fizz of hope inside her that this time, after all the pain and misery and all the spent money, their luck is bound to change.

She stares at herself as she rinses. *We would be good parents, I know it.* She raises her eyes to heaven, to whatever power is there, and thinks, *I promise I will do everything I can to be the best mother in the world and bring up a happy, loved child, if you'll only grant me the chance. No one will try harder than me. I swear it.*

She glances over at the stopwatch. Only one minute gone. How can it go so slowly? This is worse than in the gym when she has to do the plank for a minute. That is slow, but it's like a speed race compared to this.

Not knowing what else to do, she starts to rearrange the bottles of bath oil on the shelf, and then thinks how much she would like a bath right now. As it's so early, she has hours before they have to get up, plenty of time to have a nice long soak. And by the time the bath has run, she'll know whether she's celebrating or commiserating with herself.

Slowly and carefully she chooses mandarin and ginseng bath oil, a gift in her stocking last Christmas.

That sounds nice. But will it be more like a giant cup of herbal tea than a bath?

The stopwatch alarm begins to pulse and makes her jump.

That's it. It's ready.

She goes over, her fingers trembling just a little, and looks at the window. She stares blankly, confused. What does it mean? Frowning, she goes over to the leaflet and unfolds it with fingers that are suddenly stiff and uncooperative.

'If there is no line, you are not pregnant,' she reads. 'If there is a line, you are pregnant.' She stares at the stick. There is a line. Faint but there. She checks again. 'If there is a line, you are pregnant.' Joy races up inside her, an effervescent fountain of it, and she hugs herself with glee.

I knew it. I just knew it.

Putting the test down, she hesitates then pads back to the bed and climbs in, snuggling up to Dan, stroking him and kissing his shoulder until he comes to wakefulness. He grunts lightly. 'Morning,' he murmurs, then yawns. 'What time is it?'

'Nearly six,' she says. 'Well, quarter to. Dan, can I ask you something?'

'I hope it's important,' he mumbles into his pillow. 'Because I could be asleep right now.'

'Of course it is.' She kisses him again, and runs her finger over the soft dark fuzz at the nape of his neck. 'Dan . . . do you think you could ever love anyone as much as you do me?'

Dan turns over, his expression quizzical. 'Love someone as much as you? Don't be silly, of course not. I'll always love you best, you know that.'

'Well,' she says with glee, 'you're going to have to try!'

He looks confused. 'What do you mean?'

She beams at him. 'Dan, we're pregnant! It's worked! We're going to have a baby!'

He stares at her for a moment, taking it in, and then he whoops wildly. 'It's worked! We're pregnant?'

She nods, laughing with happiness. 'Yes! I knew that we'd be lucky this time. I just knew it!'

He laughs too, and they hug hard, both knowing how long and tough the road here has been.

'It's early days,' she says quickly, not wanting to jinx her chances with too much certainty.

'We mustn't get overexcited,' he cautions. 'We've been here before, remember. We'll have a long wait before we can be sure.'

'I know.' She smiles broadly at him. 'We should be sensible. But I have a feeling about this one. I don't know why. They must be lucky eggs!'

His smile freezes just for a second and then he says heartily, 'They must be. Oh my goodness, this is so exciting.'

She hugs him again. 'I love you, Dan, and I know you're going to be a great father.'

'I love you too, sweetheart.' He holds her tight. 'And you're going to be an amazing mother, just like you're an amazing person all round.'

'I can't wait to meet our baby,' she says. 'I wonder what it will be like.'

He kisses her softly and says, 'Time will tell.'

Chapter Two

Francesca sits in front of her dressing room table, smoothing cream into her face. The small white pot contains an ordinary-looking white substance that costs hundreds of dollars and promises miraculous results. This one she bought in duty-free on her way back from skiing in Colorado, so she feels she deserves it. Whether it works is another matter. But then, as Dr Schruber also tends her skin at vast cost – lasering, peeling, refining and filling, blasting it with oxygen – it's hard to know exactly which of her many treatments has what effect.

Who cares? she thinks, examining herself in the bright light that illuminates her face so that she can apply make-up perfectly. *I deserve it all.*

This is her consolation. After all, she sits here in this huge house alone. Years ago, just as her life was on the point of collapsing, she escaped London and came here to be with Walt, and become a wife and mother. Her legal career, forecast to be so stellar, was abandoned, and she became one of those charity wives, endlessly involved in fundraising, arranging glittering galas and expensive balls or auctions where rich people donated things that other rich people didn't mind paying over the odds for in the name of giving: cases of wine; use of a yacht; shooting on an estate somewhere; exclusive access to a chalet; a flight on a private plane. There was always a worthy cause to be concerned about, and always the pressure to be doing something to help. What with the charity work and the organising of family life – running the home, coordinating the children's schedules, arranging holidays – she's felt endlessly busy for years, absorbed in the bubble of life in Geneva. But now she wonders if it's been an illusion, designed to stop her realising that she made a mistake giving up her chance of a real career. Walt has always told her that she ought to go back but she's sure she's missed her chance, and besides, she is someone else now.

Francesca picks up a brush and starts pulling it through her damp hair. The house is so eerily quiet. Not that she could hear anything from downstairs, even if she wanted. Perhaps Marie-Chantelle, the housekeeper, is bitching to the maid, or maybe the gardener has come in to grumble while he drinks her expensive coffee and eats the Fortnum & Mason biscuits she has flown over. She has no idea what his gripes might be, but it's possible. She imagines herself padding down the carpeted stairs, going through the vast, smooth-hinged doors on her way to the kitchen, and then entering its sparkling whiteness touched by the gleam of chrome appliances. They would turn to her, instantly deferential, quickly returning to their work. They would melt away, the silence would descend and she'd be as alone down there as she is up here.

Alone is her regular state now. Walt has always worked all hours. The children have always been rigorously scheduled. But ever since they went away to their very expensive Swiss boarding school, she's had the most curious sense of disassociation from them. They came home from their last holidays, chattering in French and German, languages she can understand but without natural fluency, and they seemed different somehow. She looked at them and thought, *Are these people really my children?* They dressed in the way of rich Europeans: in low-key but expensive good taste. Fred had a red jumper slung over the shoulders of his white shirt and wore perfectly pressed chinos and Gucci loafers, with not a hair out of place. He greeted her almost formally, his 'Hello, Mama' subtly accented with an American twang.

He's not even fourteen years old, she thought in astonishment.

At fourteen, Francesca didn't have a tenth of his self-possession. She veered between exuberant extrovert and withdrawn wallflower, painfully conscious of her developing body, her adolescent skin, her long lank hair. And her clothes came from the high street, her attempts at fashion furnished by cheap miniskirts, baggy jumpers, black biker boots and lots of eye make-up when she could get away with it.

And then there's Olympia.

Almost twelve, but polished and sophisticated, Olympia was glued to her expensive phone. She wore make-up, discreet and perfectly applied, nothing garish or too old for her:

eye liner, mascara, a hint of blush and rosy lip gloss. Her fair hair hung in shiny sheets, pinned back with velvet-covered clips. Pearls glowed in her earlobes and she wore neat silk blouses, tight skirts, cashmere cardigans, and ballet slippers. Across her chest she'd slung a mini purse from Fendi. It held that phone, a credit card and lip gloss, and every few minutes, she held up her phone, took a picture of herself and sent it to her social media accounts with a buzzy comment underneath. 'Home for the hols, people! Looking forward to some r and r. Enjoy yours.'

Little glossy strangers.

She's amazed that she had a hand in creating them. She was so busy making herself into the new, shiny, polished Francesca – a world away from nervous, plain Cheska with her fringe and her hunched shoulders – that it never occurred to her she'd breed people like her creation and not like herself.

She leans forward to examine her skin even more closely. It's become her obsession. She judges every day by the words that are now engraved in her mind. Dewy. Glowing. Clear. Fresh. Youthful. She follows her routines religiously, cleaning, massaging, toning, applying serums, moisturisers, creams, brighteners, concealers . . . Then, only last week, she read an article in a magazine that said skin was better off without any treatments at all. That all those creams and oils clogged the pores and sped up the ageing process. 'Think of children,' the article said. 'They do nothing to their skin. And look at it!'

For a chilling moment, she felt as though all her work had

been in vain, perhaps had even been having the reverse effect. Then she thought, *What rubbish. Children have perfect skin because they're young. It all changes when they become teenagers, doesn't it? Besides . . .* She called to mind all the rich celebrities successfully holding back the ravages of time, as opposed to the ordinary women she saw on the streets. It was obvious that money and a good dermatologist got results. She would go on, she would persevere. What was the alternative? Accept the decay, the growing decrepitude? Begin to look old, tired, dull? Never. It has taken half her life to get here, to get to this place and become this person. She isn't going to relinquish all she has achieved. Not now. But sometimes she has the slightly panicky feeling that she's been heading in the wrong direction all this time, and that she hasn't properly lived yet; the sense that she still hasn't worked out if the choices she made were wrong or right. She feels she needs more time. She has to keep her options open.

But now this amazing thing has happened. She still cannot quite believe it; it's all still sinking in. But a door has opened up into a world of new possibilities.

She picks up a tube of tinted cream and prepares to anoint herself with it.

Maybe it's not going to be so lonely after all.

Walt sits across the table from her. It's a white table, and she rather hates it, but the interior designer insisted. It was that or glass, which would have been worse. Still, whenever she eats here, part of her mind is thinking how much she detests this round white table. But the alternative of sitting in the dining

20

room at the great polished mahogany table, an eighteenth-century antique set beneath a vast crystal chandelier, would have been stupid with just the two of them.

Walt is hunched over his plate, shovelling food into his mouth as though he hasn't eaten all day. She picks at the steamed fish and salad on her plate, aware of a small jet of anger in her chest, like the blast of hot air from a vent. Walt has a paunch that's growing by the year, and his skin is tough and etched with lines and creases like a rhinoceros hide. Wiry grey hairs have started to sprout out of his nose and ears and eyebrows, although his barber deals with them when they get too visible. His hair is metal-coloured and thin over his scalp. No one cares. No one judges him. If he looks all of sixty-three, good for him. He never has to obsess the way she does. No wonder he's got time to continue building his fortune when it's all he really has to think about.

'So, honey,' Walt says, looking up from his plate. 'What's the news, huh? What's happening with you?'

'Well . . .' She considers. She could tell him details from her day but they would bore him. They bore her to remember them. 'I'm working hard on the Red Cross ball.'

She knows this will be enough to satisfy him. He doesn't want to hear about tables, caterers, decorators or DJs.

He nods. 'Uh huh. That's great.'

He sounds as American as the day they met, even though he hasn't lived in the States for forty years. He was set in stone from the day he turned eighteen. If she met the young Walt, she knows he would be almost exactly the same. A little less pampered maybe – less familiar with the taste of caviar and fine champagne, less accustomed to Savile Row suits and handmade shoes – but still the same. Francesca finds it hard to understand. She hasn't stopped changing, all her life. She's always been alert to people around her, absorbing their ways, copying them, subtly changing her dress and voice to make sure she blends in as expertly as possible. Eighteen-year-old Francesca went to university equipped with the clothes she thought glamorous: tarty dresses, high heels, Topshop jeans and acrylic jumpers, suede ankle boots. She replaced them all within a term, even though it meant having to take a secret waitressing job in a rubbishy restaurant on the ring road, where she knew no students would ever come, in order to buy the lambswool cardigans, printed skirts and shiny penny loafers that would mark her out as belonging to the right set.

By the time she met Walt, she'd graduated to tailored suits, high heels, bags that were subtle designer knock-offs, hopeful that her legal career would enable her to afford the real thing. She has never stopped learning, working to fit in. She never escaped the feeling that nothing came naturally to her.

'How was London?' he asks through a mouthful of lobster lasagne.

She remembers that she hasn't seen him since her last trip. They all blur into one now, it's so normal to board the short flight and then be driven from Heathrow to their London flat. She can spend one or two days there and return before Walt has even noticed she's gone. Now that the children are away for weeks at a time, she has no one to answer to.

'It was great, thanks.'

'Who did you see?'

She considers, and then says brightly, 'I saw Olivia.'

'Oh yes?' Walt looks up. He likes Olivia. Francesca suspects he's attracted to her blonde wholesomeness, her frankness, the way she seems so unselfconscious. Olivia always moves with careless determination. Francesca has watched as she floats about the kitchen, chatting, precise yet casual, conjuring up a glorious meal while appearing to do nothing much. 'How is she?'

Francesca remembers her meeting with Olivia. She had hoped to see Dan but he wasn't around – working probably. She has been desperate to see him ever since their Spanish expedition but he's proved elusive. 'She's fine.' There's a long pause. She considers while she eats a mouthful of salad. When it's gone, she says, 'Actually, she's pregnant.'

The words sound natural enough but she feels a fizzy, almost sickening thrill as she says them. No one could possibly guess the implications and she is sure it would never occur to Walt to suspect her involvement, but she wonders if there is any hint on her face that betrays her, or a light in her eyes that tells the truth.

Walt looks up at her, surprise on his leathery face. He doesn't appear to notice anything at all. 'Really? I thought that was a no-go.'

Francesca gazes at her plate, unable to meet his eye. 'Oh . . . no. I mean . . . it's taken time. They decided to have one more roll of the dice on the IVF, and it's worked. So far.'

Her secret glee is tempered by a nasty jealousy that cuts

23

through her. No matter where the eggs came from, Olivia is growing Dan's babies inside her, feeling that fecundity as the body expands with life. *And her skin and hair.* The wrinkles fill, the hair grows thick and lustrous. Youth, for a short while, returns.

Walt sits back in his chair. 'Well, that's great news! When is the baby due?'

'Babies. Twins. They implanted quite a few eggs. Two have taken. And they're due in January.'

Walt smiles, apparently pleased by this news. 'I'll have some flowers sent. Well done, them. Although . . .' He makes a face. 'I don't envy them having babies at their age. How old is she? Same age as you?'

'Older,' Francesca says a little stiffly. She doesn't think about her age now, now she's on the cusp of forty. 'She's forty-three, or forty-four.' *That could be right.* She errs on the side of overestimating.

'Gee. They're going to be knocked out. Remember what it was like, honey?' He grins over at her, shaking his head, evidently enjoying the shared memory.

She says nothing for a moment, thinking how very little Walt's life was disturbed by the arrivals of Frederick and Olympia. 'Well, yes . . . I feel rather sorry for them. I don't think they'll be able to afford a nanny and it is so incredibly exhausting,' she remarks, wondering if he'll pick up on her meaning and congratulate her on her achievement in raising their children.

'Olivia won't want a nanny,' he says dismissively. 'She'll want to do it all herself, if I know her.'

Fury races through Francesca. *He's rebuking me. Of course she's always perfect. The fact I brought our children up without ever bothering him counts for nothing. I needed the bloody nannies, considering he never lifted a finger.* She damps down her anger. She's used to these surges burning through her, and then dousing them by force of will. But it is exhausting.

'We'll see them next time we're over,' Walt says with decision. 'I wanna congratulate them.'

'When are we going over?' She's alert. There's nothing in her mental calendar. Has she forgotten something?

'We're going to see Renniston, remember?'

The anger is back, sizzling through her, cutting and burning. She breathes out slowly. 'Why are you seeing that place? You're not serious about it, are you?'

'Sure I am. It's a dream, honey, you know that.'

'It's a white elephant!'

'I guess you know what that means, but to me, this is a very special opportunity.'

She sighs. On a plane to one of his many business meetings, Walt saw a documentary film about Renniston Hall, a vast Elizabethan house that had been a private home, then a school, and then left to decay. A society dedicated to historic preservation bought it, did some emergency remedial work and is now offering the place for sale to a private owner, on condition that the restoration of the once magnificent house is completed. Walt has been hankering after some kind of English country house for years. Fired up by the film, with its lingering shots on honey-coloured walls, battlements, mullioned windows and ornate crested fire-places, he has decided this is it.

'You don't need a place like that,' she says, trying to sound calm. 'It's a money pit. And it's going to take years to make it habitable. Why not buy something that's finished? We can redecorate in a matter of months. There are dozens of beautiful houses, closer to London as well.'

Walt eyes her stubbornly. 'But they don't have history like this one. Queen Elizabeth the First stayed there, for chris-sakes! It's the real deal, Frankie. It's the closest thing to a palace that'll ever be for sale in your country, unless they decide to sell Hampton Court! Don't you want a palace?'

She purses her lips. Of course she does. The thought of returning to Britain to a grand house, showing everyone exactly how far she's come, is tempting. But the work in-volved . . . it will be a lot more than choosing fabric and light fittings, and she knows who will be doing it. It won't be Walt. And the heritage people will be all over it. Every detail will be fought and discussed, there'll be endless applications to file, contractors to employ, permissions to seek. Walt won't understand why he can't do as he desires in his own property. He won't fathom why people in bad suits with clipboards dictate whether he can have an en-suite bathroom or not, or tell him that he's required to employ specialist craftsmen for every aspect of the refurbishment. She says, 'A palace sounds very nice, but didn't you say that part of the sale condition is that you have to let the public in?'

'Only for fifty days a year.' He shrugs. 'It's nothing.'

She stares at him. Walt does not usually have time for the

26

public. He's not been on a bus since he was a teenager. His life is carefully segregated from ordinary people: he travels in chauffeur-driven cars, sits in VIP lounges, is ushered into first class. Does he really understand what it means to allow the public access to his house?

'I think it's a mistake, when you could have something much more manageable, with bags of history too if that's what you want.'

Walt smiles. 'We're just going to see it, honey. Keep an open mind. That's all I ask.'

Francesca taps the tines of her fork on her china plate, the little twangs reflecting the strain in her mind. She knows that the great, decaying mansion is about to collide with her life. She tells herself to stay calm.

Well, I might not be able to stop him buying that ridiculous place, but I'm going to get rid of this bloody table if it's the last thing I do.

Chapter Three

Olivia feels like a well-fed python, her body bulging out around its heavy contents. Every move is slow, sluggish and difficult. Her feet are swollen and her knees ache. Her face is huge, too.

No one ever said that. They never said my face would get fat.

The change in her body is more disconcerting than she'd imagined. She hasn't altered physically since she reached adulthood, bar putting on the odd pound or two after holidays and Christmas, usually taken off without much trouble. She's watched her friends metamorphose over the years, as they started their families. Pregnancy and parenthood transformed them, making them . . . well . . . fat. And old. Some lost weight, but never quite shed the look of a deflated balloon. None ever regained their fresh, shiny, well-rested youthfulness.

Not even Francesca. Although she is the closest to looking untouched by parenthood. Maybe because she started earlier.

Olivia, meanwhile, felt immune to the transformative

effects of age. All through her thirties, she barely changed. The odd strand of grey almost invisible in her blonde hair, a faint line or two on her forehead. She'd begun to think that she was a lucky one, with some kind of genetic youthfulness that would never leave her.

Ha! What an idiot.

Now she has a feeling that she's going to discover she isn't so different after all. Already her body feels as though it's been through some great physical trauma, and she hasn't even given birth yet.

She lies back on the sofa, smiling, stroking the huge mound in front of her. 'Hello, babies. Are you asleep? You're getting very tight in there, aren't you?' She tries to discern what's under her hand – a foot? An elbow? The rounded shelf of a bottom? But she can't make it out, even when she feels the inner jabs and kicks from the babies. They're a tangle as far as she can tell, but safely warm and contained within her.

It will all be worth it.

This is what she has longed for. Now it is so close, just a matter of weeks. As the world darkens and turns cold outside, the piles of autumn leaves now rotten and slippery, the wind biting with the onslaught of winter, the babies are defying the season, growing bigger and healthier with every day, their little lungs ripening, their limbs preparing to stretch and kick, their eyes opening like mature fruit slowly bursting.

Olivia is warmed by the two little bodies inside her. She has not felt cold for weeks, even while the temperature drops. *Winter outside, but spring inside me.*

She tries to imagine what the babies will look like, but her imagination won't play ball. It provides fuzzy, generic baby faces, little bodies hardly visible inside blankets. Only once, when she was dreaming through the relaxation period at pregnancy yoga, did she see a pair of faces, little elven-featured pale visages, with deep glimmering eyes of navy blue.

Their eyes might be blue, like Dan's. I hope they are. I hope they have Dan's eyes. But she knows that they could have any colour. And a stranger's features. *Who cares? All children are a mixture of any number of genetic combinations. You never know what you'll get. It doesn't make me any the less their mother.* How could it? She is growing them inside her, her body going about the mysterious process of providing the building blocks for the cellular blueprints being constructed right now. As the babies unfurl like petals, she is nesting them, her blood running through their veins, her oxygen feeding their hearts and brains. *That's being their mother.*

The sound of the front door startles her. It slams with particular force in the winter, the blustering wind sucking it shut with a fierce bang.

'Hello!'

It's Dan, back from work. It's late then. She blinks, looking at the sodium-stained darkness outside the window. It must be after six already. She ought to be cooking, not dozing on the sofa. She's just manoeuvring herself towards the edge so she can stand up when he comes in, bringing the chill of the winter evening with him. 'Sorry, I didn't realise it was so late . . .' she begins, then catches a glimpse of his face. It's white, his mouth turned down, his eyes stern but also bewildered. She looks at the clock. It's not six. It's only four thirty. 'What's wrong?'

He sits down on the sofa beside her, and takes her hand, not meeting her eye for a moment. She thinks at once of the babies, and then remembers with relief they are safe inside her. Next she thinks of her mother, and then of her sister and nephews far away in Argentina. 'What is it, Dan?' A jitter of panic races through her.

He looks at her now, his expression serious. His hands are cold and clammy from the outside and she wants to pull her own warmth away but doesn't. 'I've got some bad news, darling.'

'Tell me, quickly.' She can't bear the suspense. If the world has been turned upside down, if someone dear is dead, she needs to know right now. She can't exist in a dream world for one moment longer than she has to.

'Okay.' He closes his eyes and takes a deep breath. 'Okay.'

They are at the kitchen table, their plates smeared with the remains of their food, sitting within the pool of golden light from the overhead pendant. They have talked so intently, they barely tasted the stew that Olivia started cooking this morning, trying out a new recipe she cut from the paper at the weekend. She's been craving Moroccan flavours lately: the sweaty tang of cumin, the sweet calm of cinnamon, the perfume of rose and the spikiness of chilli and pepper. She's dimly aware that the stew was good, but all the pleasure in its creation has gone. Dan has described the scene to her three times at least: how they were all summoned to the meeting room, then divided into groups, and how one by one they were called into separate offices to learn their fate.

'It was like being divided into fit for work, and destined for the knacker's yard,' he says bitterly.

'That might be overstating it a bit,' Olivia says with a touch of severity. 'You've got to keep it in proportion. It's not the end of the world.' She rubs her hand absent-mindedly over her full, drum-tight belly. 'You've lost a job, that's all. It happens to lots of people. We've still got the babies, that's the important thing.'

'But that's why this is the worst possible time to lose my income!' He takes a big gulp of the red wine in his glass and pours more from the bottle. He's already had two thirds of it and there's a rim of black speckles on his lips. Olivia hasn't drunk for ages now, and she's begun to lose that unquestioning belief that it's just something you do. She doesn't like watching Dan get belligerent and start ranting, his brief burst of energy followed by sudden deep fatigue and, later, by sound, snore-filled sleep. He's not at the ranting stage yet, but it might not be far off. 'We need all the money we can get now we're going to have two children to support. And all our savings are practically gone. And you're not working!' He finishes up with another gulp of wine.

'It sounds bad,' Olivia agrees. 'But it's not that grim. You're getting a redundancy package, right? A decent one, as you've been there so long?'

He nods, frowning.

'So maybe this is a good thing. You're going to be around when the babies arrive, with more than just a fortnight's paternity leave.' She starts to see it in a different light, and feels a rush of excitement. 'We'll have enough for a year or so, won't we? You'll have time to think about what you really want to do, and I'll be able to get some work in while you're home with us.'

Dan frowns, and Olivia thinks that it's almost as if he doesn't want to acknowledge anything positive. Then his face starts to clear a little. 'Maybe you're right.' Expressions flit over his face. He's only looked at the downsides. He's not used to failure of any kind, and he's stung by the humiliation of losing his job, needing to vent his anger at the people who treated him this way after all these years. But he'll get a tidy tax-free sum and can forget all the stresses and strains of his office and concentrate on the miracle of the babies and the excitement of parenthood instead. As the reality of their arrival sharpens, Olivia has dared to look ahead for the first time and consider what having twins to look after might mean. She hasn't wanted to tempt any malevolent fates, but now it seems it might actually happen. And then what? If she and Dan could do it together, how much more wonderful would that be?

She leans across the table towards him. 'This could be just the opportunity you've wanted, even though it's not ideal. I know it's a horrible thing to go through but . . . you'll be with me and the babies. We've got to enjoy this. Think how hard we worked and struggled to get here. We'll never do it again. Honestly, Dan, this is the silver lining, can't you see?'

Dan nods slowly and smiles. When his face clears, she sees the man she loves again, handsome with those dark blue eyes and thick, almost black hair. He has an Irish look about him, and indeed his father is Irish American. Charm runs in the family, along with good looks, and the attractive aura of self-confidence. Olivia still melts when Dan turns the full force of his smile on her, even after all this time. She's still thrilled by his intelligence and intellectual prowess, his sharp wit and belief in himself. Although she was prepared to adopt if the IVF hadn't worked, ready to love any child who needed her so that she could satisfy the maternal longing that's consumed her for years, it's a special pleasure to her that the babies are biologically Dan's. She almost sees it as an honour to be creating his children, even if they share half their genetic inheritance with a stranger.

Olivia goes on, eager to push home this new slant on the day's trauma. 'You know what? You can write the play you've been planning. This could be the chance you've been waiting for! You'll finally have the time to do some writing, just like you've always wanted.'

Interest flickers in his eyes, then he laughs. 'I bet there won't be much chance for writing when the babies get here.'

'You've got a breather before then. And babies do sleep, eventually!' She smiles at him across the table and puts her hand in his. They clasp each other on the scrubbed pine surface.

'But the redundancy money won't last forever,' he murmurs thoughtfully. 'We'll need to be very careful.'

'Fine,' she says, wanting everything to be all right. 'We'll cut right back. We'll work it out, I just know it. And . . .' She smiles at him, squeezing his hand gently. 'Just think. You don't have to go back to the office. Ever again. And one day, you'll probably think that this was the best thing that ever happened to you.'

He nods thoughtfully. She feels a rush of triumph that she has managed to turn his setback into an opportunity, a doorway to another life, one that he wants more than his old job.

Things are going our way. She feels sure that life is smiling on them at the moment. Luck is on their side. Fortune has spun her wheel and is whisking them upwards to a bright future after all the bad years. *Everything's falling into place. I can feel it.*

Chapter Four

The estate agent is very excited. Perhaps it's the effect of seeing Walt's Daimler sweep up the drive of Renniston Hall, or perhaps it's the thought of the massive commission that will come the agency's way if the hall is sold.

Or maybe he just likes the house, Francesca thinks. The agent jigs along, perky and energetic, beside the more laconic figure of the man from Preserving England, the heritage society that's selling the house, who's pointing out the historic features and the work already completed. Francesca remains in the background, her face inscrutable behind huge dark glasses, cutting a neutral figure in white jeans and a black silk trench coat. The attention is all on Walt, as though he is a walking wallet that can be talked open. Maybe they're right. Usually it's a woman who makes the final decision about a house, but this place is different. It needs so much capital that it's no wonder they are focusing on the probable source of it.

'Note the plaster barrel ceiling in this room,' the heritage man is saying, gazing upwards. He's exactly what one would expect: white-haired and imposing, wearing faded plum-coloured cord trousers and a tweed jacket over a checked shirt and Windsor-knotted tie. 'The fireplace is mid-sixteenth century and the plaster overmantle probably a little later, closer to 1630 or so, we believe. You can see it has a bas-relief, showing the sacrifice of Isaac.'

Walt is drinking it all in, although it means very little to him. He can't tell a pediment from a portico, but he knows that he's seeing something spectacular. 'Wow!' he exclaims. 'And whose coat of arms is that on the ceiling?'

'You'll see various arms and crests throughout the house, reflecting the many different owners since the original house was built in 1540. It's been added to several times since then, of course, so you'll see Elizabethan, Jacobean and Palladian styles . . . The families who lived here include the Vanes, the Earls of Arnandale, the Beauclerks . . .'

Francesca is half aware of the voice as they move through the great rooms, but she is in a daze as they walk around. The house has stunned her. It is beautiful, though deeply dilapidated, and more redolent with history than any place she has ever been, outside public and royal buildings. She can tell it's full of centuries' worth of ghosts: ruffed court-iers, armoured knights, cavaliers and crinolined ladies. She senses the vanished presence of dandies, nobles, duchesses and bishops, not to mention the hundreds of servants who must have kept a place like this running. It is ornate as only great houses are, the stone mullion windows embellished with carving, every column rich with entablature, and every cornice moulded in intricate designs.

But it's so . . . tired. So worn out.

The heritage man is explaining how the house was left empty for a couple of decades, put on the register of buildings at risk, served with notices for compulsory repairs to the foreign-based leisure group that had acquired it, sold on several times before the heritage society stepped in with emergency public funds and bought it. Millions have already been spent getting the house up to its current state: still not much more than a shell, but watertight, although without much in the way of plumbing or power; vast empty, dusty chambers leading one into another, and huge staircases winding upwards to corridors of doors leading into yet more rooms. Francesca is hopelessly lost after only a short time when they gain the first floor, and she walks quietly in the wake of the others as they discuss what needs to be done in this great, neglected place. It's like a gigantic beast, left untended to fend and forage for itself, its majesty hidden under the ravages of time and creeping decay, and a kind of acquired savagery. She catches glimpses of sunshine glowing on the honey-coloured stone outside, of green lawns beyond the windows. The grass is in wonderful condition. Someone has been looking after it. It is in stark contrast to the dust, cobwebs and the dirt-smeared glass inside.

She knows that Walt wants to buy this place; she can feel the desire for it emanating from him. When the heritage man mentions in passing that Queen Elizabeth stayed in the very room they're standing in, Walt almost quivers with excitement.

'Queen Elizabeth the First?'

Francesca thinks, *It's hardly going to be the other one. Where would she sleep? On a camp bed?*

'That's right.' The heritage man looks quite touched by Walt's excitement. 'She stayed here several times apparently, on her summer progresses around the country. She had a particular affinity with the place, we believe. We know that James the First visited too.'

'Wow,' Walt breathes again. 'Would you believe it?' He turns to Francesca. 'It makes history come alive, doesn't it, honey?'

'Yes,' she says. Her throat feels thick with dust. She imagines the Tudor queen lying in a huge carved bed with tapestry hangings, old and childless, feeling the glory of her reign fading. Francesca shivers with a sudden chill that crawls over her skin.

'Queen Elizabeth, huh?' Walt shakes his head. 'That sure is something. Imagine making this room just the way it was when she was here. It would be a kind of privilege.'

There is a murmur of agreement. Francesca follows the others as they leave the room.

The tour takes them up to the second floor and to the attics, then down some back stairs and into a different part of the house altogether, to a place where there are no turned balustrades or moulded plaster. Instead, they are surrounded by the unlovely tiles, ugly paint and solid pipework of an institution.

'This place was a girls' school from before the war until the sixties,' explains the heritage expert, leading them down a dark, dank corridor. 'They converted this wing into their

39

sports hall. It would never be allowed now, of course, but back then people did as they liked. Here are the old showers.' He opens a door to a long, narrow tiled room, full of the bitter smell of mould and the sour tang of old, rotten water. The floor is covered in large white tiles with blackened grout that dip down in the centre to a channel where dry drains still wait for a deluge. Shower heads stick out from the wall at intervals, crusty with ancient limescale. There are no partitions or curtains. No privacy at all.

Francesca thinks of the tour she took around the Swiss boarding school where Frederick and Olympia are studying. Olympia is in a pretty chalet-style boarding house, with views over the mountain, and a cosy, homelike environment. The plentiful bathrooms are comfortable and private.

How horrible this is, Francesca thinks, with another shudder. It's hard to believe this is in the same house as the grand royal bedroom with its panelling and great stone fireplace.

'Obviously there's plenty to do in this part of the house,' the heritage expert says, shutting the door. 'Although it's hard to know precisely what. That's why it's been left pretty much as it was.'

He takes them further down the corridor and opens another door inset with a panel of murky safety glass. Now they are in a huge chamber, its high walls tiled except at the top where there is a row of narrow rectangular windows that let in a little grey light. Francesca realises that about half of this room is below ground. In the middle of the room is a vast tiled rectangular hole sunk far into the floor, its depths filled with rubbish and filth.

Of course, she thinks, getting her bearings. *That's the swimming pool.*

She sees now that she is looking into the deep end, where a pile of leaves and accumulated litter has settled. Someone has tossed in old fittings: a pool ladder, cracked tiles, a coil of blue lane rope, some floats. The filters, thick with dirt, are falling from the sides of the pool, and the whole thing is a giant ruin.

'Well now,' Walt says, gazing about, his eyes gleaming. 'Isn't this grand?' He turns to Francesca. 'There's already a pool here! Just think, we can make all this into our own private gym.'

Francesca doesn't know what to say. The amount of work needed to bring this pool back to anything near usable is enormous. To transform it into the kind of luxurious one that Walt is no doubt envisaging will be an epic undertaking. Even then, would it ever entirely lose the feel of an institution? The size of this place is overwhelming. It's not a home. It should be a hotel or something. It makes their house in Geneva look like a cottage. This is madness.

But looking over at Walt, she knows that he wants it, and there's absolutely nothing she can do about it.

As they are leaving, going back through the great hall towards the front door, Francesca sees through a window a man working on one of the back lawns. He's carefully raking the grass as though fluffing it up to luminous emerald perfection.

'Who is that?' she asks. It's almost the first thing she has said since they came into the house. She points through the diamond-paned mullioned window. 'Out there.'

The heritage expert pauses and looks out, then says casually, 'Oh. That's William. He's been the caretaker here for many years. He keeps an eye on the building, makes sure it's secure against squatters and intruders. And he keeps the gardens in check.'

That explains the beautiful lawns. 'Does he live in the house?'

'Not exactly. He has a converted section of it that's almost become a small dwelling in its own right. There are a couple of places like that here, but William's is the only one occupied.'

'What will he do when you sell the Hall?'

The expert's tone tightens. 'Well . . . we'll see. He understands that his tenure is almost over, let's put it that way. Of course, he's not terribly happy about it. But he sees that the future of the house is best served by a private owner. Now. If we're quite done, shall we be on our way? I'm sure you have plenty to think over.'

The Daimler glides down the motorway, heading back to London, passing everything with ease, as though it's existing on a different plane from the other, more mundane traffic.

'Well, Frankie, this is going to be an adventure, isn't it?' Walt rubs his hands on his legs and pats his knees. 'I thought that place was amazing, didn't you?'

'Of course.' She takes off her sunglasses and looks at him, really seeing him for the first time in a long while. He's a coarser, fatter, older version of the man she married, and she wasn't wildly attracted to him then – at least, not in that dizzy passionate way she hungered for Dan. But she grew to enjoy his body, the way its heft provided comfort and re-assurance, and she cherished their lovemaking for the sense of safety it gave her, and the evident delight he took in her. Now she feels a tiny twinge of repulsion when she looks at him. Their sex life together is still regular enough to be called healthy, although they have different bedrooms. When he's home, Walt expects a conjugal visit every Friday and Saturday night, or on a Sunday morning, sometimes brief but often prolonged and vigorous. The days of revelling in his enjoyment of her are gone. She doesn't need him like she used to. When they first met, she felt like one huge bleeding wound walking around, her planned career faltering and her world disintegrating as she collapsed under the weight of her pain. He surrounded her in such simple love, it was like being coated in some kind of healing balm. He made the pain go away, for a while at least, and she loved him for that. But that was then. Now she feels a vague sense of being cheated, because he has never inspired the giddy feelings and desperate longing that Dan did.

Still does? She breathes deeply and turns to stare out of the window. She hardly dares admit it to herself but she knows that she still adores Dan. It seems to be something elemental inside her that she'll never be free of. It seems to be growing stronger instead of weaker as time passes.

These days, Francesca has to steel herself for the encoun-ters with her husband, trying to damp down the dread beforehand and enjoying the relief afterwards when it's over. Occasionally, if she and Walt have got on well, and if the evening has been enjoyable, or someone has flirted with her at a dinner they've attended or she's danced with someone attractive at a ball, she can get some pleasure from the activity. A few glasses of champagne help to warm her blood and give her the ability to pretend Walt is someone else. And he knows her body well enough to make sure she is satisfied. But it's not really enough.

I can't help yearning for what I should have had.

The only comfort is the knowledge of the secret that she and Dan now share, and the prospect of what the future might hold for them both. She still can't believe that it will really happen, but Olivia is getting closer and closer to her due date.

I mustn't think about it. Not yet.

'So,' she says, turning back to Walt, 'are you going to buy the house?'

'Do you think I should?'

'Does it matter what I think?'

He gives her a sharp look. 'Of course it does. What do you mean?'

She smiles winningly, always knowing when to back down. 'I only mean that your heart is obviously set on it. But I think it's crazy – you ought to know that.'

'I'll need your help,' he replies.

Of course you will. You always do. 'I'll need to recruit some people to help me,' Francesca says. 'It's an enormous

44

job. I don't have the skill or knowledge to do it alone. And it's going to take money. *Lots* of money.'

'Of course,' Walt says, unconcerned about that aspect. 'But just think of what we'll have in the end. And the contribution we'll make. We'll be saving that old place, preserving it for future generations. I'll have the lawyers start talking to the heritage people. We need some concrete numbers. And, baby –' he grins over at her – 'how about we have that royal bedroom for ourselves, huh? Fancy sleeping where Elizabeth the First got her zees?'

Francesca laughs, but the eerie feeling she felt in that room creeps over her again. She can't imagine ever finding peace in it. The image of the abandoned swimming pool floats through her mind. *Why does he want that house? What does he see in it?*

She thinks of the comfortable Kensington flat waiting for her in London, and hopes it won't be long before they are back there. She wants to put Renniston Hall as far out of her mind as she can, before it is forced on her.

Chapter Five

Renniston Hall School for Girls,

1959

Oh cripes. This is awful. Where is she?

Julia shivers in the darkness and wishes she'd thought to put her dressing gown on. She's only wearing pyjamas, thin ones, and a pair of felt slippers her mother sent from Egypt. They're not designed to keep out the cold in an English boarding school, and the chill of the stone floor bites through them with ease. She hears a noise close by and jumps violently, but it's only the wind-driven swish of the canvas sheeting the builders have put up to cover the building site that will one day be the new swimming pool. Every day, they arrive and start digging away at the hole in the ground, scooping out more mud to be carried away.

Come on, Alice. Where are you?

Behind her, the school is in silence, and Julia is alert to any noise that might be Miss Allen coming down from the boarding house at the top of the school. Perhaps she has done one of her late-night patrols armed with the little torch that she shines over the bed of every boarder, making sure each is present and correct. Julia has lain still often enough, pretending to sleep, as that ray of light shines orange against her shut lids, wondering where on earth Miss Allen thinks they might escape to. The school is in the middle of sixty acres of parkland, and the way to the road is down a long, winding drive over a bridge and several cattle grids. But Miss Allen has no thought that anyone might be crazy enough to attempt a getaway; she's taking precautions against midnight feasts or high jinks or nocturnal bullying. They've all heard the stories of booby-trapped beds, or girls dunked in icy baths, though no one in Julia's dorm has ever been brave enough to do any such thing. Not with Miss Allen in charge. Her strictness and severity are legendary.

That's why Julia is so afraid. She doesn't know what punishments Miss Allen hands out, she only knows she doesn't want one. She isn't a rebel, like Alice. The rules might be restrictive and boring, but she sees no point in challenging them for the sake of it. Life is steadier in the safe confines of obedience. She likes to be good, whereas Alice gets her kicks from being as naughty as possible.

Why did I let Alice talk me into this?

She imagines being expelled and feels sick at the thought of her mother's disappointment and her father's anger. Far away in the heat of Cairo, they think she's behaving herself, doing them credit, taking advantage of this opportunity. She's an army brat, her fees paid for by the government. Her parents couldn't afford boarding school if it wasn't for that. They were so happy when she got her place at Renniston, and when they left her at school that very first term it was with smiles and kisses and the evident hope that she would make a success of her time here. So far, it has gone well. She's been sensible and hardworking, and was even made form captain for a term. But then Alice, with her glamour and vitality, took a shine to her and decided that Julia would be her special friend.

Why can't I resist her? She's going to get me into trouble, I just know it.

But there's no denying life has been more exciting since she and Alice became best friends.

The canvas sheeting swishes again, and Julia gasps with fright. That's it. She can't stand it any longer. She's going back upstairs, no matter what Alice said. She's obviously not coming. Just as she turns to make her escape, the canvas moves again and Alice slips in from behind it, her stout school shoes looking incongruous with her pink dressing gown, the belt of which is tied tightly round her middle. Her eyes are bright in the darkness and Julia can tell she's smiling.

'Where were you?' hisses Julia, relieved and cross in equal measure. 'You've been ages!'

'Sorry,' Alice replies a little too loud for comfort. 'I forgot the time. I'm only ten minutes late, what are you fussing about?'

'You'll get us both into awful hot water. Why did you need me here anyway?' Julia is eager to get away.

'Just in case,' Alice says enigmatically.

'Come on, let's get back upstairs.'

'All right, Miss Fussy, we'll go back. Don't worry, Allen is bound to be asleep by now. She never goes on the prowl after ten thirty, don't you think I've watched to make sure?'

Julia doesn't want to argue. She just knows that Miss Allen's predictability isn't a safe bet. Miss Allen likes to shake things up and surprise people, and not in a good way.

Alice sighs happily. 'Oh, I've had a lovely time! You can't think how nice.'

She's still speaking too loudly.

'You've got to shut up now,' Julia says as they head back up the corridor. She peers at Alice in the gloom. There's a little illumination from the glow of the emergency exit sign above the doors. Alice's cheeks look suspiciously flushed. 'Have you been drinking?'

Alice giggles. 'Only a little bit of whiskey. Roy gave it to me to keep the cold out. I didn't like it at first so he had to mix it with lemonade. It was lovely like that.'

Julia is more afraid than ever. 'For goodness' sake, keep quiet and let's get back to bed.' She leads the way as they patter up the corridor, over the stone floor of the great entrance hall with the minstrel's gallery lowering over them from the darkness, and to the staircase that takes them upwards to the dorms at the top of the house. The way to Miss Allen's house is usually via the White Staircase, but they're using a different one, one that takes them to the door furthest from the housemistress's quarters. It's a tightly wound stone staircase, curling upwards inside a tower. The little arched door into the dormitory isn't the end of it; the staircase goes on and up to the roof.

They reach the doorway; it's very slightly ajar, just as Julia left it when she descended. Now is the truly dangerous bit. Her heart pounds and her breath comes short and quivery. She bites her lip to keep herself calm as she pushes the door further open, fearful that Miss Allen is standing behind it, waiting for them. But there's no one there. They slip through, and close the door behind them, the sound of the latch dropping making them both flinch. They freeze, alert, staring at each other. Alice's insouciance has worn off with the cold climb up the stone stairs, and Julia can see her own fear reflected back in Alice's wide eyes. There's nothing. They're still undiscovered. Now they can tiptoe quickly into the dorm and make their way to their own beds and safety.

Never again, Julia thinks as she slides into the coolness of her sheets and pulls her blanket tightly round her. She's kept the slippers on, to warm her feet more quickly. She closes her eyes and wills sleep to come. *I'm never helping her again.*

But she always thinks that.

The last notes of the hymn die away and the girls shut their books. It's a competition to see who can shut them with the loudest snap, and the hall is full of the sound of it, like a lot of biting jaws. Julia doesn't care about winning but feels she has to take part, so she always shuts hers with a half-hearted effort, while Alice puts everything into her snap. The Headmistress frowns from the stage where she is leading the assembly, evidently disapproving, but she seems to have more important things than hymn books on her mind.

'Now, girls,' she says in her very proper voice, sounding

like someone on the wireless. 'I want to take this opportunity to remind you that the building site is completely out of bounds to all pupils. Anyone caught going in the vicinity of the site will be subject to severe penalties. I hope that is understood.'

There's a shuffle through the room as though the girls are expressing their comprehension through their feet.

'And furthermore,' continues the Headmistress, raking the girls with a gimlet glare, as she does when she wants to make a particular point, 'it is utterly forbidden to communicate in any way with the builders who are working here.'

A rustle moves over the girls. *She's talking about men.* The thought seems to pass from head to head, and with it, pictures of strange indecencies and forbidden thrills.

'They are not to have any dealings with you. It is more than the reputation of the school is worth if it were known that our girls were consorting with Irish workmen. There will be the harshest consequences if there are any infractions of this rule.' She frowns down at the two hundred girls, from the wide-eyed, uncomprehending first form to the sniggering sixth at the back. 'And now, our bible reading. The purification of the Blessed Virgin Mary. Mabel Standish, please come forward and read.'

Alice turns to Julia and gives her a giant wink. Julia nudges her back crossly. It only takes one teacher to see, and they'll be hauled up and interrogated.

'And who, oh who,' whispers Alice, leaning in towards Julia, 'is ever going to purify me?'

Julia stares straight ahead, concentrating on Mabel Standish, and trying to shut Alice's throaty laugh out of her ears.

I'll be good, she promises in her head. *Even if Alice won't. Maybe I can be good enough for both of us.*

Chapter Six

Olivia laughs, even though she's heard the story several times before. She can't help it. Dan has perfected his imitation of his boss and the little skit of his redundancy. He manages to make himself look a bit daft, slow to realise he's being let go, but his boss appears truly stupid and pointlessly mean. Francesca throws back her head and laughs heartily as she enjoys the rendition.

'Oh, Dan,' she says, shaking her head. 'What on earth were they thinking of, letting you go? What a bloody awful way to treat you, after ten years.'

Dan shrugs as he tops up their glasses from the chilled bottle of white wine. 'It's the way the market is at the moment. Job losses all over the place, particularly in the bigger companies where they're just completely overstaffed. But even so, I was the best guy they had. I can't understand what made them do it.'

'They didn't deserve you,' Francesca declares. 'And you'll be snapped up in no time.'

'Amen to that!' Dan holds up his wine glass, and they clink before drinking.

Olivia looks over and thinks, *It's nice of Cheska to be so supportive. Dan can always count on her.*

She moves with slow deliberation between the kitchen island and the stove, half listening to them as they talk on. She didn't think she could get much bigger but there doesn't seem a limit to how far her body will stretch. Her hips feel loose and her pelvis has softened and widened to allow the babies the room they need. But it won't be for much longer. They're due to be delivered by caesarean section in a couple of days' time. Her bag is in the hall, packed and waiting. In the tiny spare room, the large white cot is set up, a cheerful mobile of painted wooden kites hanging over it. There's a changing table with baskets full of fresh supplies. Teddies are perched on the top of the chest of drawers, piles of clean muslins are on the table next to the feeding chair, and the feeding pillow is propped up against it. Giant wall stickers of floating balloons brighten the cream walls. There's nothing more to be done.

I'm ready, I can't wait . . . But there is something delicious in this quiet bubble before the babies are born. They're grown and ready for the world – that part is over – but they're also safe inside her where nothing and no one can hurt them.

Dan and Francesca seem entirely absorbed in their conversation, leaning across the table towards one another, lifting glasses of cold white wine to their mouths in a slow pattern. Francesca appears to know a lot more about all the ins and outs of Dan's office than Olivia ever has. She tried to follow it but the names of his work colleagues didn't seem to inspire anything in her imagination. There was never anything to hang on to. But, she reflects, it's probably the same for Dan and her work. While words like lupin and peony and agapanthus create bright pictures and emotional responses for her, they mean nothing to him. She has always secretly thought it is because she is not in his league of intelligence. Francesca, Cambridge educated like Dan, is one of his tribe: ferociously clever and self-confident, even if she gave up her career years ago. Olivia's always admired their self-belief, their absorption in matters of the world of business and money, but never envied it. The only world that matters to her is the one of fertile soil, and the cycle of dormancy and rebirth, the coming to fruition of things that bloom beautifully and then are gone.

I'm blooming beautifully, she thinks contentedly. She's never felt so at one with her body and so in awe of its capacity. The miracle of the tiny seed, planted in soil and fed with water and light, turning into an exquisite flower, is minor compared to the work her body is doing, without any design of hers, as it nurtures the babies inside her.

She looks over at Francesca, sitting across the table from Dan and listening attentively to him, and feels a rush of affection for her. In her great, expansive, fecund state, she feels infinitely magnanimous. Vaguely she recalls that once, she felt a little uncomfortable about the friendship between her husband and Francesca; it predates her own relationship with him, going back to their shared university days. She knows that there's never been anything more than friendship between them – Francesca's name has never featured in the list of Dan's previous girlfriends, and once she idly asked Dan if there had ever been anything between him and Cheska, and he said no. They'd just been friends. He thought of her like a little sister. He described how vulnerable Cheska seemed when she arrived at Cambridge, a mousy thing trying to find her identity, wide-eyed and lost among the more brilliant, confident students. It took a term or two for her to come out of her shell and start to prove herself. Even so, he probably never would have become her friend if they hadn't been assigned as supervision partners. Olivia finds it hard to imagine glamorous Cheska as a timid little thing.

She recalls the first time she met Cheska. She and Dan were in the sweetest part of their honeymoon phase, still wrapped up in one another but beginning to emerge from their cocoon of obsession to explore each other's lives. She had taken Dan to meet her family, and had met his parents. Now they were getting to know their social circles. Cheska made an impression because, unlike most of them, she was married. On her finger flashed a great, almost ridiculous, solitaire diamond, and a slender platinum band announced that she had taken the grave and grown-up step of matrimony, something Olivia could barely imagine for herself. Cheska was dressed in discreetly expensive clothes, everything about her expressive of money, from her haircut to the plain driving shoes in soft tan leather with the subtle designer stamp on them.

'One of my oldest friends,' Dan said, an arm around

Cheska's shoulders. 'I don't know how she put up with me. I was pretty unbearable in our supervisions, wasn't I? Acting like I knew everything worth knowing at nineteen.'

Cheska gazed up at him. Despite her sophisticated exterior and aura of self-possession, her expression was almost puppyish. It was gone in a second as she turned to Olivia and smiled broadly.

'I managed somehow,' she said. 'He wasn't that bad, honestly. He just needed a bit of taming. We're so happy that Dan's found someone like you, Olivia. Really, we are.'

Olivia warmed to her, glad of her acceptance. And yet, sometimes in those early days, she felt Cheska's stare on her and when she turned quickly and unexpectedly to meet it, she saw something appraising there, as though Cheska were studying her, trying to work her out somehow.

Protective, she thinks now. *Protective of Dan. Worried I might break up the circle of friends. Well, there was no danger of that.* Of course, that was all long ago. Now she feels she knows that Cambridge group almost as well as her own friends, and while she sees that Dan and Cheska's friendship is well worn and comfortable, she thinks that she can discern a trace of something like hero worship in Cheska's attitude to Dan, perhaps the remnant of something left over from their college days. She can imagine Dan swaggering about, making waves with his dark good looks, easy charm and humour, his obvious intelligence. He was probably the leader of their little gang, which was why she seemed to look up to him and need his approval. Well, all credit to Cheska for sticking through what was no doubt his annoying, conceited phase and getting to the other side. Dan is more mellow now, kinder, more patient and definitely less egotistical.

Though he's still got a touch of swagger about him, and that steely core. She looks over at him fondly, and then at Cheska, laughing at another of his jokes.

She's always been lovely to me. She couldn't have been nicer about the babies.

Cheska was quietly supportive all the way through the long fertility struggle, and delighted when at last it came to fruition. She'd arrived full of excitement, wanting to hear all about it, every step of the journey, from selecting the donor to the implantation of the eggs and every test and scan. She became a regular visitor, rolling up armed with bags full of goodies – treats from expensive delis, baby gifts and products to pamper an expectant mother – eager to sit and chat and share all of it. Lately, Olivia has almost begun to think of Francesca as her friend rather than Dan's. It surprises her, because their lives could not be more different. Cheska's rarefied and pampered existence in Switzerland, with the cushion of vast wealth, is something she can't relate to at all. Yet somehow, they have bonded. It's Olivia Francesca rings up and emails, and the two of them have spent hours chatting together about impending motherhood, nursery colours and the best kind of buggy, while Dan disappeared off to amuse himself with his new-found leisure.

Which is why it's nice to see them catching up. I've been monopolising Cheska a bit recently.

She stirs the fragrant Thai curry, watching the lime leaves

float to the surface. It smells delicious. They'll be eating soon, once the rice has steamed.

'Cheska, has Dan told you about his grand plan?' Olivia asks from the stove.

Francesca looks interested. 'No. What's this?'

Dan coughs and looks a little abashed. 'Oh, well . . . it's not that exciting. We've decided that I'm not going to rush into getting another job. I want to be at home with the babies and Olivia for as long as I can, and we've got the redundancy money to tide us over. And . . .' He smiles. 'I've made a start on writing that play, at last.'

Francesca's face brightens. 'That's wonderful, Dan. You must start writing! You absolutely must. What a great idea.'

'Yes, it's the right time.' Dan takes another drink of wine, then grins. 'You never know, if it all works out, I might not have to go back into consultancy at all. But there won't be much writing once the babies get here.'

'No!' Francesca laughs. 'Even one baby tends to fill up all the available space. You'll have two to contend with. But how wonderful that you'll be here for Olivia. It's worked out quite well, hasn't it?'

'Dinner's ready,' announces Olivia, lifting up the saucepan. 'Shall we eat?'

When the meal is over and Francesca is preparing to leave, she comes over to hug Olivia. The bump is so huge, she has to approach almost sideways.

'I probably won't see you again until the babies are here,' she says, kissing Olivia's cheek. Her hand lightly strokes

Olivia's bump, as though searching for the feel of the babies below the skin. 'But I'll be thinking of you. Make sure I'm on the list for an alert when they arrive, won't you?'

'You'll be the first to know,' Olivia says, returning the embrace.

'Bye, Dan.' Francesca hugs him too, then stands back, pulling her handbag strap over her shoulder, and looks at them mistily. 'You two are going to be fabulous parents. Lucky babies, to have you both waiting for them.'

'Thank you,' Olivia says, touched. 'That's lovely, Francesca.'

'I mean it.' Francesca smiles. She looks at Dan. 'You're going to be a great father, I just know it. I'm so excited to meet the babies. Bye, darlings. Take care.'

When she's gone, Dan clears up the dinner things, while Olivia sips herbal tea and rests.

'Cheska is wonderful, isn't she?' she says idly, as she sees the carrier bag Francesca left behind. It holds two expensive sheepskin rugs for the babies to play on. 'She's been so involved and so interested. She's been there for me more than anyone else.'

There's a tiny pause and then Dan says with a trace of a prickle in his voice, 'Well, I guess that's the good thing about not having to work for a living.'

'Oh.' Olivia is a little taken aback. Dan is usually nice about Francesca. Occasionally he's muttered something about the waste in giving up a Cambridge education, a law degree and a promising career, but only with fondness.

Dan looks over his shoulder from the sink, looking sheepish. 'I didn't mean that to sound unkind. I mean, she's genuine. She really does care. But she also has sod all to do these days.'

'Why did she give up work? Surely Walt wouldn't have minded if she'd carried on.' Olivia wipes crumbs from the tabletop, sending them scattering onto the floor. She ought to clear them up, but can't be bothered.

'Who knows?' He places a pan in the drainer. 'She was set to be a star. Our tutor said he thought she'd have a glittering career. But in the third year, she just couldn't seem to stay focused. Her Finals result wasn't quite as brilliant as she'd been predicted. Then she struggled at law school and gave it up before she'd finished. She was going to become a human rights advocate, but she dropped out and got a job as a PA to some businessman instead. That's how she met Walt, I think.'

'Really?' Olivia is surprised. Cheska has always seemed stronger than that to her. 'Why do you think that happened?'

Dan shrugs and says, 'No idea. Maybe she was never really cut out for work.'

Olivia can't see that somehow. 'She seems very busy in Geneva with all that charity stuff. That must be like a career in itself. And she'll find she's got plenty to do if Walt buys that place she showed us.'

Dan snorts. He's always claimed to like Walt, but doesn't show it when Francesca isn't there. He seems to scorn Walt's business success as though there is still something a little shameful in being a self-made man who didn't go to university. 'That man has more money than sense. It's a ridiculous thing to do.' He shrugs again, his hands in the sinkful of hot water. 'It's a money pit, and even when it's finished, it won't feel like a home. It's a stately bloody pile. I can tell Cheska hates it too.'

'She didn't seem very keen.' Olivia considers. 'But it'll be fun having friends with a house like that, won't it? If they do go ahead.' She sips her tea, thinking of it. 'Maybe we can spend some more time with them.'

'Hmm.' Dan doesn't sound excited by the prospect. 'Maybe. If I'm not mistaken, Walt will buy it, pour some money into it, get bored and sell it. Cheska will just wait it out. Trust me, I bet we never even see that place.'

Chapter Seven

The text comes late on a Friday night.

Walt is in bed with her, on top of her, pounding away as he grunts in her ear. She is enduring it, wondering if she should start fantasising now or if it's too late for that, when she hears her phone bleep with an incoming message. She wants to pick it up and read it behind Walt's heaving shoulders, but she's not that blatant. Instead she hurries him along, gasping and moaning, thrusting up to meet him and digging her nails into the wads of soft flesh on his back. Walt responds gratifyingly quickly, excited by her enjoyment, and hurries to his climax. As he rolls off her, she leans over for the phone. It's from Dan.

Stanley and Beattie arrived on time this afternoon.
Their mother is recovering and all are doing well. xxx

A photograph is attached but it's out of focus, showing two fuzzy bundles and two creased red faces with eyes tightly closed. Francesca squints at it, trying to make out the babies' features, but it's impossible.

'Who is it?' Walt asks, pulling a handful of tissues out of Francesca's bedside box and mopping at himself.

'It's Dan. Olivia's had the babies.' A rush of dark excitement grips her. It hasn't felt real so far, but now, here they are. The babies. *My babies*. The thought is illicit. Thrilling. *Mine and Dan's*. It's brilliant. The ultimate revenge. She can see now that she's been waiting for something like this for years, and yet she could never have imagined something so perfect. Olivia is like a daft bird whose eggs have been replaced by the cuckoo's, and is now about to devote itself to nurturing the alien brood. *Well, that's what she wanted. It would have been someone else, if not me. We'll all be happy. It's perfect*. Then she frowns. *But Stanley and Beattie. I don't like the names at all*.

'That's wonderful news,' Walt says heartily. 'How's Olivia doing? I bet it hurt pushing those two out.'

'She had a planned caesarean,' Francesca replies briefly, tapping back a suitably ecstatic response. *As I told you dozens of times*.

'Send them some flowers from us, won't you.'

'I'll do better than that. I'll take them myself.'

'You're going to London to see them?'

Francesca looks over at him. 'Of course. They're practically my oldest friends. I want to be there for them.'

'That's nice of you. Give them my love.'

Francesca barely hears him. She's looking at the message that Dan sent. It's gone out to dozens of friends, she suspects. That's why it's not personalised for her. But then, what would he possibly write? This is unknown territory. They haven't spoken a word about what they've done since Dan called her after she came back from the clinic in Spain. She was still collecting her luggage from the carousel when her phone rang.

'How did it go?' he asked. 'Any problems?'

'None at all,' she said. 'They harvested plenty. They were happy with everything.'

'Really?' He sounded almost surprised, as though this was an outcome he hadn't expected.

'Yes. They were pleased with the quality. They said it was surprising considering my age.' She hadn't been able to stop a tiny hint of boastfulness in her voice. She wanted him to know that, unlike Olivia, she had vibrant, youthful ovaries and eggs that were ripe and ready for him. The thought made her almost aroused.

'That's brilliant.' There was a tentative edge to his voice, as if he wasn't entirely certain that this was something he wanted. But when he spoke again, he sounded heartfelt. 'Thank you, Cheska. I mean it. Thank you.'

'It's my pleasure. And you don't have to worry. I'm not going to tell a soul. It will stay between us. Forever. Our secret.'

'I know I can rely on you,' he said gratefully. 'So now . . . it's forgotten, right?'

'Yes. Forgotten.' Something vibrated inside her, like a tiny internal earthquake. Perhaps it was the magnitude of their secret and what it would mean for them. After all, how could something like this be forgotten? How deeply could they bury their knowledge? Even if the fertility treatment didn't work, they would always share the secret of what they'd planned between them and the concealment from Olivia.

As she collected her luggage and made her way to the departure hall, her excitement wilted a little, replaced by a wave of dark melancholy that she quickly pushed away. The only thing to do was be patient.

Since then the promise to forget that she and Dan made hasn't been tested. It's been easy to avoid looking into each other's eyes and seeing the truth. She's not been alone with him since they agreed the whole thing, and the growing swell of Olivia's stomach always had an uncertain quality. She was high risk, an older woman with a multiple pregnancy, and they all knew it could go wrong at any time. Now that it's gone right and the plan, so dreamlike and unreal, has come to fruition . . . well, what will happen? She's excited again, thrilled by this situation and the tie that now binds her and Dan together. She can hardly believe it's actually happened.

'I'll go in the morning,' Francesca says, tapping out another message to Walt's PA asking her to book tickets on the midday flight to London.

'You're good to them, honey. I hope they appreciate it.'

'I'm sure they do,' she says, sending her message. Then she lies back and stares at the ceiling. She feels powerful, like a goddess who's summoned people into creation with a clap of her hands. She's in the mood for sex now, but it's too late. *It's a shame I didn't get the news earlier. Walt would have had a lot more fun if I had.*

'Let's open some champagne,' she says suddenly. 'Let's get up and have some champagne, then come back to bed.'

Walt looks surprised but pleased. 'Okay. Let's celebrate. Sounds good. After all, it's not every day that babies arrive.'

'Absolutely.' She smiles. 'And these ones are extra special.

Francesca is in London by the following afternoon. She goes straight from the airport to the flat, then pops out to a ludicrously expensive children's boutique owned by some European princess to pick up a whole wardrobe of clothes for each baby. She's got tiny quilted jackets, trench coats, velvety cotton bodysuits, cashmere jumpers, soft cord dungarees, pinafores and kilts, little white leather shoes. She knows it's too much and that Olivia will probably dislike most of it, but she doesn't care. Something in her wants to remind Olivia that she is a source of wealth, able to provide luxuries for the little ones. It's silly, she knows. Usually she is careful to ensure that she doesn't make Dan and Olivia uncomfortable with the disparity in their circumstances; after all, Olivia earns virtually nothing as a gardening writer and designer, and while Dan has done well enough, they're light years away from the sums that cushion Francesca's life.

Laden with crested carrier bags, she texts Dan.

Where are you? I'm coming to visit! Tell me ward etc.
So excited, can't wait to meet them. xxx

Dan doesn't reply at first, and she wanders up and down the Brompton Road, eyeing up the shop windows, wondering whether to waste an hour stocking up for the new season. At last, her phone vibrates, and she finds his answer.

Actually today not so good. Maybe tomorrow?
O exhausted. x

She stares at it in disbelief, then feels a prickle of irritation. She has assumed that she's allowed into the inner circle, one of the privileged few, as close as family. *After all, I spent enough bloody time in Olivia's kitchen, all those hours listening to her going on.*

She's been assiduous at cultivating her friendship with Olivia and, actually, is genuinely fond of her now, not something she expected to feel at first. Of course, there will always be a distance between them, but Francesca has been surprised at the way she can split herself in two: one half liking Olivia and enjoying the hours chatting and laughing together, and the other rather remorseless in her desire to win the battle that's been raging between them for years, ever since Dan brought her into their lives. It is hard not to warm to Olivia, and there's nothing personal in Francesca's desire to be close to Dan. Olivia is in the wrong place, that's all, and needs to be shunted firmly aside so that things can be as they're supposed to be.

Now she feels as though Dan has rebuked her. He is shutting her out. She's been relegated to the status of ordinary friend. A surge of anger rolls through her, but she's used to controlling her feelings, and she quickly manages to suppress it. *Fine. I can wait.*

68

She stands on the pavement, the wind lightly whipping her hair up, and taps out another message:

Yes, of course she must rest. I'll come by tomorrow.

Then she heads back to the flat, weighed down by the expensive baby gifts in their layers of white and gold tissue.

But the next day, Dan texts to tell her that they are not allowed visitors. The babies are in special care. It's nothing serious, but there's a little issue with breathing that they are confident will be sorted out. Francesca, anxious, tries to call but she can't get through, having to leave a message on Dan's answerphone instead. She spends the day drifting round the flat, worrying about the babies. She is constantly on edge, feeling involved but somehow completely marginalised. These children are closely connected to her – *my babies* – but no one will acknowledge it. *Dan won't acknowledge it.* She feels a pang of uncertainty. She realises that she has not really believed that he can wipe her contribution out of his mind, and actually convince himself that she had nothing to do with it.

The thought makes her stop in front of the long, narrow window with its view over the leafy London square. *Could he? Could he really?*

She blinks out into the afternoon, hardly seeing what's in front of her. Not once has it occurred to her that they actually might never speak of it again. She'd thought their agreement was almost a kind of etiquette, a necessary stage in the evolution of this new part of their relationship. But now she sees that it's a possibility.

He wants it forgotten, just like all the other things he doesn't want to think about. He's always relied on her docility but now she's struck with a sudden sense of her own power. *Can I let that happen? Will I?*

After all, he owes her something. He has to acknowledge that. She won't be treated like nothing.

She's absorbed in this idea when her iPad chimes with an incoming Skype call. She comes to, remembering that of course it's Sunday, and that's when the children contact her. She goes over to answer it, suddenly feeling that she has something exciting to impart to them. Then she remembers: she can't tell them about the new babies. She can't tell anyone.

She sits down, positioning her iPad as she answers the call. Olympia's face, bright and smiling, appears on the screen, and calls out, 'Hello, Mama!'

There she is. Her daughter, healthy and beautiful. Francesca feels a rush of love for her.

'Hello, darling! How are you? How is school? Tell me all about it.'

Two days later, Francesca has to return home and she has still not seen the babies. There are meetings and commitments she must get back to, and the babies are still in special care in the hospital. It's impossible to get hold of Dan, and he isn't replying to her texts, except to say that his phone is off in the ward and he'll be in touch. Then he tells her that

Olivia has been discharged, and the babies will be home at the end of the week if all goes well.

There isn't time to visit now. She sends a massive bouquet to them at home, and briefly considers trying to bluff her way into the hospital as family, to see the babies that way. But she quickly dismisses that idea – the chances are she'd be discovered, and Dan and Olivia could be there at any time. She doesn't like to picture how they would react to her arrival and attempt to get to the babies.

I must be patient. I'll have to wait. I'm good at that.

She leaves the bags of baby presents in the hall of the flat, waiting for her return.

Chapter Eight

'No lifting. I mean it. None at all.' The midwife looks sternly at Olivia. 'Promise?'

'Well . . .' Olivia is confused. 'I mean . . . how heavy are we talking about?' She has a vision of Dan having to lift her knickers out of the drawer. Pick up a spoon. Pass her a tissue.

'Nothing baby-weight, that's for sure. When they get home, you let your husband do all the lifting for at least a fortnight. Those muscles of yours need to knit back together, and if you stretch them too early, you'll do lasting damage.'

Olivia nods. She feels weak and the idea of merrily lifting anything so heavy as a saucepan seems impossible anyway. But what she mainly feels is empty. Even though her breasts are full and swollen with milk, her nipples stiff and sore, and her body is heavy with fatigue, she is hollow. The babies are gone. Her bump, once so full and ripe, is a sagging pouch with only blood and water in it, and her heart yearns for the tiny bodies she was able to hold close to her for only a day before they were taken away. She is expressing milk whenever she can with the big pump lent to her by the hospital, filling bags of breast milk that can be bottle-fed to the babies. She longs to have them latched on to her, sucking out the nourishment she can offer, but as they're in their incubators, monitored by machines, this is all she can do for now, getting them what they need while she maintains her own supply.

Dan comes in, back from the shops with a bulging bag of groceries. She looks at him gratefully. She doesn't know what she would do without him.

'Everything all right?' he asks anxiously, seeing the midwife.

Olivia nods. 'It's fine.'

The midwife gets up and puts on her coat. 'She's doing very well. And I hear the babies are coming home this week.'

'We hope so.' Dan accompanies her to the door and holds it open for her. 'Thanks for coming by.'

'That's all right. I'll see you again in a couple of days.'

As soon as she's gone, Dan turns to Olivia. 'Are you ready to go?'

They're going to the hospital. When they're not there, as close as possible to the babies, life is empty and meaningless. The only good thing is that they're sleeping deeply, recovering their strength. No doubt that will change when the babies are home.

Olivia hauls herself up out of her chair and Dan rushes over to help her. 'I'm so weak,' she says, and tears spring to her eyes. 'I'm not used to this.' She wants to sob. She's happy and miserable at the same time. She's in love with her babies and agonised to be away from them, but she also knows they're being cared for. It's hard to fight the powerful sense of thwarted longing and the misery it brings.

'Hey, it's okay. We'll be with them in a short while. I've parked the car right outside, sod the traffic warden. Come on, darling. You're doing so well.'

She sniffs. 'I'm not sure about that. I'm a mess.'

'Don't be daft. You've had a major operation and you're working like anything to keep the milk going.' He looks at the large pump in the corner. 'You'd be on that all day if you could.'

'Have you got the milk bags from the freezer?' she asks quickly.

'I'll put them in the cold box now. Then we'll get going.'

'Thanks.' She watches, full of love and gratitude as he hurries to get the milk. She's loving seeing him like this: desperate to care for her, full of love for the babies, doing whatever he can to help. This is a different stage in their lives together, a new challenge for both of them, and he is rising to it in every way he can. They're a family now. There are tiny helpless people in their lives, whose needs must be put first. She's always wondered how they'll cope, now that they're so used to their childless life, so set in their ways, so accustomed to pleasing themselves.

Perhaps we'll manage very well. After all, the babies are so wanted. But . . .

She looks out of the window at the cold wintery day, feeling far from her mother and sister. She wants them now, to be with her and share all of this. She thinks of the hot

Argentine sun, and the memory of her nephews, gurgling on a rug in the cool shade, their fat little limbs bare and kicking in the warmth.

She shakes her head. *I won't think about that now.*

'Come on,' Dan says, holding up the cool box. 'We're all ready. Shall we go?'

In the hall, they brush past the huge bunch of flowers Francesca sent. It was too big for anywhere else but the table there. They ought to be beautiful but Olivia doesn't like them. Her taste is for wild flowers, not manicured hot-house blooms in sheaves of cellophane. The heads of the lilies are already dropping rusty pollen, and one leaves a smear on the back of Dan's coat as he brushes past them. Olivia sees it but doesn't have the strength to wipe it off. Her focus is only on getting to the babies as fast as possible.

Later, in the hospital, she feels complete. She's with them. They're all together. She can hold Stanley but Beattie is still confined to the incubator, a tiny mask over her nose and mouth as the machine helps her to breathe. Olivia cuddles Stanley, patiently manoeuvring her nipple into his mouth, encouraging him to latch on and suck, while Dan stands next to Beattie's perspex cot. Her tiny fingers are wrapped around his large one, and he's gazing down at her with awe and love.

Look at these amazing babies. They're still a unit – 'the babies' – but day by day, they're dividing into two individuals.

Already she's grown to know Stanley's dark blue eyes,

liquid and blurry, gazing up at her, the shape of his mouth and the flattened button of his nose. His scalp is covered in a fine dusting of dark hair and he has long fingers. Beattie's fuzz of hair is lighter, reddish, almost invisible, and her eyes are nearly always scrunched closed. She is longer than her brother and her skull is narrower.

Who are you, little babies? Who's there, inside you, waiting to come out?

Stanley starts sucking, and she feels a rush of pleasure to be nursing him. Her nipple tingles and she thinks she can feel a gush of milk into his tiny warm mouth. This is what she has longed for, waited for. And now it's hers.

Dan is watching her, his expression soft and loving. They've come together into this new world, equally amazed and overwhelmed.

'So,' she says with a smile, 'which one do you think looks like you?'

He laughs, and gazes down at Beattie and the tiny row of fingers curled round his. 'Who knows? They look like themselves.'

'Yes.' She gazes down at Stanley and the regular movement of his jaw as he pulls and sucks for her milk. 'That's it. They're just themselves.' She had thought she would feel ownership, but instead she feels only responsibility – they are in her care, but they don't belong to her. They are themselves.

The nurse comes up to check the readings on the machine monitoring Beattie, greeting them cheerfully. 'So, you're off home at the end of the week!' she says. 'Isn't that nice?'

'Yep,' Dan says. 'We can't wait to get them home.'

'It's a miserable time of year, though, isn't it?' she says, marking on the chart hanging on the side of the incubator. 'I expect you won't want to go out much.' She smiles over at Olivia. 'Just snuggle up and stay warm at home.'

Olivia nods. Warmth is what she craves. She looks over at Dan, and wonders when she'll tell him what she wants.

Later. When I've worked it out for myself.

Chapter Nine

Francesca is pretending to read a magazine in the sitting room, but she isn't taking in a word. Instead, her mind is whirling with the impact of what happened in London. Walt comes in, chortling, just off a telephone call and returning from his study. He's merry and pleased with himself, congratulating himself on the deal he's worked out.

When he sees her, he exclaims, 'We got the place for a song, Frankie! I mean it – just under three million for a place like that? You can't get a decent London flat for less.' He sinks down in the armchair opposite her.

'Well done, darling.' She likes seeing his pleasure, even if the project has left her cold. Walt always has had infectious happiness. It was one of the things she most liked about him. The pleasure he takes in life warmed something in her when she thought she was dying. She remembers what it was like when she first got together with Walt and that wonderful feeling of being brought back to life. He resurrected her when her plans for her career had collapsed and everything had begun to fail. She thought that her life was over, and that she was whirling down a plughole towards darkness and despair. Walt brought her back into the light and made her feel whole again. He also offered her a life in which she no longer had to rely on herself for success. He would give her the trappings: the houses, the clothes, the cars. She would be a wealthy woman. Everyone would have to be impressed by that. They would notice her, and admire the way she had guaranteed herself a life they all aspired to: comfortable, safe, pleasant. And she found, almost to her surprise, that she loved Walt too. He was so straightforward and plain, the antidote to the young men she'd been surrounded by for the last few years. He lacked their preening intellectual competitiveness, and concentrated on the hard work that would bring the kind of success he valued. Money was part of it – what was success without it? – but making his mark in the world was just as important, and something in Francesca responded to his simple creed. There was nothing pretentious about it. It made sense. And his love restored her. After he made love to her, she would cry happy tears because she could feel herself reawakening a little more each time.

But she never could resist the dark addiction of her feelings for Dan. They came back to get her eventually: all that longing and need and desire. The bond between them that she felt was unbreakable, the irrefutable sense that they were supposed to be together. All of it gradually killed off her love for Walt and pushed her further and further away from him.

Walt looks over at her now. 'I want us all to go over to England, once the kids are back for the holidays. We've gotta show them the house. It'll be exciting.'

Francesca remembers that place – the dust and dirt and lack of anything that might offer any comfort at all. 'But . . .' she says weakly, 'there's no electricity.'

'Not in the main part of the house. But there are parts of it where we can stay. We'll be perfectly fine.'

She can tell that he's got his rose-coloured spectacles on. He's used to five-star hotels, not roughing it in a caretaker's cottage. *Well, he'll learn.*

'Are you happy?' he asks, an almost anxious look in his eyes. Her approval matters. She remembers that he has always looked up to her in that way. It helped rebuild her confidence.

'Of course. Very happy. You're right. It will be exciting. You've always wanted a country house.' She smiles and it fades on a sigh.

Walt frowns. 'You seem a bit low, Frankie. You've not been yourself since you got back from London.'

'No, really, I'm fine.'

'Are you sure you're all right?'

She nods. The house hardly seems to matter now. All that concerns her is what Dan told her when she was finally able to visit.

The babies had been home well over a fortnight when she arrived in a whirl of largesse, with those stupid baby clothes. And there they were – two tiny creatures wrapped up in blankets, asleep for almost the entire time. Only occasionally did they open their eyes, sleepy, limpid. They were so un-formed, a fuzz of almost invisible hair on their soft skulls, their eyebrows only faint shadows, no real shape to their plump faces, each with the same large turned-up nose, and pink, cupid-bowed mouth. Even so, she was astonished by their reality. It was more incredible than she'd expected to see them. In fact, it was hard to take her eyes off them, and she held each one in turn until Olivia grew restless and put out her arms to take them back. All the while, she searched the tiny faces for signs that they were a mixture of herself and Dan, absorbed in examining their features, hair colour, eyes, anything that might give a clue, but it was impossible to see anything. She remembered how Frederick and Olympia had been the same as infants: little doughy bundles, beautiful to her but – now that she could look back at the photographs – really like any babies.

But look at these little ones . . . they're gorgeous. Special . . . Her heart twanged as she held each one, something deep in her responding to them. She barely heard anything that Olivia said to her.

Then Olivia took the babies away to nurse them and put them to bed. Francesca watched them go with a kind of hunger inside her she hadn't felt for a long time. As soon as Olivia was gone, she turned to Dan with a joyful expression, her eyes shining. 'Oh, Dan, they're amazing.'

Immediately, she sensed a change in the atmosphere. Dan stood across the room, looking back at her impassively.

She said softly, 'They're perfect.'

'I know.' His voice was low, emotionless, as though denying her any response that she could feed off. 'We're very happy.'

'I was so worried for you all when they needed special

care. I'm so delighted they're home and all's well.' She was trying to make sure he knew she cared. That she didn't intend any harm. 'Olivia seems to be coping wonderfully.'

'She is. She's been through a lot, but she's getting better. She's been very brave.'

'I can tell.' She said nothing more, watching him. He couldn't quite meet her eyes. She'd hoped that she was wrong about her suspicion that Dan was fobbing her off and keeping her at arm's length, and that when she actually arrived – *the mother of his children, after all* – there would be an air of complicity and secret pleasure in the success of their scheme. She'd even thought there might be gratitude. But there was nothing like that. He was staying closed off, refusing to allow her to refer in any way to what she'd agreed must be unsaid.

All right. So I'll take it slowly. He'll come round.

Her gaze was caught by the mound of baby clothes on the discarded tissue paper. They were accepted with thanks but also with barely concealed amazement, as though Olivia couldn't imagine what they would use these things for. And now, they did look ridiculous. Who puts babies in cashmere?

She was determined not to let him put a dent in her enthusiasm. Maintaining a good front always got results, softening Dan, making him feel safe and comfortable. She said chirpily, 'But are you sure about Stanley and Beattie? As names, I mean. If there's time, you could think about something a bit less . . . granny chic?'

'Francesca,' Dan said quietly, his voice low with seriousness. 'I need to talk to you.'

'Of course.' Her heart sped up a little but she maintained her air of cheerful calm, at least she hoped she did. She looked over at Dan, standing by the window. Outside, Londoners drifted by, large red buses lumbered past, the endless flow of traffic flew back and forth. Out there, it was noisy and busy. In here, the flat was quiet, intense with the needs of babies. Dan was dressed in loose drawstring linen trousers, and a black jumper that she now saw was pulled on over a pyjama top, his hair messy and on end, stubble silvering his jaw and chin. He looked older and more tired but still her handsome, irresistible Dan. But he hardly ever called her Francesca. She asked tentatively, 'What is it, Dan? What do you want to say?'

She had the urge to jump up, run to him, hug him and say, 'Isn't it amazing? We're parents, we have children together, just like I always wanted. It's all wonderful!'

But he doesn't want that. I mustn't do it.

He said, 'Thank you for coming to see us. I really appreciate it, and so does Olivia.'

'Well, I am one of your closest friends. Naturally I would.' *And those babies were made with my eggs. Of course I want to see them.* She couldn't understand why Dan seemed so removed, not when it was just the two of them, alone. There was no need to pretend.

'Yes. And that's why I have to tell you that we've come to a decision.'

'Oh?' A strange swirling feeling, like the onset of nerves, started in her stomach.

'Olivia is finding all of this – London, winter, the cold, the dark – a bit of a strain. And she wants to be close to her family. So we've decided that we're going to rent out the flat and go to Argentina for a while. To be with Olivia's mother and sister, and be somewhere warm.'

Francesca blinked at him, bewildered. Then she understood. *He's taking the babies away from me.* She forced herself to keep smiling. 'What a wonderful idea. That sounds marvellous.'

He looked a little surprised, as though he'd expected her to be against it. 'Really? You think so?'

'Yes, I do. Of course Olivia should be with her mother at a time like this. And some lovely South American sunshine will be just the tonic for you all. London is miserable at this time of year.'

Dan seemed to relax. 'That's just what we thought. But . . . of course we won't be able to see you.'

'But it won't be long, will it? How long are you planning to be away?'

'We haven't decided yet. A few months probably. It's good for me too, I'll be able to get on with writing as there'll be other people there to help with the twins. I need to get going with it before the redundancy money runs out.'

'You'll get a good rent for this flat, won't you?'

'It'll help. But there's still the mortgage to pay, and all the rest of it.'

'Yes.' She nodded. 'I can see that.' Inside, her brain was processing everything as fast as it could.

Dan said, 'You do understand everything . . . don't you, Cheska?'

His question hung in the air, and she knew it was all he was going to say about their secret. He was telling her that she is to be shut out of their babies' lives, and that she must accept this and not make a fuss. She understood now that this one conversation would set the boundaries forever, and Dan had made it clear that the truth would never be mentioned. He thought it would be an easy matter to shut her up and keep her quiet and make her do as he wants. He has always thought that.

'I understand perfectly.' She gave him the warm, intimate smile she always uses to make sure he trusts her. 'Of course I do.'

But it's not going to happen again. Not this time. The knowledge shimmered through her like a familiar mantra. *I love him. We're supposed to be together.* And now there was a new and potent addition to it. *We are parents now. Those tiny babies are us, bound unbreakably together.* It gave her that feeling she had when she was first with Walt. *Restoration. Resurrection—*

'Frankie?'

Walt's voice pulls her back into the present. She shakes her head lightly and says, 'Yes?'

'That's okay with you?'

'What?'

'To organise the trip to the Hall for us all?'

'Oh. Yes. Of course.'

Walt frowns at her. 'Are you sure you're okay, Frankie? You really do seem kind of down.'

She manages another smile. 'No. I'm fine. I'll feel better

when I can see the children again. It feels as though they've been gone for ages.'

'They'll be home soon, and then you'll be longing for them to go away again!' He laughs.

She wishes she could tell him about the hollowness in her heart, and the knowledge that Dan and Olivia and the babies will soon be boarding a plane to South America, but she can't. There's no one in the world she can tell.

Chapter Ten

1959

They come back across the playing fields, red-cheeked and breathless from games, a gaggle of girls in black gymslips and white shirts, hair blown about by the wind that whistles across from the east, chilling their legs and biting their fingers.

'Why is it always so bloody cold in this place?' Alice asks, but she doesn't seem to expect an answer. She is gazing towards the building site half concealed by the row of waving evergreens that grows along the boundary of the playing fields.

Julia follows her gaze, half aware of Miss Dunleavy, the games mistress, chivying along in the rear, hurrying them all back to the changing rooms. Behind the trees, there is movement: the men working on the new swimming pool and gymnasium. They've been here since the beginning of term and still there doesn't seem to have been much progress, just a slightly bigger, muddier hole than there was before.

'When do you think it'll be ready?' Julia asks. 'It looks like it's going to be simply ages.'

'Can't take too long for my liking,' Alice replies. She pulls the band out of her hair so that her long fair locks are freed. They're lifted by the wind in long, drifting streamers. Alice is pretty, Julia knows that. She has a sweet, heart-shaped face, and blue eyes with dark lashes. Alice also knows she's pretty, and that when she looks innocent and smiles, people forgive her things. Perhaps that's why she's so mischievous. Julia understands that Alice has an appetite for naughtiness and adventure that can't be sated but doesn't know why that is. Alice says it's because she hates this place, because she can't wait to grow up and do whatever she likes, and that all the nice things about being an adult can't come too soon for her. But Julia thinks it must be more than that, because Alice cannot resist an opportunity to break a rule.

The arrival of the builders at the school was like a red rag to Alice's bull. Julia prefers the old kind of mischief that Alice used to lure her into – going out of bounds, sneaking food into the dorms, stealing from the tuck shop – to this new and more dangerous kind.

'Come on.' Alice nudges her. 'Let's try and get close to them. I want to see Roy.'

'Dunleavy is just behind us,' Julia says nervously, glancing over her shoulder.

'So . . .' Alice drops to her knee, pulls the lace on her boot undone and then starts elaborately retying it. 'Bother this boot,' she says loudly as other girls wander past. 'The laces have gone all long on one side.'

'Hurry up, Alice, please,' Miss Dunleavy says as she goes

past, 'no loitering.' But she's absorbed in counting up the bundle of bibs she's carrying.

'Yes, Miss Dunleavy,' Alice says demurely, and as soon as the games mistress is past, she reties her lace and stands up. 'Come on,' she whispers.

Julia knows there's no changing Alice's mind once she's decided. *Why do I let her do it?* She's not really sure, except that she likes Alice. She was flattered when the prettiest girl in the class wanted to be her friend, and Alice is funny and fascinating as well as glamorous. Her parents are divorced; her mother lives in London with her new husband while her father is still on their farm far away in the country somewhere. Alice doesn't talk about them much, except to tell Julia all the ways in which she's deceived them in order to enjoy herself. And even though Julia is not a great lover of danger, she can't deny that the heart-pounding mixture of thrill and fear that disobedience brings adds spice to life. But now it's all going too far.

'Dunleavy'll catch us,' Julia says, trying to make the effort to restrain Alice.

'No she won't. Come on.'

Alice veers away from the path back to the old changing rooms and takes them a little way along the treeline, then through it at a well-worn shortcut. This brings them out by the new pool site, which is, as they know very well, strictly out of bounds. The air is full of the roar of a digging machine but it stops just as they emerge from the trees, and then Julia can hear the low rumble of male voices and shouts of command. The men are standing about in working overalls, some with hard hats on, some wheeling barrows of mud, others in the great pit in the ground. One looks like the foreman, wearing a big dark jacket and a flat cap, holding a clipboard and deep in conversation with another workman.

As the girls emerge from the trees, they're noticed at once and the men turn to look and smile. One or two whistle shrilly. Julia is overcome with embarrassment. She feels young and stupid, embarrassed that they are obviously choosing to show themselves on the site. Alice doesn't seem to mind at all; in fact, she revels in the attention, swinging her hips a little and smiling coquettishly.

'How are ya, ladies?' calls one in a lilting Irish accent.

'Wouldn't you like to know?' shoots back Alice.

Julia wants to curl into a ball. She can feel her face reddening with the awfulness of it all, and she's possessed by crippling gaucheness. Her body seems an alien thing she hardly inhabits at all. She's painfully aware of the men looking at her; the small bumps of breasts at the front of her gymslip, her bare legs, and the windswept hair tucked behind her ears. Alice is more developed, more womanly, and certainly more confident. She nudges Julia. 'There's Roy,' she whispers. Then she waves and grins. 'Hi, Roy!'

Julia looks over to where Alice points. She sees a man leaning on a spade, watching them. He doesn't look happy that Alice is waving at him. He nods curtly and turns away.

'Isn't he handsome?' Alice says dreamily. Julia has caught a glimpse of a swarthy face and dark hair. Now all she can see is a broad back as Roy digs hard into the mud at the side of the pit, his workman's boots caked in it. Then she sees the other man, the one just beyond Roy. He's skinny with a boyish look about his hollow cheeks, and his black hair is long at the front, greased up like Cliff Richard's. He has a hungry expression in his sharp blue eyes and he is staring straight at Julia. She stiffens and looks away, tugging at Alice's arm.

'Come on,' she hisses. 'We've got to get back to the changing rooms.'

'I wonder why Roy won't look at me,' Alice says, staring at the obdurately turned back, the brawny arms still shovelling mud.

The foreman turns to see them, and frowns. He clearly knows they shouldn't be there. 'Clear off, you girls,' he calls.

'Let's go.' Julia turns, determined to leave Alice if she won't come with her, and heads back along the treeline towards the door to the school. They will be missed in a minute. Alice pants close behind her.

'Hold up, Julia,' she says. 'I'm just coming. What's the rush?'

'So that's your boyfriend, is it? He didn't seem all that happy to see you.' Julia is intent on reaching the still open door to the changing rooms. Once it's closed, they won't be able to slip in unnoticed.

'I shouldn't have shouted out to him. He told me not to. He said we have to keep it a secret.'

'Where do you two meet?'

'His caravan isn't that far away. He shares it with Donnie. Donnie doesn't mind making himself scarce when I'm around.'

They're at the door now. Julia can hear Dunleavy in the changing room: 'Where is Alice Warburton? And Julia Adams?'

'Here we are, Miss,' she calls, hurrying in. There's the usual smell of dirty kit, old mud, and stale water from the shower room. 'Sorry.'

'Get yourselves changed. You're going to be late for prep.' Dunleavy isn't interested in what's delayed them, and Julia has long learned the value of not explaining unless expressly asked.

As she and Alice are pulling off the black gymslips, she whispers, 'Who is Donnie?'

'He's Roy's mate, of course. He's the youngest on the site, Roy says, but works just as hard as anyone.'

'Does he have that slicked-up hair?' Julia asks.

'Yes, all greasy at the front. Looks rather good, I think, don't you? He looks like a real rocker.'

Julia says nothing as the gymslip covers her head and when she emerges, she says, 'He's all right. But I don't think you should go and see Roy anymore. It's dangerous.'

'Don't be an idiot,' Alice says with a grin.

'I just don't think it's worth it. What if you get caught? There'd be the most awful row. You'd be expelled.'

Alice shrugs. She's down to her brassiere and knickers now, her blossoming body pale and slender and pretty. She would look fragile if it weren't for the stubborn expression on her face and the wilful light in her eyes. 'So what? I hate this place. Maybe Daddy would send me somewhere better.

Besides, I'm not going to stop now, not when it's just getting interesting.'

Julia doesn't want to think what Alice means by this. She has a portentous feeling, as though something dark and menacing is approaching, and she is helpless to stop it.

PART TWO

Chapter Eleven

Two years later

The stones of the old house soak in the sunshine, thirstily absorbing it as though warming the bones of the place after the rigours of winter. Olivia wonders what winter in the house will be like. She imagines the numbness of the soles of her feet, the nasty prickle of chilled toes, the stiffness of white and purple fingers, and the way her lips become rimmed with blue. She's always felt the cold.

Oh my God. How will I stand it? Especially after Argentina.

She shivers, even though the day is warm. In fact, it's more than warm. It's properly hot. An English spring day and here she is, in this beautiful place. A dream. A dream house. A fantasy home which is now, unbelievably, *her* home. The place where she and Dan and the twins live.

Easter has just passed, and now there are flocks of daffodils nodding their heads all over the garden, banks of yellow primroses, early camellias in palest pink opening their soft frilly saucer faces to the sky. The cherry trees shake their pink and white blossom in the light spring breeze. Everywhere she looks bright green shoots are emerging. This is usually her favourite part of the year, when the work to be done outside starts to call to her and she is hungry to be out and doing. This is when gardens wake up, responding to the light and warmth and the change of season. Old friends come back, new ones emerge from the earth. Already she's thinking of dividing and replanting the bulbs of the early flowers that have come and gone: snowdrops and crocuses. Now she should be thinking of her summer crop of fruit, flowers and vegetables, and preparing the ground for new growth.

But this is not her garden. She doesn't know where the snowdrops and crocuses blossomed, because that happened before they got here. Everything about it is unfamiliar. Someone else has done all the work. She doesn't know this place, not yet. And anyway, she's rusty. It's been two years since she's experienced a spring at home, and her eye is still re-acquainting itself with an English garden, after being surrounded by the flora of an Argentinian *estancia*. She's become used to hot pinks and purples, fuchsia and mimosa and heavily scented roses, the rich dry green of the ombu tree.

All that lovely warmth. I really will miss it when winter comes back.

But by then, they will have made their bit of the house cosy and warm. The range will take the edge off the chill stone flags of the kitchen floor and begin to pump heat into the thick walls. She thinks idly that she must buy some big old curtains from somewhere to hang over the doorways, particularly the doorway into the hall.

Imagine the gusts of freezing air that will fly through the cracked old doors, whirling in to nip at necks and fingers. Really, this place is completely unsuitable for us. But ... Dan wasn't terribly keen and raised all the practical objections, but she let her reason be overruled by the romance of the house and the opportunity it offered. And the truth was that, whatever Dan said, they didn't have a great deal of choice.

A wood pigeon begins to coo overhead, the sweet, soothing sound filling her with calm just as Dan comes out of the house with that particular air of drained fatigue that comes of persuading someone else to go to sleep when one is dog-tired.

'Success?' she asks, though she's sure that the answer is yes or he wouldn't be here.

Dan nods. 'Yup. Bea was as good as gold. I put her down in the cot and she just shut her eyes and went straight off to sleep. Stan was the tricky one today.'

'He's usually so easy. I think he's still adapting.' She nods at his cup of tea, cooling on the wrought-iron table next to the bench. 'That's yours. Bit cold now, I think. I'll do a fresh one.'

'No, don't worry, it's fine. I quite like it cold. Stan was a real live wire. Finished off all the milk, even after that lunch. It took me ages to get him to stop chatting and nod off.'

'Perhaps it's a growth spurt,' Olivia says pensively. 'I think he's due one.'

Dan settles down on the bench next to her, stretches out

his long legs and sighs. 'Bloody hell. I'm bloody knackered. I never knew it was going to be this hard.'

Olivia laughs. 'Well, we could have guessed!'

'How?' Dan says with a touch of petulance in his voice. 'No one tells you what a relentless slog it is.'

'Yes they do. We just don't understand what it means till it happens. Besides . . .' Olivia finishes off her own tea, now completely cold and metallic, leaving a film over her tongue. 'It all gets better from here on in. Look at Sam and Robbie.'

Her nephews are ten and twelve, and during the stay in Argentina they were hardly seen. When they weren't at school, they were outside playing or in the sitting room on their PlayStations, necks crooked at the TV screen, eyes wide, fingers and thumbs frantically moving on the consoles. They were called to meals, ate without persuasion, went to the loo without being accompanied, cleaned their own teeth, washed themselves, read their own stories. Olivia can hardly believe that one day her own needy little children will be as independent, but the day will surely come. Already she can't really remember the hell of those early months: the blending of day into night, the desperate desire for sleep; the milk-scented, nappy-filled, feeding-obsessed hours when she and Dan just seemed to pass the babies back and forth between them as they slept in what seemed like carefully planned relays designed to prevent their parents from resting for more than twenty minutes. The best decision Dan and Olivia made was to go to stay with her sister and mother on the *estancia*. It was like flying from darkness and stress into light and rest. Sunlight, welcoming smiles and comforting arms greeted them, and suddenly life became a little easier. The mad carousel driven by panic and sleeplessness slowed. She could nap in the afternoons, leaving the babies with her mother. Someone else cooked and cleaned and returned the babies' discarded clothes washed, ironed and folded. Voices of experience calmed and soothed her, and surrounded her and the twins with affection. Slowly, she was able to return to something more like herself, and to enjoy the babies the way she had wanted to. And she had others who loved them to coo and cuddle and find them as infinitely fascinating as she did.

The time slipped easily by. Their London flat was rented out, they had no jobs to get back to. There was room for them in the villa on the *estancia*, and life was pleasant and easy. Dan could take all the time he needed to write, and Olivia felt she could breathe for the first time in a long while. She hadn't realised how tired she was of London and city life. To see sunshine and be surrounded by greenery every day soothed her deep inside, and she felt happy. Now she was able to see how hard the last few years had been, with the stress and strain of fertility treatment, the long anxious wait of pregnancy and the trauma of parenthood. The sense of restoration was seductive. Suddenly a year had gone by, and then another. Then Dan began to be restless. They had been away too long. He wanted to come home and at last she agreed. It seemed only fair, after she'd had two years with her family.

But, sitting on the veranda of the villa, under the soft blue sky, with the pampas grass stretching away into the distance, she felt a sense of horror when she imagined being back in their tiny London flat, with the small patch of green at the back and the endless traffic roaring past, the grey skies and the crowds of people. She could hardly bear the thought of going back. But, as it turned out, there was no way they could return to the flat, even if they'd wanted to.

The children sleep for the usual two hours, and while the place is quiet, Olivia goes on exploring the garden. The grounds of the house stretch out for acres, but not all of it is cultivated. Even so, there's plenty of garden to get to know. She likes the bit outside their quarters best: it's well looked after and mature, a garden that has been carefully nurtured for years and is at its peak. Beyond that, there are maintained lawns mown into contrasting stripes, carefully tended beds without a weed in sight, a rose garden and a pretty formal garden with box hedges grown in exactly symmetrical patterns, containing lavender and foxgloves and verbena within their borders.

Olivia walks the length of the garden wall nearest their door, examining the beds that run along beside it. The earth is still rather barren-looking after the long winter. Aside from the sheaves of finished daffodil leaves and the fresh crop of hyacinth and bluebell poking through, there's not a lot happening. She thinks it's already past the time to mulch here, and to turn the soil to make it a rich dark brown. Her hands itch for garden tools. Hers are back at the flat in the tiny shed. She hasn't thought much of gardening for months

– at least, not like this. She hasn't been ready to get her hands dirty.

They've been too full of babies.

In Argentina, she studied the gardens around the villa but her Spanish was too bad to talk to the gardeners who tended it. She did some research online, visited the botanical gardens in Buenos Aires, and was welcomed to some of the other great estates around the city, to look at their magnificent grounds. When the babies were asleep or being looked after, she started to draw up plans for a book on the native plants and cultivated foreign species that were now thriving in the south east of Argentina, and imagined a beautifully illustrated guide to some of the finest gardens to be seen in that part of the country. In the drier areas to the west, there were dusty stretches, with cacti and dry grasses, but she would concentrate on the lush, green areas around the famous city with its strong European influence. There were gardens based on renowned French pleasure grounds and the landscaping of Italian palazzos, each blended with its own touch of native colour and character. She took dozens of photographs – none good enough for a book but useful for her reference – and now she was beginning to write, though she wasn't quite sure of the structure yet. A year in an Argentinian garden? Or one garden studied with reference to others? It would come as she went along and discovered what it was she wanted to say.

She stops by a laburnum tree that's been espaliered against the wall. Bright green leaf buds are bursting from its dark branches. Soon they'll be out, and then the buds will come. In another month or so, the tree will be bright with golden flowers. But then . . . She puts her hand out to touch the branch closest to her. When the flowers are finished and the bees have done their work, this tree will produce pods containing rows of seeds, like small black peas. The pods will burst open and drop to the ground, and the seeds will be dispersed, ready to grow new laburnum trees, and—

'You want to be careful with that.'

Olivia jumps violently at the voice and turns around. A man is standing across from her in the garden, a mulish expression on his face. He's wearing baggy jeans covered with mud and old black gumboots, and a thick sailor's jumper that was once cream with a loose tweed jacket over the top. His hair is grey and black, greased back with a small quiff at the front, and his face is weathered and creased. It's hard to tell exactly how old he is, but he's not young.

'What?' she says faintly, still startled by his appearance.

'You want to be careful with that.' He nods towards the tree. There's a kind of lilt in his voice that she can't identify. It's not like any accent she's heard before. 'It's poisonous.'

'I know.' She looks back at the blameless-looking trunk and the spreading branches. She is already aware of the toxicity of every part of this plant. Leaves, flowers, and seeds. They can induce sickness, diarrhoea, convulsions and, in small children and animals, prove fatal. She has considered cutting it down, before the pods with their inviting row of small black seeds fall to the ground where Stan and Bea can pick them, and where little fat fingers can pluck and transfer the poison from pod to mouth, and then . . . It's too horrible to think about. Dizziness rushes through her.

'You've got little ones,' he says firmly. 'You need to be aware, that's all.'

'Yes, thank you. I know.'

The old man looks her over keenly. 'You settled in the house, have you?'

'Almost—'

'That woman's done it up, hasn't she? I saw them doing it. Weeks of coming and going. Noise and mess.' He shakes his head. 'Plenty of money spent on it, too. It's just the tip of the iceberg, though, isn't it? Has she said when they'll start on the main house?'

'No. I don't know, I'm afraid.'

'The place needs it, but I can't pretend I like it.' The old man looks around and clicks his tongue. 'I've got used to it just being me here – and the bloke who comes to look it over from time to time. Mr Howard. It's going to be mighty strange when it's peopled again.' He turns back to her, interest sparking in his faded eyes. 'Your little ones – boy and a girl, is it?'

'That's right.' Olivia is beginning to guess who she's talking to.

'How old?'

'Just over two.'

He nods. 'Thought so. Well, I like having some children about the place. They're fine ones, too, aren't they? Sturdy little chaps.' Then he fixes her with a beady look. 'Just you make sure you keep the gates and the doors closed. Don't let

105

them wander off. The garden is vast and the house is no place for little ones. There's danger in there, understand?'

'Yes,' Olivia begins, torn between pleasure at his praise of the children and indignation that she might be so stupid as to let them get lost, but he has already turned on his heel and is marching away, presumably the way he came in, through the door in the wall that leads towards the back lawn of the house.

She watches him go. He must be the gardener who has tended this place for years. What is his name?

She turns and heads back to where Dan is dozing in the sunshine. On the table next to him, a notebook lies open at a blank page, a pen next to it. He opens his eyes as she approaches and picks up the pen with a faintly guilty air.

'I just met the gardener, the one Francesca was telling us about. What's his name?'

'William,' replies Dan, and taps the pen nib on the page. He writes it down: *William*.

'What did she say about him?'

'Oh, just that they've had a hell of a time with him. He won't be shifted. He's been here donkey's years and claims that as no one but him has bothered with the house since it was left empty he has a lifetime right of tenancy here.'

Olivia looks out at the garden, and at the carefully tended shrubs beyond the walls, where the lawns stretch away. 'Why don't they just leave him here? He's done a brilliant job. He obviously wants to stay and carry on looking after it.'

Dan shrugs. 'He's getting on. He won't be able to work, and then who'll look after him?'

'So what are they going to do with him? Chuck him out?'

'I can't remember what Cheska said now. They've moved him on a bit. He was in our cottage originally. He's been shunted on to a place further away from the house.'

Olivia is struck with guilt. They've displaced him. He's been turfed out and they've taken his home. Maybe he hates them. Does that mean there's a strange, malevolent and resentful old man wandering about, wishing them harm? But then, he did warn her about the laburnum. So he must be quite safe, surely.

'I'm not sure what to make of him,' she says, frowning.

'Why not ask Cheska when she comes over? She ought to know what's going on. It's her house, after all.'

Chapter Twelve

In her study in Geneva, Francesca is on the telephone, her eyes fixed on their garden outside.

'Of course, Mr Howard. That's perfectly fine. You've seen the plans. You know what we want. You're at liberty to visit whenever you wish.' She uses the voice she employs when trying to get things done for her charity work: smooth, controlled, with quiet authority. She suspects she's going to be using it quite a bit with this man. He is already irritating the life out of her.

Mr Howard says cheerfully, 'That's very good to know, Mrs Huxtable. I will take full advantage of that, if you don't mind.'

'Of course I don't mind. I wouldn't have said it otherwise.'

'You do know that you have a very important piece of history in your possession, don't you? I'm afraid we are obliged to make sure you look after it.'

'Thank you,' she says, a touch of ice in her voice. 'I quite understand the value of our house. And I realise that all this interference is something I cannot change. Unfortunately. I'm afraid I must go now. Goodbye, Mr Howard.' She clicks the call off and sighs with annoyance. As if the renovation of a huge house isn't enough to have on her plate, she has to put up with all these complications as well. She is unaccustomed to people standing in her way; usually, they do all they can to ensure she is completely satisfied. Take the architect, for example – he couldn't do enough to make her happy. His enormous bill sits on her desk, proof of the care and attention he has lavished on her.

'Mum . . .' Olympia has slipped into the study, wheedling as usual. Now that her daughter is almost fourteen, she is constantly asking for things. Her requests seem to breed like the Hydra: fulfil one, and three more grow in its place. Her boarding school has widened her social circle to include the children of the rich jet set, and now she wants to keep up with them: their clothes, their gadgets, their holidays.

Francesca turns to smile at her. 'What is it, darling?'

'Can you ask Daddy for an extension on my credit card?'

'Ask him yourself.' She sighs with annoyance. 'You haven't maxed it out again, have you? It's barely halfway through the month.'

Olympia looks sulky. 'I can't help it. Things cost money. What am I supposed to do about it?'

Francesca looks over at her daughter. Adolescence has been kind so far: Olympia has clear skin and bright eyes; her hair is long and fashionably tousled. Her clothes are the most expensive money can buy and she is more attached to her phone than ever, now a crystal-studded model. She barely acknowledges her mother except when she wants something, which, at least, is often.

What was I like at her age?

She remembers her waitressing job in the local cafe to earn enough money to buy the few clothes she could afford. She remembers long hours in charity shops looking for second-hand bargains and loading up with used books to read in her tiny bedroom away from the noise and chaos of her family. She hated the way she looked, and went around hiding behind dyed-black hair grown long, and shrinking inside baggy clothes and heavy lace-up boots. She never had one tenth of the comfort and money that Olympia takes for granted. And yet . . . she was driven where her daughter is languid and bored. She was interested in the world, where Olympia is only excited by the doings of her tiny, privileged circle and its constant acquisition. Olympia's school reported that her results were not as good as they'd hoped: the only lesson she really applies herself to is skiing. Thousands of dollars in fees, and she can ski.

Did I do something wrong? I thought if I gave them everything I never had, they'd be happy. But it only seems to make them discontented.

'So?' demands Olympia.

'I told you. Ask your father.'

'When will I get to see him? He's never here!' shouts Olympia, cross. 'Why can't you do it? It's typical. You don't care how much I suffer.' Bursting into noisy tears, she runs out.

This is normal, Francesca tells herself. But it stabs her

nonetheless. The sheer ingratitude of it. The silly selfishness. *But she's still a child.*

A fear has begun to haunt her, that she's made a vital mistake along the way with her children that means they will grow up to be like this permanently: ungrateful and selfish. They will never understand her, nor she them. She loves them but more and more she longs for them as they used to be, as very young children, before they became so grasping. She is struck by a strong desire to go back and undo her mistakes, to be firmer and less indulgent. *It's too late now.*

She sighs and turns back to the file of correspondence on the desk in front of her. It's thick with documents. Walt's declaration that he had bought Renniston Hall turned out to be a little premature. It was only the beginning of months of long and tortuous negotiations, but once they were out of the way, the real trouble started. Architects were commissioned to redesign the house to provide the layout necessary for modern living: bathrooms for every bedroom, dressing rooms, state-of-the-art kitchen, home cinema and all the rest of it. Elizabethan houses were not created with such things in mind, and the struggle with the conservation officers began. It wasn't just them – the two men from the council she'd grown to loathe – but also the officer from Preserving England, who seems to have just as much say as anyone else, despite the fact that the house no longer belongs to the society.

Tom Howard is charming enough, and good-looking in his way, but he has an implacable will and a veneration for the past that borders on the obsessive. It would be different, Francesca feels, if so much of what he says weren't theoretical. No one exists who actually saw how the house was originally lived in or how it was run or why certain things were built. No one knows how much has been knocked down and reconstructed, or altered or changed. It's only conjecture. And yet, Tom Howard seems to think he has a direct route to the past via his imagination. He's knowledgeable, certainly, with a limitless bank of information on historic architecture. But it irritates Francesca that he seems to see no value in the present, or a place for the house to evolve into somewhere fit for a twenty-first-century family.

Sometimes she thinks she could happily wring his neck.

And, as she expected, the burden of the project landed in her lap. Once Walt ticked off the plans, he handed the whole thing over to her, and was waiting only to be told when the house was ready to move in to.

And that will be years away at the rate we're going.

But that suits her purpose now. In fact, she is doing nothing to hurry along the work. Not now that Dan and Olivia and the twins are there. She smiles to herself.

In two days I'll be with them. Dan can't keep them away from me any longer.

On the plane, Francesca is impatient. She spends the short flight to London sipping sparkling mineral water and scanning Olivia's Facebook page for news. She's been visiting it almost obsessively for two years, and finds the lack of activity frustrating. There has been the occasional picture of the babies, but after a brief flurry when they arrived in Argentina, and some photos to mark birthdays, there has been almost nothing. Olivia does post, but she tends to concentrate on plants and flowers, putting up photographs of things she has seen with a little comment about how beautiful they are, or why they are flourishing.

If I have to look at another bloody mimosa flower ... Francesca can't get excited about plants, but luckily she has discovered that she can access the Facebook page of Olivia's sister, and that she has been much better at putting up pictures of the children. There are plenty of images of her own offspring to wade through, but they have provided Francesca with a fuller picture of the lives of the twins in Argentina. She clicks there now, to look back at the library of photographs. She feels quite familiar with the house, a white-painted villa with a wooden veranda, and with the lush green lawns, the well-stocked flower beds and shrubs, and the climbing frame with swings dangling from it. The twins' boy cousins are older, skinny-limbed and brown, scampering up and down the climbing frame, diving into the pool, or playing cricket. The twins are often somewhere in the frame, waddling with toddler slowness behind, or clutching fat hands around the rope of the swing. While the bigger boys are like slender starfish, all legs and arms, in the water, the twins bob inside float suits and armbands, floppy hats shading their faces, white suncream smeared over their plump arms. Olivia is there too, holding them on the swing and pushing carefully, or in the pool, eyes crinkled against the sun, hair dark with water and drawn back into a ponytail.

She looks tired, though. Even the tan can't disguise it. Francesca is glad to see that motherhood is taking its toll on Olivia. That is, after all, only fair. Olivia is still plump from her pregnancy, her face full. Even that doesn't hide the new furrows and lines that have appeared on her forehead and the groove that leads from her nostrils to the edges of her mouth.

Dan doesn't look a bit different. She gazes hungrily at the two images that have captured Dan. In one, he has Stanley on his shoulders and the photograph is taken from below so that the little boy is outlined against the vivid blue sky, bending past Dan's head to examine curiously the camera being pointed at him. Dan is looking up and laughing, his hands wrapped tightly round Stanley's ankles. His eyes are navy against the turquoise of the sky, his skin tanned to a light coffee colour, his hair a little more silvered than she remembers. He looks happy and full of love for the little boy on his shoulders. Stanley is a podgy, golden-brown baby with soft brown curls and inquisitive blue eyes, his mouth open half in smile and half in exclamation.

He's so beautiful. She stares at the picture, even though she's seen it hundreds of time before and the image is so familiar she could practically draw it. *Our son.*

The words roll around her mind, delicious and wicked. *I shouldn't. Not my son.* Olivia's son. Dan's son. And yet . . .

Precious little thing. Isn't he adorable? He looks like Fred when he was just a baby. I'm sure that hair will darken by the time he's ten, just like Fred's did.

Something in her longs to hold the child in the picture, to

reach out and clasp him to her and savour the soft warmth of his body, the smell of his hair, and the beating of his heart next to hers. She wants to feel his existence close to her own and revel in the fact that he is here because of her.

She pulls up a picture of Beattie. Dan is in this one, but so is Olivia and so the emotional effect is more muted. Olivia is holding the little girl, who is squinting in the bright sunshine and pointing at whoever is taking the photograph. Her hair is darker than it was at birth, a golden caramel with hints of the dark brown to come. Straight and cut just above her shoulders in a long bob. *Like mine.* She can't make out the colour of the little girl's eyes, but she suspects they are the same green as her own and feels certain that this is the child whose looks could betray the secret. Of course this little girl will be like her, it's inevitable. She thinks of Olympia, who takes after Walt's side of the family with her fairness. The difference in their looks has never bothered her, except at odd moments when she's wondered how on earth she produced within her someone who looks so utterly unlike her. Now, the irony . . . that Olivia has done the same.

Beattie is the daughter I was meant to have.

The thought floats through her mind and she gasps, horrified at herself. She dismisses it at once. *Of course that's not true.* The implication that Olympia is not the right result is not one she can tolerate. But still, she gazes, fascinated, at the little girl as she sits on Olivia's hip and has the same feeling she does when she meets a friend of hers in Geneva who adopted children. It's a creeping sense that, despite all appearances to the contrary, there is something not quite genuine about the relationship between the mother and the adopted child. Of course, there is love, compassion, kindness ... but the true, profound bond of the parent to its offspring? Can that really grow between genetic strangers? She knows it's wrong to think that it can't. If she had to argue the case, she would declare that mothering a child is more than sharing its genes. But deep down, a little voice is telling her that Beattie would love her more than she loves Olivia if she only knew the truth.

She closes the Facebook page and switches off her phone. They are coming in to land. The whole thing is getting closer to her now. She's only hours away.

What are you trying to do? she asks herself. Nervousness – or fear – bubbles in her stomach. *What's your plan?*

There is no real plan, just a slow movement towards whatever is meant to be. She has crazy fantasies sometimes, ones she knows would be intolerable in real life. She conjures them at night in the darkness when she can't sleep and is possessed by a kind of wicked excitement. A strange and enticing future beckons, one that means certain key people have to be disposed of. In fantasy, she can casually wipe them out, but in real life that would be impossible. Not to be considered. Very, very wrong.

But things are working out very strangely. She remembers the way the return to England was broached. How it came about. An email from Olivia, not from Dan, who has not been in touch at all beyond a few cheery greetings and replies to emails she sent him, in which she was always upbeat and friendly and never mentioned the thing that lay between them.

Hello, Cheska

Olivia picked up the nickname from Dan, and although Francesca doesn't really like her using it, there isn't much she can do about it.

So it looks like our time in Argentina is coming to an end. There are all sorts of reasons why it's best to come home now, even though I'm going to miss it like crazy. It's been such a brilliant start for the twins, with family around to help out and keep us all from going insane. I've really loved being able to share their babyhood with my mother and sister, too. Really special. But . . . time for a reality check. It won't be long before they start school, and we need to think about what's going to happen next.

The thing is, we've got a problem. Our flat is rented out, as you know, and it just doesn't make any sense to go back there when it's bringing in an income. I can't face London, anyway. So we are looking for a place to live. We could go near Dan's parents but I can't quite face that either. You know that his mum is in a home and doesn't know who he is anymore. His dad is devoted to her, and that's great, but I have a feeling that if we were nearby, we'd be on caring duty for both of them, and I can't manage it right now. Besides, they're pretty far north and you know how much I hate the cold. And, more to the point, Dan doesn't particularly want to be near them. So . . . we're just trying to think of nice places to live – a house with a garden, a good school nearby, all the usual stuff – and I remember that you used to live in Gloucestershire, didn't you? What was that like? Would you recommend? I know it was a while ago and things may have changed, but any advice is gratefully received.

Hope all is well with you guys. One of the upsides of coming back is that we'll get to see you more often, and you can spend a bit of time with Stan and Bea. They are so sweet, they really are. You must meet them properly. I'm loving it, even if it's all completely shattering!

Speak soon.

Lots of love,

Olivia x

Francesca read and reread the email, trying to work out what was between the lines. The implication was that they needed the money that the London flat was bringing in. Did that mean that Dan hadn't been able to find another job, or that he didn't intend to? If Olivia had decided not to live in London, it would be tricky for Dan to find a job in the sphere he'd worked in before.

Gloucestershire? She instantly conjured up the home where she grew up, a tiny house in a large estate on the edge of a big town. Her primary school had been all right, but her secondary was a massive place in which she'd felt out of place and mostly ignored. Except there had been Mrs

Patterson, who had encouraged her and made her feel she could achieve something. Mrs Patterson had seen her love of reading, and pushed her towards books and authors she'd never heard of. Soon, Francesca was retreating to Mrs Patterson's classroom whenever she could, to read quietly and study harder. Mrs Patterson had told her that she should apply to Cambridge University, and that she could get there if she worked as hard as she could. Not far from her huge, concrete, sprawling monolith of a school two bus rides away from home, there was a private girls' school, housed in an elegant Victorian brick building behind neatly trimmed hedges, playing fields for hockey and lacrosse stretching out beyond it. Francesca had seen the girls walking about the grounds or heading home in the afternoons. The older ones wore their own clothes, and they seemed like impossibly graceful creatures in their floating skirts and printed blouses. All of them seemed to be so polished, so elegant. She'd wondered if it was because they had money. But it couldn't just be that, could it? Were they taught different things inside their exclusive, closed-off world? Were they taught how to live in that easy, confident way, and were secret rules of existence divulged to them that meant they could belong and she could not? But she wanted to belong. As thousands of kids poured through the gates of her school each morning, boys whooping, running, grubby schoolbags bouncing, uniforms skewed, girls caked in make-up, skirts hoisted up, Francesca felt lost in their chaotic sea of humanity. She yearned to be in the other place, where life looked calm, quiet and ordered, and where rules were respected, where people seemed to matter. She knew then that Cambridge was the way to find those people and join them, and she decided that she would go there, if she possibly could. That was the beginning of her journey.

Gloucestershire? She shivered at the thought of her twins being taken there. Of course, Olivia envisaged quite a different version of it: a Cotswold cottage with a verdant garden, a village primary school with small classes and lots of outdoor space. But Francesca could only think of the place she'd been so desperate to escape.

Dearest O

I'm so excited that you are all coming back! I'm sure life in Argentina was wonderful but you're right to return and get settled before the twins start school. It's never too early to find the right place. I hope you don't mind if I make a suggestion for you to think about. You know Renniston Hall, don't you? That place I showed you the brochure for all those months ago? You probably thought the whole thing had fizzled out, and it nearly did, but in fact we have completed the purchase and it won't be long before renovation begins.

Here's what I'm thinking . . . part of the house is suitable for living in. I think it was quarters for a housekeeper or something. It has its own bit of garden – quite a large bit – and is more or less separate. How about if you and Dan live there with the twins while you think about where you want to go eventually? It has all the space you need. There will be some building work going on, and you and Dan could do me a favour by being on site to keep an eye on things. In return you wouldn't need to worry about rent. It's a very special place, I'm sure you would like it. And there is a nearby school with an outstanding nursery attached to it.

You don't need to let me know right away. Have a think and talk it over with Dan. The offer is there if you want it.

Can't wait to see you all.

Love, F

xxx

That had been enough to set the ball rolling. Because how would she see enough of them if they were out in the middle of the countryside somewhere? This way she would be pulling them closer to her, wrapping them up in her world.

As long as Olivia couldn't resist the lure of the house and garden, and the idea that all of it was free. Francesca didn't know what discussions or negotiations took place between Dan and Olivia, but after the initial grateful thanks for a hugely kind offer, there was a wait of a fortnight or more before Olivia wrote back, asking if there was a way they could take a look at the house.

That was when Francesca knew the plan had worked.

Chapter Thirteen

'Dan, please, take them outside and play with them while I get this finished. Cheska will be here any minute.'

Olivia is flustered, rushing about to make it all look as tidy as possible. They haven't long been in, just over a week, and there are still boxes everywhere, the things from their flat in London having been delivered by a courier from the storage unit. The twins' relentless routine has meant that unpacking has been relegated to nap times and in the evenings, when Dan and Olivia are both tired from another long day of guarding two energetic toddlers.

'Okay, okay.' Dan scoops up Bea from her booster seat, where she's been playing with the remains of her pasta and tomato sauce, smearing it lovingly over the pale blue polka-dotted oilcloth on the table. 'Come on, monsters, let's go out and leave Mummy to it.' He looks over at Olivia as she hurries at the tomato sauce with a damp cloth. He unclips the little black belt holding Stan in his place. He's begging for a biscuit loudly. 'Don't get yourself too het up. It's only Cheska, not a royal visit.'

'I know but I want her to see that we can look after this place, that's all.' Olivia scrubs away at the red stain but it's already sunk in and left a pale orange mark behind. 'Oh, bother this bloody sauce.'

Dan laughs. 'For crying out loud, this is the best bit by far! Have you not looked at the rest of the house?'

Olivia laughs too. She sees his point. Beyond the door that links their bit with the big house lies a huge dirty emptiness that she only glimpsed once, not long after their arrival. The scale seemed overwhelming. Their quarters are much more modest and they are lucky to have them. There was no sign that Dan was going to get another job, and when she asked him about it, he was evasive and then bullish about the fact that they still had half of his redundancy money left after they had lived so cheaply in Argentina. They paid for the flights, contributed towards the bills and covered the cost of their food, but Olivia's sister didn't charge them for their stay. When she said anxiously that life wouldn't be so cheap back in England, Dan said that he needed longer to work on his play. He had a unique chance to devote himself to writing, and once he went back into corporate life, it would be impossible. Besides, he was enjoying being with the twins at this precious stage of their lives. She saw his point, even if she couldn't help wondering how much longer the play would take when he'd already had two years, but it didn't solve the problem of how they would manage. Her own freelance career has been completely quiet since she had the babies, and her plan for a gardening book of her own has a hazy, half-formed aspect. Besides, it would bring in very little money, certainly at first. She's had a bit of success with gardening books and journalism, and that means she has some royalties every six months, but not enough to live on. So when Francesca offered them free accommodation in a beautiful part of the country, it was not something to be turned down lightly. Just a few more years, and then the children would be at school and Olivia would be free to re-energise her own career. And by then Dan would surely have got the play he is writing out of his system. He seems convinced that it will solve all their problems, that staging it will be straightforward and that an inevitable success will follow its first performance. It happened to a friend of a friend of his, so why shouldn't it happen to him too? All he has to do is write the damn thing, but it's harder than he imagined and the going is slow.

'Writing isn't easy, Olivia,' he said one hot afternoon on the *estancia* when she asked after his progress. They were lying in their bed in the villa while the twins were out playing with their grandmother in the garden. They'd taken the opportunity to retire to their bedroom and make love: intense, rather sweaty and rapid, as it had been since the babies had arrived. They seemed to have lost the knack of leisurely pleasure, but no doubt it would come back as the children granted them more time to themselves. 'Creative writing is particularly demanding. It needs time and nurturing.'

She prickled a little at the implication that her writing was easy but then, maybe it was. She could no more write a play than she could fly, but she found plenty to say about the habits of hardy annuals or the best kinds of shade-loving bedding plants. Making things up must be harder.

She said, 'So surely living rent-free at Renniston is the perfect solution. You can carry on writing and we don't have to worry about earning more money right away, with what we have left over from the flat rental.'

'I don't know,' he answered, frowning. 'Is it worth all the upheaval of moving there and getting ourselves settled in a part of the world we don't know?'

'But it's a great offer,' Olivia countered. 'I've looked up the primary school and it really does seem just what I'd hoped for. Outstanding, according to Ofsted. The pressure would be off for a couple of years at least.'

'The play won't take me that long,' Dan replied, his hands tucked behind his head, his elbows pointed out like a pair of bony wings on either side. She could see the feathery fronds of hair in his stretched armpit. It made her think of a woodlouse on its back, its many legs in the air. Dan's chest, shoulders and torso were resolutely white but the rest of him had tanned to a light brown in the Argentinian sun. He looked healthier than he had in London, where he'd had the pallor of the office worker, and his eyes shone bluer against his darker skin. She turned over to him and ran a finger lightly over his chest and circled one of his nipples.

'Of course it won't. But I like the idea of being able to stay if we need to. I'm sure I can find some garden design work. I've already researched some local companies, and I liked the look of one in particular. They might be interested in taking me on for a bit. And the house . . . well, it looks magnificent, don't you think? What an amazing place for the children to spend some of their childhood.'

Dan frowned up at the ceiling, where a metal fan hung above them, whirring and slowly spinning, keeping cool currents moving through the room so that they didn't stifle. 'Yes. But—'

'I know what you're going to say. It's my only real worry,' Olivia said, turning back to lie on her pillows. She pushed her hair away where damp tendrils were sticking to her cheek. 'The place might be dangerous for little ones. And if there's any building work going on . . . well, I can't do it if it's a building site. Cheska seemed to imply we'd be quite separate from any of the work, though. So I think we should go and see it.'

Dan laughed shortly. 'All the way to England just to look at it? I don't think so.'

Olivia sighed. 'You're right. We'll have to find another way.'

Dan rolled over and stared her straight in the eye. 'But are you sure? Do you really want to be . . . so . . . close to her?'

Olivia blinked at him in surprise. 'Close? To Cheska? She's in Geneva!'

'I know, but . . .' He made an impatient click with his mouth. 'The place wouldn't be ours.'

'Because we can't afford one right now.'

Dan looked away and sighed. 'Okay, okay. It's fine. Don't worry about it.'

'I don't imagine we'll see much of her,' Olivia soothed.

'If you're worried about your work being interrupted.'

But he didn't reply.

In the end, their viewing of the Hall was done over Skype, with Francesca taking her tablet around the living quarters so they could get a feel for where they might live, but it was difficult to envisage the place as a home. It was almost empty and the dull winter weather gave everything a dirty grey tinge. Outside the garden looked large and with potential but it was dormant, everything bare and bleak.

'You can make it so lovely,' Francesca said over the connection, her voice disembodied as she carried the tablet around. 'I'm going to renovate it and furnish it anyway, so don't worry about that. My plan was to use it as extra accommodation and maybe a holiday let at some point. As long as you don't mind my taste.'

'Of course not,' Olivia said quickly. 'That would be amazing, if you're sure.' Secretly she wished she could do the choosing – Francesca's taste veered more towards the glossily perfect than her own – but that was a very ungrateful thought. 'There's just one other thing . . . the building work. Where will that all take place?'

'Don't worry about that for a moment. For one thing, your bit of garden is completely enclosed. And for another, any works would be based on the other side of the house. It's a bit difficult to show you the scale of this place, but you can be sure that you'd hardly be aware of them. You'd have to go looking for them. Really. This place is the size of a school, remember.'

That had been enough to reassure Olivia. After that, she had to work on Dan, who remained strangely reluctant to take up the offer, despite the fact it seemed perfect, the answer to their prayers.

'Maybe,' he said at last, when she'd pressed him again on why he was negative about it, 'it's because I don't want us to be so beholden to Cheska.'

'Really?' She stared at him in surprise. 'Why not? I mean, you're such old friends. Why wouldn't she try and help us if she can? And from the sounds of it, we'd be doing her a favour too, seeing as she can't be there all the time. She obviously wants someone she can trust to be at the Hall.'

'Yes.' He pursed his lips, frowning. 'I just mean . . . in case there are any problems. We don't want to ruin a friendship.'

She laughed. 'Ruin it? How? I suppose if we burned the house down or something, she might be a trifle narked. But there's no way Cheska will hold it over you. She seems really eager to help us. And let's face it, she can afford to, so why not let her?'

Dan sighed and said, 'I suppose you're right. And it needn't be for long, if I can just get this play finished.'

'How close are you?' she asked. He'd never let her see anything he was doing, and quickly closed the computer screen whenever she came near him while he was working. He told her he was sensitive about anything being seen and taken out of context before he was ready.

'Getting there,' he said vaguely. 'Making progress. Sometimes it's a two steps forward, one step back kind of thing, you know?'

'I suppose so,' she replied, though she'd always found the process of writing more straightforward than that. 'Well, you should take the time you need. So that it's right.'

Dan nodded. 'Absolutely. It has to be right. I knew you'd understand. Honestly, it's not that far off being a complete first draft. I'll show it to you soon, I promise.'

Six weeks later, they boarded a plane, each holding a twin, their copious luggage safely stored in the aircraft's belly, and headed back to England to live in a place they'd never seen before. Francesca wasn't able to be there when they arrived, so she had posted them the key and sent a long and complicated email about how to let themselves in. It was pitch-dark and all of them were utterly wrung out and exhausted by the trip when they arrived in a minibus taxi arranged by Francesca to pick them up at the airport and bring them and all their stuff up the motorway to Norfolk. Thank goodness for Francesca: when they finally managed to find their way to their quarters, there was a hamper of food waiting for them, the place was beautifully furnished and equipped, and everything seemed fully functional. Olivia had only a vague sense of a vast thing attached to their tiny bit of the house – the cottage, as she quickly began to think of it – as though they were in a tug boat that was towing a huge empty liner along after them through a dark sea. Only once had she looked inside the main house, but she was too overwhelmed by the scale of what lay beyond to go very far while she was still so busy sorting out their new home. She was curious about the Hall, but she preferred the cosy warmth of the cottage and the safety of its enclosed garden to the dusty, abandoned grandeur beyond. Then she discovered that it was actually much closer than she'd realised all along.

Now, with Dan in the garden with the twins, she checks the time. Francesca is due any moment. There are still a few boxes stacked against the kitchen wall, but that's not too bad. The ceilings are high and the boxes don't take up too much space. Olivia runs to the sitting room, picks up a blanket and rushes back to drape it over them. Does that look better? She's not sure. They just looked like boxes before, and now they look as though they might be hiding someone, a large square red and white checked presence standing like a sentry against the wall. She takes off the blanket, and they go back to being neatly stacked boxes again.

She darts a glance around the room. All is tidy. She was afraid that Francesca would make this place look very modern, like the house in Geneva, which she saw once featured in a prestigious interiors magazine, all gleaming surfaces, designer furniture and white walls. But she hasn't. It's been furnished with vintage charm – a large pine table, an oak dresser, old-fashioned armchairs and bright rugs. Everything is new, of course, and clearly not the cheapest either, but it looks inviting and homely, which is exactly what she'd hoped for. She feels a rush of affection and gratitude to Francesca for giving them this opportunity, and she wants to do all she can to be worthy of this kindness, and repay it in any way she can.

Just then she hears voices in the garden. An exclamation

in a female voice, a loud male 'halloo'. *She's here.* Olivia whips off her apron, drops it over the back of a chair along with the blanket and hurries outside.

At first she blinks in the sunshine, which is unexpectedly bright after the cool dimness inside. Then she sees Francesca, who is kneeling in the garden, regardless of her expensive-looking jeans and the smart blue blazer she is wearing, her arms open to Bea, who is tottering across the grass towards her. Francesca is beaming, her attention entirely focused on the little girl as she gets closer. 'Come on, sweetheart,' she is saying, 'come to me . . .'

Olivia smiles at the sight: Francesca's pleasure is pure and guileless – there is no doubt that she is happy to see the children. Dan is walking slowly behind Bea, watching her proudly, Stan in his arms and watching the new arrival with solemn curiosity, as though he is glad that his sister is there to go ahead of him and assess the danger before he gets near.

'Hello, darling!' coos Francesca as Bea reaches her. The little girl's hair glints brightly in the sunshine, and she is wearing a sweet blue pinafore dress, a gift from Francesca that Olivia put on her as an acknowledgement of the generosity. Her tiny feet, looking too small to support her toddler plumpness, carry her the last few steps before Francesca can no longer resist, but scoops her up in her arms and holds her tight.

How wonderful that she loves them so much, Olivia thinks. *I'm so pleased.* She is happy to think of the twins' world peopled by adults who love them and whom the children can trust. There are no godparents, but Olivia wants as many friends and supporters in their lives as possible.

'Hello!' she calls out, walking over towards them. 'You made it.'

Francesca is showering kisses on Bea's cheeks and the little girl is enduring them, an expression of muted curiosity on her face. She pulls away slightly as she sees Olivia approaching and puts out her arms towards her mother, as if she feels she has fulfilled her social obligations and would now like to return to the comfort of the familiar.

'Yes, yes.' Francesca is examining Bea with rapt absorption, as though taking in every centimetre of her soft skin, the colour of her eyes, the miniature perfection of her ears and nose. 'The journey was fine.' She turns for a moment towards Olivia, her eyes shining. 'Haven't they grown? They're so different from the photographs, you just can't tell from those . . .' She stares back at Bea and then looks towards Stan, who is still quiet and suspicious in his father's arms. 'Hello, darling! Aren't you gorgeous? Goodness, he's changed so much, it's hard to believe these are the same little babies I met last time.'

Bea has started to whimper, stretching out her arms so far that she is in danger of toppling out of Francesca's hold altogether, and Olivia, only half thinking, leans in to take her, pulling her daughter free. She is surprised to find that Francesca holds on, and for a moment, she is tugging at Bea and then suddenly Francesca loosens her hold enough for Bea to slip out of her arms and into Olivia's, where she nestles, tucking her head onto Olivia's shoulder. Francesca smiles at

132

her, putting out a hand to her and saying softly, 'But aren't you beautiful?'

Then she turns to Dan. 'And this is the divine Stanley!'

Stan is still eyeing her, blue eyes round and assessing in the unabashedly judging way that small children have. He doesn't smile.

'Come and have a hug from Cheska,' Francesca wheedles, holding out her arms to him. 'Aren't you such a big boy? His eyes! So like yours, Dan. Come on, sweetie, come for a cuddle.'

His eyes still fixed on the stranger, Stan seems to shrink into his father's arms, then turns his face away completely, burying it in Dan's neck. There is clearly no question of a hug. Francesca laughs it away as Dan leans in to kiss her cheek.

'Ignore him, he's a shy bunny,' he says, dropping first one kiss and then another, and Francesca presses the corner of her mouth to his cheek in return. 'How was the trip?'

'Oh, fine. I picked up a car in London, and the traffic was pretty good, considering.' She turns to Olivia, and leans in for kisses. 'I haven't even said a proper hello to you yet! How are you? You look absolutely blooming!'

'Oh, well . . .' Olivia gives an embarrassed laugh. She knows that she is a different version of her old self. She's in a loose shirt dress that is forgiving of her plumper figure, and it's been ages since she had the time to blow-dry her hair properly or put on make-up. It doesn't seem all that important now, but she can't help feeling the contrast with

Francesca's polished looks and elegant outfit. 'Thank you. You look marvellous, as usual.'

It is true that Francesca has barely changed in years: her skin is as smooth and unlined as ever, she's youthfully slender and her hair is still a glossy brown cut in a chic layered bob with a feathery straight fringe.

Olivia goes on, bustling to hide her slight discomfort, 'You must come inside and have some tea or something. I know it's sunny out here, but it can be surprisingly chilly when the wind gets up.'

They all head into the kitchen, Dan and Olivia carrying a child each and Francesca talking merrily about her very early flight from Geneva, every now and then a hand reaching out towards the child nearest to her as if about to stroke them, or hold their hand. But each clings to the parent holding them, quiet in the face of the new arrival. Olivia feels vaguely as though they are not being welcoming enough, and that this will offend Francesca.

They're often shy around strangers, she thinks, *and life has been so full of new experiences lately.* The twins might be wondering where the extended family has disappeared to, and why they are no longer on the *estancia*, although in reality they seem much the same as ever. As long as they are with Dan and Olivia, they don't seem to mind much where they are, settling down in their cots after milk and a story, just as they did in Argentina.

'Oh, you've made it look wonderful,' Francesca exclaims as she comes into the kitchen.

'Well . . . only because you furnished it so well,' Olivia

says shyly, putting Bea down by the box of toys kept at the far end of the room. There's a jug full of daffodils on the oilclothed table, and she's rearranged dishes on the dresser, putting out a bowl of fruit to add a dash of colour to Francesca's restrained white tableware. She goes to the kettle, fills it and switches it on. 'You've really transformed the place.'

Francesca laughs lightly as she sits down, and says, 'It's not entirely . . .' then her voice fades out as she watches Dan settle Stan on the rug next to Bea, putting some toys in front of him. The little boy scrambles up at once, his bottom high in the air as he pushes himself upwards, and then trots to the box to see for himself what he'd like to play with. Olivia likes his independent spirit, the way he wants to be certain that he's got the pick of the bunch to amuse himself with. Bea is chattering to Dan, a stream of gibberish mixed with sense delivered in a high fluting voice with a slight stammer.

'What were you saying?' Olivia asks, getting mugs from the dresser.

Francesca blinks, looks away from Stan and then shakes her head. 'Sorry, I lost my train of thought. I . . . I was about to say that I wanted the place to be nicely done so that we can use it as a holiday let or for staff once you've found your own home.'

Olivia feels a tiny stab of offence at the idea that they've been put in to test-run the staff quarters, and then rebukes herself. That's just stupid. They hardly need the place for guests, not with a house the size of Renniston.

'That's why I wanted top quality stuff,' Francesca says, smiling at her. 'And I'm thrilled it's come in useful for you all.' She smiles at them, almost mistily. 'You seem so at home here.'

'We are,' Olivia says honestly. 'I like it very much.' It's true, she realises. She does like it. The cottage has gone from the neatly impersonal to the lived in and homely in a very short time. It's begun to feel like theirs. *It's probably a good thing that Cheska is here, to remind me that it's not. It's just temporary. I mustn't get used to it.* 'And what are your plans for the main house? Should we expect builders soon?'

'Oh,' Francesca says, suddenly vague. 'Things will happen in a while. We're still getting permission for the architect's plans. It's so incredibly long. Every new bit takes weeks and weeks to agree, and then there are the endless site visits. You might see conservation officers and various people from Preserving England wandering around. I'll tell them to let you know whenever they plan to visit, just so you're not surprised.'

Olivia remembers the old man in the garden warning her about the laburnum. 'Whatever happened about that caretaker? William, isn't he? He's still around.'

'Yes,' Francesca says, though it's clear her mind isn't on what she's saying. 'He's proved a bit tiresome. He seems to have various tenancy agreements and promises that means he can stay as long as he likes. A bit of a bore, really, but it's hardly worth spending a fortune fighting it when he might pop his clogs at any moment, and then the problem's solved.'

Olivia gives her a startled look, surprised at the callous sound of this solution, but Francesca is out of her chair and down on the rug with the children, chatting to them and joining in with their game as much as they will let her. Olivia looks over at Dan with a smile, trying to signal her inner thoughts: *I have a feeling the twins are making Cheska broody!*

Dan is looking at the group on the rug, unsmiling, and he doesn't catch Olivia's eye. The kettle boils and she goes back to making the tea.

Chapter Fourteen

Francesca is on a high, but she's trying to hide it. Excitement bubbles up in her every time she looks at the children, and she can hardly take her eyes off them. She is hiding it well, she believes. A lifetime of schooling herself in control and concealment has given her the gift of preventing others from knowing what she is thinking. Besides, she is careful. She makes sure to ask Olivia about herself, and to question Dan about how he enjoyed life in Argentina. He starts off talking to her almost warily, his sentences short and closed, as though she is the interrogator and he is intent on avoiding her questions, but soon he warms up, and seems to forget that there is anything other than complete normality between them. They slip back easily into their past relationship. Their past pretence.

In fact, there were two distinct stages to their relationship – before and after Olivia. Before . . . well, it was a shaky, difficult time that only began to improve when Francesca found Walt. After Olivia, it all seemed mysteriously healed. The first time she met Dan's new girlfriend, he put his arm around Francesca's shoulders and introduced her to Olivia as his oldest friend, and after that they had a tacit agreement that what went before would never be mentioned again, and that it would be ignored forever. It was almost as though they learned to see themselves as Olivia did: old friends, bound by their university experience, with a long, untroubled, platonic friendship that stayed firm through the vagaries of their romantic lives, the girlfriends and boyfriends that came and went, before Francesca found Walt, and Dan found Olivia. Francesca joined in with the facade because it was the only way she could stay close to Dan; if she began to make waves or remind him of things he'd rather forget, then he might pull away and be lost to her forever. And if Olivia ever suspected, she might well prefer it if Francesca stayed far away. So that was how it had been ever since.

And now there is another stage. The birth of the twins, and everything that brings with it.

It has not developed as she imagined. It's been making her so anxious that she's lain awake at night, darkness pressing against her eyes as she plays through scenario after scenario, wondering why Dan has turned cold on her: vanishing to Argentina, taking the twins, cutting off contact, not sending emails or photographs as she had hoped he might. Then she understood that he is staying true to form, simply ignoring whatever makes him uncomfortable or doesn't fit with his version of reality. He wants, and needs, Olivia to be the mother of his children. So he had to wipe her, Cheska, out of the picture, certainly at first, or the scale of his deception, the con trick he's pulled on Olivia, might prove too much. He might have to look at the truly awful thing he's done, and he might feel compelled to confess and ruin everything, unless he can convince himself that it never happened. And she knows he is very good at doing that.

If my experience is anything to go by.

She recalls how beautifully and neatly Dan has always managed to forget everything in the past. And then he asked this momentous thing of her – *well, all right, I offered, but still* – and so perhaps she shouldn't be surprised that he has decided to forget that too.

But he can't. He'll find that out. He can't.

So she has played the long game, the careful, patient waiting game, and that is something she is very good at indeed. It helps that she now has the priceless gift of access to the children. The only question is how much time is left, because that is a precious resource these days, and she can't afford to squander too much of it. Things will need to happen before too long.

She sits now in the kitchen of the living quarters that she so carefully prepared for Dan and Olivia and the children. It might look artless but there is design in its rustic simplicity: she consulted one of her favourite interior designers on every aspect, trying to make sure it would prove irresistible to Olivia. She was delighted with the (expensive) result, and it is almost a little galling to see how Olivia has changed things, and spoiled some of the finish with her own additions, but Francesca has to admit to herself that the effect is pleasant. The atmosphere is of a cosy cottage, a family home. Only the height of the ceilings and certain touches of grandeur – the diamond-paned windows with a few coloured crests in them, the large slabs of limestone that make up the kitchen floor and the studded oak doors – give away the fact that this is actually part of the larger house, cut off into a separate dwelling years, if not centuries, before.

The children are back in their booster seats, eating their supper of strips of roast chicken and peas, accompanied by potato and carrot mashed together with nuggets of golden fried onion and a top of crisp cheese. Bea is trying hard to feed herself, digging her spoon into the orangey mash and scooping up what she can, then aiming it for her mouth. The lumps in her hair and smeared over her face show that her success is only partial, but she is enthusiastic.

'Yum, yum,' she says loudly when she eats a mouthful.

'Come on, Stan, old chap,' coaxes Dan, trying to get the boy to eat the food heaped on the end of the spoon he holds, but Stan keeps turning his head away, his lips pressed shut. 'This one's an aeroplane, look, it's zooming into the airport . . . here it comes, down into the airport . . . open the airport, for pity's sake, Stan, the passengers are going nuts right now!'

Francesca laughs as she watches, fighting the urge to join in.

Olivia looks tired now that she has rustled up another toddler meal, served on time with its correct balance of nutrients, but she is still alert, still on duty. Francesca recalls how grateful she once was to the nannies who took this tedious, repetitive task off her hands. She would often be busy and gladly hand the children over as the grizzly after-noon session began, right through suppertime to when the children were sitting happy and full in their baths, splashing in bubbles; or even beyond, until all she needed to do was go in and drop kisses on their soft, warm, sleepy faces as they lay in their cots, and whisper goodnight.

Perhaps I should have tried harder, she thinks, as she watches Olivia swoop in to make sure that Bea eats some chicken and drinks a mouthful of her highly diluted juice. In a way, she would love to be back there now, when Olympia and Frederick were sweet, soft-haired, smiling toddlers who were happy with whatever they had, and who reached for her hungrily, giving and receiving kisses and hugs without the accompaniment of requests for money or clothes or holidays. At the time it seemed like hard work that would go on forever. But actually, it was easy. And it was over in the blink of an eye. And now, gone for good.

'Shall we have a glass of wine?' Olivia asks, inadvertently brushing a blob of mash into her hair as she wipes a stray strand from her forehead. She looks up at the clock, a vin-tage French station clock Francesca had shipped from a dealer in Aquitaine, and makes a face. 'The sun is over the yard arm as far as I'm concerned. Anything after five o'clock is civilised!' She smiles over at Francesca. 'I've got some cold Gavi in the fridge.'

'Sounds lovely,' Francesca says. 'But . . .' She raises her eyebrows warningly. 'Only one. I'm driving later.' She turns to Dan. 'So, Dan, how is the writing going? When will we be allowed to read the play?'

Olivia goes over to the fridge and starts looking for wine glasses (*The long-stemmed crystal ones should be in the left-hand cupboard*, thinks Francesca, but Olivia goes to the glass-fronted cupboard where the mugs previously were and takes the glasses from there) while Dan looks uncomfortable.

He clears his throat. 'Well, no one's read it yet. Not even Olivia. I'm not quite ready to show it to anyone. It's kind of . . . sketchy. You know. Words here. Words there. A lot being formed as I go along.'

'How many scenes have you completed?' Francesca presses. She remembers suddenly that at university Dan was writing a novel. Everyone was very impressed. Novel writing was for sometime in the future, when life experience and maturity gave them something worth saying. The novel went on and on being written, even after university: written, edited and never finished, until one day Francesca realised that Dan must have thrown away far more words than he'd ever retained. Perhaps he'd even thrown away two or three novels' worth of words. And still there was not one complete chapter to read. And then it was forgotten.

How long has he been working now? she wonders. *Two years? I suppose he's had the babies taking up a lot of working time, but even so* . . . She is aware suddenly of Olivia listening carefully as she quietly uncorks the bottle and tips out the wine into the glasses.

'It's not really that easy to define a scene,' Dan says, frowning as though thinking hard. 'I mean, of course, I've got scenes. But until I reach the fifth act . . . you know, it will be hard to see exactly what *work* the earlier scenes are doing, and they'll probably need to be completely rewritten. So there are scenes, and yet there aren't.' Then he laughs ruefully, as though realising how ridiculous he sounds.

'So have you got anything finished? Any bits of scenes you're happy with? I mean, in the first act, say?' Francesca says. She thinks it's fine for Dan to take the time he needs as long as he finishes eventually and the pattern of the abandoned novel is not repeated, but she knows Olivia is listening and suddenly has the sense that she has been under the impression that the play is more complete than Dan is now revealing. Olivia comes over quietly and puts a glass of wine in front of Francesca, slipping into the seat next to Bea, who is singing to herself as she chases peas around her melamine plate. Stan is banging his cup on the table as he munches his way through a mouthful of chicken. Over the noise, both women are listening hard to Dan.

Dan smiles his killer smile at her, the one that always melts her. 'None I'd want to show you, Cheska. Not with your insight and judgement. I don't want you to see it until it's perfect, just in case you hate it.'

She smiles back at him, warmed by his praise. 'I'm sure it's brilliant, whatever stage it's at. Is it a comedy? Are you going to say what it's about?'

Dan looks thoughtful as he loads a plastic spoon with more food from Stan's plate, ready to deliver the next mouthful as soon as Stan has finished the last. 'It's a kind of . . . it's a black comedy. A bit satirical. A bit . . . you know, punchy, modern, relevant, absurd. A bit tragic too.'

Tragical-comical-historical-pastoral, she thinks, and won-

ders where that's from. *It's a quote but from where?*
Shakespeare, I think . . . about something ridiculous. 'Wow.
I can't wait to read it.'

'I hope you'll also get to see it,' Dan says, with a modest
smile. 'Even if it ends up being staged in the top room of
some east London pub.'

'You should get in touch with Rupert,' Francesca says.
Rupert is one of their acquaintances from Cambridge who
once directed student plays and is now a celebrated and
award-winning producer. 'Although I suppose he's more film
based these days.'

'Yeah, I was thinking about that, but Rupert was always
a bit of an idiot. I'm not sure I really trust his judgement, if
I'm honest, not after he went and did that musical.'

'Yes,' Francesca agrees. 'It was something of a sell-out. I
suppose the money and the A-listers were too hard to resist.
We can't blame him for that.'

Dan snorts, as though he absolutely can blame him for
that.

Olivia rolls her eyes lightly and says, 'Money isn't always
a dirty word, Dan. It's actually quite useful.'

Dan shrugs. 'But what's the point in anything if you just
give up and take the cash?'

Francesca feels a tiny stab of something painful, as though
Dan is referring to what happened to her: the promising
career in human rights law that faltered and died, before
she became a rich Swiss housewife. She rushes to hide her
awkwardness and suggests a few other names of their con-

temporaries who now have positions of influence in the arts: a couple of actors, a theatre director, a script editor, a literary agent, quite a few who are now important at the BBC. It's a reminder of how gilded they all were, and how much potential they all once had. *How much was handed to us because of our university and the* entrée *it gave us? And the connections we made there?* She recalls that two of the women at university who went on to be well-known actresses had famous parents. Nearly everyone from the circle she mixed in – bright, privately educated, privileged – had contacts to call upon. Even though she had no family connections, Francesca still had the name of her college to drop into conversation like a little magic talisman, her degree ('From Cambridge? Goodness, you must be clever!') and the name of her well-known tutor, a man who wrote bestselling books and presented television and radio programmes, who put her in touch with helpful people when she began her law studies, getting her work experience in chambers specialising in human rights. *But it wasn't only that*, she reminds herself. *It wasn't just leg-ups. We all worked hard to get where we did.*

And then, for her, it all came to a shuddering halt. A blanket of deep sadness drops slowly over her. How did that happen? She's never wanted to think about it. She's always felt that she took the only path open to her, in order to survive. Anything else is too much to consider.

Olivia stands up, as though she is suddenly bored with the conversation. 'Come on, Cheska, let me show you round the rest of the house. Dan, can you give Bea her yoghurt?

She's finished, haven't you, sweetie? You've eaten it all, you clever thing! Isn't she clever?' She leans down to nuzzle the little girl, who beams and crows loudly with pleasure at her cleverness.

'Sure,' Dan says, scooping up more for Stan, who is still slowly eating and now interested in the food in the trench at the bottom of his bib.

'Stan can have one too when he's finished.' Olivia picks up her wine and cocks her head towards the door to the rest of the cottage. 'Follow me, Cheska.'

Francesca stands up, also picking up her glass. She'd like to stay with the children, and was planning to offer to help Stan eat his yoghurt, but she's also interested in the bedrooms. She wants to be able to visualise where the twins sleep. 'Lovely, yes please.'

Olivia leads her out of the kitchen, nursing her wine glass against her chest, one hand on the bowl and one on the base of the stem. The condensation makes a dark stain over the blue of her top. 'We're so grateful for this, you know that. Lucky for us you wanted to use this for a staff annexe or a holiday let, it's been furnished so nicely.'

'You're so welcome. I'm happy to help.' Francesca looks around curiously. She can see pictures and books, familiar from the flat in London, and yet different in this new environment. The previous neat impersonality of the cottage is now full of the presence of individuals, from the photographs on the hall table to the bright orange folded-paper-like lampshade, a massive piece of origami, that's now suspended in the stairwell and looking unexpectedly splendid, like a

Cubist sun beaming above them against the mellow stone of the old walls as they climb the stairs that turn back on themselves to reach the first floor. Olivia talks about the villa in Argentina as she shows Francesca around, and Francesca half listens, nodding and asking questions but actually looking as hard as she can. There are three bedrooms; the one at the front with the view of the garden has been turned into the twins' nursery, with two large white cots on either side of the room, two small white wardrobes against each wall, and a shared changing table in between. There are bright framed posters on the wall – Barbar floating over a country in a convoy of balloons, the Gruffalo and Beatrix Potter – and alphabet letters adhered at jaunty angles. *I hope those come off.*

'Oh, isn't it sweet!' Francesca exclaims. 'It's perfect.'

'They love it,' Olivia says, her tone content. 'And in the evenings I can hear the wood pigeon cooing them to sleep.' She leads the way out of the bedroom and into the hall, down towards the spare room. 'Now, this one I've barely touched, as we don't need it right now. Until we have visitors, anyway.'

Francesca peeps in. It is indeed just as she left it, with the double bed neatly made, a quilt of pale country floral squares over a snowy duvet, piled with white pillows and pastel cushions. A cream armchair with more cushions sits in the corner. On the dressing table are a few essentials any guest would want: a jar of cotton wool balls, a box of tissues, a nail file and some upmarket make-up remover, along with an expensive hand cream. At the window is a pretty view towards the side of the garden – not as pretty as the front view but still acceptable. This edge of the west wing of the house is on the side that has been less altered. Perhaps a school caretaker or elderly teacher lived here. At any rate, the other wing is far more like a school, with its swimming pool and abandoned gymnasium. This side is more homely. It reminds Francesca of holidays in the Lake District, where she was taken when she was young. Their only holiday of the year: a week's walking in the Lakes, staying in the cottage of a friend of the family who charged the bare minimum. But she loved it, being away from home, seeing the beauty of the countryside and the grandeur of the hills. This place makes her feel the same way: comforted, refreshed and renewed.

'And we,' says Olivia, turning back to the hall again, 'have unashamedly taken the room with the en-suite shower. I mean, it has no windows so no view, but the luxury of the shower meant we had to have it. And here we are.'

Olivia opens the door and Francesca looks in with that strange tingle she has always felt when she's caught a glimpse of Dan's marital bed. It's blameless enough: the bed she, Francesca, chose, but now with Olivia's bedding – a faded ticking stripe duvet and matching pillowcases, a floral quilt folded at the foot, going rather well with the taupe buttoned headboard that was already there. But despite the appearance of utter normality, Francesca knows that this is where Dan and Olivia share their most intimate moments, and she can't stop herself imagining them as she looks: the kisses, slow at first, growing in intensity, the exploration of

149

each other with hands and fingers, and the meeting of their bodies, the movement growing more urgent until it's over in a rush of ecstasy. Francesca pushes the image out of her mind, but in the moment that she and Olivia stand there looking in, another takes its place. She recalls an evening when the old crowd were all assembled at Dan's flat, and the evening turned drunken and riotous. As usually happened, Olivia retired to bed and eventually the others left, while Dan and Francesca stayed up until close to dawn, opening another bottle, lighting up cigarettes long after they'd both given up smoking, and talking intensely about times past (though they never mentioned *that*, because they never did). At last Francesca crashed out on the sofa, Dan offering her a blanket to go with the rough Navajo style cushions before he staggered off to bed. She woke, dry-mouthed and heart pounding, at around 8 a.m. and realised she needed to get home and restore herself to normal. The cigarettes that she rarely touched had given her mouth a particularly foul taste and her headache a violently thudding quality. On her way out of the flat, she had to use the bathroom and as she tip-toed past Dan and Olivia's bedroom, she glimpsed through the door that stood slightly ajar their naked feet emerging from their bed. The reality of their sleeping together hit her anew like a punch to the stomach, and she was crippled by the feelings all over again – the ones she's tried all these years to subdue: jealousy, outrage, injured pride, fury . . . She stared for a long minute, then found the bathroom, and eventually crept away. The glimpses of Dan's private life were the hardest things of all to cope with, when it was all still so raw.

All of that flashes through her mind now, as she looks in at the bedroom. Olivia is beside her with an air of expectation, as though waiting for her verdict on a room that Francesca considers more or less unchanged.

'It's . . . wonderful,' Francesca says a little weakly, wondering what Olivia wants for a room that's not exactly the Brighton Pavilion. 'Such a special room.'

'Then you know the secret,' Olivia says jauntily.

'Secret?' echoes Francesca.

'I didn't find it right away.' Olivia goes into the room towards the back wall. She's right that this room has no windows, so it has an enclosed, removed feel, rather dark and close.

Is that what she means?

'It was only the day before yesterday that I realised,' Olivia continues as she reaches the wall beside the right-hand side of the bed that looks like the rest of the panelling covering the walls. She puts out her hand and pushes down, and suddenly the wall moves, opening outwards into a twilight gloom. 'There's a handle here, but it's very easy to miss. And here we are.' Olivia goes through the doorway that has appeared in the panelled wall, and disappears. Curious, Francesca crosses the room in three strides and looks out through the doorway. They are on a wooden balcony that she can see, in the evening dimness, stands above a part of the house she knows, but she's having trouble orienting herself. A moment ago, she was in the cottage, now she's somewhere else entirely, in the main house. Actually, she's in

151

the great hall, at the far end, high up and looking down into the room.

'Can you see?' asks Olivia, laughing at Francesca's face. 'We're in the minstrels' gallery. We're connected by a secret door.'

'I didn't know,' Francesca says, surprised.

'Well, it's very hard to see that handle. And to be honest, I wish I hadn't noticed it. I've not quite felt the same about our bedroom since. When I'm in bed, I keep thinking I hear it move, even though I know there's no one there. It feels ever so slightly creepy to be connected to the rest of the house right by our bed like this.' Olivia smiles at her conspiratorially. 'But it's empty. Silly, isn't it?'

For a moment, they both look out over the huge hall with its vast empty fireplace at one end, the chill rising from the stone floor. Francesca is assailed suddenly by images of the past – the Tudor lords and ladies, the Jacobean nobles, all the way from the fourteenth century to early in the twentieth, when the last great house parties took place. They're all gone now, every soul who was entertained here, who danced across this great stone floor or warmed themselves at the fire. Francesca shivers again.

Why did Walt buy this house? It's so full of the dead past.

'Come on. I'm cold.' Olivia turns back to the warmth and normality of the bedroom. Francesca follows, slightly stunned by the unexpected coalition between the cottage and the main house. She takes a gulp of the cold white wine as they go. Olivia goes in and sits on the bed, beckoning Francesca over as she takes a sip from her own glass. 'Come and sit down,' she says. 'I want . . .' She pauses while Francesca sits down a little gingerly beside her, almost as though afraid of defiling the place where Dan and Olivia perform the intimate rites of marriage. 'I want to thank you for sorting this out for us. I'm only just beginning to realise how incredible this place is, and how lucky we are that you offered it to us. You could be getting amazing money for it from any number of holiday people. And we've got it for free. We won't take advantage, I promise. We'll be gone as soon as we can.'

Francesca blinks at her, hoping she is hiding the start of pity she feels. Olivia actually seems to think that she and Walt need the few hundred pounds a week that a holiday let would bring them. 'Don't be silly, you can stay as long as you like, you know that.'

Olivia smiles, her gaze sliding away. She clutches her wine glass with one hand and the other plucks a little nervously at the duvet cover. She sighs. 'Thanks. It means a lot. Francesca . . .'

'Yes?' Francesca's heart begins to beat nervously. She is suddenly aware of the size of the secret she has inside her. It sits on her tongue. With a few breaths, a few vibrations of her voice box, a quick series of movements of her mouth, the secret would be out, free to wreak its havoc. She has to keep it in, even though she has the wild impulse to release it and see what happens. *Don't tell. Don't tell.*

'What do you think of Dan?' Olivia asks suddenly.

'I . . . I . . .' Her heart flutters with nerves and her breathing quickens. 'What do you mean?'

'This play. It doesn't sound like it's anywhere near

finished.' She frowns anxiously and plucks at the duvet cover. 'I thought . . . it's just he's spent so many hours on it. We agreed that he would take this opportunity to see what he could make of writing.' She pauses, a look of uncertainty on her face, as though she's afraid of sounding disloyal. She shrugs and laughs lightly. 'I'm being silly. He'll do it, of course he will. And then either he'll make a huge success of it, or he'll go back to doing the job he did very well. And, thank goodness, we've got this place in the meantime.' Olivia suddenly reaches out and grasps Francesca's hand, gazing at her straight in the eye. Francesca is aware of the candour shining out of Olivia's blue-grey eyes, the rim of long dark lashes around them, the little blood vessels creeping in from the edges of her whites. 'You've given the children a home,' she says in a low, urgent voice. 'When we needed one. Thank you.'

No. You gave my children a home. Thank you. Francesca smiles. 'You're welcome. After all, what are old friends for?'

She is in the kitchen again, while Olivia does the bedtime story for the twins. In a moment, she'll be back, and then it will be the usual dynamic: the three of them round a table, eating Olivia's food and talking brightly, or intensely, or laughing, or sharing experiences. But they won't be able to say what really lies at the heart of everything. Olivia is in the dark. Dan has chosen to wipe it from his mind. Francesca holds the power of havoc in her hands.

Doesn't he realise I could undo everything if I chose?

Perhaps he does and that's why he's so afraid of meeting her eye.

Francesca sits sipping her wine while Dan washes up the dishes from the children's supper. There is a dishwasher, but he seems happy to fill the sparkling white butler sink with water and suds and do it by hand. She watches him, his broad back inside the blue T-shirt he's wearing, the way his firm body fills his jeans. A tremor of lust pings through her, catching her unaware. Her attention has been so taken up by the children that she hasn't noticed Dan in the way that she usually does, but suddenly she is almost convulsed with the old longing for him: he's tall, firmly built and masculine, strong across the shoulders and solid where he should be. She thinks of Walt, older now, sagging and paunching. His kneecaps are wrinkled and his buttocks droop, and his belly hangs heavy with a fatty pouch in front. *Not that he was ever exactly an Adonis.* Dan has always inspired a lust that's all the stronger for its simplicity. She finds him irresistible.

Along with the desire, which jolts through her, leaving an empty yearning in its wake, she feels a twinge of the old anger at being condemned to a life with Walt when it could all have been so different. Quickly she suffocates it, reminding herself of the old mantra: *It was my choice. It was what I wanted.*

She takes another sip and says softly, 'Dan?'

He turns slightly in acknowledgement. 'Yes?'

'I just wanted to say . . .'

He stiffens, then turns back and continues washing up. 'Yes?'

'Well . . .' She lets the word hang in the air for a moment. 'You know what we need to talk about.'

'I'm not sure I do,' he says quickly, defensively.

So I was right. He's convinced himself to forget the truth. She will have to talk to his back. But maybe that's best. Perhaps it works better for both of them if they don't have to look into one another's eyes when they let the secret out.

'You're not to keep me out, Dan,' she says in the same soft voice, removing any hint of menace from her tone. 'I don't want much. Just to see them now and then. That's all. Don't deny me that.'

He says nothing, but there is a tension across his shoulders and the angle of his neck.

'I know you don't want to talk about it, and that's fine. I'm happy with that. But don't stop me from seeing them. That's all.' She sips her wine again. He still says nothing.

And then, at last, he mutters, 'I understand.'

She smiles, even though he can't see her.

A moment later, Olivia is coming into the room on a sigh and a smile, and their evening can begin.

Chapter Fifteen
1959

Alice likes to make her excursions on Friday nights. Julia wonders if it is because that is the evening when there is a special service in chapel, with candles lit and the chamber choir singing an anthem. There is a vaguely romantic air to the whole thing, and Julia thinks that perhaps it gets Alice in the mood.

But when she asks, Alice says it is only because that is the night that Roy says he will see her. Friday is pay day, and a lot of the men go down to the pub in the village to spend whatever part of their earnings they're not sending back to Ireland. That means the caravans are usually empty and no one is there to spy her sneaking into Roy's.

'What about the other chap?' Julia asks. They are in the library, supposedly working on their Latin, but actually whispering as quietly as they dare, hoping not to rouse Miss Johnson, who sits several shelves away at her desk by the door. 'The one we saw at the building site.'

'Oh.' Alice raises her eyebrows. 'Donnie. The Cliff Richard one. Fancy him, do you?'

Julia blushes. 'Of course not.' But she has been thinking about him. The hollow cheeks, the sharp blue eyes and the greased-up quiff with the hair separated into stiff dark tresses that look like the sagging bars of a cage. 'Anyway,' she says quickly, as a distraction from her pink cheeks, 'I'm surprised you still want to go and see him, after that time.'

Alice ignores her, suddenly absorbed in her second declension conjugations, her eyes hard with annoyance. She doesn't want to talk about the time that she came staggering back through the canvas sheeting, into the passage where Julia was waiting.

'What is it?' Julia hissed when she saw Alice crying, her hand clutched to her face.

'Roy was angry with me,' Alice sobbed as quietly as she dared. 'Because we went to see him working.'

'I told you we shouldn't have gone,' Julia burst out before she could stop herself. 'It was obvious he didn't want you shouting and waving at him.' Alice sobbed again and Julia stared at her compassionately, feeling rotten for telling her off when she was in this state. 'What did he say?' she asked, trying to remember to keep her voice down. 'Did he shout at you?'

Alice sniffed, and tried to muffle her sobs. They subsided into small hiccups. 'Not at first. He was all right at first. We drank some whiskey and we had a laugh and then . . .' Her blue gaze slid to Julia and then away again. 'Well, you know, we messed around. But Roy started talking about us coming to the site. He'd drunk quite a lot of whiskey and he got ever so angry. I couldn't quite understand why he was so cross now, after he'd been so nice to me and said such lovely things. But he was. He shouted, and said I wasn't to risk his job like that again, and didn't I understand what was wrong with it and then he . . .' Alice choked again on a sob and took her hand from her cheek. In the dim light, Julia could make out a shadow along Alice's face. 'He hit me.'

Julia gasped. 'Oh my goodness! Alice, he didn't! That's terrible . . . I can't really see it, we'll have to take a look in the light.'

'It doesn't hurt as much as it did at first,' Alice said miserably. 'It was just a slap, I suppose. Not so very bad. Is it awfully noticeable?'

'I think so. Come on, let's go to the lav and take a look.'

They crept upstairs in the familiar way, but took a detour to the girls' lavatories on the first floor, where they dared to turn on a light and look in the mirror.

'Golly,' Julia said as they both stared at the bright livid mark stretching over her cheekbone.

'Maybe it will be gone by morning,' Alice replied, gazing at it with a kind of horrified fascination.

'I don't think so. It'll probably look worse. What will we tell Miss Allen?'

They turned to look at one another, each reading the other's fear in their eyes.

Alice had stopped crying, her hurt evaporating in the face of this crisis. She said stoutly, 'I'll tell her I fell out of bed, right onto my face.'

Julia giggled because it sounded rather funny, and she tried to imagine someone falling onto their face. It was ludicrous.

Alice's lips twitched and then she laughed too, but without much mirth. 'All right,' she said, 'I'll tell her I hit the chest of drawers on the way down.'

'That's better,' agreed Julia. 'Come on. We should get back quick as you like.'

So in the morning, Alice told Miss Allen that she had bashed her face on the drawers and Miss Allen sent her to Matron for a cold compress, although by then the redness was speckled with blue and purple, with yellow climbing up under Alice's eye, and there wasn't much to be done but wait for it to heal.

Julia was so relieved. She hadn't wanted Alice to be hit, but perhaps she now understood how stupid it was to risk everything for a man like Roy. And for two weeks, Alice didn't go to the caravan on a Friday night. When she told Julia she was sneaking out again, Julia was horrified.

'But he hit you!'

'No he didn't, not really,' Alice replied loftily. Her memory of the evening had faded with the bruise. 'Well, not much, and I had annoyed him. Besides, he'll be sorry now, he'll be missing me so much.' She smiled to herself and her eyes sparkled, as if envisaging some private pleasure that would be enhanced by her absence. 'I want to see just how badly he is missing me.'

'Don't go,' Julia begged. 'You've left it this long. They'll have finished that blessed pool in a bit, and then they'll go away and you can forget about him.'

Alice turned to Julia, her blue eyes cold. 'But I don't want to forget about him. Don't you see? He's the only thing I've got in my life that's mine, and I don't want to lose him. You don't have to meet me if you don't want to. I don't care.'

But Julia wasn't able to lie upstairs in the dorm wondering. She was afraid now that one day Alice might not come back, and so she played sentry, guarding the entrance and waiting for her friend to return, the scent of whiskey and cigarettes hanging around her. Roy was very happy to see Alice again, and apologised for the blow, and there was no question that Alice would not go again. As long as the builders were there, she would continue her forbidden jaunts.

'You do fancy Donnie, don't you?' Alice whispers suddenly, looking up from her Latin.

'No, I don't,' Julia shoots back.

'Oh, you do. No need to pretend, I can see it written all over your face. Why don't you come with me next time?' Alice's tone is suddenly wheedling. 'I'll ask Roy if Donnie can stay back in the caravan, and I'll bring you, and we can have a party.' The idea has taken hold and she bounces slightly in her seat. 'Oh, go on, it'll be fun.'

'No!' Julia exclaims more loudly than she meant to.

Miss Johnson looks over from her desk, and stands up so she can see over the shelves. 'Quiet, please! Silent study.' She disappears from sight as she sits back down in her chair.

Julia drops her voice to a whisper again, as she bends over her book pretending to write. 'I wouldn't be such an idiot.'

Alice smiles. 'You never know. You might like it.'

*

I don't know why I'm doing this, Julia thinks as she follows Alice through the canvas sheet that leads out into the building site where the new pool will one day stand.

'Mind the hole,' Alice whispers. 'It's pretty big.'

It's cold as soon as they step through into the darkness, and a chill, hard wind is blowing. It's early November, and the weather has turned from autumn towards winter, though there are still leaves being whisked from the trees, and the grounds are thick with dank, rotting piles of them.

'It was easy when it was lighter,' Alice grumbles, 'and before this hole got so bally big.' She pulls a torch from her dressing gown pocket and shines its small beam at the ground so they can find their way. 'Come on, follow me. I know the way pretty well.'

As they pass the great dark pit, Julia glances into the cavernous shadows. It's taking forever to burrow out the tons of soil to make the pool. It's hard to believe it will one day be a clean, shiny, tiled rectangle, full of bright blue water. She imagines herself gliding downwards through the turquoise warmth, kicking out her legs, her arms pushing her forward as she nears the bottom. Then she shivers, afraid she might fall in if she's not careful.

'Hurry up, slowcoach!' Alice is full of excitement that her little dream of a party is coming true. She's even put on a frock under her dressing gown. Now they are beyond the site and heading out towards the fields behind the school where the builders have their caravans, separated from the main buildings by a thick hedge. The caravans are barely visible from the school itself, which is no doubt the plan, but there is an easy footpath to the living quarters made by the stomping boots of the workmen as they tramp through the mud at the start and end of each day.

Really, it's not so hard to get there, Julia thinks with surprise. Each time Alice set out, Julia imagined her on a kind of quest, passing through dark forests and over dangerous terrain in order to reach her destination. But, in fact, she's only had to tiptoe along this path and be taken straight to the caravans. The only downside is the cold and the disorienting effect of the darkness.

She shivers as another gust cuts through her dressing gown and cotton pyjamas and whips her skin with cold. A picture of her parents comes to mind: they sit on the terrace of their house in Cairo, her mother fanning herself and complaining of the heat while her father sips at his gin and tonic, and reads the newspaper, a cigarette held in the fingers of one hand. What would they think if they could see her now, out in the darkness, sneaking off to meet some Irish builders?

It almost makes her want to laugh, in a ghoulish fashion. They'd be apoplectic. And so disappointed. What would Alice's parents make of it all? Julia can't imagine. The chilly beauty who arrives in a large car to collect Alice at the end of term seems like a statue of marble coldness. No wonder Alice wants to seek out warmth, even if it involves such risk. Or maybe, because it does . . .

They pass through massy shadows that rustle and move – the large hedge that borders the field of caravans. Now the torch beam falls on large curved shapes, like a herd of huge, silent cattle. The caravans, empty while the occupants are drinking in the pub. Only one shows the glow of a light behind a square of curtain.

'That's the one, that's Roy's,' Alice says excitedly. 'Come on!'

Julia is afraid now. What has she done? What is she saying by going into that caravan? That she is like Alice, ready to drink whiskey and do all the other things Alice does – whatever they may be?

Why am I here?

It's partly because she has never been able to say no to Alice, whose powerful methods of coaxing and ordering by turn have always impelled Julia to obey eventually. But it's more than that. She wants to protect her friend, and there is a strong impulse in her that believes her presence will be a buffer between Alice and danger, though how on earth that could be, she doesn't know. She is fourteen and dressed in trousers and a jumper over her pyjamas that have ponies on them. Some kind of guardian angel she is!

She doesn't even want to admit what else might be bringing her here.

Alice hurries forward as they get closer. She climbs three small metal steps and taps at the door of the caravan. 'Roy! It's us.'

Julia stands below, anxious, her heart thudding, fighting the desire to run back to the school and up the stairs to the safety of the dormitory. *But it's too late now.*

The door swings open and there, huge in the small frame, is Roy. He makes Julia think of a giant from a storybook, as he bends his head to look out at them and grins.

'Hello there, girlies!' His voice is deep but with a cheerful sing-song quality that eases Julia's nervousness just a little. 'You made it, I see. Glad you could. Now come on in, it's warm in here and cold enough to freeze your britches out there.'

He retreats back into the light and Alice skips up the steps after him. Julia trails behind, her desire to be in the warm overcoming her trepidation. The next moment, she is in the small space of the caravan. Immediately in front and to her left are two small doors, closed tight. To her right is a miniature kitchen space – a Formica countertop below a window with a plastic sink sunk into it, with storage space underneath and a shelf above. A small gas hob with two burners sits on the counter, connected to a tank that stands by the door. Dirty plates and pans are piled in the sink, and the air is ripe with the smell of something meaty, along with the staleness of well-used bedding and unwashed clothes, and a layer of cigarette smoke on top of it all. Opposite the kitchen counter is a tabletop slotted between two built-in benches, meagre cushions on top to buffer their hard sur- faces. But Julia's eye is drawn beyond this to the back of the caravan, where a built-in seat follows the three sides around, and thin curtains with faded zigzag patterns hang over the small windows. The air is full of cigarette smoke that stings her eyes and burns her nostrils, and she blinks against the acrid haze. One side of the seats is used as a bed, with a pile of pillows and blankets messily stacked at one end. In the furthest corner sits the thin boy she saw at the building site that day, staring over at her, a cigarette hanging off his lips, his hands clasped together and his foot, encased in a long leather shoe, tapping. He's listening to music on a transistor radio held close to his ear, but it's hard to hear much through the static.

Donnie, thinks Julia, and she is surprised to find her insides leap and contract with a hot squeeze of excitement. He's good-looking, with that thin face, the staring blue eyes and the dark quiff teased upwards. His gaze rests on her and she has the same sensation of not being entirely in her own body, the one she had when they went to the building site that day.

In the middle of the low-ceilinged caravan, Roy stands, stooped to prevent his head banging on the ceiling. He's wearing old brown trousers and a slightly grubby white shirt that looks like a vest to Julia, and he's holding up a whiskey bottle.

'Will you have a little drink then, ladies?' he asks with a grin. Without waiting for an answer, he uncorks the bottle and starts to slosh out the amber liquid into tin mugs that sit on a small table, alongside an ashtray full of pillowy grey ash and bent discarded butts.

'Thanks, don't mind if I do,' Alice says in an odd voice. Julia glances at her friend, who holds herself stiffly, her lips pouted and her eyes wide. 'But put a bit of lemonade in mine, won't you.'

'Anything you say,' Roy says, and winks in her direction. Alice giggles, fluttery and silly.

What's wrong with her?

Roy turns to Julia. 'And you? The same?'

'Just lemonade, please,' Julia says, her voice sounding ridiculously prim. She wants to cower away from Roy's overwhelming presence: he seems so big, so old and so intensely male, with his chunky body and dark hair that covers his bare arms and climbs the back of his neck. There is thick black stubble over his jaw and up his cheeks. His hair is cut short, as though it's the only bit he bothers to tame.

'Just lemonade?' Roy laughs. Even his laugh has a lilt to it. 'Ah, come on. You want a little fire in you, don't you? Try it. You'll like it. I'll just add a touch so you can get acquainted with it.' He pours a bit out into the last mug, then takes the lemonade bottle and tops up the girls' drinks with the fizzy liquid. The boy in the corner watches, without saying anything. Roy hands the girls their mugs. 'There you go.' He looks curiously at Julia. 'Now what's your name then? Alice only said she was bringing a friend.'

'Julia.' It comes out sounding strangled.

'Joo-lee-a,' he repeats, the slightest hint of mockery in his voice, and holds a mug to her. 'Well, delighted to meet you.' She takes the mug and he clashes his own against it. 'Cheers! Here's to old friends and new.'

Julia stares into the tin mug. It's only half full, the bubbling lemonade tinted pale brown. Alice takes a swig from her mug and starts chattering to Roy as Julia lifts hers slowly to her mouth. She's never tasted alcohol before. Just before the rim of the mug blocks out her view of anything but off-white enamel, she looks straight at the boy on the seat, and he is staring at her, watching her every move. He lifts a hand to his mouth, takes the cigarette from his lips and blows out a cloud of smoke. Julia tips the mug and she can no longer see him. The liquid touches her tongue: it's fizzy and sweet with a peaty undertone, a taste like old brown honey with a hint of lemon. It is quite pleasant, she thinks, as she swallows. A feeling of relief comes over her. She'd feared that one taste and she'd be on the floor, drunk, or violently ill with the disgusting flavour. Instead, she feels quite normal. It's fine. She looks over at Alice, who has taken a big gulp of hers.

'Hey, Donnie,' Roy says as he passes him a tin mug. Donnie puts down his radio and takes it. 'You haven't said hello to our guests yet!'

'Hello there,' Donnie says. His voice is lighter than Roy's bass, without the rich lilt but with an accent of some kind.

'Joo-lee-a and Alice.' Roy gestures at them with his mug.

'We've already had the pleasure,' Alice says in the strange, grown-up voice she's used since they came in.

'Aye,' Donnie says.

'H . . . how do you do?' Julia says, unable to think of anything else.

Roy laughs. 'How do ye do? How do ye do, eh, Donnie?'

Donnie doesn't laugh, but looks back at Julia, solemn. 'I'm well, thanks. And you?'

She can't make out what he said and echoes him with a question in her voice. 'Andrew?'

Roy bursts into louder guffaws. 'She can't understand you!' He turns to Alice. 'You never said you were bringing a duchess here, darlin'.'

Alice sashays over to the seat and takes her place along from Donnie. 'Oh, she's no duchess, are you, Julia? Just an ordinary girl. I'm afraid she's not very experienced.' She flutters her eyelashes at Roy. 'Have you got a cigarette?'

Roy grins. 'Anythin' for you.' He hands her a packet and she lifts one out by its white tip.

Julia stares, really shocked now. Alice hasn't said anything about smoking and here she is, her lips pursed around the thick stem of the cigarette as she leans forward for a light from Roy's match. She pulls in a breath and instantly releases it in a puff as she sits back, holding the cigarette stiffly in the air.

'Do you want one?' Roy asks, offering Julia the packet.

She shakes her head. 'No . . . no thank you.'

'Sit down. Go on.'

Alice pats the cushion. 'Next to me.'

Julia goes around the table to sit between Alice and Donnie, and Roy says, 'Now we'll get things going! Turn your music up, Donnie. I don't mind it, even if it is your American rock nonsense.'

Donnie leans forward to turn the dial upwards and the beat of the music fills the room, a wailing voice over the top. 'Elvis,' he murmurs.

'Now,' Roy says, winking again, 'we can get the party started.'

The party is the least fun one Julia has ever attended. It consists of sipping at her lemonade while she watches Alice continue to behave in a fashion she has never seen before, winsome and girlish, and then with the strange pseudo-sophistication that involves that odd voice, and her head cocked on one side, the eyelashes fluttering. It looks, Julia thinks, ridiculous but Roy doesn't seem to mind it. He squeezes his great form in beside Alice, one hairy foot crossed up over his knee, one arm stretched out behind her on the seat cushion, the other lifting the mug of whiskey to his mouth, and looks down on Alice with his broad smile, the one that somehow softens the overpowering masculinity of his presence.

The tinny music beating out from the radio fills the small space, along with the hiss of static. Julia is painfully aware of Donnie at her side, and his still tapping foot on the floor, but she doesn't turn to look at him. They sit, two silent observers of Roy and Alice's flirting, Julia wishing with all her heart that this could be over and she could leave, drag Alice back to the dormitory and tell her, sternly, that never ever again should she go to the caravan. There's something here in the caravan that she doesn't understand; she only knows it's a powerful force that she and Alice should not be tampering with. They are out of their depth.

Donnie mutters something occasionally, and she realises that he is saying the name of the musicians that they are listening to. 'Little Richard,' she hears. 'Johnny Mathis.' She's never heard of them or listened to their music before.

There are refills of everyone's cups, but Julia stops drinking hers, just letting bubbles pop on her tongue when she lifts the mug. Her mouth is numb and her head a little fuzzy, and she knows that she must have had more of the whiskey than she guessed.

It must be only half an hour after they arrived, but it feels like much longer when she notices that Roy is bent into Alice, his face in her neck as she giggles and drinks, two cigarettes now smoked and stubbed out. Then she sees, with a swift sideways glance, that Roy is kissing Alice, his big, stubbly man's mouth on hers. Julia is horrified, and looks away, mortified that she has seen this and shocked that Roy would think it all right to kiss a girl who is still in the fourth form.

Why, he's old enough to be her father! What's he thinking of?

She stares at the floor, appalled and frozen, not knowing what to do. She wants to pull Alice to her feet and drag her away, but she knows how much Alice would hate that, and besides, what if Roy gets angry? *They must know when to stop – Alice always comes back. But how long? How long can I stand to wait here like this while they do . . . that?*

A hand on her arm makes her jump. It's Donnie, no longer lost in the music, his blue eyes fixed on her. He says nothing, but indicates the door with a turn of his head, and gets up, skinny legs stepping round the table and heading out. She stands and follows, the two on the seat behind apparently oblivious as they nuzzle, murmur and giggle.

Donnie has opened the caravan door and is sitting on the metal steps that lead down from it. He's lit another cigarette and is blowing out the first stream of long smoke, white in

171

the night air. Julia stands above him, looking down on his dark head.

'Close the bloody door!' roars Roy behind her.

'It's freezing,' calls Alice, a slur in her voice, and then she laughs wildly, as though she is being tickled.

Julia steps out into the cold night and pulls the door to behind her. There is still light from the windows and she can see Donnie half lit by it. Clambering down the steps, she crouches down until she is sitting gingerly on the icy metal.

'Want one?' Donnie asks, looking at the burning end of his cigarette.

'No thanks.' Julia shakes her head. 'They make me feel sick.' Inside, her stomach has churned in rebellion at the bitter smoke. Out here, in the cool air, it's almost fragrant. She looks down and realises she's brought her tin mug out with her. Automatically she lifts it to let the bubbles play on her lips, then gasps as the mug is violently knocked from her grasp. It curves through the air, a ribbon of liquid erupting from it, and hits the grass with a thud as the lemonade splatters down.

'Don't drink that stuff!' barks Donnie.

'Why'd you do that?' she asks, shocked.

'Don't drink it, that's all.'

'I wasn't.' She's filled with indignation. 'I was just pretending. I don't like it, it makes me feel sleepy.'

'You look like you've been drinking it happily enough,' Donnie says accusingly, turning to look at her. His eyes are dark, just the whites glimmering in the half-light. 'Just like your friend.' He shakes his head and takes a terse puff of his cigarette. 'I don't know what you girls are playing at. What would your mothers say?'

'I don't know,' Julia says miserably. 'Nothing very good. She'd be furious.' Then her outrage returns. 'But this wasn't my idea, you know! I'm only here to look after Alice. I didn't want to come. I think it's awful, and we'll be expelled if we're caught, both of us—'

'You want to stop her. You'd better,' Donnie says roughly. He picks a strand of tobacco from his tongue and rubs it away.

Julia stares at him. He's turned away and now she can see his profile: the long, slightly beaked nose, the high cheekbones and the fine shape of his eyes. Something in her quivers. 'Why?' she whispers.

He shakes his head and is silent for a while, then turns to look at her. 'I don't know how your sort lives. Maybe it isn't true what they say about ladies and how gentle and precious you all are. Maybe you're all at it, all the time. But it's not what my mother hopes for for my sisters, I know that, and she'd tan their hides if she thought for a second they'd done what that girl does, at her age. Drinking, smoking and . . . all the rest of it.'

'The rest of it?' Her voice is high, almost plaintive. 'What are you talking about?'

'You've seen it. What they're doing in there.'

'Kissing?' Julia stumbles over the word in her embarrassment at saying such a thing to a man.

He laughs, a short, joyless sound. 'Yeah. Kissin'. And . . .'

The caravan suddenly erupts with sound. The radio has

been turned up full blast. A moment later, there is a strange rocking, and Julia feels the steps shifting slightly underneath her.

'And that,' Donnie says, cocking his head towards the caravan's interior. 'He's a loony but I guess he's far from home. Away from his wife and kids. Wanting what all the men want. He's just lucky enough to get it. But if he gets caught . . .' He puffs violently on his cigarette. 'It'll be a bloody mess, that's all.' He shoots a look at Julia. 'And you and me . . . we'll get caught up in it, even if we both think it's no good.'

'You mean . . .' Julia's struggling to take in what he's saying. 'He's married?'

'Course he is. His fifth kid is on the way.'

'I've got to tell Alice,' she says, getting up quickly. Donnie reaches up and grabs her hand, his blue eyes shining in the refracted light.

'No,' he says urgently. 'Don't go in there. All right? Don't go in.'

'But what are they doing? Dancing?'

'Oh, Holy Mary,' Donnie says and laughs under his breath. 'No. Not dancing. You can't go in. It'll be over soon enough. Wait out here with me.'

She looks down and realises he is still holding her hand. It's smooth and warm, encompassing hers with ease. A strange feeling creeps upwards from her toes. Everything becomes concentrated within her hand and the sensation of its being held by Donnie. It's making her dizzy.

'All right,' she says, sinking down beside him.

'Good girl.' He lets go of her hand. She wishes he would hold it again.

They sit together in the cold, looking out into the night as the caravan rocks and rocks and rocks, and the sound of the music wails in the air.

Chapter Sixteen

Olivia wakes in bed, luxurious, replete with sleep. She has just had a delicious dream, but she can't remember what it was about. She yawns, sighs and thinks. Then, suddenly, she is wide awake. She rolls over to the broad white expanse of Dan's back curving away from her. They generally start the night spooned into each other and wake back to back. She shakes him lightly. 'Dan!'

He grunts, and is then alert, turning towards her. 'What?'

Since the twins were born, they have both developed the ability to snap awake. Olivia thinks it's like a superpower, the way they can hear, in the depth of sleep, the faint mosquito-buzz wail that means one baby has woken up. Then there's the race to get there before the other stirs and wakes too.

'Listen,' she whispers, and they are both still, straining to hear something in the silence.

'What is it?' Dan asks. 'I can't hear anything.'

'Neither can I.' She laughs, low and throaty. 'That's the point. It's five to seven. And there's not a peep.'

Dan looks at his watch and laughs too. 'Oh my God. Do you think it's started? The long walk back to a civilised life?'

'It might have. It's the first time but it's a start. Right?'

'Yep.' Dan yawns loudly. 'But you could've let me sleep a bit longer. I was just about to get Scarlett Johansson's number.'

'Oh dear.' Olivia runs a finger along his arm. 'I suppose you'll just have to make do with me.' She slides her hand along the smoothness of his back, over his waist and downwards. 'Well, well, you certainly were happy to get that number, weren't you?'

She has his solid morning erection in her hand, caressing its smoothness as she drops her lips on his shoulder. He turns to her and presses his lips on hers. They both luxuriate in the warmth of the bed, the closeness of their skin, and the softness of their mouths. She catches the slight staleness of his breath and doesn't mind it. One of the things she loves about Dan is how he always smells good to her, even when he ought not to. She likes him sweaty and tangy from the garden best of all but now, with the fragrance of their bed in his hair, he's still delicious. It's always been that way, right from the start. She dates the beginning of her love for him from the first time he gave her his jumper to wear and she smelled its honeyed scent.

'I didn't get her number, remember,' he murmurs against her mouth, his voice buzzing on her lips. 'That's the point.'

'But you were pleased to see her.' She laughs again, grasping him hard. His mouth opens on hers and they kiss properly. It's sleepy and sweet for a while, then, at the same moment, they are both possessed with need. Sex has been relegated to whenever they're less tired than usual, and even then it's become more perfunctory than ever before. She vaguely recalls a time when they made love several times a week, and regularly spent hours at the pursuit. She can't imagine that now. How on earth did they have the time, let alone the energy?

But in this moment, triumphant in the twins' late sleeping, she is seized with some of the old vigour and enthusiasm. Dan seems to feel the same way. He dips his head to her breasts and takes a nipple in his mouth. *Not quite the same breasts as they once were*, she remembers ruefully, thinking of the way they have shrunk and lost their firmness, and she hopes they still do the job as far as Dan is concerned. He always used to love them so. *Still, he seems quite happy right now.* He's rolling his tongue around the nipple while his hand grasps her other breast. She is quickly and thoroughly aroused, and wants to have him as soon as possible. She pulls his head upwards so that she can have his mouth again, and they intensify their kisses. Dan shifts and she makes way for him, so that he can lie between her thighs and rest his chest on hers. They revel in the sensation of skin on skin, and Olivia grasps him tightly, wrapping her arms around him, knowing he likes to be held like this. When their mouths part, she inhales the sweet smell of his neck and bites lightly on the skin there. He manoeuvres himself so that they can be, at last, joined together and as he presses down, Olivia sighs happily, closing her eyes and giving herself over to the feeling of completeness she always gets in that first moment, when her body accepts his. Then they start to find a rhythm, moving back and forth to meet each other. She loves the weight of his body on her and the solid strength of his thrust. Her mind turns loose and fluid as she relinquishes conscious thought for animal enjoyment. They start to gather pace, feeding off one another's excitement. Dan's panting whooshes in her ear before he returns to her mouth to kiss hard and thoroughly. Her limbs begin to tingle and she feels the rising of pleasure from deep inside.

There is a shout from down the corridor. 'Maaaa-meeee!'

They stop, staring into one another's eyes, panting.

It comes again. 'Maaa-meee! Daaaa-deeee!'

'Oh God,' groans Dan.

'Ignore it.' Olivia pulls him close to her again and wriggles her hips to reinvigorate him. 'Come on, we're so close . . .'

'Okay.' He kisses her, and begins to move again, grunting with the pleasurable effort, and then buries his face in her neck, his breath loud in her ear.

She pushes up to meet him, straining to recapture the feelings of surrender and enjoyment. *Don't listen*, she tells herself. *We only need five minutes . . .*

'Maaa-meee! Daaa-deee!'

They're both resolute, pressing on. She rubs her hand down his back to his buttocks, urging him to continue.

Another voice joins in. 'Maaa-meee, we're awaaaaake!'

'Oh God,' Dan says again, and he stops, his eyes apologetic. 'I'm sorry. I don't think I can. I can't concentrate.'

'I know what you mean.' Olivia sighs. 'Nor can I.' They

gaze at one another in regretful understanding. 'Oh well. It was nice while it lasted.'

'Same time, same place, tonight,' Dan declares and gently lifts off her.

'It's a date.' She smiles. It might happen, but they are usually too shattered at bedtime to do much more than read a few pages of their books and pass out. They move apart and a moment later, they are both pulling on pyjamas, ready to respond to the treble voices piping along the hall.

'Daaa-deee! Come and get us!'

'Coming, you rascals!' roars Dan. 'Are you ready for the Daddy monster?'

Shrieks and giggles burst from the children's room as Dan heads out, throwing a resigned look at Olivia over his shoulder as he goes. 'Later,' he mouths, and she nods with a smile.

Olivia lies back in the rose-scented bubbles and lets the warm water wash over her. She and Dan have an agreement. One lazy Saturday or Sunday morning each. One gets up and deals with the twins single-handed, getting both changed and dressed and breakfasted and taking the morning shift up until eleven. The other is free to do what they like: read, sleep, watch a movie, go for a run, take a bath ... With Olivia, it nearly always ends up with the bath. She never cared much for baths in the past, preferring the swift efficiency of the shower, but now she adores them: the long, fragrant soak, the replenishing of hot water, the slow business of shaving her legs or buffing her skin with a loofah, the magazine from the Saturday paper to provide any entertainment she needs. But since they moved here to the Hall, she's found stimulation enough in simply looking at the high ceiling, the decorative cornice like the icing on some elaborate wedding cake, and the window that stretches upwards in a huge stone arch. It has panes of stained glass in it, coloured diamonds that glow azure, rose, green and orange. She wonders what this room was once, long ago, before someone managed to install pipework and waste systems and a hot water cylinder.

I bet they could never have imagined what life in the future would be like. She wonders what the future holds that she cannot imagine. *But that's the point. If I could imagine it, it would hardly be unimaginable.* She recalls from somewhere that Italian princes of the very early Renaissance, as early as the fourteenth century, already had hot and cold running water. *I expect Dan told me that.*

That's been the pattern of their relationship since they first met: Dan is the clever one, the informed one, the one with the Cambridge degree, while she is instinctive and bright without being overburdened with knowledge. It was partly the reason why she was so reluctant to give him a chance. As soon as she met him, she thought that he was everything she liked least. For one thing, he was far too good-looking and she'd long learned not to trust the really handsome ones. In her experience, they tended to be conceited, self-absorbed and of the opinion that a woman ought to be grateful they'd deigned to notice her. For some reason, she found herself the target of the handsome men, not – she was sure – because she was a great beauty but because they could sense that she was a challenge and they were determined to conquer her. After all, if they were so irresistible, it was a given that a moderately attractive blonde would thank her lucky stars to get the attention of a truly good-looking man. Her evident imperviousness to their charms seemed to fire up their seduction reflexes. The whole thing bored her silly. She liked men who amused her; the ones who thought just enough of themselves not to need her to fill a gap in their self-esteem, but not so much that they wanted a meek, hero-worshipping trophy.

When Dan came up to her at a party, she saw the determined look in his eye and thought, *Oh dear, here we go. How am I going to shake him off?*

The first few gambits of his conversation only solidified her preconceptions. He tried to amuse her with an abstract joke about Dante's rhyme scheme. She had no idea what he was talking about but smiled indulgently and then said she really had to go and talk to her friend, and walked off, leaving him open-mouthed. A little while later, he was at her side again, a little less ebullient but still trying to impress her and to find out if they had any common ground. 'Were you at Cambridge?' he asked.

'Only for the day,' she said sweetly. 'Perhaps you remember me from that.'

He laughed, a touch sheepishly, as though he wasn't sure who should be embarrassed by the admission.

He followed her around all night, but she'd already seen him with his gang of friends: loud, confident, thinking they were something special because they were among the latest few thousand to graduate from Oxbridge. She didn't care about all that. She'd opted out of intellectual competition years before, when she'd abandoned A-levels to do a diploma in gardening at a local college. She'd always longed to be outside, working with the earth and everything it could provide, learning about the beautiful, infinite variety of plants, and the needs and patterns of the growing world. For years she'd met no one who'd gone to university but she'd learned marvellous lessons and ancient wisdom from the people who trained her. She'd spent a few years at Kew as an apprentice, and been asked to contribute to the gardens' literature. A chance appearance on a television programme set there had given her a path into broadcasting too. Before she knew what was happening, she was writing a column for a national newspaper, involved with the Chelsea Flower Show and appearing on gardening programmes. Not long after, a literary agent took her on, and she wrote her first book about gardening through the seasons. That was what had really brought her into the world of the cocky, overeducated, arrogant men who thought that they knew it all, and that she was their willing pupil.

When she shook Dan off that night, she thought that was the last of it. Yes, he was attractive. She pictured his face as she rode the night bus home to Dalston: classically handsome, with dark hair and piercing blue eyes. *But too arrogant for me. I don't want to be talked down to. No thanks.*

Nevertheless, when he phoned her, she was pleasantly excited to hear from him. It wasn't going to go anywhere, but it might be fun while it lasted. He was attractive, there was no doubt about it, and when he dropped his lofty, intellectual act, there was an unexpected sweetness about him. They went on a few casual dates: drinks in a pub, walks along the river, and, at his suggestion, a viewing of an exhibition of gardening paintings. Away from his circle of university friends, he seemed to relax and return to some version of himself that didn't need constantly to score points, as though life was a general knowledge game show where the winner had accumulated the most information, relevant or not. She didn't mean to play hard to get, it was simply that she didn't see a future for them. Even when her initial indifference turned to a kind of friendly affection – when she realised she was storing up jokes and stories to share with him – she still kept her distance. He wanted to kiss her, she knew that, but until she had finished weighing up whether that was a good idea or not, she wouldn't even let him hold her hand. He seemed mystified by her behaviour, but also intrigued by it. She noticed that wherever he went, women's eyes followed him. She began to see that if he was buying drinks at the bar, he'd be served quickly if it were a woman behind the counter. Waitresses appeared quickly at their restaurant tables. He took her to a party and girls flirted heavily with him throughout the evening, ignoring her presence at his side.

Then she started to understand why he was so tenacious with her. He wasn't used to doing the chasing. He was chased all the time. Now she was making him work. As he wooed her, he dropped the showing off, the obscure jokes designed to reveal his intellectual prowess, and the tendency to look down on anyone who hadn't been to Cambridge. Instead he showed a charm and kindness she had not previously suspected. When she was ill, he sent a courier round with a box of carefully chosen gifts to help her feel better: a packet of Lemsip, a pot of honey, a miniature of whiskey and some lemons, a copy of a comic novel and a hot water bottle. He turned up himself that evening, having found his way to her flat in Dalston, with a bunch of flowers and the ingredients for dinner which he insisted on cooking for her. When he left, he made sure she had a cup of herbal tea to take to bed.

Without meaning to, she started to open herself up to him. She treasured their long Sunday afternoons together, lazing in a London park, wandering around a gallery, or watching a play or film together. She liked the long evenings over glasses of wine, with vigorous debates about things they'd seen. Then one night, as they walked back along the riverside, the coloured lights of the South Bank gleaming in the blue darkness, she kissed him, and felt the deep inner chime of connection: intimate, physical, intense. After that, they kissed all the time.

As she began to realise that Dan meant something to her, she became afraid. If she loved him, she'd have to deal with the constant feminine attention he attracted, and she feared it would make her paranoid. Already, despite herself, she felt pangs of jealousy when he was stared at or approached. She was afraid that she'd always worry that someone would come along to take him away from her. She decided it was too much to live with, and, before she got in too deep, she told him it was over. It had been fun and she liked him very much, but there was no future and she needed to get on with her life.

She was surprised at the depth of Dan's devastation at her decision. He refused to let her dump him, doing his best to win her back, slowly but surely. She resisted at first, but the flowers and letters, the antique gardening books delivered through the post, even poems composed and carefully written out in cards, all worked their magic. She agreed to spend the day with him and they headed off to Brighton one gusty clear morning. In the afternoon, they ended up sitting on a bench by the sea, gazing out over waves whipped by a tangy coastal wind while they ate hot, salty-sweet chips from a paper cone. She was cold. He took off his jumper and gave it to her. Its soft warmth melted the last of her resistance and as they laughed and ate together, she knew that they would spend that night together. They haven't parted since.

How long ago was that now? She stares up at the ceiling. The water is cooling around her and she debates whether to add more hot, but the wrinkled state of her toes decides her against it. *It was sixteen years ago.* She was twenty-nine and he was twenty-five. There seemed to be endless time back then, and she wanted to do so much before they settled down and had children. Even so, she couldn't have forecast what would happen: that by the time they wanted to start a family, it was already too late. But of course, it took a few years of trying before they admitted that it wasn't going to happen naturally. Then the investigations began, and the reassurances that it would probably be all right. The suggestion, at last, that they ought to begin to consider IVF – as if there was still all the time in the world. Olivia always clenched her fists tight with anger when she thought of it. They listened so closely to every word the doctors uttered, did exactly as they were told, remained calm and patient when advised to. And yet, at every stage, when their hopes were dashed again, there seemed to be the implication that the doctors had known all along that this would probably be the case, and what a shame that they had wasted so much time already, as though it had been Dan and Olivia demanding that things slow down so they could spend another six months going down closed-off avenues. It made her furious to think of it, so she tried to shut it out of her mind. Then, when the prospect of parenthood seemed so far away as to be an impossible dream, Dan asked her to marry him.

She had never felt the urge to be married but when Dan proposed, she knew it was what she wanted. He was still committed to her. The lack of children didn't mean their relationship was worth any less. He loved her, no matter what. It was a joyous day: a London register office, a riotous lunch with friends and family, an evening party with everyone else they wanted to be part of their celebration. But when the euphoria had worn off, there remained a bleakness below it all. They didn't know then what a long road there still was to travel, and how many more compromises would have to be made.

She has a flash of memory of the terrible moments in her relationship with Dan, but shakes her head to lose them.

They're over. Gone. They've got through the worst. Everything from here will be better.

From the cooling bath, Olivia hears shrieks from downstairs and tenses, listening. They sound harmless. The children must be playing some game of chase. She sighs and smiles. That's why, perhaps, she's never minded the sleepless nights or the relentless hours. Yes, she gets tired but she never minds it, not deep down. Because this is being a parent, something she feared she would never be, and the hectic, demanding days will pass as surely as everything else. They must be seized and experienced and lived.

As for the twins' heritage – she never gives it a thought, except vaguely in passing. Plenty of mothers look nothing like their children, and plenty of children have characters that are not a bit like anyone in their family. No one knows what they will get or what genetic mix will emerge. Sometimes she spots bits of Dan in the children, and she loves to see them. The fact that nothing of her will ever be seen in them is something she dismisses. *They might learn my mannerisms, my tone of voice. They'll love gardening because I do. I'll teach them about music and good food and how to look after animals and to be decent, honourable people. That's more important than sharing a hair colour or a gait or something.*

She stands up in the bath, water cascading from her as though she's Venus rising from the waves. She looks down at her body: it's certainly different now, with its folds of flesh and added layers of padding. One day she'll do something about it. Meanwhile, she feels rather magnificent – an earth goddess who has borne children and is now literally greater as a result – and Dan doesn't seem to mind. She feels so lucky for everything she now has and all the opportunities in life that still await her further down the line, and she can't wait to get stuck into it all.

She steps out of the bath and reaches for a towel.

Chapter Seventeen

The ladies, each perfectly turned out and polished with glinting blow-dried hair, sit eating salad off white china and sipping mineral water, waiters flitting around them attentively.

'Well, I think it's a great shame,' one says with a smile, looking over at Francesca. 'You will be missed!'

Francesca gives her a rueful look. 'That's sweet of you. I'm so sad about it. But it's just a necessity at the moment. I'm sure I'll be back on board in due course.'

'But,' says another, pushing away her lunch of barely touched leaves, 'I know exactly how it is. When we had our chateau in France to restore . . .' She rolls her eyes. 'My goodness, the work involved! It was non-stop for me, for a year or so. So I'm not surprised.'

They are talking in English but there are many different accents around the table. Francesca's is the only British one.

'I hope,' says a blonde German heiress who looks nothing like her fifty years, 'that you'll have us all over to see the work. I looked up the house on the internet after you told us about it, and it is certainly magnificent. But you'll have your hands full. How many rooms, remind me?'

'I'm not sure. A hundred and eighty? And around forty bedrooms!' Francesca laughs. 'I can't think of anything nicer than having you all over to visit – when I have some bedrooms I can actually use, instead of forty useless ones. But until then, you do understand that I'll be travelling back and forth all the time? It won't be practical for me to be on the committee, I simply won't be around enough.'

'Of course.' They are all smiling, all understanding. Most of them have properties across the world and they know that sometimes it's necessary to devote one's time and attention to one or other of them.

'And Walt?' asks one of the Spanish ladies, looking particularly fine in a red blazer that sets off her dark, low-lighted hair. 'Will he be helping?'

'You know men,' Francesca says, spearing a pea shoot with her fork. 'He's so busy he hardly knows what country he's in. No doubt he'll drop in and take a look from time to time. But it's frantic for him right now. I've barely seen him for weeks. Once the house is done, we'll take a lovely long vacation there and he can enjoy it.'

'Good idea!' enthuses another of the circle, a Swiss lady with a mink-collared sweater. 'We all need a little time together, don't we? To keep the marriage healthy. It's only sensible.'

The wealthy wives nod in understanding. They all know the importance of a well-nurtured marriage and the comfort and security it brings.

*

Back at home, Francesca packs carefully, in between checking messages and stopping to fire off emails. It's only a week or so since her trip to Renniston but she's heading back there as soon as she can. All she needs is the excuse, which is why she's arranging for the Preserving England man and the architect to come to the house, and for builders who specialise in conservation to come and give her quotes. She's already had a few round to inspect the work, but it can't do any harm to have more. After all, there has to be a good reason for her to spend a few days at the house.

She has to resist the impulse to pack up mountains of things for the children. That would not be wise, given Dan's state of mind. She can't pay too much attention to the twins or do anything to make him defensive in case he decides to move the family out and somewhere else beyond her reach. There is still the option of returning to Argentina, and she has to be sure that it isn't taken. As it is, she is probably going back a little sooner than she ought to. But it already seems an age since she was with the babies and she misses them with a hunger she hasn't felt since her own children were tiny. It's so invigorating to feel this rush of maternal need; it takes her right back to the time when she had that yearning to be near Frederick and Olympia, when she herself was young. That is nearly sixteen years ago now.

Thank goodness for the children.

They took the pain away, or at least, most of it. Their presence and her ability to lose herself in her love for them removed the devastation of what had happened before their arrival, before her marriage to Walt. It was such a dark time that she'd done her best to forget it almost entirely. It wasn't as though she had to talk about it – only one other person in the world knew, after all – and there was nothing to remind her about it, unless she chose to remember. And for the most part, she let it go and looked to the future and the choice she had made.

Only once has she been ambushed by its sudden and unexpected resurgence. Six years ago, Dan rang to tell her that he and Olivia were getting married. It was not a surprise, when they'd been together so long and had shown all the signs of considering themselves a permanent couple. Before the engagement, when she'd asked Dan why there was no wedding, he'd said that Olivia didn't believe in marriage, a statement that made her prickle, as though her own choices were being judged and found wanting.

'Why not?' she'd asked.

'Oh, you know,' he'd said vaguely. 'She doesn't think a piece of paper makes a difference to how we feel about one another.'

Francesca had thought of all the wives she knew who cherished that piece of paper and the security it gave them as time marched on and made them vulnerable to being replaced.

Still, Francesca had thought, *if Olivia doesn't want to marry Dan, all the better.*

It was just not a position she could ever imagine taking herself.

She heard of the engagement with resignation tinged with a hint of bitterness. She sent a card of congratulations and awaited the wedding invitation that came in due course. She was surprised by the card inviting her to Olivia's hen party, held on a hot day in London, with a big lunch at a restaurant and drinks in a pub with a beautiful garden, and then dancing in a nightclub. At the lunch, Francesca felt out of place. Most of the people there were Olivia's friends – from school, her gardening career, her writing world – and there were a few from a side of Dan's life she didn't know. One or two of the Cambridge crowd were there, or their wives or girlfriends. Everyone seemed vivacious and interesting but Francesca found it hard to engage. She was struggling with her emotions about the whole thing. They were celebrating the imminence of Dan's marriage, and that was something she couldn't bring herself to think too much about.

'Have you seen this?' It was the woman to her right, a merry, dark-haired person – Alex, she thought her name was. She passed Francesca a white leather album. 'It's so cute! You need to write in it too.'

She saw that it was a record of reminiscences and the thoughts of Olivia's friends on the occasion of her forthcoming marriage, looking back to the past and wishing her all the best for the future. Some people, forewarned, brought photos to be stuck in, or drew little pictures on their page. The lunch was already at the empty-plate-and-refilled-glasses stage. Francesca took her time flicking through the pages, learning more about Olivia than she had ever known before. She'd been cautious about being too pally with Olivia before now, not knowing what Dan might have told her. An entry in the book caught her eye.

I am so glad you two are getting married because you are totally and completely perfect for each other. I remember Dan when you first got together – oh my God, it was ten years ago! – and Dan was just in this state of utter happiness, and he told me he'd met an amazing girl who made him laugh and talk and think and, of course, had the body of his dreams. I'd never seen him like that before! I knew even before I met you that you were someone special, Olivia, and now I'm privileged to be your friend. Every best wish for all the happiness in the world, you gorgeous couple!

Claire xxx

Francesca stared at the page, reading it twice. She tried to calm herself down. *Wedding hyperbole.* Then it came, rolling upwards from her depths – a great wave of black, grief-filled anger. A flood of dark misery. *Why? Why her? Why not me?*

Amazing girl.

But I could have been that for him. He wouldn't let me! Laugh ... talk ... think ... why couldn't he do those things with me? We had all that together, we always did!

Body of his dreams.

The words burned in her mind, causing an actual physical pain in her stomach as though she was clenching up with some awful cramps. She was possessed by the feelings that had threatened to swamp her all that time ago: dark, wild, frantic despair that wanted to whirl her down into nothingness.

Ten years.

Ten years!

Francesca remembered only too well how things were for her ten years ago. While she was in agony, Dan was sampling the sweet delights of falling in love. She was his for the asking but that wasn't enough. He rejected her: everything she'd fought so hard to become, the struggle to learn how to be the right kind of person, the battle from that tiny house on the edge of town to the golden Cambridge college . . . it all meant nothing to Dan. She might as well not have bothered. He'd never wanted her, not in the way he wanted Olivia. There in the restaurant, as they celebrated his forthcoming wedding, an urge to scream possessed her. She teetered on the brink, almost overcome by the impulse to stand up and yell, turn over the table, smash the glasses, throw plates, let out all her misery and frustration and the pent-up jealousy that had poisoned her being for so long that she couldn't remember what it was like to live without it.

She steadied her breathing and calmed herself, using all her powers of control. She glanced up the table to where Olivia was talking and laughing with a friend; she looked so pretty, her blonde hair pulled up, darkish below and fair strands escaping at the edges. She looked so young, younger than the majority of them even though she was older than most, with her clear complexion, the glow on her cheeks and her slenderness. She wore a pale blue dress with a grey cardigan falling from her shoulders, a gold necklace with an acorn pendant hanging from it. Simple and yet effortlessly attractive. Francesca felt bulky and overdressed in a navy jacket, expensive T-shirt and white jeans. She was slender too, but in the stringy manner of someone who restricts all but the most vital foods. Olivia had a wholesomeness about her, as though she delighted in the good things of life and in return, life liked her back and let her stay young and healthy and fit.

It's wrong to hate her, Francesca told herself. *This isn't her fault.*

She knew that. Her rational brain could still inform her of the fact, and yet she couldn't stop the anger and resentment that needed a target from flowing towards Olivia.

She breathed long and slow again, smiled at Alex and said, 'Can I borrow a pen?'

Dearest Olivia
You have worked marvels for Dan. He has become the person he is meant to be, because of you. We are lucky to count you among us as a real friend and everyone is the better for your presence. I hope you two have many, many years of happiness in front of you, and that we'll all be together to share it with you.
All our love,
Francesca and Walt xxxx

And somehow she got through the rest of it, though she left before the nightclub, at the end of her tether, full of leaden sadness at the way it had worked out, and eaten up with jealousy of Olivia.

A month after the wedding, which had passed by in a

haze of sorrow that she hid with a manic cheerfulness and too many glasses of champagne, Dan confided in her the story of their fertility problems. It was the only thing that was able to lighten her mood, and after that, she began to feel better. After all, the amazing body could provide nothing in the way of offspring, while her lesser being had produced two beautiful children. It was a comfort of sorts.

Walt is home, as she discovers when she goes into the sitting room to look for a book she wants, and finds him there reading a newspaper.

'Oh!' she says, surprised to see him. 'You're home.'

'Yes.' He looks up at her over the folded-down corner of a page, giving her a beetley look from beneath his sprouting brows. 'Didn't Anastasia tell you I'd be back?'

'Perhaps she did.' Francesca gets torrents of emails from Walt's personal assistant, most entitled 'WAH movements', which always make her think of a baby's cry. They inform her of Walt's whereabouts and soon-to-be-abouts but she finds it impossible to hold the endless itineraries in her mind. Usually she focuses on when he is to be home and holds on to that. But that must have slipped her mind too.

'I'm surprised you weren't expecting me,' Walt says, putting down his paper.

'Why is that?' She goes to the bookcase and starts scanning it for a volume she promised to lend to Dan. It's a good idea to take it with her.

'Because the children are coming home?' He says it in a

half-ironic questioning tone, like a character in an American sitcom.

She goes still, startled and confused. 'Are they?'

He laughs with an edge of disbelief. 'Yes. Of course. It's in the diary. Anastasia sent the usual reminders. But you don't need those normally. Have you forgotten?'

She stands there, confused. She has completely forgotten. In fact, she has scarcely given the children a thought since she got back from England. Her whole mind has been focused on her return to Renniston and her need to get back there as soon as she can. She knows she has to speak. At last she says, 'Well, that's very strange. I must have got my calendars confused. I haven't had the usual reminders.'

Walt stares at her quizzically. She hasn't needed reminders like that, ever. The return of the children is always anticipated and planned for, with arrangements made for their stay. This time, she remembers, they have a long weekend away from school. Those are easier to forget, without the usual kerfuffle and packing and awkward gear that comes at the end of term. As she is processing this, and mentally making last-minute plans, Walt speaks.

'Frankie, are you okay?'

'Yes.' She speaks brightly, a smile over her face. 'Of course I am.'

'Really?'

She laughs now, a merry, pealing sound. 'Of course! What on earth could be wrong?'

'Well, now, I don't know.' He puts down the paper and sits forward in his chair, regarding her with a mixture of solemnity and affectionate concern. 'Why don't you sit down for a moment?'

She hesitates, eager to be off, wanting to return to her own private world. But she's spent long enough learning to subsume her desires when Walt is around to be able to put that on hold. 'All right.' She sinks down on the edge of an armchair, as though poised to leave at any moment. 'What is it?'

'How long have we been married now, Frankie?'

'Sixteen years, darling.' She smiles warmly at him.

'I think I've got to know you a little in that time.' He returns her smile. When he does, his face brightens, and the sagging jowls lift a little. The sparkle in his eyes reminds her of the Walt who attracted her all those years ago: never handsome, but with a vitality and a good humour she found soothing. He was going places, she knew that. The ride would be a good one, and he would make her life easy, both materially and as a companion. Not being wildly in love would be an advantage. It would protect her from the pain that went with passion.

'We've got to know each other,' she replies.

'Yes. I hope you've been happy, Frankie.'

'Of course,' she says, as though incredulous it could be any other way.

'I'm glad. You've made me happy too. But . . .' His eyes take on a hint of sadness. 'I've wondered if something is wrong lately. You're not yourself. I heard you've resigned from the Red Cross committee. You've been so distracted too. I know I'm not about all that much but when I am, it's as though you're completely absent, even when you're in the room with me.'

'Oh, that's silly,' she says, a tiny ripple of apprehension rolling through her stomach.

'And now you've forgotten that the children are coming home.'

'No, no, I remember now,' she says quickly.

'So have you arranged to have them met at the airport?'

'I . . . I'll check on that right now.' She stands up, wanting to be away from this interrogation.

Walt frowns. 'And for the weekend? What are we doing? I have in my diary that we are possibly going skiing.'

'Oh.' She sighs with a touch of irritation. 'No, we can't do that now. At least I can't.'

'Why not?'

'I'm going back to England tomorrow morning.'

Walt looks astonished now. 'You can't do that! Fred and Lympie are home. We should be together as a family.'

'Please don't call her that, you know I don't like it. The children will be fine.'

'What are you doing there that's so important?' His voice is rising a little and he's sitting forward in his seat, looking up at her as she hovers, keen to be on her way.

'I'm trying to make the arrangements for this house you've bought. Remember? That's why I've resigned all my committees. I'm going to be spending all my time overseeing the renovation. So,' she says tartly, 'perhaps you should have thought about that before you bought the old wreck.'

'I thought that's why we've got Dan and Olivia there – so they can oversee it,' Walt protests.

'They can't do everything. We still haven't hammered out the details, and they can hardly approve the architect's revised plans, or decide which contractor we're going to use.' She feels she's managed to turn things around so that she is coming out on top. No longer the bad, forgetful mother, but the harassed wife, overwhelmed with the organisation of practical details and arrangements.

Walt stands up, his knees cracking with the effort of lifting his frame upwards. 'You can go on Monday, can't you? There won't be anything to be done on a Saturday, will there?'

She thinks about this. He's right, of course. Her appointments are for Monday and Tuesday, arranged precisely so she can spend longer with the twins. She could go out on Sunday night, when Frederick and Olympia are on their way back to school, but that would mean putting off the moment she has been yearning for, when she will see the babies again. They've been in her thoughts constantly, filling her dreams and her waking hours with memories of their faces, the piping of their voices, the sweet smell of their skin and hair. Then she remembers. 'Mr Howard from Preserving England is going tomorrow afternoon. It was the only time he could make for weeks. That's why I need to be there.'

'Call him. Rearrange.'

'I'm not sure that's possible—'

'Come on, Frankie. You can't tell me you'd rather see that conservation guy than our kids! You said only the other day how annoying you find him. Call and postpone.'

She stares at the floor, following the pattern of the blue silk Persian rug with her gaze. She can't bear the thought of putting off what she's been looking forward to so keenly. But her duty is here, she realises that. And she would like to see Fred and Olympia.

Of course I would.

'I'll think about it,' she says briefly, then strides towards the door. 'I've got to see about collecting the children now. We'll talk when I get back. Can you ask Anastasia to book somewhere nice for dinner? Marie won't have time to make anything now, so we'll have to eat out.'

She marches out, frustrated that she now won't see the twins as she has been longing to.

Not for long, though. I'll be with them as soon as I can.

Chapter Eighteen

Olivia can't pretend to herself that she's not glad Francesca won't be coming until Monday, and not till late as all the morning flights were booked. Even though their days are no longer governed by the strict timetable of the working week, there is still something special about the weekend. They can't help sticking to the rituals – a luxurious supper cooked by Olivia on Friday night with plenty of wine, watching a film together on Saturday night, a roast lunch on Sunday. The repetition is comforting and something she looks forward to. Even though it would be perfectly nice having Francesca here – and they can hardly say no, as it is her house and there is an unused spare bedroom awaiting a guest – she prefers being on their own.

On Friday night, gleeful that they have been released from the impending visit for another forty-eight hours, she cooks with particular relish: steak in a peppercorn cream, potatoes *persillade*, and purple sprouting broccoli with snippets of anchovy and globules of melting butter. Dan opens a bottle of shiraz and they celebrate the best part of the day: the twins safely upstairs and fast asleep, and two or three lazy hours to themselves to eat and drink and talk. He goes to watch a cricket match he's recorded while she cooks, and Olivia takes occasional sips of her wine, enjoying the peaceful, harmonious atmosphere as she prepares the food.

Not so long ago, this ritual became strained and difficult. As the years of unsuccessful IVF took their toll, their relationship suffered. At dinner, they would sit in silence with the radio on so that they did not have to talk about what was dominating their lives. It wasn't only the pressure of their desire to become parents and the continual dashing of those hopes; the powerful and uncontrollable currents of artificial hormones surged through Olivia, making her morose, weepy, and hopeless with a hair-trigger temper. Dan tried to be understanding but he soon lost sight of the fact that these feelings had been created within her and there was little she could do about it; they were beyond her control. He lost patience and fought back, grew equally as tetchy and cross as she was, argued furiously and became cold and distant when she wouldn't – couldn't – snap out of it.

'For God's sake, I don't know if this is worth it!' he yelled during one of their most fierce confrontations. 'Do you know how long we've been living like this? Do you?'

He stood across the kitchen from her, his blue eyes flashing and his dark eyebrows set in hard arches. She stared back, eyes pricking with tears, trembling with her own anger, not sure any longer what they were fighting about or why, or what she felt about anything except miserable.

'I'll tell you.' He took two steps towards her and she

cowered a little, even though she knew there was no way he would hurt her. His desire for confrontation was what frightened her. 'It's been years. It's been fucking *years*. Where has the joy gone? We're so eaten up with this thing, it's taken everything good out of our lives together. When did we last have sex without thinking about conception and babies and ovulation and all the rest of it?' He stared at the floor and then shut his eyes, an expression of agony on his face. 'Shit!'

She wasn't able to do anything but cry. She didn't have the strength for anything else. All she longed for was his arms around her, comfort, kindness, understanding of the sapping nature of this journey they were on, with no promise of a destination. Her hands were over her face, tears soaking into her palms, but she didn't utter a sound. No arms enfolded her. Instead, she heard him turn and leave, and a few moments later, the slam of the front door. When he came back, she was as cheerful as she could be, and he didn't mention her tears or ask how she was. That night, they lay back to back and didn't touch or speak. When she felt him relax into slumber, she wept again that he could sleep without resolving things, telling her he loved her or trying to make it better.

For the first time she began to wonder how well she knew Dan. Their love had been a happy, indulgent thing that had brought them both pleasure and happiness, and she believed it was strong and true, made to face anything. But now she felt that in a time of trial and difficulty, when she needed him desperately, he was not able to stand firm and give her the patience and generosity she craved. In the talks about parenthood, she felt a distance grow between them and sensed that there was something deep inside Dan that he was concealing. When they talked about adoption, he agreed with her that it was a definite option, said how much he would be in favour of taking on a child from abroad, and yet she felt that he was not quite sincere. She could not help suspecting that sometimes he said things he did not mean to keep her happy. Frustrated, she pushed harder, asking more questions, trying to find out what he really thought, but he kept slipping away, staying elusive, saying the right things but leaving her with the uncomfortable sensation that he was prepared to hide what he really thought. He would fudge, obfuscate, even, perhaps, lie to her. It was a horrible thought that she could not quite credit, and she tried to ignore it.

The next morning, peace gradually returned and they carried on as best they could, knowing that the next Slough of Despond was not far away. Then came the dreadful day when they were told that her eggs were no longer viable. There was no way she could become a mother, at least, not a genetic one.

They walked away from the Harley Street clinic, where their life savings had been spent, in a state of shock. She was thinking, *If only I'd known! If only someone had told me that it could all run out like this*. She remembered the years of trying to stop conception: the contraceptive pill, taken for over a decade; the morning-after pill prescribed several times after accidents and forgotten pills; the jittery wait for a period after an illness that might have interfered with the process of contraception. *What was it all for? I should have grabbed the opportunities while I could, while there were still eggs to fertilise, while my body still had the capability. It's gone . . . it's over. I missed it. But how? How did that happen?*

For over a decade, she and Dan had talked themselves out of having children because, for one reason or another, the time wasn't right. They had thought they were in control of the process, and that her body would wait obediently until they decided, for whatever abstract reasons, that they were ready. The flat, she remembered, was part of it. They'd thought there wasn't room, or that it wasn't in a fit state – as though a baby would arrive and immediately criticise the decor and demand its own nursery. And all along, while they dithered and delayed, her body had been in the process of winding down its fertility. It had been ready for motherhood since she'd turned fifteen and now, its blind biology unconcerned with things like school, careers, bank balances and steady relationships, it considered she'd had long enough to sort things out. The babies had been there, a potential child every month, and if she hadn't done her bit, that was it. During the decade of indecision, over a hundred chances had come and gone.

More than a hundred potential children. I'll never know even one.

She was struck by the fiercest sense of loss she'd ever known, greater than when her father had died. All that possibility, wasted. She reeled under the blow.

Dan walked beside her, morose, his collar turned up. 'So that's it.' His voice was terse, low, sad and full of finality. 'It's over. The end of the line.'

As soon as he said it, she heard a voice sounding loudly within her. The word it spoke reverberated through her. *No.* She would not accept this. Something powerful refused to let that happen. She would fight it and win. Her grief wrapped itself up into a ball and tucked itself away in her heart. She felt hope fill her, pulled in from some invisible and unknown source. Stopping in the street, facing him full on, she said fervently, 'No, Dan. No. It's not the end. We're going to take a different path. But we will still be parents.'

'What are you talking about?' He looked bewildered.

'There is another option. We can use an egg donor!'

He frowned, his lips tightening. When she'd mentioned this possibility before, he'd never responded, just brushed it away and changed the subject.

Olivia went on: 'I've read about it on the internet forums, and researched a bit too, just in case. I'll show you when we get back.'

Back in the flat, they opened up their laptops and started surfing through websites of clinics and agencies that offered egg donation, some for eye-watering fees, and it seemed a straightforward process – although nothing with fertility treatment so far had been straightforward.

But when she told Dan this was what they must do, he refused point-blank.

'Absolutely not. I don't want to bring up a stranger's child. I want our baby made up of us. You and me. I'm not

209

interested in mixing my genes with a woman whose history, whose family, whose nature I do not know.'

They talked for hours, Olivia getting more emotional as she realised that Dan was adamant on this point. She'd reached an inner, obstinate core of him she'd never seen before, where there was no compassion, no give at all. They moved around the kitchen, facing each other in mini stand-offs.

'So you don't think nurture has anything to do with it?' she demanded. 'Don't you think environment is important? More important than whether you inherit the ability to sing or write with your left hand?'

'Actually, I don't think nurture is everything, now you mention it. It's important, I wouldn't argue with that. In fact, nurture is vital. But all the nurture in the world isn't going to make a silk purse out of a sow's ear, and what if you get a sow's ear?'

'A sow's what?' She sighed with exasperation. 'They're eggs! So we can use your sperm to make a baby who'll be ours! You know as well as I do that the eggs coming from one person guarantee nothing. What about my great-grandmother who went mad and got put in an institution? What about my aunt who had depression and killed herself? What if my eggs got a hefty dose of mad suicide genes instead of liking gardening and being good at art? There are no guarantees, but at least this way we get a baby, and it will be related to you and your family, if that's what matters.'

He stalked about, cross, his brows knitted, and said, 'No. I can't do it. I'm sorry. I can't stand the idea, and that's all there is to it. I don't think I could love a child who was half a stranger to me. At least we know about your great-grandmother and your aunt. With this option, we'd know nothing. Not least about hereditary diseases and all that. What if we had a baby and loved it and lost it to some dreadful condition we hadn't realised was in the family?'

'I want to take the risk!' Olivia screamed. 'You can't deny me that!'

'I don't want it, and I won't do it because I'm ordered to!' he yelled back. 'You can't force me to!'

They rowed for hours until, in a mess of misery and tears, Olivia went to bed to weep hopelessly into her pillow, while Dan bedded down in the spare room. She thought that night that maybe this meant they would split up. Would they be able to reconcile their opposing views, and if he won, would she ever be able to forgive him for robbing her of the chance to bear a child?

She didn't think, in her heart, that she could, even though she loved him so much.

The next week was terrible. They barely spoke, both aware of the seismic shock to their relationship. They had always been so together and such a team, and now they were riven apart and unable to see the way back, neither able to yield to the other.

She began to think seriously that they would separate over this, and she was lying in bed late, with Dan out somewhere, wondering if he was thinking the same thing, when she heard the door slam. He moved around the hall and kitchen for a bit, and then came to find her in bed, opening the door quietly until he saw that the bedside lamp was on, and then padded in to sit beside her.

He took her hand in his and said, 'If you really want to do the egg donor route, then I'm behind you. We'll do it.'

She sat up, happiness washing through her as his words sunk in. 'Really?'

'Yes. I want us to vet the donors really carefully. And I've done some research and found a clinic we could use. It's in Spain but it comes really highly recommended and it's cheaper than the London ones. Would that be all right with you?'

'Yes!' she cried joyfully. 'Anything, I don't mind! But . . .' She smiled at him, searching his face. 'What made you change your mind?'

'I want you to be happy,' he said, kissing her and holding her close. 'I can't bear us to be apart.'

'I'm so glad. I can't bear it either,' she said, hugging him back, filled with love and gratitude. And they began the process the very next day, using the clinic that Dan had found.

But she's never really understood what changed his mind when he'd been so entrenched against the idea.

The steaks are ready now, oozing red-tinged, fat-blobbed liquid on their resting plate. The potatoes are fried into hot, crisp little dice, speckled with garlic and parsley, and the broccoli is glossy from the steamer, scattered with snippets of spiky brownness.

'Dan!' she calls, dropping cutlery on the kitchen table. 'It's ready.'

He comes through, bleary-eyed from the television. 'Mmm, smells fantastic.' He sits down, gazing appreciatively at the table as she moves the steaks to the plates. 'Wow. My favourite.'

'Of course.' She sits down opposite.

'You're amazing,' he says, and looks at her tenderly. 'Is there anything you can't do? You're an incredible mother, a magical gardener and writer, and a fantastic cook. You must have had some pretty good fairies at your christening.'

'Don't forget the bedroom fairy,' she says with a coquettish smile.

'How could I?' He smiles back, and they remember their interrupted lovemaking of the previous weekend. They never got back to it. They both know that tonight – after the sumptuous meal and the blood-warming red wine – they will make up for the long wait. They are close again now, emotionally and physically, and she has done her best to forget that steely, unbending, cold-hearted Dan who, at their darkest moments, repelled her. The arrival of the twins decontaminated their relationship and renewed it, and she has pushed away the doubts she had about him.

'Aren't you glad Francesca isn't coming?' she says with a laugh. 'I mean, we can hardly stop her, and she's bound to turn up occasionally. But somehow I never expected her to be staying with us, not with the enormous house at her disposal.'

'Mmm.' Dan is engrossed in cutting his steak, revealing the pinkness within. 'We forgot to take into account the fact that it isn't habitable.'

'Yes. Of course, Francesca is lovely company and she clearly adores the children . . .' Olivia eats a tiny hot cube of potato, then says, 'and I was wondering if we ought to make her a godmother.'

He glances up at her quickly and says, 'I thought we didn't want godparents.'

'I don't – not *god*parents. I'm not a churchy person, you know that. But she seemed so . . . *into* the twins. Didn't you notice? She could hardly keep her hands off them. It was kind of sweet. It crossed my mind that it could be a nice gesture to ask her. Besides . . .' Olivia laughs a little sheepishly. 'I think she'd be pretty good at birthdays and Christmas and all of that. She already spoils them with presents. In a very material way, it would be rather nice for them to have a rich godmother. It's not just that, of course – she'll love them and they'll love her.'

Dan says nothing but chews slowly on his food, still staring at his plate.

Olivia sips her wine, and looks at him. Eventually she says, 'Well?'

Dan swallows and sits back. 'I can see what you're saying. But I would say no. We decided on no godparents. We'll only offend all the people we haven't asked if we ask one person. And I reckon Francesca will always be generous, godmother or not.' He frowns, hesitates and says, 'I'm not sure I want her to be in the twins' lives all that much anyway.'

'Really?' Olivia is surprised. 'Why not?'

He shrugs, making a face. 'Dunno. No real reason. Just

214

. . . that part of her life is over now, you know? I don't want her deciding she wants to do it all again with our two.'

'What?' Olivia laughs disbelievingly. 'Why should she want to do that? I think it's sweet, how much she loves being around them. I expect that now her two are grumpy teenagers, she rather likes being around toddlers.'

'Yeah. But still . . .' Dan leans back in to his plate, cutting another chunk of steak. 'I don't think we should get too settled in here. We're at her mercy. I don't want her taking over, that's all. The less we see of her, the better.' He puts the steak in his mouth.

Olivia is puzzled, but there is, she supposes, a certain logic to what he says.

Perhaps it wounds his pride a little to be accepting Francesca's generosity like this. It makes us look a bit like the poor relations, I suppose. But I'm in no hurry to move on. I feel we're really settling in. I can see us belonging here – for a little while longer at least.

Chapter Nineteen

Francesca finds the delay of her journey back to Renniston only whets her appetite for the twins. The fact she can't take a morning flight out on Monday is deeply frustrating and for a moment she considers chartering a private plane to fly her back to England, but dismisses that as over the top. It would be hard to explain to Walt why she felt such a desperate need to get to a house she doesn't like all that much. As it is, she can rearrange most of her appointments but Mr Howard can only do the Monday before she gets there, so she sends an email to Olivia asking her to show him whatever he needs to see in the house.

The children arrive home in a flurry of overnight bags and chatter, and she comes down to greet them with hugs and kisses. These days, they change subtly every time she sees them: another centimetre of growth, or a different way of styling their hair. As she embraces them and asks about their journey and how school is, she feels a strange foggy distance between her and them, but the children don't seem to notice.

They're happy to be home, even though it seems like they only just left after the Easter holidays.

The disconnected feeling continues all evening, throughout the family dinner in the restaurant in town. Francesca eats with her usual restraint and measured carefulness, and says almost nothing. While Fred talks ebulliently in his suddenly much deeper voice, Francesca is half back in the garden at Renniston, with Bea tottering towards her, her eyes wide, her soft hair lifted in the wind. Olympia picks at her food, one eye on her phone, on which she taps out messages every now and then. Walt fills in any gap with his stream of questions about lessons, friends and boarding houses.

'This term is less fun,' says Fred. 'It's always more boring when there's no skiing.'

'All the more time to spend on your academic goals,' Walt replies gravely. 'You've got exams coming up, young man. I don't want to see you flunk them in favour of a couple more hours on the mountain. Olympia knows how I feel about that. She's got a lot of catching up to do and I don't want to see the same thing happen to you, Fred. These exams really matter.'

'Yes, sir,' Fred says respectfully, cutting his pizza into slices while Olympia rolls her eyes at her father's stuffy attitude.

Francesca feels even more remote from her little family. She cannot ski as well as they can, having come late to it, and she doesn't have their devotion to the sport. In fact, she doesn't like sport at all. She blinks at each of them in turn. *Who are these people? What am I doing with them?*

She feels displaced, as though she ought to be reading a bedtime story to Bea but has been wrenched through space to this other version of her existence.

'And what about you, young lady?' asks Walt, turning to Olympia. 'How is the school work going?'

'We've got new house parents,' she announces, deftly side-stepping the question of her academic progress.

'Really? This late in the year?' Walt is eating Wiener Schnitzel with a mountain of well-dressed salad and he takes a bite, frowning. 'That's unusual. Don't they tend to see out the last term?'

They talk on, Francesca drifting on the outskirts of their conversation as her imagination takes her back to the house in England and the children there, living at the edge of the great hall. She thinks of the cottage as a beating heart of warmth and life in the middle of a huge, cold body. In fact, it is not just the rest of the house that's so dead and uninviting, it is the whole of the rest of the world.

She catches herself up at this thought, half appalled, and tries to remind herself of what else matters. She looks at Fred, her son. Her boy. His arrival began to heal her properly. She adored him. Now she can see the man he will be – a softer, taller version of Walt with all the polish his boarding school can provide – and she understands that the most intense part of their relationship is over. He is already gone from her side; he belongs more to the world than he does to her. She looks over at Olympia, still so young, so absorbed in the intensity of her small universe and the relationships within it; her daughter is discovering all the many ways to judge and evaluate herself, already believing she is a competitor in some intense and never-ending race. *She has so much already. She has no idea of how lucky she is. If only she can think enough of herself in time. If only she can avoid what happened to me.*

Francesca gazes at her daughter's unselfconscious beauty. *They're both so beautiful, they don't know how marvellous and forgiving youth is.* She's stabbed by grief for her own younger self, who tried so hard to be worthy of love, and almost . . . almost succeeded.

The memory takes her back to Renniston and the little people there. They are a healing gift. They make everything right. They are . . . recompense.

She looks at Frederick and Olympia as they talk and eat, perfectly confident in the security of their world.

Forgive me, darling children. You don't need me so much anymore. I have to be with the others now. You'll understand one day. Everyone will.

After everyone has gone to bed, she stays up in the snug, an old black and white film playing on the huge television screen mounted on the wall, hoping it will block out the pictures spooling through her mind and help her relax.

Her phone rings, startling her, and she picks it up. The screen displays the caller name: Renniston Cottage. She quickly pauses the film and presses the phone to her ear, anxious in case it is news of the children, in case something is wrong. 'Hello? Olivia?'

'No. It's Dan.'

'Is everything okay? Are the twins all right?' Her heart is racing, her palms clammy with fear. Already she is imagining what might have gone wrong.

'They're fine. They're asleep. And so is Olivia.'

'Oh. Thank goodness for that.' She smiles down the line, enjoying the sensation of relief. 'You frightened me for a minute.'

There's a pause.

'Dan?'

'Yes. I'm here.'

'Well? What is it? Everyone's asleep here too.' There's a moment of cosy complicity: the two of them, alone in their respective homes, joined by this secret telephone call.

'Cheska, I'm going to come straight to the point. I don't want you to stay here.'

'What? Why not?' She wonders if the children are ill after all, with something infectious perhaps.

'I don't think it's right. Stay nearby, by all means, if you need to visit the house. But I'm not comfortable with you being in the cottage.'

She lets this sink in, her skin prickling as she realises what he is saying. She had half expected something like this, but not so soon. He's making a defensive move, trying to keep her away from the children in case, somehow, the secret should slip out. *Or more likely that he'll be forced to think all the time about what he's done. My presence won't let him forget.* She answers softly. 'I don't think you really mean that, Dan.'

'I'm sorry, but I do, Cheska. You and I both know that it's

not a good idea for you to spend too much time around the twins. I'm trying to protect you as much as anything, because you might not be able to help yourself becoming too involved.'

'That's sweet of you, Dan, but you don't have to worry, honestly.'

'Even so.' She hears his voice take on the steely tone he uses when he's made his mind up. 'I think you should call Olivia tomorrow and tell her you've decided not to stay here.'

He thinks I'll do as he says. He thinks that all he has to do is twitch my strings and I'll perform just the way he wants. But it's not like that anymore. I'm not the obedient little Cheska I used to be. And I hold his whole family in my hand. But she doesn't want to destroy anything. She just wants to be happy, to be close to Dan and to the children. She laughs lightly and presses her mouth a little closer to the phone.

'Now, Dan. Let's get something clear. You're living in my house. I don't think you're in a position to stop me visiting if I want to. I don't mean any harm, you need to understand that. But I don't expect you to stand in my way. I want to know the children – know them properly. And you're not going to stop me. So let's not argue about it anymore, all right? Now, I'll see you on Monday. Night, darling.'

She clicks off the call with a delicious tremor at the sense of her own power. For the first time, she senses that the tables have turned.

After all this time, now he has to listen to me. He has to do what I want.

Chapter Twenty

The weather takes a turn for the colder, the blue skies turning a wintery grey and a chill wind blowing up. The spring blossoms look exposed and shivery, daffodils drooping away from a murky sun and blossom trembling in the icy gusts. In the fields near the house, the sheep sit, looking like fat cushions, their lambs nestled in beside them, slender legs tucked up underneath.

Dan is working in the little downstairs room he's commandeered as a study, so Olivia bundles the children up in their coats and scarves, looking out the woolly hats she thought had been put away for a while, and takes the children for a walk. They leave the grounds by the side gate that gives the best access to their part of the house, where they park the car Dan picked up second-hand from an advertisement in a local paper, and come out on a lane. They've already explored a little way along this lane, which leads past some pretty cottages and down to a farm, then onwards to open fields, where they've made some excursions. But it will be cold on the exposed brow of the hill, she thinks.

Besides, it's quite a long walk and as she's on her own, she won't be able to carry both children if they get tired.

'Let's go the other way,' she says to Stan and Bea. The children don't mind one way or another, although Bea says, 'Baa baa sheep?' as those are what she most likes seeing.

'There might be. We'll have to see. It's a new walk, isn't it?'

They wander out in the other direction, but progress is slow. The children are distracted by puddles and mud, and both stop to pick up sticks that take their fancy. Olivia keeps up a constant stream of chat as they walk along: 'Oh, what a lovely stick, Bea, that's a splendid one. No, don't hit the puddle with it, you're splashing Stan with all the muddy water. Oh dear, now his coat is dirty, we'll have to put that in the wash when we get back, won't we. That's a bit of a bore. Luckily I think we have another one just in case, the old jacket Aunty Charlotte gave us that she had left over from the cousins. Stan, don't go up that bank, there are nettles there that sting you. Don't go there! Please come back. Listen to me, Stan, when I talk to you. You won't like stings, they hurt. They're ouch, Stan, remember ouch? That's right, now come and hold my hand for a bit while we go along here.'

She is absorbed with them, just as she has been for two years now, ever since they were born. Her world revolves around them and their needs, and the task of filling their universe with experiences, words, explanations and knowledge. It is a task she intends to fulfil to the very best of her ability; it cost so much, in every way, to get here and she takes her parental duties very seriously – not because she wants to glorify herself through the children, shining in the reflected light of their intelligence and achievements, but because she feels she owes it to them. They've been summoned into existence at her command and she must ensure that existence is as rewarding as possible.

They are walking beside a high hedge that borders the front of the house, which seems to go on forever. She's already considering turning back, as it will take even longer to retrace their steps as the twins get tired. They're chattering and babbling away, but lunchtime isn't far off and soon they'll start moaning and she remembers that she hasn't brought any rice cakes with her. Then, suddenly they are at a gate: high, black, wrought iron with elaborate twists and turns and gilded leaves at the top. Behind the gate, which is about two metres wide, is the house. Renniston Hall, in all its glory. Olivia stares, trying to take it in. She hardly ever sees the house from this perspective. Usually she catches glimpses of bits of it, from windows and from the garden, and she saw the impressive picture on the front of the brochure that time when Francesca showed it to them in the flat. When they were deciding whether to live here, she scrolled through pictures on the internet, from old engravings to bright colour tourist-information photographs, and, of course, it looked magnificent. But now it is real. She half whistles as she looks at it. The house is not set back from the road – there's no tree-lined avenue through miles of parkland, and she has the sense that at one point, there was more land with the house that's now no longer part of it. The short drive feels truncated. In front of the house is a large gravelled circle, a grassed roundel with a fountain on it in the centre. And then, a broad expanse of honey-coloured stone, with a dozen huge windows set in it, and a magnificent stone portico, carved and ornamented, set over the huge oak front door. This place is enormous. Their little cottage must take up just a tiny part of it.

Francesca owns this! Well, she and Walt.

Olivia only has a hazy idea of Walt. They've met a few times – he was at their wedding and some of the occasions that have brought them all together over the years – but if she hadn't met him, she could almost believe that Francesca had made him up. He is her invisible partner, the husband who is never there. His work, whatever it is, takes him all over the world and his wealth keeps him in Geneva, where he parts with as little of it as possible. He must live in Switzerland for tax reasons, she supposes, which is a position she rather despises, although she has always liked Walt when she's met him. He radiates good humour and tolerance, and laughs in a loud, unselfconscious way at his own off-colour jokes, though she can imagine he's less fun in a boardroom or a business confrontation. He makes an odd partner to the slim, polished Cheska with her vague air that somewhere, something is clenched.

Striving. That's a word that comes into Olivia's mind when she thinks of Cheska, as though she's on her way somewhere, trying to keep it all together as she goes implacably onwards, never daring to stop in case of . . . *what?*

And now she has this. What on earth are they going to do

*with it? There are only four of them. What kind of madness
makes them want to live in this huge house? It ought to
belong to the National Trust or something.*

She can see it now: open to the public, with a tea room,
and a shop that sells fudge and tea towels and decorated
garden tools, along with big illustrated hardbacks about the
house's history. She can see weddings held in the great hall,
marquees on the lawn for anniversaries and literary festivals
and genteel gardening courses. There ought to be a car park
and public loos and guides on hand to point out interesting
features, and the rooms furnished in the right period and
hung with portraits of previous owners. People ought to
swarm the corridors, children running down galleries, the
place alive with activity, everyone able to experience and
enjoy this place.

Four people living here?

She remembers that the place will be open to the public,
once the restoration is complete. Perhaps there will be
guided tours arranged privately by appointment. Not exactly
guaranteed to bring the punters in.

'Mummy, I'ms hungry . . .' Bea is pulling at her hand.
Stan is singing to himself, swinging on the iron gates, his feet
on the cross bar between the upward rails. 'Biscuit?' Bea
asks, smiling sweetly, showing her rows of tiny, perfect teeth.

'Yes, yes, let's get back,' she says. It's going to take a good
twenty minutes to walk home. Something in her is a little
stunned that this place is their home. Her bedroom has a
door that leads into this extraordinary place. She is astonished at the thought. Even, she realises, a little afraid.

'Come on, off we go!' She takes Stan's hand and pulls him gently off the gate. Bea slips her hand into Olivia's other one.

They start their slow meander back down the road.

Dan has lunch ready when they get back: plates loaded with little crustless sandwiches, chopped cherry tomatoes, carrot sticks and boxes of raisins. There's a tub of grapes and some little round cheeses in red wax coatings. Typical toddler fare.

'What are we having?' Olivia asks with a laugh, when the children are settled and eating.

'Err . . .' Dan looks about. He picks up a bowl and offers it to her. 'Tuna mayonnaise on crackers?' he asks.

'Maybe. Or I can get some soup on. It won't take a moment – there are some parsnips withering away that I can stew up with an onion and some curry powder.'

'Sounds good.' Dan is scrawling a list on a pad on the table. 'We'll need to get to the supermarket at some point, we're running low.'

'And Cheska's arriving later,' she reminds him.

'Oh yes. I forgot.' He makes a face.

She laughs again. 'You look like you can't stand the thought! I don't understand it, you two are such good friends. Why have you gone off her all of a sudden? Is it because she's become our landlady or something?'

Dan's eyes harden. He shrugs and says nothing for a moment. Then he says, 'Maybe. Something like that. She always likes playing Lady Bountiful.'

'Does she?'

'You know, arriving with armfuls of presents, picking up the bill at restaurants, sending us lavish hampers at Christmas, all of that.'

'I thought she was just being generous. Spreading a bit of her money about when she knows we haven't got as much as she has.'

'Yeah . . . maybe.' Dan is quiet again, pensive. Then he smiles and says, 'Maybe I'd just rather it was only us. We've been living with your family for such a long time. I've kind of enjoyed being on our own again.'

'I know what you mean.' She goes round the table and hugs him. 'I like it too. I don't even want to go to the supermarket.'

He hugs her back, dropping a kiss on the top of her head. 'Then stay here. I'll take the kids.'

'I have to stay anyway,' she says into the warmth of his shirt. 'That conservation man is coming, the one Cheska wants me to meet.'

'Ah. I forgot. All right, you stay here. I'll go shopping after the children have had their naps.'

Olivia savours the warmth and security of his solid body, bigger and stronger than her own. She looks back at the table and sees Bea's green eyes fixed on them, watching solemnly as she chews on her sandwich.

Where did those green eyes come from? she wonders idly. She has blue-grey and Dan has dark blue. Then she remembers. *There's no knowing. They could be from anywhere.*

*

The knock on the cottage door comes right on time at two thirty, not long after Dan and the twins have left for the trip to the supermarket.

She answers it, a little nervous. She's not quite sure what she's supposed to do, and Francesca speaks about the conservation officers as though they are agents of the devil, engaged on a mission to thwart, disrupt and destroy her plans at every opportunity.

A man holding a buff-coloured folder stands on the doorstep. He's well dressed in a smart coat and dark trousers, a bright red scarf around his neck, his chestnut leather shoes shiny. He has an open expression, soft brown eyes behind a pair of tortoiseshell-framed glasses and a longish face, his bottom lip fuller than the top and a dimple in his chin. His brown hair is the only unkempt thing about him: it's wavy and rather long, with a touch of mad professor about it.

'Hello!' he says in a brisk, friendly tone. 'Are you Mrs Felbeck?'

'That's right.'

He sticks out his hand. 'I'm Tom Howard. Good to meet you.'

'Hello, Mr Howard.' She takes his hand and he pumps it up and down briskly.

'Call me Tom.'

'Call me Olivia.'

'Thanks. I will.' He grins with a pleasant beam of friendliness, his eyes crinkling up at the edges. She notices that there's a touch of green in the brown of his iris.

'Sorry,' she says after a moment, 'please come in. Would you like a cup of coffee or something?'

'Well now, I would, very much. This is just about the hour for a bit of reinvigorating caffeine.'

She laughs and leads him into the kitchen, and puts the kettle on while he looks about.

'This is very cosy,' he says, and taps his foot on the floor with appreciation. 'Very fine local limestone. Wonderful stuff.' He shakes his head. 'This place is full of treasures. What's it like to be living here?'

'It's hard to say,' Olivia replies, getting coffee and mugs together. 'We've not been here very long. We're still settling in.'

Tom Howard is looking about, scrutinising the walls and ceiling, as though noting every light fitting. Olivia feels oddly nervous, as if she has allowed him in against Francesca's wishes. Did she get permission for all the work in here? Or did she not need to? *It's a Grade I listed building. I imagine she needed permission for every plug and every pipe. No wonder it's taken years to get this thing moving.*

'You're looking after the place for Mrs Huxtable, are you?' he says, his eyes moving over the room. 'Did she finally manage to get rid of old William?'

'We're not exactly looking after it, but I think she's glad to have someone on the property, especially once work begins. And William is still around. I saw him only recently.' She has caught glimpses of the old man in the distance and she saw him yesterday, emerging over the top of a distant hedge, trimming it carefully with shears. She wondered what shape he was maintaining and told herself she must go and look at the gardens again sometime soon. The life in them was beginning to call to her; she was being tempted to venture beyond their own section of walled garden.

Tom Howard nods, looking interested. 'I don't think they'll ever get rid of him. Not now.' He glances around the kitchen again. 'Of course, he must miss this place.'

'Yes. I feel bad that he was chucked out and now we're in. How long did he live here?'

Tom frowns. 'Oooh, I don't know . . . I'm told he's been here over thirty years. It was a girls' school in the fifties and sixties, and it got hit by some big scandal to do with one of the girls getting pregnant. It limped on for a bit but closed down in the early seventies, I think. Then it was bought by a foreign businessman who never did a thing with it and hired William to be a caretaker while he was abroad. Goodness knows why he wanted it, he never spent much time here. Then he got caught up in some revolution in his own country and more or less disappeared. It was left to rack and ruin. William stayed on to look after it as best he could. You can imagine what kind of a job it was to keep an eye on this place on his own. I believe the owner kept sending cash to pay him and to maintain the fabric but that stopped once he lost contact. But William carried on anyway.'

Olivia pours out the coffee and hands him a mug. 'Milk's in the jug if you'd like it.'

'Thank you.' Tom takes the mug and then sloshes in some milk. 'This is just the ticket.'

Olivia persists. 'So are you saying that William has

worked here for decades and decades . . . for no pay? All alone?'

'That's about the size of it. If he hadn't, goodness knows what would have happened. As it is, there was lots of decay and damage. When we got hold of the place six years ago, it was in a sorry state. It took over a year just to mend the roof and stop the worst of the water getting in. Luckily William had dashed about with buckets and stuck up polyurethane when the holes got too bad, and he kept everything he could when it fell. Chunks of plaster, joists, bits of shattered statue.' Tom smiles, the skin around his eyes crinkling behind the glasses. 'He deserves a medal, he really does. He used to roam the house with his torch at night, to make sure there weren't any vandals getting in.' Tom laughs. 'For all I know, he still does.'

'Poor old man,' she says thoughtfully. 'Alone here for years and years. No family, no nothing. And he's being sacked?'

Tom Howard sips his coffee slowly, as though gaining a little time while he considers. 'I rather thought you'd know all about it – as you're working for Mrs Huxtable.'

'I'm not working for her,' Olivia says quickly. 'We're her friends.'

'Of course. Sorry. I didn't mean to offend.'

'You haven't. But I don't know anything about what's happened to William.'

Tom looks about again. 'Well, when he lived here, it was a good deal less comfortable than it is now. Not so much in the way of dishwashers and so on. A bit less gingham. I suppose he must be in one of the estate cottages now but they're little more than sheds. Unless the tenant farmer has given him a place. I don't suppose he minds very much. He only wants to be close to the house, that's all. I've never seen such dedication in anyone.'

Olivia is full of guilt. What must the man think of her and Dan, moving into his house after he's been thrown out, and never lifting a finger to look after the house? How could Francesca do it, after everything the old man had done for the place? Couldn't she have kept him on, or renovated a place for him? It would have cost her nothing in the grand scheme of what this place was surely going to require.

Tom has finished his coffee in three easy gulps, not seeming to mind its scalding heat. 'That was delicious, thank you.' He puts down his mug. 'Now. Shall we go and see the house?'

In his folder, Tom has detailed plans of the house that seem to go on forever. He consults them as they walk around, muttering to himself and gazing about. Olivia follows behind him, staring with amazement at everything she sees.

'But this is incredible,' she says, awestruck. The house is an extraordinary piece of history, she can see that, full of beauty and magnificence. She has never walked around a place so redolent of the past before.

'Haven't you looked around already?' Tom asks, surprised.

'No. We haven't. Not really. It's taken all our time settling in to the cottage. And we have small children. Two. Twins.'

He blinks at her blankly, as if that's no excuse for not exploring a house like this when it's on your doorstep. 'Oh. All right then.' He begins to talk as they go. 'That is a plaster barrel ceiling – an amazing example of early sixteenth-century work. Really quite stunning. Of course, it's gone through extensive renovation. I was part of the team overseeing the work here, and really you wouldn't believe how much has been done. It was just the tip of the iceberg, if you'll excuse the cliché, but at least it stopped the rot. Our hope now is that Mr and Mrs Huxtable continue the good work.'

'What I don't understand,' Olivia says as they walk along a gallery with views over the formal quadrangle behind, 'is why this has gone to a private family. Surely it's a national treasure. Why hasn't it been taken on for use as a public space? It should be open to everyone, all the time.'

Tom stops and turns to look at her, a sigh escaping him that he tries to hide. 'Believe me, I think the same. This place is like Hampton Court, or Blenheim Palace, never really designed as a private home but rather as a magnificent setting for courtly life. But people higher up the food chain thought that the best thing for the place was for it to go back into private hands, even though that caused half the trouble in the first place.'

As he talks, he takes a pencil out of his pocket and scrawls a red line over a small section of the plans.

'Are you going to approve the changes that Francesca – Mrs Huxtable – wants?' Olivia asks, observing him scribble. 'It seems a bit contradictory to let a private family buy it and then refuse to allow her to turn it into a family home.'

'I can't say at the moment. Our decision will follow in due course, once we've considered all the impact the proposed changes will have on the historic fabric.' He is suddenly all professional, his language rehearsed, his phrases well worn.

Olivia feels a rush of annoyance and a hot flush rises to her cheeks. Before she can stop herself, she blurts out, 'Well, where were you all when this place was falling down? When only William was here to stop the rot? What did you care for the fabric and impact then? Now someone has actually put some money into the place – millions probably, with millions more to come – you're all over the joint. Suddenly it's more precious than anything in the world! And now you're laying down the law, when not so long ago you were perfectly happy to let the rain gush in and the ceilings fall down and the thieves break in!'

Tom stares at her, his expression solemn. When she has finished, she is immediately embarrassed by her outburst, wondering where it came from.

'Of course we weren't happy,' he says. 'But it belonged to someone. It was only the fact that we could force a purchase that saved the place at all. Before then, we had no legal right to enter.'

'And now it belongs to Francesca,' Olivia replies, 'and you seem to have retained all your legal rights.'

There is a pause, and then Tom laughs, a rich, merry sound. 'Are you sure you don't work for Mrs Huxtable?' he asks. 'Because you're certainly putting her case pretty well.'

Olivia laughs too. 'I don't want the building harmed any

more than you do. But it seems to me that a few bathrooms and some proper heating and all the rest aren't going to hurt it. It was a school, didn't you say?'

'That's right. For girls. It opened after the war and closed down thirty years later, after it had sold off most of the land.'

'Then I suppose it was messed around with pretty well then.'

'There are some dreadful bits,' Tom admits. He raises an eyebrow at her. 'All the more reason to stop anything else being spoiled.'

Olivia gazes back. He smiles, and she feels her annoyance ebb away. *After all, what does this matter to me?* But her unwitting involvement in William's eviction has made her feel part of all of it and not in a good way. 'Do you need to see anything else?' she asks. 'My husband and children will be back soon.'

'That's fine for now,' he says, closing his folder. 'I'll have to come back, though. I'll call you direct, if that's all right. So that we don't disturb Mrs Huxtable unnecessarily.'

'Of course. She'll be here for a few days this week, if you want to see her. She's arriving later today.'

'Yes, she said on the telephone.' He tucks his folder under one arm. 'Perhaps I'll call back then. I might as well take the opportunity, if she's here.'

'Of course.' Olivia is disoriented, but Tom knows the way. She follows him out of the long gallery, already anticipating the return of the children. They haven't been far from her mind the whole time, and she's yearning for them, the way she has since they were born.

Since before they were born. Since forever.

Chapter Twenty-One

The car takes Francesca straight from the airport to Norfolk. Her cases are in the back and she wonders how she will explain the amount of luggage considering she is only supposed to be staying a few days. One large bag is devoted to gifts for the family: some expensive cosmetics for Olivia, books and a leather-bound initialled notebook for Dan, toys and clothes for the children. Perhaps it's a clumsy attempt to buy their affection but she can't help herself. She's grown used to the role of generous provider, the good fairy who arrives with delightful presents and whose arrival is therefore always welcome. She still gets a thrill from her buying power, just like the tingle of excitement she felt when Walt gave her that shiny silver credit card and she realised she had money to spend. She'd always intended to have money because she understood that the basic division between those graceful girls in the pretty brick school and the hordes of children in the big, grey comprehensive was wealth. It took money to enjoy the pleasant things in life, and if she were ever going to belong to that crowd, with their easy confidence and their certainty that they were entitled to the best, she was going to need money. That was partly what took her towards a legal career, where she would be certain of earning a decent living and supporting herself. But she wanted more than just the money, which was why she chose to specialise in human rights. She wanted a notable career, to make her mark, to rise in her profession and prove herself. She wanted to make a difference in the world.

But I didn't. I gave it all up. I turned my back on it.

She knows that it started at Cambridge, from the time she met Dan. She can recall with absolute clarity the day she walked into her supervisor's room and saw him, lolling in an armchair, idly glancing over the essay he had written. He was the most beautiful boy she had ever seen, with his tousled black hair, the chiselled features and romantically hollow cheeks, the strong brows and the deep blue eyes. She almost gasped with the impact of him. Then he looked up at her, gave her the full force of his most charming smile and said, 'You must be Francesca. Hello. You must excuse my essay, the ink's barely dry. You'll have to do the brain work, I'm afraid. I soused myself in beer last night, and I'm fit for nothing. I'm sure you're much more respectable.'

But when the supervisor came in and asked Dan to read his essay, it was, of course, brilliant. Afterwards they went for a coffee together and when the waitress brought it over, she said with a smile, 'Oh, aren't you a pretty couple!'

Dan laughed and said, 'Nice of you, but we're not a couple.' Then he winked at Francesca. 'Yet.'

That was that. She was head over heels from that moment.

*

He must have known from the start that she adored him. He flirted with her sometimes, making her tremble with pleasure, or acted like a protective older brother. Occasionally, there'd be a touch of scorn in the way he acted, or he'd make her the butt of a joke, sending a rush of scarlet to her cheeks, but he'd always see her mortification and later make up for it with a whispered compliment or an affectionate hug. She never really knew how he felt about her, though he went through strings of other girlfriends, mostly gorgeous. She would have given up if he hadn't kept that conspiratorial attitude towards her, that cheeky warmth that hinted she knew him best of all. Maybe he cultivated her so that when he really hadn't done an essay, she would lend him notes, find him books in the library, make his excuses for him. Once, knowing he had stayed out two entire nights before a supervision, she even wrote a whole essay for him just in case he needed it, getting up at dawn to make sure it was ready in time. She imitated his style as best she could. But he pulled a sickie and didn't show up anyway. When she gave it to him, he laughed, thanked her and took it. She never knew if he handed it in or not. But she didn't mind. She'd do anything for him, even at the expense of her own work. Instead of being able to settle and concentrate, she would trot around the faculty, college and university libraries looking for him, under the pretence of talking about their work, but really so she could spend time with him.

When her results began to suffer, her tutor asked her if anything was wrong. Was something interfering with her work? She said no, of course not. She could hardly admit even to herself that she was prepared to put her passion for Dan ahead of her studies. But the truth was, he took precedence over everything. He became more important than her friends, her degree, and eventually, even her career.

I would have sacrificed everything if he'd asked. Everything.

And in a way, she had.

Francesca stares out of the window at the English countryside. She's lived away from the land for so long, it feels almost as foreign as Swiss mountains once did to her, but something in her responds to the rolling patchwork of green and yellow fields, the white dots of distant sheep, the ancient hedgerows cutting across hills and bordering roads. Once she wanted to leave all this behind; now she is starting to envisage a future here. But what is it? There are misty pictures in her mind, little snapshots of a life that might await her.

The car races up the motorway, the engine a smooth hum, the driver silent and concentrating on the road. Francesca lets her mind wander over the dreamlike images that are assembling in her mind.

She sees the house: it's been transformed into a splendid and comfortable home. Fred and Olympia are there, healthy, happy, positive and behaving like perfect, civilised teenagers. But Walt . . . where is he? He's a benign presence still – he'll always be that, she can't imagine him any other way – but he's not exactly there. He's away somewhere else. But Dan is there, smiling, happy, realising, at last, that all along they were meant to be together. Olivia is somewhere else too. That's not specified. She doesn't want to think about that. And what's this? Two beautiful little children, the wonderful creations that unite her and Dan. They have made him understand why he and Francesca are destined for each other. Life will be wonderful. At last, she'll begin to live the way she was supposed to. It will be like coming home.

Francesca blinks, realising her eyes are full of tears. She sniffs. *Don't be so silly. It can't happen like that. It's impossible.*

But that picture of bliss is so very hard to resist.

It would make everything right. It would show that all along, it's been worth it.

It's teatime when the car draws up at Renniston. As they pass the gates, she glimpses the stunning frontage of the building and has a sudden rush of excitement that this is hers now.

What a long way I've come, from that tiny, noisy house in Gloucestershire, to this.

Then the car turns to the side, and pulls up in the space next to a muddy vehicle that must be Dan and Olivia's. It has certainly seen better days, and next to the Daimler, it looks positively decrepit. She hopes it's roadworthy enough for the twins to be driven in; two large seats in the back seem to indicate that their safety is taken seriously, at least. Giving Dan and Olivia a new car might be a more tricky proposition.

'Can you bring the bags in, please?' Francesca asks the

driver as he holds the door open for her to emerge. 'Just one case to start with. Then wait five minutes, and bring in the other bags. Thanks.'

She picks up the bag loaded with gifts and carefully makes her way over the muddy drive to the gate in the wall that leads into the cottage garden. Her cream ballet slippers are not exactly suitable for this so it's a good thing she brought a pair of walking boots with her, along with a warm waterproof jacket. Her anticipation builds as she opens the garden gate and steps through. Her heart is pounding and she's filled with a kind of delightful nervousness, knowing she's about to see what she most longs for. The first thing she notices is great patches of white hanging in the air, and then realises that they are sheets hanging out, drying in the spring wind. Olivia is there, pegging out the last one. Now she can see, emerging from behind one of the flapping white squares, a child sitting aside a riding toy, pushing it along with their feet. The caramel-coloured hair is tied up in bunches – *it's grown! And she's got curls at the ends* – and the little body is wrapped up warmly in a bright spotted coat. *Bea.* Her heart swells with love for the tiny girl. *Where's Stan?* She spots him at once, crouching over one of the borders, digging in the soil with his fingers. For a moment more, she enjoys the scene of their innocent play, and then she calls out.

'Hello! I'm here!'

Olivia turns from the washing line she's strung up over the old paving stones in front of the cottage, and waves, a big smile on her face. 'Hi! You made it!'

'Is it okay if Richard here takes the bags up?' Francesca

says, as the driver comes into the garden carrying her case.

'Of course. Go upstairs, turn right, and it's at the end of the corridor.' Olivia walks towards them, homely in jeans and a flowery shirt with a cardigan over the top. She's completely natural, her hair pulled back and her face bare.

And still not yet lost the baby weight.

'Hello, darling,' Francesca says, and kisses Olivia on each cheek. 'You look lovely.'

Olivia laughs. 'I know I don't but it's nice of you to say. Come on in. How was the journey?'

'Oh, fine, I barely notice it now, I'm so used to it.' She holds out the bag. 'I come bearing gifts and you shall have them in return for a proper cup of English tea.' She is studiously keeping her distance from the children but she is aware of them at every moment. Bea has stopped riding and is observing the new arrival with no sign of recognition. Stan is still absorbed in his earth works.

'You shouldn't have, Cheska!' Olivia exclaims, a little abashed at the sight of the loot. 'You really do spoil us far too much. But how kind of you. Come on, let's go in and I'll get you that tea.'

Richard has made his journey up to deliver the case. He catches Francesca's eye as he heads back towards the car and she gives a small nod. It won't be too much trouble for him to slip past with the rest of the luggage.

'Here are the children!' she cries, sensing this is the moment to notice them. 'Hello, sweeties, are you having fun? Do you like playing in the garden?'

'Come and say hello,' Olivia urges Bea, who is closest.

Bea climbs off her yellow plastic ride-on and trots over obediently.

''lo,' she says and smiles at Francesca. A wave of fierce love surges through her for the child. She drops to her knees, releasing the bag of gifts and hardly noticing the cold grass underneath her, and holds out her arms to her. Bea approaches, understanding that she is to be hugged, and submits to Francesca wrapping her in a tight embrace and kissing her cheek.

It is a wrench to let the child go, but Francesca releases her after a moment. She's deeply, intensely moved. *My daughter. My little girl.* She looks up at Olivia, smiling. 'Isn't she just beautiful?'

Olivia gazes down at Bea, her eyes full of the same pride and love. 'Yes, she is. Bea, you take Cheska inside, I'll get Stan.' She looks over at her son. 'Oh my goodness, those fingernails of his are going to be caked with mud.'

'Yes, you take me inside, Bea.' Francesca takes up the girl's small hand. 'Let's go to the kitchen. Would you like some juice and a biscuit? I'm sure Mummy will say it's all right. Come on.' The desire to have Bea to herself even just for a moment is so strong that she's prepared to ignore Stan for the time being. She barely even notices when the driver murmurs that the bags are unloaded and he'll be on his way. Everything is centred on the small child at her side, and the way she longs to feast on the sight of her.

They are at the kitchen table, the presents spread out in front of them. The twins are playing with their toys, sitting on their play mat and talking to each other in a mixture of words and babble that seems to make perfect sense to them. Francesca thinks that they are clearly bright.

'This is really too much, Cheska, I mean it. You shouldn't have.' Olivia looks at the small mountain of expensive cosmetics that Francesca has brought her: oils, creams, tinted moisturisers, shimmery cheek colour and lip balms. 'I really don't bother with most of this stuff anymore.'

'You will,' Francesca says wisely. 'Believe me, I know what it's like. One day, you'll suddenly realise that you've got some of your life back and you'll want to start restoring yourself.'

Olivia laughs with a touch of embarrassment. 'If you say so. My old self seems so far away now, I don't know how I'll ever get it back.'

'Don't be silly. Of course you will. You just don't have time to think about yourself. It'll change, I promise. Besides . . . now that I'm here, I can help look after the twins. You can have a bit more time to yourself.'

'That's very nice of you,' Olivia says, and takes a sip of her tea. 'I'm sure that would be lovely but you're not here to do my childcare for me. There's obviously plenty here for you to oversee. Tom Howard called by earlier, as promised.'

'Oh. Yes.' Francesca remembers the ostensible reason why she is here. 'What did he say?'

Olivia describes the visit, passing on all that Tom Howard said. 'So what exactly is going on at the moment?'

Francesca sighs. 'It's such an endless palaver – we submit plans, they consider them, then object or demand changes or more explanation. Then we resubmit and it all goes through the same process, over and over. And you can imagine how much we want to do here.'

'I saw the place for the first time really. It is extraordinary.' Olivia frowns and smiles at the same time. 'But I don't really understand how it's going to be a home. It's just so . . . large. How will you do it?'

'We're planning to do what the great houses do – have a comfortable family wing and very grand state rooms for big occasions,' Francesca replies. She likes the way that sounds. As though that kind of life is second nature to her. 'And we'll collect whatever we can that's related to the house's history, for visitors to see.'

Olivia nods slowly. 'That makes sense. But what made you want a house like that? Where you have to let the public in?'

Francesca shrugs. 'Walt wanted it. He loves history. Owning a place like this is his dream come true. Did you see Queen Elizabeth's bedroom?'

'No. I didn't know she had one!'

'There's nothing in it. But it's worth seeing. I'll show it to you sometime when we've got a moment.'

'And what's your plan while you're here?' Olivia asks, sipping her tea again, regarding Francesca with her clear blue-grey gaze. 'Are you staying long?'

A flutter of panic goes over Francesca. She wants to be evasive but she knows she can't be too vague. She has booked some appointments to make sure she has a purpose here and she goes over them quickly. 'So all that should keep me busy.' She smiles at Olivia. 'I hope I won't be under your feet too much.'

'Don't be silly, you're very welcome! You can stay as long as you like. Consider this your home from home.'

'Thank you.' She smiles at Olivia, glad she has conveniently given the answer Francesca lined up for her. 'That's so sweet.' She looks about. 'Where's Dan?'

'Working. He's requisitioned one of the small rooms down here as his study. He's in there most of the day when he isn't looking after the twins. I'll call him – but he asked me to let him go for as long as possible before disturbing him.'

'Oh no!' Francesca holds up her hand. 'Don't call him on my account. There'll be plenty of time to see him later.'

For the first time, she has something that takes precedence even over Dan. She turns to the twins chatting away to each other on their mat. Stan is pushing one of the toy trains she brought, while Bea works away at slotting the track together. She looks back at Olivia with a bright smile.

'If you need to go and finish the washing, I'll play here with the babies.'

'All right.' Olivia puts down her mug and gets up. 'It's certainly easier to get things done when I don't have to watch them all the time. Thanks, Francesca.'

'You're very welcome. Think nothing of it.'

The three of them are absorbed in the game: Francesca has set up the railway track and now they are pushing the engines along the rails in a haphazard but generally good-natured way. There have been some squeals and squabbles over favourite trains or a preferred route – the bridge is particularly popular – but Francesca has calmed them down and sorted it out.

There's a real connection between us. I can feel it. I know it's there. And I think they can feel it too.

They've responded to her with a total acceptance of her authority. When she sorts out the argument, they are both content with the outcome, especially as she is careful to be absolutely fair. What startles her most is how alive she feels when she is near the children; it is almost as though the world begins to hum and vibrate in such an intense way it shakes her from within. Their beauty and the perfection of their features is almost overwhelming, too much to bear. She is unable to take her eyes off them, studying each one for her own likeness, or for the combination of herself and Dan. Stan has the blue eyes but his colouring is lighter than Dan's. Bea – Francesca is full of silent, secret glee – Bea has clear green eyes like her own, with a dark brown rim around the iris. Her hair is definitely darkening towards Francesca's own brunette. The slight toddler curl in her hair will disappear as it grows heavier and thicker, and then . . . *She'll look like me. I wonder if Olivia will notice. Surely it's practically impossible not to see it . . . but she won't, of course.* The one who notices will be Dan.

The door to the outer hall opens and Dan strides into the kitchen, as though summoned by her mental mention of his name. For a moment she feels like a witch who is conjuring strange and powerful spells, with power over who people are and what they do.

'Olivia, when do we— Oh.' He stops dead, gazing over at the play mat, where Francesca and the children are engaged in playing.

Stan looks up and sees him, immediately holding up his new prized possession. 'Daddy, Daddy, Daddy, look, look, train, train, train . . .'

Dan hardly looks; he is staring at Francesca, his expression hard to read. It is not joyful, that much she can tell. She's been wondering how he will react to her act of rebellion and refusal to do as he says. 'Hello,' he says at last, his tone neutral. 'I wasn't sure what time you were coming. Good trip?'

'Yes,' she says, 'thanks.' She's pleased to see that he appears to have accepted the situation, but she can tell he isn't listening, he's looking quickly around the kitchen.

'Where's Olivia?' he asks.

'In the garden. She went to finish hanging out the washing.' Francesca realises she's been gone a while now. She must have been distracted. 'Come and look at our train track.' She wants Dan to join them on the mat, and play as well. She wants to feel a part of that complete unit: *Mummy and Daddy and babies, all playing together* . . .

'I . . .' He looks reluctant. 'You're obviously having a good time. If Olivia's not here, perhaps I ought to get back to work.'

'How is the play going?'

'All right.' She can see that he's in a quandary. He doesn't want to stay but he also doesn't want to leave her alone with the children. And he's not going to say anything about her desire to get to know them.

You shit. The sudden violent words startle her. The rush of fury that engulfs her is not a feeling she usually associates with Dan, but here it is: boiling anger at the way he is treating her. *I gave you these children. You wouldn't have them except for me. I won't be pushed aside. I won't be ignored.*

But as usual, she knows that control will be the only way to get what she wants. She mustn't be angry. She must be charming and sweet and make sure he has no idea of the dreams and desires she nurtures.

'Go back to work,' she says sweetly. 'I'm fine here. Listen, there's Olivia now.'

So everything's fine now, isn't it?

Or is it?

You'd better get used to me, Dan. Because I'm not going anywhere.

Chapter Twenty-Two

1959

The heat of Cairo is wonderful after the bitter chill of England and the endless freezing draughts in Renniston Hall. Julia feels herself relax in the warmth, and loses herself in the sights and sounds of the city. Her mother takes her shopping, and they go past one of the oldest souks in Cairo. Through arches of golden stone, she catches glimpses of shining metal, colour and fabric. The smells are spicy, rich and dense. One stall holder has hung metal lanterns up the high walls of the souk, some burning with lights inside their hammered copper or brass fretwork. Another stall sends plumes of fragrant incense into the air, and another is heaped with bright patchworks: rugs, blankets and decorative pieces. There's no end to the noise and colour and sheer mountains of things for sale. No one sells just one of anything; everything is piled in abundance, from baskets to hookah pipes, from carved figures to inlaid furniture. And then there is the food – this is the most exciting of all. At home, food is ceaselessly bland: all grey, washed-out green and turgid brown or beige. There hasn't been much of it either, never enough to feel full with, even if you could stomach more boiled cabbage or stewed mutton. Here, there are great baskets heaped with spices of amazing colours: rust red, magenta pink, bright yellow and orange. Enticing scents fill the air, and the sight of tables laden with vividly coloured fruit and vegetables is almost overwhelming. There is so much: sacks of onions, crates of bananas and oranges and lemons. Her mouth waters to see it all.

They walk down a narrow alley with chairs and tables squeezed on either side, the doors and windows of cafes open behind them. Men sit at the tiny brass tables and the air is full of the aroma of coffee. Julia sees a waiter carrying a plate of sweetmeats – pink, yellow and green confections – and she feels quite faint with desire to taste sugar melting over her tongue.

'Ugh, these crowds. Filthy,' mutters her mother, striding at a pace down the alley with Julia following afterwards as quickly as she can. She notices how eyes follow her mother in her smart white dress and high heels, her neat calves and ankles perfectly visible. There is a white scarf wrapped around her head and she wears a pair of cat's-eye sunglasses and looks, Julia thinks, incredibly glamorous, like a film star. There are mutterings as they pass, but Julia understands not a word. She only hopes they are being nice, but perhaps they are not. Lately she is entirely confused about the relationships between men and women. Once, it had been so clear. You went through life waiting to meet the one, the man destined to be your husband. Then there was a romantic courtship, a marriage and grown-up life began, with children in due course, somehow, but all with the proviso that you were suitably worshipped by the handsome man whose heart you held in the palm of your hand.

Was that what it was like for Mummy and Daddy?

She thinks of her parents and their perfectly calm, quite sedate relationship in which her father's work is always of the utmost importance. His frequent absences are only to be expected when he is so high up in the army, and it is right that they follow wherever he leads – although in Julia's case it has taken her all the way back to England and boarding school.

'Mummy . . .' She pants after her mother, who can walk awfully fast these days.

'Yes, what is it? Come along, Julia, don't dawdle. We'll be late for Mrs Alexander and we must get through all the arrangements for the Christmas party.'

Julia tries to speed up, wondering why her sensible sandals don't go anywhere near as fast as Mummy's high heels. 'Do I have to go back to Renniston? Can't I stay here with you for a bit? I'm sure it wouldn't matter if I missed a few weeks.'

'Don't be silly, Julia, of course you can't. You can't dip in and out of your education, you know that. I understand that winter is miserable at school – games are harder and the cold is rather awful – but it will get better.' Her mother throws her a smile over her shoulder, her eyes invisible behind the dark lenses of her glasses. 'Honestly it will.'

Julia says nothing but puffs on behind her mother, thinking that it won't get better, not for a while yet.

'Mummy?'

'What is it?' Her mother sounds exasperated, bored with it all.

'Can you ask the school when the swimming pool will be finished? Can you telephone them or something?'

'What?' Her mother laughs in disbelief. 'The swimming pool? What on earth are you talking about?'

'I'm just so . . . so keen to swim again and I'd love to know when it will be done. The builders have been there forever and it's not finished yet.'

'Be patient, Julia. Of course I'm not going to make a very expensive telephone call to the school just for that. They'll think I've gone barmy for one thing. And besides . . .' Her mother strides on, determined to get to Mrs Alexander as fast as possible. Julia wishes she could stop to examine the fascinating stalls they are passing but there's nothing for it but to race on. 'You don't even like swimming.'

At Mrs Alexander's house, cooled by whirring fans, she can catch her breath and have a little peace while her mother and Mrs Alexander discuss Christmas parties. It seems so odd to celebrate Christmas in this hot, foreign land where there aren't any churches – at least, not the kind she is used to – but she's sure that there will be all the usual things to eat, including Christmas pudding. She can't imagine wanting it in this heat, all rich and claggy and filling. A strawberry sherbet would be much nicer.

A servant brings her a cool glass of lemonade and she wanders out into the garden to drink it, sitting down by a tinkling fountain to watch it play. She dips her fingertips into the water and paddles it, seeing tiny fish swimming about below the surface.

Here, at least, she can forget the thing that rules her life back at school. Alice was delighted to have a real partner in crime once Julia had been out on the excursion with her. She was jubilant on their return to the school and couldn't understand Julia's muted reaction at all. She teased her about it the next day, when they were out on the lacrosse field, chasing the ball for miles and miles. Whenever it disappeared up the field, they found a quiet place to talk and wait for it to make its way back again.

Alice hit the ground with the handle of her stick as if trying to dig up a divot. 'Come on, Julia, you spoilsport. Didn't you enjoy it? Don't you think it's a blast – boys, whiskey and music and all that? It's just like being grown-up!'

'I didn't enjoy it one bit,' Julia retorted, pulling at the leather strings of the net on the end of her stick. 'I don't want to go again, and neither should you. It's dangerous. What were you and Roy doing when I went outside with Donnie?'

Alice laughed. 'What were you doing outside with Donnie while I was inside, eh? Get up to a bit of hanky-panky your-selves, did you? Any smooching?'

Julia remembered Donnie's disgust at the way she and Alice were behaving. He didn't even seem to accept that it was all Alice's idea and nothing to do with her.

'Did you know Roy's married?' she demanded.

Alice shrugged. 'I suppose he might have mentioned it. But there's no way his wife will find out, she's back in Ireland.'

'Well . . .' Julia was flabbergasted by her insouciance. 'Don't you care? Don't you think it's wrong? You . . . you let him kiss you!'

'Oh Julia, you baby, what does it matter? I'm not going to marry him myself, am I? He's just a builder!' Alice looked up the field, then lifted her stick and started to run off. 'Come on, they're on their way! Aren't we supposed to be defending or something?'

But I can't believe she doesn't care. I just can't believe it.

By the end of term, Alice's mood had changed a little. She lost some of her ebullience and did not suggest a trip out to the caravan after Friday evening chapel for over a fortnight. Julia was glad. It was colder and darker than ever as the year drew to its close. Soon term would be over and she would be taken to the airport to catch a plane for Egypt all on her own, and she was nervous at the prospect. It would be her first time alone but her parents thought that she was old enough and responsible enough now. Nevertheless, she was aware of the downward swoop in Alice's spirits. It was a pattern she was familiar with: a period of high spirits and devil-may-care energy, followed by a mood of lethargy and gloomy pessimism. It was just how Alice was. Usually she tried to cajole her friend out of her low spirits, but not this time. If it meant Alice was not in the mood for naughtiness, then it was all to the good. The builders might finish the pool and be gone before her mischievous side returned,

257

although they were working on the gymnasium, the pool still a large dirty hole in the ground.

The only, tiny regret she had was that there was no way she was going to see Donnie. His image frequently played across her mind, and she whiled away many chapel services and duller lessons thinking about him and the feeling of her hand held in his. Roy, she thought, was repellent – so hairy and huge and manly, like a real grown-up. But Donnie was a romantic-looking boy, a rebel, a bit like James Dean with his hair long at the front and an air of dissatisfaction at the way things were, a longing for how they might be different. When they read *Romeo and Juliet* in English lessons, she imagined Romeo as looking like Donnie, and when she made herself into Juliet, she was covered in chills of excitement. The play became fascinating to her, because it came so terribly alive when she pictured them in the roles, Donnie talking to her as Romeo did to Juliet. She even read it in bed to herself. Her copy was tucked away in her suitcase back at the house. Reading it brought her closer to Donnie, even though she knew nothing of him except what she had learned that evening in the caravan.

She sips her lemonade in the hot Cairo afternoon, runs her fingers through the cool water, and wonders if he ever thinks of her, and if she will see him again. Much as she wants Roy gone and the danger past, she can't help hoping that Donnie will still be there when she gets back.

But it's hopeless. Nothing can happen. And besides, he doesn't like me. Not one little bit.

*

The Christmas holidays are over in a flash, and it seems like no time before Julia is returning home to cold, dark England, the sights and smells and light of Egypt still in her mind. She wonders how she will get through the next few cold, bleak months without being in utter misery the whole time. Not only that, her mother has said that the trip to Cairo for Christmas cannot be repeated until the summer. She will be spending all the rest of the holidays at school, or with one or other of the teachers, whoever can be persuaded to offer her houseroom. It's a bleak prospect.

The night before term begins is the usual noisy affair, with cars pulling up in front of the school, parents wandering around looking bewildered, the Headmistress on show, girls rushing everywhere, shouting and laughing and squealing with the excitement of seeing each other again. Trunks are piled up against the walls, there are mountains of sports equipment and shoes and bags. The housemistresses stalk about, being polite and oily to the parents, and shooting ghastly looks at overexcited girls in the hopes of calming them down. Julia retires to her bed, her things unpacked and her trunk left outside to be stored away in a box room until it's next needed.

Goodness knows when that will be. At least the others know they'll be leaving again at half-term. I don't know how long I'll be here, stuck in this horrible place.

She reads a book while she waits for Alice to appear. It is not until supper is about to be served – a late and light affair of eggs boiled until they're bullets and some slices of toast

– that Alice arrives, her mother and stepfather on either side of her looking cross and tired.

Julia sees them walk past the dormitory, and Alice glances in for long enough to catch her eye and turn her own to heaven in an expression of utter weariness. Sliding off the bed, Julia hurries over to the door and listens.

'We're so late,' she hears Alice's mother say. 'I'm sorry. Alice got terribly car sick. We had to stop at least half a dozen times. I hope she's not coming down with something.'

'Matron will keep an eye on her,' Miss Allen replies. 'How are you now, Alice?'

'Much better, thank you, Miss Allen.'

'Good. Will you want some supper? Perhaps an egg or two will do you good.'

'Oh . . . no thank you, Miss Allen, I'd rather go to bed if that's all right. I'm sure I'll feel better in the morning.'

Julia hears murmured goodbyes and muted kisses, and then Alice's mother and stepfather make their way back downstairs to exchange a few words with the Headmistress and be on their way. She tiptoes quickly back to her bed and picks up her book, just in time. Miss Allen appears with Alice a moment later.

'Ah, Julia. It's suppertime, didn't you hear the bell? Off you go. Alice is going to bed early. You can swap all your holiday news in the morning. Right now she needs her sleep.'

Alice doesn't look at all well, now that Julia can see her properly. Her face is grey and haggard, and there's a slumped look about her shoulders.

'Yes, Miss Allen,' she says, getting off the bed. 'See you later, Alice.'

'Yes,' Alice says and sighs.

Oh dear, Julia thinks, as she makes her way down to supper. *She's no better at all. If anything, she seems worse than before. What an awful term this is going to be.*

And just to make matters worse, she noticed on the way in that the building site at the side of the school looks just as it did when they left. The pool isn't finished. The builders are still here.

PART THREE

Chapter Twenty-Three

There is plenty of mirth around the table, and lots of wine too. Olivia has already stacked six empties outside and there are several more bottles on the go. It's been so long since she's spent time with Dan's Cambridge crowd, she's forgotten how they all drink like fishes. But now she remembers the irritation she used to feel when they came round to the flat after a night out, and she knew it would be drinking and debating till dawn. More often than not, she would bow out, leaving them to it, retiring to bed with her earplugs, knowing that Dan would come crawling in at some point and join her. The only uncertainty would be who she would find on the sofa in the morning.

But she likes the feel almost of a family celebration this evening, the sense of reunion. There is Jimmy, Dan's best friend from Cambridge, once a slim Young Turk and now a well-padded publishing executive, grown rounded on too many lunches, and his wife Katy, an editor in the same publishing house that Jimmy helps to run. Each has a failed marriage behind them – Jimmy married soon out of Cambridge to Claire, another of their circle, but she has been erased and Katy has taken her place. Olivia knows that Jimmy and Katy met at work and had a wild affair while they were both still married, which culminated in the two divorces and remarriage, and now there are stepchildren on both sides. Katy has fitted in so very well and gets on so easily with everyone that it is sometimes hard to remember that there ever was a Claire, or that Katy was not one of the original crowd. But in fact, Claire was around for years and Olivia liked her and invited her to her hen party. Not long after that, Jimmy's affair was discovered and Claire wasn't even at the wedding. She wonders suddenly why they've never been in touch, and resolves to contact her one of these days, if it's not too awkward.

Then there's Stevie, a Yorkshireman who says very little but drinks with an almost studied determination, and listens hard. He'll suddenly butt in with a joke or retort that reduces them all to helpless laughter, or he'll command complete silence to tell an extraordinary story before lapsing back into taciturnity. If Olivia knows him, he'll drink red wine until he's sunk two bottles, and then ask Dan to bring out the whiskey. It's a dangerous mixture and Olivia thinks that it signals pretty clearly that Stevie is a doctor, as doctors are almost invariably the hardest drinkers she meets. Stevie's solo tonight – his girlfriend is at home looking after their children.

Here with her husband is Alyssa Grant; she is Italian, with long dark hair and eyes that droop a little at the edges, giving her a permanently melancholy expression. She is not quite of the inner circle of Dan's friends but always welcomed because she is from a distinguished family and has become a noted textile designer. Her husband Dave is a pleasant man with a lantern-jaw he conceals with a covering of stubble, who likes nothing better than talking at length about the complicated property deals he is continually on the brink of pulling off.

Last of all, sitting across from them, her eyes alight and her face beaming with pleasure at the reunion, is Francesca.

'It's pretty bloody rich, Francesca,' says Stevie suddenly, a slight slur in his voice, 'that you invite us to your house, which has to be one of the biggest I've ever seen, and even though you've got about a hundred and fifty bedrooms, you can't put us up for the night!'

They all laugh.

'Sorry, Stevie,' Francesca returns. 'I admit, it's ridiculous but the local hotel is very comfortable. And you all have to come back next year when this place is a bit more hospitable.'

Next year. Olivia is smiling but she looks down at her plate to hide a slight frown. *I wonder if you'll still be staying here then, Cheska.* Then she mentally rebukes herself. *It's not been that long. Only two weeks.* But it is beginning to drag a little and she's wondering when Francesca plans to go home. Not only that, but it's not entirely evident what she is actually doing here at all. The architect has made a few visits; Tom Howard returned – happy to see her, cheerful company – and he and Francesca disappeared on another tour of the house; a building contractor came to evaluate a job so he could submit a quote. Apart from that, Francesca has spent her days helping around the house, chatting and playing with the children, seemingly without very much else to do at all. Dan has been disappearing into his study from first thing in the morning until late at night, reappearing for meals, and she is missing him.

'You've got Cheska,' he said when she mentioned it as they lay in bed together reading, and she sensed, just for an instant, something closed off about him.

'I know, and that's nice. She's good company and has helped me out such a lot. But it's hardly the same,' she replied. 'I like it when it's us – you, me and the twins.'

He sighed. 'I know. Me too. When she's gone, we can get back to normal. In the meantime, I can press on with the play, and get as much done as I can. At least it's useful in that respect. You can share a bit of the childcare.'

'Yes. She adores it,' Olivia said, and gave a little half-laugh. 'I mean, she honestly never seems to get bored of them. I know you're supposed to pretend to like other people's children as much as your own, but she actually looks like she does. I found her reading a story to Bea yesterday, and she had her on her knee with one arm round her, and she had her head rested against Bea's, and the look on her face, it was like . . . like . . . she really loves her.'

Dan stared at her, his blue eyes impossible to read. His voice, when he spoke, was flattish, almost uninterested. 'Everyone likes babies. Women do, anyway.'

Olivia was taken aback by this. It didn't sound much like

something Dan would say. But he turned back to the book he was reading, making it clear the conversation was at an end. There was nothing after that but sleep either. With Cheska at the end of the hall, they didn't much feel like making love, even though it was unlikely she would hear anything.

And still Francesca stayed on, with no mention of a leaving date. Olivia arranged this evening half in the hope that it would mark some kind of turning point, almost a farewell, so that she could be on her way.

'That was a marvellous meal, Olivia,' Alyssa says, putting her cutlery down neatly. She is the last to finish, even though all the men have had seconds. 'You must give me the recipe.'

'Thank you, I'm really pleased you liked it.' Olivia stands up to clear, and Alyssa and Katy go to help. 'No – please sit and chat. I'm happy to do it. I'll call for help when I need the pudding things put out.' Olivia takes the stack of empty plates over to the dishwasher, while Dan refills glasses and reaches for another bottle.

'So, Danny, how's the writing life?' asks Jimmy, leaning back and looking expansive. 'Finished your masterpiece?'

Dan laughs. 'It's almost there.'

'How long have you been writing it?'

'Just over two years.' There's a tiny tone of defensiveness in Dan's voice. Olivia is alert to it at once. Jimmy's and Dan's worlds have never collided before, but now Dan is writing, and that is Jimmy's territory.

'Two years? You'd better get a move on, mate. We get a book a year out of most of our authors – and I'm talking a hundred thousand words, not a fifty-page play.' Jimmy is teasing but even loading plates into the dishwasher, Olivia can tell that it's not going down that well.

'It's an entirely different discipline,' Dan says stiffly.

'Of course it is!' cries Alyssa. 'Don't listen to him, Dan. It takes time to create a masterpiece. And as for working when you have small children, it's almost impossible! Creativity needs quiet and concentration. I find that when I work on my designs. Silence and calm are vital.'

'Jimmy, you know sod all about writing plays. Or books, come to that.' Katy is being the sunny-natured peacemaker as usual. She leans over towards Dan. 'Jimmy likes to pretend that because he works in publishing, he knows a literary masterpiece when he sees one. Actually, all he knows how to do is count the beans, and every now and then take an author out for lunch. I know that writing takes as long as it takes, and that's all there is to it.'

Jimmy is more than a bit drunk. 'Rubbish!' he shouts. 'You're turning into a house husband, Dan. I bet the lovely Olivia is keeping you, isn't she? She's done quite well with those gardening books – I always said you should come and be published by us, Olivia – and no doubt the royalties are keeping you in cornflakes and nappies!'

'I'm sure Dan's play will be a success,' Katy says placidly.

'Oh wait, it's really Cheska you should be thanking, Danny, isn't it!' roars Jimmy, laughing. 'She's provided you with this terrific place to live. In fact, between them, Olivia and Cheska are looking after you very nicely indeed, aren't they? Lucky for you that your killer charm hasn't quite worn off yet, eh? You can still reel 'em in when you need to. I remember how you used to keep Cheska sweet so that you could scam her essays off her!'

Olivia looks over at the table, which suddenly has the frozen quality of the tableau. Francesca has a strange, twisted half-smile on her face and is staring at the tabletop. Dan is hunched, his eyes set hard as they are whenever he's angry. Alyssa is frowning at Jimmy, her mouth tight. Only Dave and Katy, the non-Cambridge people, seem unaffected. Stevie pushes himself to his feet a shade unsteadily, his chair scraping over the stone floor.

'I'm going outside for a fag. Want to join me, Dan?'

Dan hasn't smoked for years, as far as Olivia knows – not since before they started trying for a baby. 'Yeah, why not?' He gets up, slides his hands into his trouser pockets, and slouches out behind Stevie. A gust of cold air comes in as they pull the door to behind them.

Jimmy makes as if to follow but Katy puts a hand on his arm. 'Leave them for a bit,' she says.

'What did I say? Dan knows I'm only joking.' He looks over at Cheska, his head moving jerkily with the drink. 'Cheska, you know I'm joking, don't you?'

Francesca says nothing but takes a sip of her wine.

'I think it's best if we just move on and let it go.' Katy pours water from the jug into Jimmy's glass. 'Drink that, darling, and give the wine a rest for a bit. Olivia . . .' She turns, cheery and bright, always there to pour oil on troubled waters. 'Are you sure we can't help?'

Dan and Stevie come in ten minutes later, their clothes

bringing in smoke-tinged cold, and Stevie has worked his magic. They are both laughing and the awkwardness is forgotten.

Relieved that the evening is back on track, Olivia serves up pudding of ginger and lemon cheesecake with a rhubarb syrup that gleams pale pink on the creamy top. They eat with relish, and drink a little more wine, and talk loudly about their lives, their children, the old days and jokes from long ago. Olivia has heard some of the stories so often she can almost believe she was actually there, and that makes her feel she belongs. Once Katy came along, she was no longer the new girl, and no longer one of the few non-Cambridge people allowed in. Now that her experience of the group predates Katy's, she feels as though she's taken another step into the very heart of it. Except that, every now and then, she senses that there are events and happenings that still have a resonance all these years later, and which she knows nothing of.

Perhaps it's better not to know, she thinks, spooning the lush creaminess of the cheesecake into her mouth. *I always knew that Dan had a past – and I'm sure he used his charm to great effect when he wanted to.*

She looks over at him now. He is restored to the old Dan: smiling, joking, holding his own and being brilliantly amusing. He and Jimmy have a good double act, batting stories back and forth, setting up jokes for one another. She's glad. He needed a good dose of his old life and his old self. Perhaps it might bring him out of the study a little bit more and remind him that there is a life beyond this place and the play.

Pudding is finished to satisfied sighs, and coffee and chocolates are brought out. Dan and Stevie go out for another cigarette and then, when they return, Dan fetches the Talisker and they all drink a measure – or several, in the case of Jimmy, Stevie and Dan. Francesca, too, is drinking. Her cheeks are flushed and a few beads of sweat shimmer on her nose. She's become talkative and excitable.

'So, how about you show us round the house, Cheska?' asks Stevie, draining another measure.

'It's late!' exclaims Francesca, shaking her head. 'We should have gone earlier, when it was still light.'

'Oh no,' rejoins Stevie. 'This is the best time. You're not telling me the place isn't haunted, are you? I bet you've got tons of ghosts out there – a house like this must be thick with them. What is it, sixteenth century? You're gonna have some tragic cavaliers or a walled-up nun or something.'

'I don't have a clue,' Francesca says. 'I didn't want to know about ghosts and I didn't ask.'

'That's why you've got to give us the tour,' Stevie says, with a grin. 'A torchlight tour. It'll be fantastically creepy.'

'Brilliant idea,' agrees Jimmy, all enthusiasm. 'We'll do it. Have you got a torch, Dan?'

'I think we've got one, in case of power cuts,' Dan replies. 'I'm up for it if you are.'

Olivia can see the drama of the dark house by torchlight appeals to him. 'And we can take a candle each, there are plenty of those.'

'Excellent historical touch,' agrees Jimmy.

Dan turns to Francesca. 'Will you do the honours, Cheska?'

She looks touched to be asked. Olivia realises that Dan has hardly said a word to Francesca this evening, no doubt distracted by the presence of Jimmy and Stevie, his old muckers and partners in crime. In fact, now she thinks of it, he has said very little to Cheska in the last few weeks. He's been unusually cool. *Probably encouraging her to get on her way.* But it's not like him. Not at all.

'Of course.' Francesca stands up. 'But put your coats on. It's cold in there, and it might be too draughty for candles. We'll see.'

As they get ready to go into the main house, Olivia pulls Dan to one side. He has a stack of candles in one hand and a box of matches.

'I'll stay here,' she says. 'You'll probably all want some tea when you get back, and anyway, someone's got to stay with the children.'

'I'm sure they'd be fine,' Dan says, 'they're fast asleep, and we'll only be gone twenty minutes or so. You should come along, I bet it will be quite an experience.'

'You go, Olivia,' Katy says, hearing the end of their exchange as she comes out of the loo. 'I'm an absolute chicken. Anything like the hint of a ghost and I'm a mess. I think it's my Catholic upbringing. I utterly and totally believe and I don't get any fun from it. I'll stay here with a book and you go. I want to ring for our taxi as well – we should be on our way to the hotel before too long, and we'll take Stevie with us.'

'There, all decided,' Dan says. Olivia feels it would be

274

rude to turn down Katy's offer. 'Get your jacket and we'll get going.'

They leave through the secret door in Dan and Olivia's room, filing through one by one. Already, it's skin-crawlingly creepy, as they find themselves high above the empty and silent great hall.

'The minstrels' gallery,' announces Francesca, shining the torch beam about. 'I expect there were some sights to be seen from up here – kings and queens and lords and ladies dancing and intriguing down there.' The light falls on the cavernous space of the old fireplace.

Olivia looks down into the room below. A hand on her waist makes her jump and gasp.

'Only me.' Dan's voice murmurs in her ear. 'Are you okay?'

She nods. She hasn't drunk all that much but enough to feel her imagination is a little more heightened than she would like.

'Take a candle.' Dan hands them around and lights them, each one casting a flickering golden light onto the face of the holder, giving them hollow, shadowed eyes. The little flames gutter in the invisible currents of cold air that swirl around them.

'Let's go downstairs,' Francesca says, directing the torch beam towards the dark mouth of the staircase. 'And have a look around.'

'Please be careful, everyone. And once we get there, I think we should stay on the ground floor,' Olivia says, suddenly aware that a party of drunken guests climbing staircases in the dark is not a good idea.

'All right. Shame to miss the Queen's bedroom, though.' Francesca leads them to a narrow wooden staircase that winds down to the great hall below. They troop after her.

'But this is stunning!' says Alyssa when they emerge. The light of five candles is surprisingly strong when they all stand together, but as they separate to look around, it diminishes to little golden glows moving about the room. 'Did they keep any of the old fabrics? Imagine what some of the tapestries and hangings must have been like!'

'Nothing like that,' Francesca says. Their voices echo around the huge empty chamber. 'It all disappeared years ago, before it became a school. Goodness knows what happened to it. Some of it might be upstairs in the attics – there's tons of rubbish up there. But it will probably have mouldered away by now.'

'What a shame,' says Alyssa.

'How much did you say this place is worth, Francesca?' enquires Dave.

They wander around the hall for a while, their shoes tapping on the hard stone, Jimmy's voice booming around and Francesca answering questions as she illuminates bits of the room – the windows, black against the night, the chimney breast, the panelling around the walls.

Olivia wishes they could go back. She doesn't like being away from the warmth and cosiness of the cottage, or too far from the twins, even though she knows that Katy is there listening out for them. But it seems the tour is going on for a while longer – the others are interested and keen to continue.

Francesca leads them out of the great hall and along a corridor that is so completely pitch-black it almost appears to suffocate their paltry lights, and then out into a series of rooms, with magnificent plaster ceilings and fine fireplaces. They walk along, more accustomed to the darkness now, gazing around in awe at whatever their candlelight reveals, their footsteps loud on the polished wooden floors while Francesca explains how much has been restored by Preserving England and what the place used to be like. Olivia is interested, despite herself. They must have walked the entire length of the front of the house, she thinks. They linger in another grand room that Francesca announces was once an eighteenth-century library, now lacking its books. Then they move on, Olivia last, her attention taken by the carved fruit and vines around the window panels. She wonders whether the candlelight is enhancing their intricacy as she hears footsteps move away, voices fading as they leave the room. Then she realises quite suddenly that she is completely alone. The others have vanished.

She walks quickly to the door they left by, and finds herself in another of the dark linking passageways. 'Dan? Cheska? Where are you?'

Standing stock-still, her little candle flame flickering valiantly and illuminating the patch where she is, Olivia strains to hear voices but there's nothing. A rush of fear climbs up inside her but she quickly controls it. They are playing a joke on her. She mustn't panic; they're watching and laughing from somewhere nearby. And they can't have gone far. They agreed to stay on the ground floor after all.

If I turn around and walk back the way we came, I'll be at the great hall and that means I can easily find my way home.

Annoyance starts up inside her.

This is just like Dan when he gets together with Jimmy and Stevie. He would never do this to me if it weren't for them. They're such a bad influence on him.

'All right,' she says loudly, certain they are hiding somewhere close. 'Very funny! You're completely spooking me out, if that's what you want! Could you come out, please? I don't much like being on my own here in the dark.'

She waits, listening out for a stifled giggle or a whisper, but there's nothing. A blanket of complete silence seems to have fallen over the house. She feels uneasy, pressed in by the dark. Where have they gone? Why can't she hear so much as the tap of a shoe on stone, or the distant boom of Jimmy's voice? They are definitely hiding.

'I don't think this is very friendly at all!' she says, her voice trembling a little. 'I'm feeling a bit picked on. Please come out.'

Again she waits and still there's nothing. She is aware of the vastness of the house around her, empty room after empty room, and the cosy cottage with the sleeping children and the warm kitchen seems very far away. Her imagination supplies a sudden ghastly image: a ghoul, a demon, approaching her, its mouth stretched in a silent scream. It's a ridiculous bit of fantasy, she knows that, but even so, she turns to hurry back the way she came, intending to run through the long stretch of rooms all the way back, when she hears a noise. Ahead of her, down the passageway, there's a distinct thump and the sound of footsteps.

There they are!

Relief rushes through her and she sets off in pursuit, hurrying forward into the darkness, listening as hard as she can for more giveaway sounds of where the others are. When she reaches the end of the passageway, there's another door that stands open and leads into another passageway, this one running across. She can turn left or right. 'I'm coming!' she calls. 'Where are you?'

Listening hard, she thinks she hears a sound to her left, and turns down that way. The candle flame flickers and drags in the draught as she strides down the corridor in a little slice of light, the dark pressing close all around her.

Where are they? Panic is rolling around her stomach, making the ends of her fingers prickle and her heart race. *This is horrible, horrible. How could they do this to me?* She longs for their familiar presence, the safety in numbers. She's always considered herself a rational person, but she can't help the power of her imagination, and the nasty pictures it's feeding in her mind, the legacy of fairy stories, ghostly tales, and horror films.

Why didn't I turn around when I had the chance? She suddenly sees how stupid it was to go on, and turn off the path she knew. *Where am I?* She has a horrible feeling that if she goes back the way she came, she might miss the doorway back into the front of the house. A dry sob of fear starts in her throat and she forces herself to be calm. She is still moving forward, still straining for the sound of the others, unable to believe that they really have deserted her like this, or that they are not looking for her.

Another thump, louder this time.

She gasps and stares ahead into the darkness as far as her candle will let her. Now she doesn't know whether to continue on or turn back. Then footsteps echo in the darkness ahead.

'There you are!' she cries, relief flowing over her. 'This is the most horrible practical joke anyone has ever played on me, I hope you know that!' Her voice sounds strong in the silence, and she tries to make it normalise the situation. 'Some thanks for cooking your dinner, I must say!'

There's no answer. She starts to walk briskly as though by acting as if she isn't frightened, she won't be. But soon, she slows. There is silence again. The footsteps have vanished.

Olivia stands still again, the nightmarish feeling returning. For a moment she was able to persuade herself everything was all right, but here she is, still stuck in the horror of being alone at night in a vast and empty house, abandoned by Dan and the others. She looks about, sensing that the house around her has changed: there are no more elaborate panels or carved window shutters. The walls are covered in peeling paint and a couple of large institutional pipes travel along it. The floor is tiled, she realises. Then she sees a faint, glimmering light to her right, the first she has seen that isn't her own candlelight. She is looking through a door. It's closed but there is a glass pane in it and the light comes from further in. Half unthinking, she pushes at the door and it opens stiffly. She advances slowly, her candle flame now guttering wildly in the breeze that rushes up the corridor.

Where is that light coming from?

The corridor echoes with her footsteps as she walks on the tiled floor, drawn irresistibly forward by the light. A chamber lies ahead of her, she can see that now, and at the top of it are narrow windows. It's from them that the light is coming. The moon must be out, and providing the silvery light that floats in through the windows. Now she is standing at the entrance of the huge room, trying to make out what is in its heart of blackness. She starts to move forward, confused by what she can see, as the room seems to be in layers of some kind, with another wall towards the back of it but sunk down below the floor level. She frowns.

What is it? What's in there?

'You!'

The booming shout resounds off the walls and makes her shriek, and in her fright, she drops the candle, which hits the floor and fizzles out at once. Olivia spins round to see a figure holding a torch, the dazzling beam trained straight at her, blinding her so that she cannot see who it is.

It shouts, 'What the blazes are you doing here?'

She screws up her eyes against the glare. 'Please, I can't see!' Fear and confusion whirl through her, but she also knows, at least, that it's no ghoul beaming a torch in her face and shouting. It's not the spirit world way.

The light is dipped. She blinks hard to regain her vision and as she does, the figure moves towards her and resolves itself. She knows it.

'William,' she says with relief. 'Thank God.'

'What are you doing here?' the old man demands. 'It's the middle of the bloody night. You're all wandering around like a bunch of loonies. I thought there were vandals in the house. I sent them all back to the cottage where they belong.' He mutters to himself. 'Half drunk, with a load of candles in my house. Fools.' He looks up at Olivia again, his face craggy in the shadows produced by the torchlight. 'They were in a tizz about losing you. I said I'd find you. How did you get yourself here?'

Olivia glances around the room, now less frightening than it appeared when she was alone. 'What is this place? What's in the middle?'

'This is the pool room,' William says roughly. 'It's empty now. It should be left as it is. Don't come here, do you understand? Don't let the kiddies come here. Stay away, for God's sake. It's not safe.' He swings the torch beam back to illuminate the way out. 'Now come on. Let's get you home.'

Chapter Twenty-Four

Francesca feels that quite enough fuss has been made over Olivia. It's a damp squib end to the evening when they all have to sit waiting in the kitchen while William goes to find her, Dan in an agony of guilt and Jimmy apologising for a prank gone wrong.

'It was only going to be for a minute,' he says, suddenly sobered. 'I wasn't to know she was going to go haring off.'

Dan can't sit down; he's pacing around. Katy is soothing everyone, putting on the kettle for restorative cups of tea while Stevie goes outside for another cigarette, and Alyssa and Dave get their things together. Their cab is waiting in the driveway, the engine having already been idling for twenty minutes.

Francesca sits at the kitchen table and watches, disappointed that the dinner has ended this way. The impact of her house has been lost. They won't remember the grandeur and the wonderful atmospheric effect of candlelight on old stone. They'll recall it as a place where Olivia got lost, and feel sheepish about their part in it. 'Please all come back another time,' she says loudly. 'You ought to see it in the daytime to get the full effect.'

'We'd love to,' Alyssa says, well wrapped up in her black coat. She leans down to kiss Francesca's cheek. 'Amazing house. See you very soon, darling. Let's meet in London when you're back there, yes?'

'Of course.' She accepts Alyssa's kiss, then Dave's. Then they move to Dan to ask him to apologise to Olivia for not waiting, and to give her their love. They leave in a flurry of goodbyes while Katy brings over mugs of tea, putting one down in front of Jimmy with a look of fond scolding.

'Poor old Olivia,' she says, sitting down. 'I think you've all been very mean.'

'For Christ's sake, Katy,' Francesca says coldly. 'No one meant for her to get lost. She should have come back the same way instead of disappearing off into a place she has absolutely no knowledge of.'

Katy raises her eyebrows but stays good-humoured as she lifts her mug to her lips and blows gently across the surface of her tea. 'All the same,' she murmurs, 'I'm glad it wasn't me.'

The door opens and Stevie comes back in, a smile on his broad face. 'Look who I've found,' he says, and behind him is Olivia. She is a little breathless but smiling, with only a faint air of reproach. Francesca feels a surge of irritation: here she is, the heroine again. Such a wonderful meal, such a lovely cottage, such beautiful children.

But this is my house. I decorated this cottage, it's all my work. And those are my children!

She feels something inside herself harden, something that up until now has remained pliable, flexible and feeling. Now she will stop trying. It's almost a relief.

I've had enough of her taking my life.

As the others crowd around Olivia, exclaiming, showering her in apologies and asking how she is, Francesca stays back, still sitting at the table and observing. Olivia has all the attention as usual, revelling in it, pretending to be modest.

'Thank goodness for William,' she is saying. 'I was about to walk head first into an empty swimming pool, like an idiot!'

'Where is he?' Dan asks. 'I want to thank him.'

Oh, for crying out loud, don't bring that old man into the house. I don't want to see him. Francesca is the only one who knows the extent of the fight to evict William from the estate, and the way he's steadfastly refused to go, with the power of Preserving England behind him. They seem to think he has some right to be here, because of the service he gave the house in the years when it stood empty. They are of the opinion that he should continue working if he wants to, even though he's in his seventies at least.

'He's just outside,' Olivia says. But when they look outside the back door, he has gone.

'What was he doing wandering around at this time of night?' Francesca says with a laugh. 'He's like an old ghost himself.'

'He thought someone was in the house without permission.'

'They were,' says Francesca. 'Him!' She laughs again and there is a tiny silence among the others. Then Katy puts a cup of tea into Olivia's hand.

'Well, we're all jolly glad he was. And now you're back safe and sound, so that's all right. Alyssa and Dave had to go – they said thank you and lots of love – and now we have to get on our way too. It's almost one o'clock in the morning. The hotel will be wondering if we're ever coming back.'

'Yes,' Dan says. 'I think we could all do with turning in. Children don't care what time you went to bed. They always want to get up at the same time, no matter what.'

Francesca looks over at him, but he is attentive to Olivia and, she suspects, is determined not to catch her eye. He's been giving her the cold shoulder ever since she got here. Perhaps he thinks she hasn't noticed, but she has. He doesn't flash that smile at her, or ask her opinion on things, or engage in the old banter. He's making it plain that if she doesn't behave, he'll withdraw his affection from her.

Fine. Have it your way. But it's a dangerous game, Dan. You've given me too much power to piss me off. We'll see what will happen . . .

Francesca sleeps badly, tossing and waking before sinking back into sleep, sometimes too hot and at others too cold. It's probably the whiskey, she thinks, when she is wide awake at six thirty. She hardly ever drinks spirits and mixing it with wine was not a good idea.

She lies in bed, staring up at the ceiling, thinking about Olivia. She knows that nothing has so far been said about when she, Francesca, might be leaving. It's a delicate subject, as this is her house after all.

But they'll be within their rights to ask soon. And I can't keep staying on for no reason.

The thought of leaving the children fills her with dread. They have become the twin suns of her existence, almost as though her whole world revolves around them. She thinks of them constantly from the time she wakes until after they are in bed, and she is sure that they are responding to her differently. Something inside them recognises their link to her, she is sure of it. Only yesterday Stan came up crooning at her, 'Teska, Teska,' and held up his arms for a lift and a cuddle.

Children just don't do that with virtual strangers. They can feel the connection. They know it. It's inevitable.

But Dan stands in her way. Olivia is too stupid to realise the truth, but Dan knows and he isn't about to let her ease herself into his family unit. He's made it plain that as far as he's concerned, she's going to be excluded. Unless she finds a way to convince him, but at the moment, she can't think what that might be.

She wriggles under the covers, hot again and searching for a cool place, then she hears a little babble coming from the children's room.

They're up. They're awake.

She slips out of bed and opens the bedroom door, listening. Yes, they are talking quietly to one another in their high voices, a mixture of words and sing-song sounds.

Such good children. Aren't they wonderful, just amusing themselves until everyone else wakes up?

It can't do any harm to play with them. Dan and Olivia will appreciate the lie-in after the late night. She tiptoes downstairs and prepares two beakers of milk, warming them quickly in a pan of hot water, then returns. When she opens the nursery door, their little faces turn towards her, eyes wide with curiosity. They are sitting in their cots, Bea playing with a soft toy and Stan with his feet poking out between the bars, watching her.

'Teska!' Bea laughs, drops her toy and stands up, holding on to the rail of her cot. She looks adorable in a dotty sleep suit, her soft light hair ruffled into feathery curls, her cheeks pink with just-woken warmth.

Stan hauls himself up and starts to jump up and down. His sleep suit is stripy and his hair stands up on end like a soft brush. He has spotted the beakers in her hand. 'Milky, milky, milky,' he chirps and holds out a plump hand for his.

'Here's your milk, darlings,' she says. The residual bad mood from last night disappears and she is filled with a sense of completeness, serenity settling on her and happiness warming her. Everything is right here, with these wonderful little people, these surprising and unexpected gifts. When she made her spur-of-the-moment offer to Dan all that time ago, she didn't really believe it would work. She didn't really want it to. She still thought the best outcome was for Dan and Olivia to be denied parenthood. When he actually accepted the offer of her eggs, she thought that was the only triumph she needed. She never expected the whole thing to actually happen.

But now, as she holds Bea's hand and watches her suck on the beaker of milk, and as she ruffles Stan's swan's down of hair, she realises that Dan has actually given her peace. When she's with these children, she's happy, as though she's seen the reason for her own existence, the thing she fought for so hard her entire life. It was for these small people that she abandoned her family, worked so hard and got to Cambridge. It was for them that she changed everything about herself and created a new person. It was for them that she stayed true to her love for Dan, despite everything he did to her.

Because in the end, these two little people are the mingling of us, and look . . . look what we made.

She has a fierce impulse to run to him in his bed, to ignore Olivia, and shake him, shouting, 'Look what we made! It's come late, we've wasted so much time, but look what we've got now!'

Surely he'd start to understand then.

This place and these tiny people are all that's real and good. Geneva and her life there, the other family . . . it all seems as though that is a dream, a fleeting process she had to go through to get here, to where she was supposed to be all along.

It's taken so long. But it's here now.

Francesca spends a happy hour with the children, taking them out of their cots, getting them dressed and going down with them to the kitchen. She buckles both into their booster seats and makes their breakfasts, mixing up their oaty porridge and adding banana slices and a drizzle of honey. They eat obediently while she makes herself a cup of coffee. It's all perfectly innocent but she can't help getting an illicit thrill from it, as though she is doing something forbidden. She has never gone quite this far before, taking over the morning routine from Olivia. But she is *helping*. Olivia cooked for them all last night and this is a little thank you. To make her point, Francesca unloads the dishwasher and tidies away all the dinner things, returning the clean glasses to their cupboard and putting away the serving dishes on the dresser.

All too soon, she hears pattering feet on the staircase and Olivia enters in her nightdress, her expression questioning before her eyes fall on the children with a look of relief. 'There you all are!' She goes over to kiss the children. 'Has Cheska made your breakfast? How nice of her! Delicious banana porridge, yum yum . . .' She looks over at Francesca, her smile a little stiff. 'What time did they wake up? I didn't hear a thing! We both slept a bit late, I'm afraid.'

'Don't worry, it's fine.' Francesca smiles back beatifically. 'They woke quite early but I was already awake myself, so I got them up. I hope you don't mind. They've been terrifically good.'

'Of course I don't mind. It's very kind. You didn't have to—'

'It's my pleasure. Coffee?' She goes to the jug still warm on the counter and pours a mug for Olivia. When she hands it to her, she sees that Olivia is regarding the children's clothes.

'Thank you. Just what I need,' Olivia says brightly. 'How nice. You've dressed the children in the clothes you brought them. They look very smart.'

'Don't they,' Francesca agrees. She'd noticed that the lovely things she brought from Geneva were carefully put away and not touched. Saved for good, she supposed. But on a whim, she took them out: a pale yellow dungaree dress over white tights for Bea, and for Stan a blue and white striped top with navy blue dungarees. 'Do you mind?'

'Of course not. They're very lucky to have such nice things. I just hope they don't make a mess of them, that's all.'

'Better that than never wearing them at all,' remarks Francesca and sips her coffee. There's a small silence which is filled by the sudden ring of her mobile phone, startling them both. She looks down and sees Walt's name on the screen. 'Oh, excuse me, I'd better answer this.'

Getting up, she takes the phone and wanders out into the hall, glad of her slippers against the cold limestone slabs. 'Hello, darling.'

'Frankie? When are you coming home?'

That's like Walt. Direct and no nonsense.

'Soon, soon. I'm being kept very busy over here. Olivia is struggling a bit all on her own. She needs me and I'm very happy to help out with the twins. They are so sweet, Walt, you wouldn't believe! Both as bright as buttons and incredibly active.'

'I'm sure they are, Frankie, but we also need you here. Marie-Chantelle keeps coming to Anastasia for orders about how to run the house, and Anastasia has no idea how to do things and nor do I. As for the children, they've been asking why you haven't been around to Skype them as usual, and Olympia is inundating me with requests for things I have no idea what she's talking about . . . and I miss you, you're not here when I get home. You've been gone for too long. We've got some dinner parties and engagements coming up, and are you coming back for those, or what?'

She can hear the resentment in his voice, and she feels a kind of cold contempt that surprises her.

So now perhaps you understand how much you owe me, and how hard I work to keep your life running smoothly. You've never had to think about what menus to plan or how to keep our family ticking over and your social life going. It all just happens, because I do it. You've taken me for granted for years. Now you might start to appreciate me.

She keeps her tone soft. 'I know, honey, it's a little unusual, but it won't be for much longer, I promise. Listen, I'll ring Anastasia today and go through everything with her. We'll have a nice long chat about all of it and sort it out. If I can't make any of the social stuff, I'll get her to make my excuses. It will be fine, you'll see. Maybe you should take Anastasia to the opera do – she'll enjoy it. Buy her a nice dress to wear and she'll be in seventh heaven.'

'Frankie . . .' Walt sounds puzzled now. 'What is this? What's going on? Have you left home and don't want to tell me?'

She laughs merrily. 'Of course not, what a funny idea! I'm just so busy, so taken up with everything that needs doing on the house – this planning stage is crucial, you know that. I'll be able to be much more hands-off when all that's behind us. And meanwhile I've got the twins to look after. They need me.'

'Those aren't your kids, honey,' Walt says. 'You don't have to stay there and look after them; I'm sure Olivia is perfectly capable of doing it on her own. You've got your own, remember?'

She is momentarily stunned into silence, as she recalls that the outside world still believes that the twins are not her children.

'I'd like you to come home, okay? Go back to the Hall when you're needed but I don't want you living there away from us.'

'You should have thought of that before you bought it, darling,' she says sweetly. There is a tiny pause as her barb travels over the line to him, and then she says quickly, 'Actually, there is a reason why I need to be here for just a little longer. I had a builder here and he's going to be able to make a start on the pool. Mr Howard says we don't need to wait for formal permission for that, there's no concern about the heritage situation. And I thought, well, we may as well get going on whatever we can. So I need to be here to start proceedings off. Then I'll come home.'

'Well . . .' Walt sounds as though he is trying to be reasonable. 'Okay. How long will it take?'

'Only another week,' she says, her tone placatory. 'Then I'll be home.'

'I hope so, honey. Aren't the children due some holiday soon?'

'Oh . . .' She racks her brain to recall the term dates. 'Yes . . . half-term. I'll be back before that, don't worry.'

'All right. Another week. I miss you, Frankie.'

'I miss you too, darling. Now, tell me how work is going.' She sits down on a hall chair and prepares to listen.

If I have to take it one week at a time, that's fine with me. But I'd better call that builder today.

Chapter Twenty-Five

Olivia finds she cannot stop staring at the children sitting at the table, dressed in those ridiculous outfits, eating their breakfasts with Francesca sitting there, overseeing everything. The clothes are nice enough, if far too expensive for what they are, but they're just not suitable for the twins' lives. The blue dungarees don't have poppers so the whole thing needs to be taken off for nappy changing, and white tights and a pale yellow dress are going to be filthy in about five minutes once Bea gets down on the floor.

Olivia can't help feeling a stab of anger. *They're my children. I'll choose what they're going to wear.* She likes Bea in trousers – warm and practical – and she likes the well-worn nature of her nephews' hand-me-downs that work equally well for both twins. She's determined not to dress her daughter in pastels and frilly skirts, and she is quite happy to see Stan in so-called girls' colours. She proudly dresses him in a shocking pink anorak when they go out.

After breakfast, she says again how nice the children look but as she doesn't want them to get these lovely clothes dirty, she will go and change them. It's a relief to see them back in their usual scruffy things.

I mustn't dwell on it, she thinks, as she gets dressed herself. Dan is in the shower and the twins are playing on the double bed, half watching as she pulls on her jeans, a long-sleeved T-shirt and a jumper. She can't remember when she wore anything else. 'Come on, monsters, let's go outside and hang out the washing.'

By the time Olivia gets back downstairs, Francesca has gone, leaving the kitchen neat and tidy. As she gets the twins into their jackets, Olivia wonders what the call from Walt was about. It's odd, the disconnected nature of Francesca's marriage. She never mentions Walt, and doesn't appear to think much about him either. Olivia can't imagine not being intimately involved with Dan. If they were apart, she would think about him constantly, and talk to him every day. As it is, there's a constant stream of communication, even when they're together. She sends emails to his computer when he's working and she doesn't want to disturb him but needs to flag something up.

Perhaps that's what Francesca is doing too, but I just can't see it. They might be messaging all the time for all I know. Perhaps they talk on the phone long into the night while we're asleep. And what about her children? When does she ever see or talk to them? Horrible boarding schools, with their enforced separation. It doesn't seem right. I suppose they don't mind it. Maybe there will come a time when I don't need to see the twins every day, and when my life goes back to being all about me. But it's hard to imagine it at the moment.

Outside, the air is blustery but warm and the sunshine heats the walled garden, the stones reflecting its rays. The garden is blooming, with all sorts of treats and surprises bursting out through the soil. She must find the time to investigate properly. And, she reminds herself, she hasn't looked at the rest of the garden for a while. She is intrigued by the hedges she spotted and wants to see what shapes they've been trimmed into. The children play happily as she pegs out the washing in the same endless ritual, her fingers clumsy with the tiny cold wet socks, small outfits waving in the breeze like a row of miniature scarecrows.

Her fears of last night when she was lost in the house seem silly now, but a nasty chill creeps over her skin when she thinks of it. Whatever happened, it wasn't nice. She still finds it difficult to believe that Dan let Jimmy persuade him to leave her there and hide, but he was drunk and he can be an idiot when he drinks. The atmosphere of schoolboy jape must have been too much to resist. He was certainly apologetic afterwards, clearly grasping how unpleasant it was to be alone there in the dark. She was mollified. It was all right. He was forgiven.

The strange thing was how cold Francesca was over it. *She's been so lovely lately, she can't do enough for me. And suddenly, last night, she went all prickly.* Olivia recalls that right from the off, as she started preparing the meal, Francesca grew distant. She didn't offer to help – not with the cooking, or with the table, or even clearing away afterwards.

It was almost as though she were trying to relegate Olivia to the status of housekeeper, while she played the lady of the manor.

Maybe that's what she's used to at home. Olivia wrestles with a pair of Dan's heavy wet jeans, tethering them down to the line with several pegs.

Francesca seemed to enjoy herself during the evening, revelling in the old jokes and stories, and joining in whenever she could. Her attention was firmly focused on her Cambridge mates, but that was how it should be. It was why they were there, really. And she was in her element when they went on the tour of the house. But afterwards, she seemed thoroughly pissed off.

And then back to normal this morning. Emptying the dishwasher, feeding the kids, clearing up. Just the same old Cheska, smiley and chatty and nice.

She bends down to the washing basket and gets more clothes. The line is dipping under the weight already, but the warm air will soon dry out the worst of the water. As she takes out some sleep suits, she considers.

What is normal for Cheska, though? What do I really know about her?

She has always been around, for as long as Olivia has known Dan. A fixture in his life. A platonic female friend with whom there has never, apparently, been a spark of romance.

Olivia laughs to herself. *Well, it's possible. I mean, Dan has a magnetic effect on lots of women, but some have got to be immune to him. Look at the others . . . Claire, Katy,*

Alyssa . . . they've never seemed to respond to him like that. And nor has Cheska.

And yet, now she thinks about it, she remembers how she once used to feel vaguely uncomfortable about Francesca and the intimacy she shared with Dan. She believed him when he said that they'd been no more than friends, but always wondered if that puppyish attitude of Cheska's had spilled over into something romantic. When she playfully asked him, he laughed and said he didn't think so. Still there was something intimate between them . . . *But he was close to Claire too. What's the difference?* She thinks hard, frowning as she pegs out another T-shirt, hearing the children chatter at her feet as they play with the pegs in the bag. *It was because Claire was absolutely and irrefutably in love with Jimmy. They were a couple. The intimacy with Dan was a close friendship. But Cheska is in a couple too, married to Walt. It's the same thing.*

Her mind plays over it again, what it was like when she met Francesca, how she absorbed the story of Francesca's marriage.

It wasn't really like Claire and Jimmy, because Walt was never here. We never saw him. It was always Cheska on her own, except very occasionally, like at our wedding. He was there then. She remembers him, a portly businessman with a merry smile and a loud American accent, a little out of place with his handmade shoes and tailored suits and solid gold cufflinks. She liked him. But it was hard to visualise him at Francesca's side as her partner. It was more like she'd brought a distant relation along.

Why did she marry him? I can't see it somehow.

But the marriage has lasted so far, with two children and a home in Switzerland and now this house, a project that will see them into the next few years at least.

Suddenly she recalls the moment last night when Jimmy said something in particular. What was it? Something about Dan still being able to reel them in, and he mentioned Cheska in particular. Then it went quiet and everyone was a bit odd, just for a moment, until someone smoothed it over.

She stands still, the damp clothes swaying on the line beside her.

What did that mean? She shrugs. *I'll just have to ask Dan. I'm sure he'll tell me.*

Once she's finished with the washing, there's still no sign of Francesca or Dan. He must be working. Her eye is caught by a sudden movement, and she gazes upwards to see Francesca standing at the window of the twins' bedroom, looking down while she talks on her mobile phone. When she sees that Olivia has spotted her, she waves merrily and makes a gesture to show that she is deep in a conversation.

What's she doing in there?

Olivia picks up the washing basket and takes it inside, leaving the twins playing. Then, on a whim, she gets her coat and slips on her boots. They will take a walk into the garden of the main house. Why not? It might get her creative juices flowing again. It's been fun poking around in the cottage garden, and she's spent some happy half hours weeding and clearing and giving the shrubs some space to breathe.

But I need to earn some money soon. Dan's redundancy won't pay the bills forever and despite what Jimmy says about my royalties, they don't amount to all that much.

She should think about a new book. The Argentinian one can't go ahead now that she's left and there probably wouldn't be much of a market for it either. 'A nice how-to guide always goes down well,' her literary agent would say. 'That's what they like. Simple, pretty and lots of lovely pics.'

She hasn't heard from him for months. He's probably forgotten all about her.

Well, there might not be a book in Renniston, but I'm sure I could do some articles for a gardening magazine or a Sunday paper. I'll pitch something to my old contacts and see what happens.

Feeling a little brighter, she takes a twin by each hand, and they skip out of the cottage garden, singing one of their favourite songs as they go. She soon realises they don't need their coats; the weather is properly warm. They are well into May and there's more than a hint of the coming summer.

'Isn't this lovely?' she asks, as they walk along the gravel paths and she begins to take in the garden. The trim paths are bordered by lavender and purple sage with small round rosemary bushes in between. Behind are taller plants, stocks in white and mauve, white-green balls of hydrangea, fluffy-headed phlox, with shaped evergreen shrubs adding structure. Where paths divide, bay trees stand guard, their trunks sturdy and bare, their leaves trimmed to glossy green orbs on top. Jasmine, clematis and honeysuckle climb the old stone walls, some of their flowers already out, speckling the

301

shaggy growth with colour. Some borders have tiny cut hedges of their own to enclose a mass of blooms, or a rose bush. It's old-fashioned but lovingly set out and cared for.

Does William really do all this on his own? How incredible! He must work so hard.

The children are entranced by the gravel and she has to stop them picking up handfuls to toss at each other and over the borders. Then they come to a smaller enclosed garden, set out with formal patterns, with a pond in the middle.

'Stay away from the water,' she says strictly, and diverts them from their instant run towards it. 'No, you naughty things! We're not getting wet today. It's not that warm.'

Then she sees it. The topiary, in the garden beyond. 'Look, look!' she cries, laughing. 'What can you see?'

Bea and Stan look where she is pointing but they don't know to lift their gaze and it's only when she holds them both up that they see what she is talking about.

'Wabbit!' cries Bea, pointing too. 'Wabbit, wabbit!'

'Wabbit?' asks Stan wonderingly, then sees it and shrieks. 'Cat!'

'No, rabbit,' Olivia corrects, and then she sees the cat as well. 'Oh my goodness, it's a pet zoo. Come on, let's go and look.'

She puts them down and they make their way out of the far end of the formal garden and into a wide avenue at the back of the house. Here, at the eastern end of the Hall, is the topiary: a row of green hedges cut into the shapes of animals.

'Squiwwel!' cries Bea, and laughs.

'Yes, a squirrel. And a bear, how hilarious. What made him put a bear here? And . . . what's that? An owl?'

The row of green leafy animals has been carefully trimmed and maintained. Each animal is neat and easy to identify. They spend a happy hour wandering among them, pretending to feed them, and talk to them, and the children make up names for them. Then Olivia realises it's time for lunch and chivvies the children back onto the path for home.

How lovely to find these animals, she thinks. *It makes up for that horrible experience last night. The house doesn't seem so bad when it's got this little menagerie here.*

As they head back towards the cottage, she thinks she sees someone watching them over the low wall of the formal garden, but when she turns to look, there is no one there.

When the twins have eaten and Olivia has put them down for a sleep, Dan emerges from his study for lunch. Olivia is just sitting down to join him for a bowl of soup at the kitchen table when Francesca comes in to say she is catching up on admin this afternoon and could she borrow the car to go to town. 'I'll get some lunch there, and do some grocery shopping if you need anything.'

'No problem,' Olivia says. 'Of course you can borrow the car. And the list is on the wall over there, take it with you. I'd be ever so grateful, I can't stand the supermarket.'

'Happy to. I'll see you later.' She takes the car key from the rack and goes out.

Olivia raises her eyebrows at Dan as they hear the car engine start up. 'There we are. Peace at last.'

'Are the kids napping?' he asks, looking about as though he has just noticed they aren't there.

Olivia nods. 'Fed and fast asleep. We had a very nice morning in the garden.'

'That's good,' Dan says absently, and brushes the crumbs on his plate into a little pyramid. He frowns. 'We've got to get rid of Cheska. I don't want her here anymore. I really don't.'

'I can't say I'm ecstatic about it, but how can we?' Olivia tries to sound reasonable. 'This is her house. What can we do about it? She'll have to go eventually.'

'Or we do,' Dan says brusquely.

'Leave? But go where?' Olivia knows she doesn't want to leave. She likes it here: the old cottage and its sunny garden, the mysterious great house beyond. 'We haven't got the money to rent somewhere like this.'

'We don't have to live in a place like this. We could take a flat in the town. Or get a modern house that doesn't cost as much.'

'I . . . suppose we could,' she says cautiously. 'But would we be as happy?'

'We'd be a darn sight happier than we are sharing our lives with Cheska!' he bursts out.

She leans towards him, anxious at the sight of his strain and the way his fists are clenched. He looks so tense. 'Is everything going okay with your writing?' she asks.

'What?' He scrunches up his face as though he can't understand a word, then says, 'Oh. Yes, yes. It's fine. I mean, it's not finished, I don't know when it will be finished.' He releases a hard puffing breath through his nose. 'Look, the redundancy money is almost gone. The rent from the flat is paying our bills. Obviously it's good that we don't have rent to pay on top of that. But one way or another we need to sort out our future. And I just don't think it's here, Olivia. I'm sorry. It's best that we come to terms with it sooner rather than later.'

'We could sell the London flat and buy a cottage,' she suggests. 'Somewhere like this – rural and pretty with a garden . . .'

'But where will I work?' he says slowly in a tone of exasperated patience, as though pointing out the screamingly obvious. 'If my writing doesn't come to anything, I'll need to find something like my old job again. And that means London.'

'No. Not London.' She's determined. She doesn't want to take the twins back there, to the noise and the traffic and the struggle to go anywhere. 'We have to be able to make it work. Surely. I'll start coming up with some proper book ideas. I'll go to town for the day and see my agent and talk it over with him. I'll get some pitches for articles ready.'

'All very nice possibilities. If they happen, then maybe we could live off them. But we can't be sure.'

He's in one of his negative phases – nothing she suggests will inspire hope. He'll knock it all down. She tries to think of what she can do in the short term to improve his mood, and places a hand over his, rubbing the tops of his knuckles gently. 'Listen, I'll talk to Francesca and ask her what her plans are. Maybe we can explain that we really need some time together as a family. She must know what that's like, she's a mother.'

Dan looks suddenly even more miserable, his blue eyes darkening and his mouth turning down. 'No. Don't do that. We don't need to risk upsetting her. Leave her be. She'll go in the end. It's just . . . draining.'

Olivia stares at him, still rubbing her hand over his. 'Dan . . .' she ventures. 'I know I asked you before but . . .'

He flicks his gaze up at her; it's hard and unyielding. It reminds her of the dark days. The arguments. The tears and shouts and desperation. The sense that he might be a stranger to her. She feels momentarily cowed, then decides to press on.

'You and Francesca . . . did anything . . .' She tries to pick her words carefully. 'Did anything ever happen between you? Romantically?'

He hesitates, and as soon as he does, a strange feeling washes over her, a prickling, buzzing feeling as though her world has just shifted. 'Did it?' she asks, her voice tight with sudden strain.

He looks up, his stare unwavering. 'No,' he says firmly.

'You would tell me, wouldn't you?'

He pauses again, and she is back on tenterhooks. 'Look, I don't know . . . back in the day, she might have nurtured a little crush on me. But if she did, it was a lifetime ago and it never went anywhere. It was over long before I met you. She was going out with Walt practically as soon as we left university and soon after that she got married. That's all there is to it.'

'That's it?'

He nods. 'Yep.'

She wonders why she still feels a sense of unease, as though this is not the whole story. Dan obviously doesn't want to say more.

'Do you promise?' she persists.

He looks away, clicking his tongue with annoyance. 'For God's sake, Olivia, what did I just say? Of course I promise. There's nothing to it. Can you please just acccpt it?'

He gets up, pushing his chair away from the table with unnecessary force, and she watches him go, heading back to the study and the demands of his play.

Chapter Twenty-Six

Francesca finds it is a relief to escape the cottage for a while and drive into town. She doesn't have all that much to do. She's already been on the phone to Anastasia for most of the morning, and sorted out all the details of her domestic and social life. An hour or so of emailing helped her deal with other arrangements. It looks as though the builder she met last week will be coming back to start work on demolishing the old gym and swimming pool. It all has to be rebuilt.

It's a bit mad to start on a pool when they don't yet have anything like a working house, but at least something will begin. And it justifies her continued presence in the house.

As she parks the car and wanders into the small town, she admits to herself that the settled bliss she felt so recently is wearing off. In many ways, she wouldn't mind returning to the privacy and luxury of the London flat. She would quite like to be back home in Geneva. Talking to Anastasia and to Marie-Chantelle has brought her old life vividly to mind and she is surprised to realise that she misses it after all. There is an order to it, a smoothness and a predictability. She is free to do as she likes there. And what's more, others do what she wants. She loves the twins with a deep passion but she has forgotten what hard work toddlers are – and how obstinate and determined they are too. She's always calling out, telling them to stop, racing after them, trying to prevent them from eating worms, or falling in puddles, or smearing food where it should not be. They are constantly dirty, requiring endless changes of nappies and clothes, and hungry when they shouldn't be and then refusing food at meals.

Olivia should stop feeding them all those snacks when they beg for them. They don't need all those rice cakes and animal biscuits. It only fills them up and stops them eating dinner. It's so British.

She catches herself up and laughs despite herself. She's been too long in Europe, where the children of her acquaintance are like little adults, perfectly at home in restaurants and at smart dinner tables from an early age. Then she frowns again. *And why isn't she potty training them? They are surely old enough to be out of nappies by now. I'm sure Olympia and Fred were.* But the memory is a little hazy and unreliable now. She can't be certain how old the children were when they learned to be dry.

Francesca walks along the high street, past the endless chain shops, looking for a nice place to have a decent coffee, but she can only see Starbucks and a bakery cafe serving up monstrous iced buns with violently red cherries on top, or huge chocolate muffins studded with dry-looking chips. Eventually she sees a deli that has tables out the back and goes in for a black coffee and a look at the homemade cakes, which she carefully refuses. Sitting at a table, she takes out her phone and scrolls through the photographs she has taken of the twins. There are reams of them, but she loves them all. The children are surely worth the price of being here.

What a shame I can't take them back with me. The thought floats into her mind, and she sits up straight, imagining suddenly a life in which she has the twins at home in Geneva, with their laughter ringing through the house. It would be so marvellous! She would be able to enjoy all the fun, and someone else would do the work. Her old nanny might even be available. For a moment, Francesca considers ringing her to check her availability. Then she shakes her head ruefully. *It can never happen. How could I even start to get custody of them?* For a moment, she wonders idly what the legal position would be, but she soon dismisses it. She's well aware that the law would recognise Olivia as the children's mother no matter where the eggs came from and besides, there is the matter of the disclaimer, signed in the Spanish clinic, that waived all rights to the children.

No. It can't happen like that.

So how can it happen? Her mind wanders over the possibilities but nothing is realistic enough to capture her imagination.

There really is only one solution to all of this. Somehow, I have to replace Olivia. That's all there is to it.

As she drives back to Renniston, the bags of groceries in the back, she feels calm again. It is as though life has become a series of little moments of resolution. Yesterday, she let go of the part of herself that has tried to understand and excuse Olivia for things that are not her fault. She's not going to bother with sympathy and understanding anymore, they only stand in the way of what she wants. Today she has understood what has to happen for her aim to be realised. There are more conclusions to come to, she is sure of that, but they are unknown for now. At least she has confidence that she will receive them in time. Gradually, the way will become clear.

She parks the car at the side of the cottage, and takes some of the shopping bags from the boot to haul inside. Olivia's list turned out to be quite long and there are several bags full to bursting. As she struggles with two of the heaviest, she becomes aware of someone watching her and turns to see William, the old gardener or caretaker or whatever he is, staring at her. He is just the same as usual, in old brown trousers and a saggy tweed jacket, his white stubble rampant and his faded eyes beady.

'Well?' she snaps. 'What do you want?'

He says nothing but only stares at her, observing her as she staggers under the weight of the bags.

What have I packed in here? Lead? Oh God, I wish he'd stop staring at me.

She snaps, 'If you wanted to help, you could bring a bag or two.'

'I don't obey your orders,' he returns, his voice gruff. 'I thought you understood that by now.'

'All right, all right. I don't give a shit, if I'm honest.' Francesca rather enjoys releasing a casual swear word. She's sure

311

that he's of the generation that would be shocked to hear ladies swear.

He takes a step towards her, his eyes blazing. 'Why don't you leave these people in peace? What are you doing here? I've watched you with those kids, you're all over them. She's their mother, the other one. Not you. You go off somewhere else. It's not right, latching yourself on to them like this, and you know it.'

She narrows her eyes at him, resting her bags on the muddy ground. 'You know sod all about it, so why don't you just piss off? You can stop spying as well, and if you don't, I'll report you for harassment, and then we'll see how much support you get from Preserving England. This is my house and my land. I know you don't like it, but that's the way it is, so you'd better get used to it.' She realises she's enjoying the spiky confrontation and letting loose a little of the acid that's collected in her veins lately. 'The sooner you're away from here the better. The builders are coming in a day or two and all this will start to change, whether you like it or not. Your day is over, understand?'

Bending down, she picks up her bags again and heads for the cottage, while he stands there and watches.

As soon as she gets into the kitchen, Francesca senses the change in atmosphere. Usually, Olivia would give her a big smile and a friendly greeting. Now, from her place at the stove where she is stirring something that smells delicious, she turns with a smile that doesn't reach her eyes and says in a cool voice, 'Hello, you're back.'

They don't want me here anymore. They've discussed it. Francesca is certain. 'Yes,' she says brightly. There's no way she's going to acknowledge this change in mood. Everything is absolutely normal, as far as she's concerned. 'I got the shopping.'

'Oh, thanks. That's splendid.' Olivia comes towards her, wiping her hands on her apron. 'I appreciate it.'

'Don't be silly, it's nothing. I'm glad to help.'

'You must let me give you the money.'

'No, don't bother, consider it my contribution to the board and lodging.'

'But,' Olivia says stiffly, 'it's your lodging anyway. Remember?'

Francesca smiles again and gestures over her shoulder. 'There's more in the car but I might send Dan out to get it. The old gardener bloke is out there and he gives me the creeps.'

'Really?' Olivia brightens, her mood softening. 'I'll just go outside and have a word. I need to thank him properly for last night.'

Before Francesca can ask where the children are, Olivia has disappeared out of the door. She puts the milk in the fridge and looks around. The play mat is tidy and the table is set for the twins' supper. She goes out into the hall, and hears the blare of the television coming from the sitting room at the end, the room below her bedroom. She goes towards the sound and opens the door. Bea and Stan are sitting on the floor, their backs pressed against the sofa, transfixed by the bright moving pictures on the screen in

313

front of them. Dan is with them, but his head is tipped back, his mouth open and his eyes closed; he is breathing deeply.

The twins look round briefly as she comes in but when they see it is her, they return their gazes to the television, where a vividly coloured cartoon about birds is unfolding. Francesca is filled with calm. This is peace.

Very gently, she goes to the sofa and sits down next to Dan. He doesn't wake. With one hand she reaches down and strokes Stan's head. Her thigh is almost, almost pressed against Dan's, but not quite.

Here I am, she thinks happily. *With my family.*

The pleasant, peaceful idyll is brought to an end by Olivia's shout from the kitchen that the twins' supper is ready.

'Come on, little ones,' Francesca says. 'Dinner!'

Dan jerks awake and stares at her, surprised by her presence. Then a look of something like horror comes over his face. 'What are you doing here?' he asks in a hoarse whisper.

She smiles sweetly. 'Just watching television with our children, darling. What's strange about that?'

'Our children?' he repeats, going pale.

She shrugs lightly. 'The children, if you prefer.'

There's another shout from the kitchen. The twins don't move, still absorbed in the television. Dan blinks hard and leans towards her. She thinks about how his nearness would once have sent her into a frenzy of hard-to-conceal agitation and desire. Now she simply feels the rightness of their being close. Like any couple. Like any parents.

'Listen, Cheska,' he says in a low, urgent voice. 'I don't

know what you're playing at but you know what we agreed.'

'What? I've forgotten.'

He stumbles, not sure what to say next. Has she really forgotten, or is she playing by the rules and pretending there is no secret? Is she forcing him to say out loud what is supposed to remain unsaid? She can't help feeling gleeful as she watches these thoughts play across his face as clear as the cartoon the children are watching.

Dan gathers his thoughts and starts again. 'You need to go soon, okay? Olivia and I need some space. You're welcome, of course, but we're a family—'

'I know we are,' she says innocently.

'No. Olivia and I – and the children – that's the family. You know that. You've got your own family and you should think about getting back to them. Okay?'

She reaches out and gently puts her hand on the thigh of his jeans. 'Or . . . we could share?' She smiles at him. 'There are no hard feelings on my side, Dan, over . . . the past and all that happened. We can still make it right.'

He frowns. 'What are you talking about?' He shifts awkwardly under her hand but doesn't push it away.

'Perhaps there's a way we can all have what we want. After all, we are a family. Daddy and Mummy.' She leans in so that she is very close to his face, looks at his mouth, then up to his eyes, laughs throatily and whispers, 'And Mummy.'

He gazes back as if hypnotised by her, perfectly still under the hand that rests on his thigh.

The door opens and Olivia is there, looking frazzled. 'Can't you hear me?' she demands and then takes in the scene before her: Dan and Francesca close on the sofa, her hand on his leg. Francesca swiftly removes it in a smooth, guiltless way, as though it had been there only an instant. She shifts away from Dan in a small but obvious movement. Olivia blinks and opens her mouth to speak, but says nothing.

'Sorry, sweetheart,' Dan says, standing up quickly. 'We were just coming.' He picks up Stan, who whimpers with resistance, his eyes staying firmly fixed on the screen as Dan carries him off, scooping up Bea as he goes. A moment later, they are all gone, leaving Francesca with just the television for company, playing on regardless of its lost audience.

She stares after them, and thinks she might possibly have found how to get Olivia out of the way.

Chapter Twenty-Seven
1960

The winter term is always a subdued one, full of icy fingers and chilled toes, girls huddled around tepid radiators and wrapped in scarves. It is about endurance, more than anything else, hunkering down and putting up with all the discomfort until spring finally arrives to relieve the pressure.

Julia wakes up to the bell and groans, getting herself out of bed, aware that this is the last time she will feel warm all day. Washes are quick in the morning, and she gets dressed rapidly before making her way down through the freezing corridors to the dining room for breakfast, where at least it is a little less icy.

Who thought this place would be a good school? she wonders as she hurries down the stairs with everyone else. *It's too big and cold to be tolerable.*

Perhaps if there was a decent heating system, it might help. But then again, the swimming pool and gym at the end of the east wing are still being constructed, so huge gusts of winter air come in all the time to chill the place even more.

Lessons start at nine after assembly and prayers, but she

can tolerate those. At least they are inside, where it's possible to dig fists deep into pullover sleeves and warm up fingers that way. Lunch is hot, and they eat as much as they can, even of the horrible stuff, like rice and gristle stew, or what they call tubey soup, because the lumps of meat in it are full of little white tubes, whatever they might be. But the afternoon, and sometimes even the morning, brings games. The walk to the changing rooms has the air of the condemned about it. The painful stripping of warm clothes and the replacement with kit, far too skimpy for the weather outside, and then the horrible run from the school to the frosty playing field.

'Come on, girls, let's warm you up. Run around the perimeter, please!' Miss Dunleavy bellows, but she looks freezing herself and not at all keen to be outside. They run but Julia feels only marginally warmer afterwards. There are stretches, then they're divided into teams, and then they start the match. Julia has only a vague idea of what the game consists of, and spends most of the time shivering on the side of the pitch, using her lacrosse stick to strike tiny snowstorms of frost off the crisp blades of grass.

'What's up with Alice?' asks Sophia Buxton, who is her opposite number. Sophia jumps up and down a few times, her cheeks bright red with cold. 'She's not herself this term.'

'She's not very well,' Julia replies. 'I'm not sure what's wrong with her. She's been under the weather since we got back. That's almost two weeks now. She keeps going off to Matron.'

'They'll be sending her home at this rate. I heard Matron

tell Jennifer Mason that this isn't a hospital. Jenny's been ill three times already with flu, she can't seem to shake it.'

'I expect Jenny would be better off at home,' Julia says. 'At least she'd be warm and get some decent rations. It's no wonder she can't get well here.'

'So, do you think they'll send Alice home? I've not seen her at one games lesson so far this term. They won't like that.'

Julia and Sophia swap meaningful looks. They both know the almost religious fervour of the school's approach to games. No one can miss too many lessons without questions being asked.

'I suppose they might,' Julia says. She has hoped not, but lately she's begun to think that it might be for the best. Alice is evidently not herself, and the black mood doesn't seem to have lifted at all. In lessons, Julia sneaks looks at her, and often sees her big blue eyes swimming in tears, and a look of abject misery on her friend's face. But when she asks what's wrong, Alice won't tell.

Later, as they come back across the field, a little warmer now after the game, Julia sees the small dark figures of the men working over by the gymnasium. The builders went home over Christmas and New Year, but now they are back and hard at work on the construction of the gym. The dugout pool has been left while the shell is constructed round it. Julia strains her eyes to make out Donnie, or even Roy, but she can't see that far and can only guess which of the little figures is Donnie.

I wonder if I'll ever see him again. I don't think I will, somehow.

Sadness grips her for an instant, and then she pushes it out of her mind.

Perhaps someone has a word with her, or perhaps she just feels a little better, but a day or two later, Alice rallies. She dries her tears and even smiles at Julia over breakfast, and teases her about her hair, which means she must be feeling better. Things seem a little more normal, and Julia is happy and relieved. She's missed Alice, even if life is less risky without her high jinks to cope with.

'What's the matter?' she asks over lunch, when there are just the two of them left at the table. 'You've been awfully ill, haven't you?'

Alice sighs, an air of melancholy enveloping her again. 'Yes. I'm all right today. And perhaps I will be tomorrow, but I don't know when I'll be completely better.'

'It's funny because you actually look a bit healthier in lots of ways,' Julia says, trying to offer some comfort.

'I do?' Alice lifts her eyes to Julia's questioningly.

'Yes. I mean, you're . . . you're definitely fatter than you were. Not . . . not horrible fat. I mean, healthy fat.'

'Really?' Alice starts to laugh. 'That's terribly funny.'

'Is it? Why?' Julia smiles at her, finding Alice's mirth infectious.

'Why? It just is!' Alice laughs harder. 'I can't explain. But they don't think it's my body anyway. They think it's my head. I've had to see two different head doctors already, men with glasses and clipboards and pencils and a big desk and a sofa I have to lie on.' She leans forward to Julia, still laughing. 'Not like Roy's sofa. Not like that at all. They don't touch me, they make me to talk to them. But they may as well not waste their time, because I'm not going to say anything. Not a sausage.' She puts her finger on her lips and says, 'Shhh.'

'What are you talking about?' Julia says helplessly.

'Girls, quiet please, finish your lunch!' It's Mademoiselle, who is in charge of the dining room today.

Alice refuses to say anything more and then lunch is over and they don't speak of it again.

Julia thinks about the head doctors all afternoon. What does Alice mean? A psychiatrist, she supposes. Perhaps that's why she's so depressed – anyone would be if the grown-ups had decided you've gone round the bend. *But it's awfully unfair, considering that they're the ones who've made her that way. If her parents had just cared about her a little bit more, she probably wouldn't be like this.*

She wants to tell Alice her conclusion and tell her how sorry she is, and how unfair it is, but there isn't a chance. They sit far apart in Latin and are in different sets for Maths. Then they are outside for the afternoon lacrosse match, and Alice is attack, while she is defence, so they don't cross paths for long enough to talk.

It rained the previous night and there was no frost, so the ground is soft and muddy, easily churned up by lacrosse boots and sent splattering up legs and over arms. They are all filthy when they get back from the field.

'Showers, please, girls!' yells Dunleavy, and there's a universal groan. Everyone hates showers. They don't have them very often because it means the girls are slower getting dressed again, but it's inevitable today. Julia looks over at Alice and sees a look of horror on her face. Julia feels the same – she detests the humiliation of the shower but there's nothing for it. They have to do it.

Julia strips off her kit until she is in her gym knickers and vest. This is the most awful moment. She can't bear revealing herself to the eyes of the others, even though she tries not to look at them and is sure they feel just as she does. She quickly pulls off the vest and then the knickers, picking up her towel and shielding herself with it as she pads along the cold tiles to the showers. They are all on, hot water and steam filling the narrow room, with its rows of heads bent over the one single channel. Nowhere to hide. No privacy. Miss Dunleavy stands at the door, taking towels from girls as they pass. They are supposed to shower using the small white bars of soap in the little cubby holes by each shower head, and then return via Miss Dunleavy for their towel on the way back to the changing room. Julia reaches the games mistress and hands over her towel, then runs for the nearest shower, staring at the floor. The only good thing about the whole process is that the water is hot, hotter than anywhere else. Perhaps it's closer to the boiler room or something. She faces the wall and stands under the stream of water, letting the mud on her legs and arms melt and flow away. Then she notices that someone is under the shower next to her, and she can't help glancing over, her gaze still lowered, to see who is there. She sees a naked form facing the wall as she is, with slender legs and a neat behind, a straight strong back and fair hair curled up into a rough bun to keep it from the water. But that is not what draws Julia's eye. Instead she finds herself following the curve of the belly as it protrudes outwards from just above the pubic mound, sticking out before rounding upwards towards the breasts, like the side of a pear.

Julia's gaze continues up and she meets the candid and yet deeply sad eyes of Alice, staring back. She makes the same sign she did at lunch, pressing her finger to her lips, mouthing, 'Shhh.'

Oh no, thinks Julia as she understands what she has seen. *Oh no. It can't be. Can it?*

Alice knows she knows, but nothing is said. Julia can't think what to say, or who to tell, or how to ask for help. No one else has noticed. Not even Dunleavy, as she held out a towel and Alice scampered past, her arms folded across her front until she was able to snatch the towel and hide herself. She tries to imagine going to a teacher, or writing to her mother, or to Alice's mother, but she can't think of what she could possibly say, or how it would help matters.

But how much time have we got?

She realises how little she knows about what is happening to Alice. She knows the theory of human reproduction and has looked at the biology textbook line drawings of tubes and ovaries and sperm ducts like everyone else, but she has only the vaguest idea of the practice, or how it all even starts, except that intimacy must take place, whatever that might be. Kissing, she supposes, and touching of some kind. Whatever happened in the caravan when she and Donnie were outside. That must have caused it.

An idea bursts over her with a rush of inspiration.

Of course. Donnie. And Roy. That's what I have to do.

Julia finds the journey undertaken on her own much more terrifying than the excursions she made for Alice's sake. It is strange and frightening to be setting off alone to sneak out of the dormitory and down through the cold, empty school to where the canvas sheeting is still tacked over the door. It goes against her nature to be so wilfully disobedient, but it is the only thing she can think of to do in this awful situation. There's less wind now that the walls of the gymnasium and the pool room have gone up, with holes left for windows at the top. She is glad to discover that there is not yet a door for the back of the gym, just a makeshift piece of wood that is easy to push open wide enough to slip through. Then, with the help of her pocket torch, she follows the route she remembers from the last time she did this, when she followed a flighty Alice through the hole in the hedge.

It's Friday again and the campsite is quiet, as she'd hoped. It's easy to recognise the caravan at the back of the field with the metal steps where she sat with Donnie. A light is on in the interior, the flimsy curtains drawn. Julia shivers as she picks her way over the dark field towards it. It's so cold and the sky feels low and heavy. When she reaches the door, she pauses and listens. The sound of tinny music comes from within. Surely that means that Donnie is there. She is excited and scared at the same time, and more than a little shocked at her own audacity in coming out here alone without being asked. After all, she has only met him once, weeks ago. For a moment, she wonders what on earth she is doing here. Then she remembers Alice's burgeoning belly, taps lightly on the door and waits. There's no answer and she wonders if her knock could be heard over the noise of the radio, so she knocks again with more force. A moment later, the music stops abruptly and footsteps cross the caravan. The door opens a touch and she sees a face peering out through the gap.

It's him.

Her insides curl in a somersault that makes her blood rush and her head spin. Now what is she going to say to him? How on earth can he help her? But she is sure that he is the only person she can tell who will understand.

The door opens a little further, and Donnie is there, looking out at her, a little stooped in the doorway, an expression of astonishment on his face.

'You,' he says in surprise.

'Yes.' She manages a small smile. 'I know you weren't expecting me. I need to talk to you.'

'To me?' He frowns. 'What about?'

She looks beyond him into the caravan but can see nothing. 'Is Roy there?'

'He's down the pub,' Donnie says briefly. 'With all the others.'

'Why don't you go down to the pub?' she asks shyly.

He shrugs. 'Not my cup of tea. I'd rather stay here and get a bit of peace. Listen to my music.' His accent is gentle, not as strong as Roy's, but still there. 'So . . . what do you want? I'm afraid I don't have whiskey, if that's what you're after.'

She flushes. 'I don't want that.'

'Then what do you want?'

'I told you. To talk to you.'

He laughs drily. 'What can you have to talk to me about?'

Julia stares at him, and bites her lip. An expression crosses his face that she can't quite read, but she knows he's guessed something of what she's come to say.

'All right,' he says finally. 'You'd better come in then.'

Inside, she sits on the cushioned bench underneath the window where she sat the last time she was here. The place seems bigger without Roy's vast size in it. She's relieved he's not there.

'So what's the trouble?' Donnie asks, handing her a tin mug of tea he's brewed up for her. 'Your girl's in a bad way, is she?'

Julia takes the tea and nods. 'I'm afraid so. She's been very down in the dumps for ages. I thought she must be ill or something, or else in the most frightful bad mood there's ever been. But then, yesterday, I guessed what it is. And I don't think she's going to tell anyone either. But they're bound to find out sooner or later, I'm just amazed no one's noticed already. She's learned to hide it, I suppose, but she can't do that forever.'

'Young girls can go the whole way and never show,' Donnie says wisely. 'I've seen it.' He shakes his head. 'Poor lasses. It's never a good way to be.' He lights a cigarette and blows out a stream of smoke. 'It takes two to make the baby, but only one of 'em has to carry it, and that's the one the world blames.'

Julia looks over at him, not knowing what to say. She is hopelessly shy about these things and when she remembers that she is sitting across from Donnie, the boy she has been dreaming of all winter, she can hardly believe that they are talking about babies. It's as though she's been transported to the grown-up world in a blink of an eye, without really knowing enough about it.

Donnie puffs on his cigarette again, his foot tapping as though his music is still playing.

Perhaps he's hearing it in his head.

'So the poor girl is in the club. Why'd you want to talk to me about it? I don't know what I can do.'

'I thought . . . I thought perhaps you could tell Roy and he might know what to do.'

Donnie laughs incredulously. 'He won't have a clue. He's got four kids already; last one was born over Christmas but it died. He's been drinking like a fish ever since he got back here. It's shaken him up. He's lost his appetite for having his parties with your friend, anyhow. She'll get no help from that direction.' He shakes his head. 'I'm sorry for your girl and all, but she must have known she was taking a risk. I suppose the school will be shot of her. Her family will have to look after her. She'll have money if she's at a place like this. She'll be all right. It's worse for the girls who have nothing, and who end up in homes, with their kids taken away from them, and ruined for life.'

Julia blinks at him. She's never heard of such places or dreamed that things like that can happen. What did Alice do to get herself into this situation? Surely they would take Alice's baby away from her too. How on earth could she keep it? And would she really have to leave school? All the questions she hasn't yet considered flood her mind, and they sit in silence for a moment.

At last she glances over at Donnie, and says, 'Should we tell Roy about it? It's his baby after all.'

Donnie shakes his head. 'No. We mustn't tell him, not unless he really needs to know. Does she want him to be a father to it?'

'No,' Julia says, embarrassed. 'I don't think so.' She thinks of Alice's breezy dismissal of Roy as being just a builder, and doesn't want to repeat such a thing to Donnie.

'Well then. It'll only make him mad. Their little fling is over now.' He makes a face. 'I always knew it would end up in no good. Someone was going to suffer. I'm sorry it's your friend.'

'What do you think will happen to her?'

He shrugs. 'She'll be smuggled away to have it. The kid will be adopted. She'll be okay. I told you, she's got money. It buys the way out of trouble.' He glances over at her.

'You'd better tell her mother. That's the only thing there is to do.'

'I can't do that,' Julia says unhappily. 'Alice would never forgive me.'

'Then persuade her to do it herself. Better to do it now than wait for everyone to notice.' He stubs out his cigarette. 'Come on. You shouldn't be here. I'll walk you back to the school. No point in you getting yourself in trouble as well.'

He stands up and puts out a hand to her. She takes it and he helps her to her feet. They gaze at each other for a long moment, their hands still locked together, warm and smooth, aware suddenly of their physical connection and the feelings it is provoking in them. For an instant, she thinks he will pull her towards him, bend his head and kiss her, and she wants him to with everything in her. But he doesn't. He releases her hand, looks away awkwardly and says, 'Let's go then.'

They walk back across the field, past the dark caravans. Julia wonders what it is like when the place is full of men, the caravans crowded and noisy.

'How long do you expect to be here?' she asks. 'When will the work be finished?'

'Another three weeks or so,' Donnie says. 'Not too long. It's slow at first, then it speeds up. You'll see.'

They reach the new pool building and he says, 'I'll leave you here then.'

'Goodbye,' she says. 'And thank you.'

'You're welcome. Tell your friend good luck.' Then he turns on his heel, his hands stuffed in his pockets and trudges away, back towards the caravan field. Julia watches him go, then hurries back inside, to make her silent dash for the dormitory.

The strangest atmosphere exists between her and Alice now. Whenever she looks at her friend, she sees not just Alice but the burgeoning life inside her. A baby. What does it look like, tucked up inside Alice's body? Is it half finished, like the clay head she was moulding in pottery but never got round to adding the finer details to, or is it perfect but in miniature, simply amplifying by the day? Julia has so little idea of how these things come about, and while it has never seemed important or relevant before, it does now.

One lunchtime, by unspoken consent, they walk around the grounds where they are permitted to go during breaks, and Julia knows she must say something, before the opportunity is lost.

'You know you mustn't do games anymore,' she says as they walk down one of the gravel paths bordered by lavender plants that are stringy and brown in their winter dormancy. Above them the sky is a yellowish grey.

'Yes, I know,' Alice says. 'It is getting tricky. I can't seem to run as fast as I used to.'

Julia gives her a sideways look. 'As if that matters. The point is that it can't be good for the baby if you run around.'

'Mmm.' Alice does not seem shocked, either by the casual mention of the baby, whose existence has not yet been acknowledged out loud, or by the thought that activity might not be good for it.

'But also,' Julia continues, 'it's bound to be noticed. You can't hide it so well in kit, and then there are the showers . . .'

At least, she reflects, *it's a comfort to know how little we are looked at. Dunleavy didn't notice. But it can't go on like that.*

She asks in a rush, 'How have you hidden it so far? Didn't your mother see it?'

Alice laughs with a touch of bitterness. 'No. I've covered it up in jumpers. If you don't know what to look for, it's not very evident, really.'

'But it will be soon.' Julia feels desperate. Why won't Alice think about the reality of her situation? 'Someone's bound to find out. And what about when the baby starts to come? Do you know when it's due?'

Alice shrugs. 'I'm not sure. I don't entirely know when . . . it . . . happened.'

They stop, Julia facing Alice, her hands in the pockets of her coat. 'So . . .' she says, her face heating up with the embarrassment of it all. 'You and Roy. You . . . you did that.'

'Yes.' Alice tosses her head defiantly. 'I let him do it to me. It wasn't rape, if that's what you're thinking. I wanted to do it! At least he loved me, in his own way. I felt special. He said I made him feel like no one else in the world, and he told me I was beautiful and amazing, and his gift from God. He said I was a consolation.'

Julia gazes at her, open-mouthed. She feels helpless in the face of this. On the one hand, she can understand the power of being loved and wanted. In her secret heart, she has thought that if Donnie loved her and asked her, she would do the same with him that Alice has done with Roy. But she can also see the futility of it and the danger. What is the point of a love that can never be, when its consequences are so dreadful? Roy, with his wife and children, and the absolute impossibility of the relationship. 'But,' she asks at last, confused, 'do you love him? Roy?'

Alice sighs dreamily. 'I love to be loved, and he loved me. And even though – if you want the truth – it was horrible, it was also lovely, because it showed me how much he longed for me.'

'Even though it only lasted for a short time?' Julia asks quietly. She is thinking of the way Roy hit Alice and wondering how that can be reconciled with the love she thinks he showed her.

'Oh no,' Alice says. 'It lasted ages and ages. I thought it would never end. You'll see when it happens to you.'

Julia feels odd to think it might. She can't imagine it. It must be years off.

They walk on together in silence for a while, Alice still dreamy and disconnected. Julia says, 'I think you need to tell your mother.'

Alice is startled out of her reverie. 'What?'

'Tell her about the baby. What else are you going to do? If you don't know how far along you are, you can't know when it's coming. You can't have the baby here at school.'

Alice frowns and says irritably, 'I do wish you'd stop going on about the blessed baby.' She begins to stalk away along the path. 'You're like a stuck record!'

'But what are you going to do about it?' persists Julia,

hurrying after her. 'If you won't do anything, I'll have to. I'll have to write to your mother, or tell Miss Allen, or *something*.'

Alice halts and whirls around, sending a little flurry of gravel into the air. Her expression is furious, her eyes blazing. 'Don't you dare!' she shouts. 'Don't you dare do anything, or tell my mother. I'll decide what to do, and no one else, and that's that.'

She storms off back towards the school and Julia can only follow.

Snow comes that afternoon, as the winter darkness is falling. They are in a history lesson, Julia sitting by the window when she sees the first swirl of flakes through the diamond panes. The big radiator that her leg is pressed against is giving out a mild heat.

Snow, she thinks. *How pretty.* If it gets too thick on the ground, there will be no games but they'll be allowed to go out and amuse themselves in it with snowballs and building snowmen. Such activity now seems so innocent, the pursuit of another time, before she had to nurture Alice's deep, dark secret.

'Pay attention, please,' says the teacher, as the girls begin to notice the whirling snow with a murmur of excitement. 'I'm afraid that the Civil War is more important than the weather. Now, who can name the first battle of the conflict?'

Julia looks down at the page in her notebook where she has been scribbling. There is nothing about the Civil War there. Instead there is the beginning of a letter.

Dear Mrs ?

She will have to find out Alice's mother's new name, as she is sure it isn't Warburton anymore, now that she has remarried.

I'm afraid I have to tell you some news about Alice.
She

Here she stopped, unable to think of how to continue. It seemed indecent to write it down. Beneath are suggestions for the rest.

She is in an interesting condition . . .
She isn't well . . .
She has had an accident and is expecting a . . . an
event that . . .

Oh dear. None of it is right. She tries to remember what Donnie said and writes that down.

She is in the club.

Will Alice's mother understand that? It seems too obscure. She might think Julia means the stamp-collecting club, or the woodland craft club. Julia glances over at Alice, who is gazing dreamily into the middle distance, tapping a pencil on the desk with light, regular strokes. Is she thinking of the child inside her, imagining its future? Perhaps she is feeling a kick or a movement that is reminding her of its presence. Or, more likely, she is pretending that it doesn't exist and never will, and forcing herself to forget.

At that moment, as Julia looks over at her friend, Alice starts and goes very still. A look of horror appears on her face and an instant later, she turns and looks at Julia. The expression on her face is one of terror tinged with something else. A word springs into Julia's mind.

Triumph?

But what on earth could she take as a victory from this awful situation? Then Julia thinks she might understand. Alice has taken her disobedience to the limit. As scared as she is, she is also exultant because now they will find out just how naughty she has been.

Oh, Alice. It's all too serious for that. Why can't you see?

But Julia will have to help her. There is no other way.

The moment the lesson ends, Alice runs to the lavatories and shuts herself in a cubicle. Julia follows, skittering along the corridor after her, and into the loos. She knocks on the door.

'Alice? Alice?' she hisses urgently.

Other girls come in, glancing at Julia standing outside one of the stalls, but they ignore her as they drop their books, use the lavatories, wash their hands and leave. There are only a few minutes between lessons, and there is one more class before the day is over. Julia grabs one of the girls as she is leaving.

'Clara, tell Miss Brown that I'm taking Alice to Matron, will you? She's not a bit well. She's throwing up in there, and when she comes out I'll take her to the sanatorium.'

'All right,' Clara says without interest. 'But you'd better get a shift on, you know it's not allowed to miss lessons because of someone else.'

'Yes, I know, but it's urgent,' she says impatiently.

Clara shrugs and heads out. They are alone again.

'Alice?' Julia raps on the door.

'What?' The voice is muffled and strained.

'What's going on? Are you all right?'

There's another long pause, then the flush of the lavatory and the door opens. Alice is pale but seems normal. She smiles. 'I'm fine, of course.'

'No, you're not. I saw your face. Something's up.' Julia scans her face anxiously. 'Has it started? Is the baby coming?'

'No, no. I just had a cramp or something, that's all. Come on. We'd better get going, or we'll be in trouble.' She heads out, leaving Julia to follow behind.

All that afternoon and evening, Julia keeps a watchful eye on Alice but can learn nothing. Alice remains pale and is apparently studious in the last lesson of the day, keeping her face firmly turned down to the desk. Once, Julia thinks she sees Alice stiffen and her knuckles whiten as she holds her pencil in a tight grip, but it passes and there is no other sign of any trouble – no moan or exclamation of pain.

Perhaps I imagined it. It must be nothing.

The process of pregnancy is a mystery to her, beyond the knowledge that the woman carries the growing child inside her and then pushes it out down below in a painful and lengthy process. If Alice were having the baby, surely she would be lying on the floor and screaming by now. As that isn't happening, Julia concludes that nothing is out of order. Perhaps Alice was telling the truth and she really did have a touch of cramps.

That might be normal, for all I know.

All she can do is watch and wait.

Darkness has descended even earlier than usual and outside the windows of the school the snow is falling ever more thickly, quickly blanketing the lawns and hedges, the fountains and stone balustrades. The world outside is a mass of eddying flakes, and inside, the mood is excited but also muted. They will be snowed in, and that could last days and days.

Supper passes and Alice barely eats, but that is not so unusual. She often goes through periods of hardly touching food. Julia feels she should urge her on for the sake of the baby, but that seems an odd thing to do, and besides, how could she, when they're surrounded by the other girls, not to mention the staff?

When they say goodnight, and curl up in their beds in the dorm, separated only by flimsy low walls, Alice seems even paler and has begun to look genuinely ill.

'Are you sure you don't want to go to Matron?' Julia asks, worried, as she looks over the low partition into Alice's section. 'You don't look at all well. How are the cramps?'

'I'm fine,' Alice says, but her eyes are tired and her cheeks look hollow. Nevertheless she smiles. 'It's going to be all right. You'll see. I'll be all right in the morning.'

Julia curls up in her bed and waits for the cool sheets to grow warm so that she can sleep, listening for any sound from Alice, but there's none. Before long, she can't listen anymore as she drifts off into half-consciousness, thinking of the snow and the warmth of Egypt.

She wakes suddenly, and knows at once that something is

wrong. Jumping out of bed, shivering in the chill air outside the blankets, she runs lightly to the partition and looks over it. Alice is gone. Her bed is empty.

Oh no! Where is she? Panic races through her as she stares wildly about the dark dormitory, as though hoping to see Alice in the shadows. *I have to find her.*

As quietly as possible, she opens her drawer and pulls out her weekend clothes: trousers, a blouse and a thick jumper. Then a pair of socks and her coat and hat. It's so cold in the school, she'll need all of that to keep warm. Then she picks up her boots, gets her torch from its hiding place in her bedside table and tiptoes out of her cubby hole and into the main dormitory. There is not a sound. She is sure that Alice is not here.

Her instinct takes her the way they have always gone when sneaking out of school: down to the end of the hall and out through the little arched door onto the stone staircase. 'Alice?' she whispers and it seems to hiss down the stairs. There is no reply. She bends to put on her boots, her cold fingers stumbling over the laces, and then starts slowly down, switching on her torch so that she can pick out each step as it curves away from her. Where can Alice be? Where has she gone, and why?

Julia knows that there is only one place that Alice would be heading.

But why? Why would she go there?

She catches herself up with a rush of unexpected sadness. *Where else can she go? Who else can she tell?*

But would it really be so bad to go to Matron, or Miss

Allen or any of the other women here in the school? They're not monsters. When they saw Alice in trouble, in desperation, surely they would help her. But Alice lives by her own rules and her own idea of what the world should be. Whatever she sees in her future, Julia can guess that it is not being the naughty schoolgirl who surrenders herself in pregnant disgrace to the tongue-clicking disapproval of the spinsters in authority. She will want something grander and more dramatic than that.

Julia is on the ground floor now, and she tiptoes along, following the wavering beam of her torch, looking for signs of her friend, hoping that she has got onto her trail before she has gone too far. But there is no trace of her all the way past the changing rooms and out through the canvas sheeting into the pool room. Julia crosses it quickly, noticing that the wooden door at the end is already pushed ajar, and draws in a sharp breath as she looks at the world beyond. The snow has stopped and the sky is clear, shining with a huge silver moon that sets the snow glittering with millions of tiny twinkles. Across the fresh virgin snow that has fallen over the dirty building site, hiding its mud and filth and mess, there is a set of deep footprints leading towards the boundary between the school and the field where the caravans are.

Julia can't help gasping in horror. So she was right, the baby is coming. Why has Alice decided to set off like this? What can she hope to achieve? She hurries on, scrunching through the fresh snowfall, her breath coming in puffs of icy smoke, feeling afraid of what she will find at the end of this fantastical journey. She hardly needs her torch now, as the moonlight reflects on the snow's surface and lights up the way as if showing her the route to Alice.

The caravans are silent and dark as usual, each with its own heavy counterpane of snow under which it seems to snuggle. *Like bugs in a rug*, she thinks, and presses on towards the one at the back that belongs to Roy and Donnie.

As she rounds the corner of the van, she sees her: Alice, huddled in the snow, half crouching, half lying, her face twisted and her teeth bared. She is wrapped in a fur coat, one that Julia remembers her bringing back from home after Christmas, laughing about how she took it from her mother's wardrobe without asking, and the fur is sprinkled with clumps of snow as though she has been rolling in it, like a winter bear taking a bath.

'Alice!' She dashes forward as fast as she can through the snow, drops her torch and kneels down beside her friend, touching her gently on the arm as if half afraid to cause her more pain.

Alice is grunting and panting, her skin whiter than ever, her hair wet with sweat, her lips pale. She opens her eyes and sees Julia, a look of relief passing over her face, but cannot speak while the strange stifled moan is in her throat. Julia holds her, wishing desperately that she can remove the pain somehow, but she has no idea what to do. Fright races through her. This is serious. This is birth. What can she do?

Some of the tension leaves Alice and she relaxes a little into Julia's arms. 'You found me,' she whispers with a smile.

'What are you doing, you idiot?' Her fear makes her

sound petulant, but she knows Alice understands. 'Why did you come out here?'

'I wanted to . . . I wanted to have the baby on my own. So that . . . So that I can give it to Roy.'

'Roy?' Julia is astonished. 'But what makes you think he wants it?'

'It's my . . . gift. My . . . consolation.' Her eyes close and her face twists into a rictus again. A great groan comes up from within her, and she clenches her fist with the pressure of keeping it inside. Her mouth is tightly shut. Only a high, quiet sound comes out on the night air. Julia guesses that Alice is doing all she can not to wake the occupants of the caravans.

'You can't stay here,' she says, as soon as she sees that the pain has passed. 'It's freezing. You can't have a baby out here in the snow. Come on.'

'I can't move,' Alice says, her tone almost cheerful. 'I can't walk any further.'

'All right. Then you'll have to wait here for just a moment.' Panic flares in Alice's eyes. 'Don't leave me!' She grips Julia's hand with a tight, cold grip. 'I thought I could do this alone. But I can't.'

'I won't leave you – not for more than a minute. But we have to get some help.' Julia scrambles up in the snow and heads for Donnie's caravan. Instead of knocking at the door, she goes round to the back to the window. There's no time for tentativeness now – she raps as hard as she dares. A few seconds later, the curtain is pushed aside and she sees Donnie's face, bleary with sleep, looking out at her.

She mouths one word. 'Help.'

He rubs his eyes, squinting at her, and then seems to grasp that this is an emergency. He mouths back, 'Two minutes,' and disappears from view. Julia goes back to the door and waits, her arms wrapped around herself, hopping on the spot against the cold. She can only think of Alice, worried for her in the snow alone, and she hears the low muffled wail of another rush of pain.

How long now? How close is she?

The door opens and Donnie stands there, dressed but without a coat. 'Hell's fire,' he says, shuddering. 'It's freezing out here. What are you doing here?'

'It's Alice. She's over there. She's having the baby.' Julia points to the strange huddled shape in the snow that's rocking gently. 'We have to get her inside.'

'What?' A look of horror crosses Donnie's face. 'The baby's coming? She can't have it here!'

'She can't have it in the snow,' Julia says firmly. 'We're coming in. You have to help me, she can't walk.'

Donnie gapes at her, and then sees that she is not to be denied. The seriousness of the situation will not allow it. 'Holy Mary,' he says, looking suddenly like a young boy. 'All right. Come on then.'

They go over to Alice, and find her in a strange state, almost as though she is asleep, although the whiteness of her face makes her look more like a corpse. Julia is panicked until she groans as Donnie struggles to get an arm underneath to lift her.

'You take her other side,' he directs, panting a little. 'We can both do it if we lift together.'

Somehow they manage to hoist Alice up, supporting her with their arms beneath hers. Her head lolls a little and she is a near dead weight, so they half carry, half drag her across the snow to the caravan, and then up the steps and through the open door. Once inside, Donnie lowers Alice gently to the floor and looks over her at Julia.

'You're going to have to do it,' he says. 'You're a woman. You know about these things.'

'I don't know anything!' cries Julia in a panic.

'You know more than I do.'

'What about Roy? Where is he? His wife has had children, he'll know what to do.'

Donnie looks grim. 'First off, he's lying in his bed through that door and he's flat-out drunk. He's had near on a bottle of whiskey tonight; he wouldn't wake if it was the Second Coming itself. And second, if he was awake, he'd be useless. No man sees the birth of his children, it's not right. We need a woman, and you're it.'

Alice starts to moan again. The force of her pain silences them both: they can only witness it, watching the animal nature of it, and the startling way her body won't be deviated or stopped. It has a job to do, and nothing will prevent it now that it has begun.

Donnie and Julia look at each other. 'You'd better get her things off,' he says. 'The baby is coming.'

*

It's the beauty of it that strikes her the most. She's always imagined that childbirth must be ugly, but it isn't at all. In the light of the lantern, Alice's belly is velvety smooth, huge and ripe. She lies on the old blanket that Donnie puts down for her, and, clutching at Julia's hand, she allows herself to surrender to the mysterious forces possessing her. She never screams, but moans and wails with her mouth closed as pain grips her in ever closer pulses, and yet, she somehow relaxes too, as though she knows that she can deliver the baby, now she is sheltered and cared for. Donnie walks around the tiny space of the caravan, most of it taken up with the two girls, occasionally looking but mostly trying not to, as though he wants to preserve Alice's modesty, even though she is lying naked on the floor, her belly rising and clenching with the force of the contractions.

Julia doesn't know how long they are there. It could be one hour or four. Time seems to concertina, shrunk by the patterns of Alice's labour, the wracks of pain that come and go, closer and closer together, until she is squeezing her eyes shut, her mouth wide, her hands painfully tight on Julia's, pushing down and down.

Julia looks at the junction of Alice's thighs, where everything is red and stretched and unrecognisable as any part of anatomy she has ever seen. It is so alien that it doesn't strike her as obscene or disgusting; it simply is what it is, and in the middle of the work it can and must do. Then she sees it. The curve of a skull coming down through the dark red orifice and out into the world. It halts its progress as Alice

344

gathers her strength for the next onslaught and then, as she pushes, the little head presses further out.

'It's almost here! Oh, well done, Alice, well done! Another push, another push!' Julia has washed her hands and now she reaches down, ready to take hold of the child when it emerges. Donnie hovers nearby, tension all over his face, expectation in his eyes.

Alice allows a cry to escape as she pushes down again, and suddenly it happens more quickly than Julia can anticipate. With a sudden slither and a gush of water and blood, the body slides out of Alice's and into Julia's waiting hands. It is tiny and perfect, a thick purplish cord connected to its small round belly and then wrapped around its neck, where its face is perfectly still and blue.

Chapter Twenty-Eight

Olivia is quietly furious.

'What was going on in there?' she says, spooning food into Bea's mouth. She has no patience with her daughter's attempts to feed herself today, but Bea doesn't like being deprived of the fun and is whining and resisting.

'Nothing,' says Dan. He is feeding a more compliant Stan, who likes being fed and is opening his mouth for the spoonfuls of rice and stew.

'She had her hand on your leg!'

'She put it there for a moment. It doesn't mean anything. You know what she's like, touchy-feely and all the rest of it. Besides, if you'd give me a chance to explain, I'd tell you that I've actually asked her to go.'

'You have?'

Dan nods. His expression is cross and sulky. 'Yes.'

'And what did she say?' Olivia asks, diverted from the source of her anger and fear. The sight of Francesca and Dan on the sofa together has shaken her. It has given her the unpleasant notion that something is going on between them of which she knows nothing.

'She was about to tell me when you came in. But I think she's going to give it some thought.' He shoots her a wry look. 'You never know, we might get our lives back sooner than you think.'

Francesca has left them to it, perhaps sensing that the atmosphere is less than welcoming. She is normally keen to offer a hand when it comes to feeding the children and positively relishes the bedtime routine, the one that floors Olivia every evening: the supper, the cleaning up, the baths, stories and sleep rituals that the twins like to draw out for as long as possible.

'Can you ask her again?' Olivia urges. The idea of life without Cheska, even if it means less help with the childcare, seems very appealing. It's been too much and too long. And, now she thinks about it, too intense.

Dan sighs irritably again, but says, 'All right. I don't want to get her back up, that's all.'

'I'm sure you won't. She is such an old friend after all. And, according to you, she might still have a sweet spot for you.' She looks up quickly to see how he will take this little needle.

He shoots her a look. 'I didn't say that. I said that years ago she might have had a little crush on me. She's just a friend now. Okay?'

'Okay, okay . . . Bea, please, another mouthful for me. Please.' She slides more rice into Bea's mouth and changes the subject. 'I thought I might go to London actually. I sent an email to my agent to see if I could have a chat with him about some future projects and ideas I've got.'

'All right. If you think it will help. When will you go?'

With a little yellow spoon, Olivia stirs the stew in the bowl she is holding and bites back a comment. It's always been like this. Her work has always been considered less than his because she didn't wear a suit and leave the house at 8 a.m. every day and stride off importantly to an office. It didn't bring in as much money as his, and it didn't have a regular pay cheque. And even though it was writing, which he rather admired, it was just garden writing, nothing intellectual. Not like his. But it was still her work and it helped to provide for the family. Now, in fact, it is all they have coming in. She wonders suddenly if Dan is jealous. She's been a moderate success, with her gardening books selling well enough to bring in some money each year. And she has an agent in London – a fairly useless one, but still – and now that Dan is embarking on a writing project, perhaps he suddenly and unexpectedly feels inferior. She thinks of Andrew, her agent, in his office in a tall building near Piccadilly Circus. She sent him an email today and he replied at once, somewhat to her surprise, offering to take her for lunch any day this week. He has an unusually quiet diary and can accommodate her whenever.

She says, 'I thought I'd go down the day after tomorrow. Is that okay?'

'Fine with me.' He shrugs. 'Whatever you want. I suppose Cheska can look after the kids, if she's still here.'

She glances over at him, cross and resentful. She has given

him all these hours to write a play that she hasn't yet laid eyes on and which appears to be no closer to being finished than it was when they arrived here. Now it seems as though he can't even be bothered to look after the children himself.

The image of him and Francesca close together on the sofa comes into her mind. *Should I leave them alone?* she wonders. Then she pulls herself up. *I'm being stupid. Dan has been off Cheska for ages. There's no way he wants anything to happen.* Then she thinks, *But what about Cheska? What does she want?*

She pushes the thought away. 'All right. I'll book my train ticket.' Then another thought crosses her mind. She will send another email tonight, one she's been meaning to send for ages. Perhaps it will help to answer the questions turning over in her mind.

Two days later, Olivia waits in the reception area of her agent's office. It is not a glitzy building and she has to climb three flights to get to his floor, but there is something undeniably glamorous about it. In the small entrance area are bookshelves with the recent work of the company's clients neatly displayed: picture books, paperbacks and weighty, serious hardbacks. There's nothing by her, of course. Her last book was too long ago to be out on show.

Behind the desk, a friendly girl, who has provided Olivia with water, taps away at her keyboard and, without warning, answers calls through her headset. The first time this happened, Olivia thought she was being spoken to and when the girl said, 'How can I help you?', she started to reply, saying, 'I'm fine, thank you, the water is lovely,' only to have the girl talk over her with, 'He's in a meeting right now. Can I ask him to call you back?' and then she guessed. It was embarrassing.

So now she keeps quiet and hopes it won't be too long before Andrew is ready to see her. It is a relief to be away from home. The atmosphere has been distinctly odd, ever since she walked in on Francesca and Dan on the sofa. Something about Francesca is distant and yet gleeful, while Dan seems both cross and on edge, as though something might set him off at any time. She can't understand why things seem to have changed, when they were all so harmonious just a short time before. *It's the price of living with people*, she thinks. *The strain starts to tell in the end. Maybe marriage is really just finding someone you can bear to live with full-time. Even then, it's hard.*

Dan drove her to the station this morning, still mulish and silent. It's the side of him she likes the least, when he decides to inflict his bad mood on her but won't tell her what caused it.

'Will you be okay today?' she asked, unable to shake the habit of concern for his welfare even when he's being sulky.

'Of course.' He sighed as he turned the car into the station car park and looked for somewhere to park.

'And you know where I left the twins' lunch? In the green tub on the bottom shelf of the fridge. Three minutes in the microwave, stir and leave for a minute. Check it's not too hot before they eat it.'

He shot her an annoyed look. 'I know. I've done their lunch before. We'll all be fine.'

'At least Cheska will be out of your way. The builders are going to start bulldozing the old pool, aren't they? She'll be overseeing that, I suppose.' She tried to sound cheerful. 'Let's hope we can't hear it when they start.'

Dan grunted.

'I'd better get my train,' she said. She leaned over to kiss his cheek, and then climbed out of the car and that was that. She can only hope he's snapped out of his mood by the time she gets back.

I'll go shopping in Piccadilly after this, she thinks, *and get him something nice as a present, to make up. I hate it when things are chilly between us.*

The girl at the desk suddenly says, 'Yes, I'll send her right in.' Then she looks over at Olivia and says brightly, 'Andrew will see you now. First office on the left down the hall.'

Andrew is happy to see her. He's changed a little since they last met, with markedly less hair, but he is a friendly, talk-ative man with a seemingly ceaseless interest in his business. They chat in his office, catching up with what's happened over the years since the twins arrived, and then he takes her out to a brasserie down a back street, not far from the bustle and grinding traffic of Piccadilly Circus. They weave through groups of tourists who stare up at the advertisements for Sony and McDonald's as though this is what they have come to London to see.

Lunch is very pleasant, the kind she hasn't had for a long

time. She eats a game terrine with fresh French bread and cornichons, and then a duck breast cooked with prunes and Armagnac, served with pureed potato and green beans. It's hearty, traditional stuff, and Andrew orders a bottle of very good red wine to go with it. She drinks two glasses and enjoys the light-headed feeling. It seems so decadent to be here, thinking only of her own pleasure, when at home Dan is doing the usual demanding routine of looking after two small children.

I will definitely get him a present, she thinks, feeling even more expansive after the wine. *Something really nice. Something he really likes.*

'So tell me about your possible projects,' Andrew says, turning to business as their plates are cleared. 'There's no reason why we can't get you a decent deal for a book if you've got an idea. The last did well. You're in a good place.'

'Well . . .' She feels a little shy, but she begins by talking about the research she did in Argentina.

'I like that idea,' Andrew remarks. 'There's not a massive amount of mileage in it as a how-to book but it would make a lovely coffee table piece. That's a definite maybe.'

Olivia feels more confident. 'And then there's this house we're living in right now,' she begins, and starts to tell him all about Renniston. His ears prick up at once, and when she starts telling him about William and the animal hedges, he's beaming all over his face.

'This is a wonderful story. And stately homes . . . well, we all know the very healthy market for those. A garden restored. A garden saved,' he corrects himself. 'One man's labour of love. A garden through history.' He nods. 'You could really do something with that. Do you have any photos?'

Olivia brings out her phone and scrolls through some of the pictures on it. She's taken some of the cottage garden and a few of the Hall gardens. There are plenty of the children too, which naturally distract them from the garden project.

'Who's this lady?' Andrew asks, pointing at a picture of Francesca holding Bea, the two of them smiling into the camera. 'Is that your sister?'

Olivia laughs. 'No. That's Cheska . . . I mean, Francesca Huxtable. She's the owner of the house actually. I'd need to get her permission to do a book on it, but I'm sure that won't be a problem. Why did you think she's my sister?'

'It's only because of the resemblance.'

'With me?' she asks, surprised. She's never thought they look at all alike.

'No, not with you. With the little girl. They've got the same colour eyes.'

'Have they?' She bends over the phone for a closer look.

'Yes. And they're both dark.'

'Oh. Yes. So they are. Well, Bea's not really that dark, it's just the light. But I can see why you would think that.'

Andrew sits back and picks up his wine glass. 'But as you're not related, it's obviously a coincidence,' he says. 'After all, you're their mother.'

'Yes,' Olivia says slowly. 'Yes, I am.'

*

Afterwards, when she and Andrew have said their goodbyes and she's promised to send him some material, she begins to walk down Piccadilly. Her happy mood over lunch has evaporated, although she is not entirely sure why. Still, she is determined to get Dan a present. First she walks into a gentleman's outfitters, a purveyor of country clothing, and spends a while browsing through the ties decorated with pictures of pheasants, and the plus-fours and plus-twos that look as though they have come from a P. G. Wodehouse story. She buys a pair of thick socks that she thinks will help combat the cold floors of the cottage, but nothing else is suitable. Dan isn't a country gent and isn't about to start wearing checked shirts and red cord trousers now.

Out on the street, she gazes into shopfronts and thinks about what he might like. She mustn't be too extravagant but she has enough money to get him something nice. Maybe a box of chocolates from Fortnum's. Then she checks her watch with a gasp. She'll be late. She almost forgot her other appointment. She puts Fortnum's out of her mind and hurries on towards the Patisserie Valerie on the edge of St James. As she gets closer, she sees a familiar figure sitting at a table in a window, the curly head bent over a magazine, and she rushes in.

'Claire, hello, sorry I'm late!' She drops her bag and sits down heavily in the chair opposite.

Claire looks up with a smile. 'Don't be silly, you're not.' She leans over for an embrace. 'It's lovely to see you, Olivia. It's been far too long! I'm so glad you emailed me. So, how on earth are you?'

Olivia has worried that the meeting with Claire would be awkward after all this time, but it isn't. In fact, it's lovely to see her. They talk quickly for a few minutes, while the waitress takes Olivia's order and then brings tea. Then Olivia starts to describe everything that's happened lately and, for the second time, she pulls out her phone and shows her favourite pictures of Bea and Stan to Claire, ones that don't feature Francesca.

'They're two and a half now,' she says proudly.

Claire looks up at her, her eyes sparkling with tears. 'I'm so happy for you, love. I remember what it was like for you in the early days, when it all looked so hopeless. I always prayed it would come right for you and Dan, and it has. They're beautiful. Doesn't Stan look like you? I mean, he's got Dan's colouring but there's a definite look of you.'

'I don't think so,' Olivia says with a soft laugh. 'They're IVF but not with my eggs. We had to use a donor in the end.'

'Really?' Claire colours lightly. 'I didn't know. How silly of me. I really did think he looks like you.'

'Good! Maybe he's getting some of my expressions just by being round me.'

Claire hesitates, then says, 'Do you mind me asking . . . what's it like? Having children who you know aren't related to you? I hope I don't sound like a buffoon, but I can't help wondering.'

'No, it's fine.' Olivia thinks for a moment. 'I suppose it's like having adopted children, but more intense. First, I know that they have a big bit of Dan in their make-up – how much is yet to be revealed. And second, I grew them inside me and gave birth to them, so they feel like mine. I mean, really and entirely mine. The hair colour and . . .' She suddenly remembers Andrew's comments about Bea's eyes and it shakes her, although she's not quite sure why. 'Well, all that doesn't really seem to matter,' she finishes a bit lamely. 'So it's all good. And how are *you*?'

Claire talks a little about her life since the divorce from Jimmy and the problems she's had with her oldest child and the strain of moving to a smaller house in a less convenient position, while Jimmy has moved into his new wife's ex-marital home in a very smart area of Islington. 'It sticks in the craw somewhat,' Claire says. 'His midlife crisis rewarded him with a younger wife, a nicer house, more money and only having the kids every other weekend, which is exactly how he liked it when he actually lived with us.'

'I'm sure he misses them,' Olivia says.

'Maybe.' Claire shrugs. 'So, what have I missed with the gossip? How is everyone? How is Cheska?'

'Cheska . . . well . . .' Olivia wonders where to start. A couple of months ago she would have said, 'It's all just the same – Cheska is one of our best friends.' But now she doesn't know quite how to answer. She tries to explain a little about the new arrangement and how it came about, realising as she does how strange it sounds.

Claire holds up a hand. 'Wait, hold on. Are you telling me that Cheska is now living with you and Dan and the children? In her house?'

'Not exactly living. Staying.'

'How long so far?'

'I don't know – three weeks or so? Maybe four.'

'And is she planning to leave any time soon? I mean, she still has a home in Geneva, right?'

'I don't really know when she's going. She told Dan soon, apparently. But builders have just arrived at the house, so she might be with us a bit longer.' She leans in towards Claire. 'If I'm honest, that's partly why I got in touch. I'm finding it all a bit weird. And I can't help wondering why she wants to muscle in like this. She's always been a bit of a mystery to me, and I thought you might be able to tell me a bit more about her.'

To her surprise, Claire starts to laugh, almost guffawing.

'What is it?' Olivia asks. 'What's so funny?' She frowns, a little hurt that she has been the source of such amusement. 'Claire . . . what's so funny?'

'I'm sorry! It's not funny at all. In fact, it's tragic. It's just—' Claire struggles for breath. 'It's just that after all these years, Cheska's dream is finally coming true.'

'What dream?'

'You must know!'

'No. About what?'

'About how she feels about Dan! I wondered if it had faded away over the years – I mean, she seemed relatively normal for ages – but obviously not. Hasn't he told you?'

'Well . . .' A nasty sick feeling is growing in the pit of her stomach. 'He said that she might have had a crush on him at some point in the past. At university. But I got the impression that it hadn't lasted beyond then.'

Claire rolls her eyes. 'Well, I never said anything because it didn't seem right just to bring it up apropos of nothing at all. You and she seemed so close as well, so either you knew, or it wasn't appropriate to mention it. Francesca did not just have a crush on Dan. She was obsessed by him. *Obsessed!* Well, you know that Dan was a bit of a babe magnet. He had girls after him all the time, he could take his pick at college. Jimmy and I used to laugh about it. He'd go to a party and look at a girl, and boom, she was his for the night. He literally didn't have to try at all. Of course he was handsome but it didn't hurt that he was also clever and funny and well read and all the rest of it. And then there was Francesca, who was such a timid little thing at first, in the same year, the same college, reading the same subject as Dan, and they were supervision partners.'

'Yes, she said that.' Olivia remembers Cheska talking about it, laughing about how she could never understand a word of Dan's essays.

'So they were friends and Dan obviously liked her. But not like that. At least . . .' Claire frowns and trails off.

'What?' Olivia asks, almost fearful.

Claire looks pensive. 'He . . . he was really fond of her. Almost protective at times. Because when she arrived, she was a bit of an outsider. Shy. Dressed incredibly tartily at first, in very silly high heels and tight skirts when everyone else was wearing Converse and jeans, but then acted like a maiden aunt half the time. She was odd.' Claire is evidently thinking back, remembering. 'She was clever, though, and quirky, and a bit different, and seemed to be going places.

Dan liked that. And he used her shamelessly, getting her to do half his work for him. I suspect he rather liked her puppy-ish adoration, the way she followed him around, obeying his orders. Once he bet Jimmy he could get her to go all the way to the cafe at the end of town to fetch him a particular kind of bun. Cinnamon or something. And she did. All the way there and back, to get Dan what he wanted. He could be a bit unkind.' Claire laughs suddenly. 'I remember seeing her trailing from library to library, trying to find him so she could sit and study with him. And at a party, she'd have her eyes glued to him, watching him work the room and pick up whoever he fancied. You could almost feel her agony. Poor thing, I did feel sorry for her. I don't even know if she realised how obvious it was.'

Olivia takes it all in, the picture she has had of Dan and Francesca's friendship resolving into something new and different. Perhaps she has always sensed that there was something like this below the surface, because she isn't surprised. It makes things fall into place, even while it raises new questions.

Claire says, 'Jimmy always thought that Cheska didn't get the First she was predicted because she spent so much time mooning over Dan. She was supposed to become a hot-shot lawyer, but that never happened either.' Claire shrugs. 'I don't think that was anything to do with Dan, though.'

Olivia says slowly, 'So Dan just . . . accepted her adoration, did he?'

'I think so. I don't really know, Olivia. I got the impression something happened between them – some kind of showdown. There was a scene at the May Ball, the last one we all went to together. Francesca and Dan went off alone for a very long time, from before midnight, and we didn't see them again until almost dawn. It looked like Francesca had been crying, but she was also happy and Dan had his arm around her. I wondered if they'd got together, but Jimmy was certain they hadn't. He said Dan just didn't fancy her. But . . .' Claire's expression becomes dreamy, remembering. Olivia can tell that she is seeing them all again, as they were years ago: young and dressed up in their ball gear, the future ahead of them, long before midlife crises and messy divorces and the pain of breaking up. 'She did look lovely that night.'

'Cheska?'

'Yes. She looked so pretty, I remember it. I think I have a photo of us all, on our way to the ball. I remember scanning it in to Facebook. If Dan was ever going to fancy her, it would have been that night.'

Olivia feels something cold in her chest, like a stone. All this is almost too much to take in. She feels torn between anger that she's never known the truth, and pity for Cheska's thwarted passion. She knows in her heart that Cheska is no threat. Dan doesn't love her, she's sure of it. *So why does she have some kind of hold over him? I can sense it. The way her hand was on his leg, it was like she knew she could do that and he couldn't say no.*

It didn't square with the picture of them at university: Cheska his faithful lapdog, him the swaggering Casanova, deciding whether or not to slake her passion.

She feels Claire's hand on hers and looks up into her sympathetic eyes.

'I'm sorry, Olivia, I didn't mean to upset you.' She looks remorseful. 'Cheska's nuts. She should have put it all behind her years ago. I can't believe she's still crazy about him after all this time.'

'You haven't upset me. Really. I didn't know, but it's not a shock. I know very well what Dan was like. Don't forget, I was almost put off by his arrogance.'

'I'm glad you weren't. I meant what I said, that stuff I wrote in your hen party book. He's been a better person since he met you. Honestly he has.'

She manages a smile. *I'm not so sure. Maybe he's just learned to act better.* 'Thank you.' Then she says, 'Do you know anything about her marriage to Walt? How that came about?'

Claire shakes her head. 'Not really. Only that it was sudden. Not long after we left university. She met him and almost immediately she got engaged. But if I'm honest, I don't think she ever stopped loving Dan, even though she pretended that was all in the past. I mean, we all just let it go and accepted that Cheska now loved Walt and her feelings for Dan had mellowed into friendship. Dan got together with you, and Cheska seemed fine with it.' Claire's expression changes swiftly, and she frowns.

'What?' presses Olivia. 'What is it?'

'Well, I just remembered your hen party. I caught an expression on Cheska's face when she was reading your book. It was . . . *pain.* I wondered if she had a headache or something. But now . . .' Claire looks over at her, her expression grave. 'Maybe her passion for Dan has never changed after all. If I were you, I'd get her out of the house. Or get yourselves out. But get away from her somehow. It's just not healthy.'

'No. You're right.' She realises that at this very moment, Francesca and Dan are at home together, with the children. Just the four of them. Without her. She has an overpowering need to be there, right now. Putting down her cup, she stands up, breathless. 'I'm sorry, Claire, I have to go. I've got to get my train. I need to go at once.'

Claire looks at her knowingly. 'Yes, you should. Take care, Olivia. I'll see you before too long, I hope.'

On the train home, Olivia cannot quell her feeling of anxiety. There is no more reason to be afraid now than there was this morning, she tells herself, and she was perfectly happy going off then.

She checks her phone but there is still no message from Dan. She phones him on his mobile but he doesn't pick up and she doesn't want to call the landline, just in case Francesca picks up. Instead she leaves a message on his phone.

'Hi, honey. I'm on my way home. I hope you had a good day and all is well with the twins. I'll be at the station at around five-ish, if you want to pick me up. I'll text the exact time when I've checked it. See you later, bye.' She rings off, wishing he had answered. The ability to communicate all the time is wonderful except when there is unexpected silence. What if something has happened to the twins and he is at the hospital with them, unable to check his phone? What if there has been a fire, and they are all lying in the ashes, the phone melted?

For goodness' sake, Olivia, calm down, you're being stupid. Everything is all right. In a couple of hours you'll be home and you can talk about everything with Dan.

She sits back in her seat and takes a few deep breaths, grateful that there is no one in the seat beside her and she can enjoy some privacy. The trolley comes past, pushed by a steward, and she buys a small bottle of white wine and a packet of peanuts. She wouldn't usually drink on the train in the afternoon but she feels the need to take the edge off her anxiety, so she pours out the drink, and opens the nuts. The wine is warm and bitter and she abandons it after just a sip or two, but she manages to eat the nuts, flicking through the day's news on her phone. Then a text pops up and she rushes to read it. It's from Claire.

Hi, Olivia. Lovely to see you today. Made me realise how long it's been. Let's keep in touch, I've missed you. Don't worry about Cheska, she's not all bad. By the way, take a look on Facebook, that picture is in my photos. I've sent you a friend request. Love Claire x

Olivia goes to Facebook and sees Claire's friend request. She accepts it and at once is able to access Claire's page and all her information. There are her photos, and she scrolls down through them until she sees the one she wants.

There they all are, familiar from photographs in Dan's

collection, standing in front of a college, dressed in their finery. It must be early in the evening as they all look well turned out and sober. She spots Claire in a bright red dress with matching lipstick, her hair up in a haphazard style.

Ouch. That's a bit nineties.

Then she spots Francesca, and remembers how Claire said she had looked really pretty that night. *She wasn't wrong. She looks lovely.* There's something timeless about her style: innocent and sweet, with a vintage charm. She's always thought of Francesca as polished and well turned out rather than attractive, but in this photo she looks rather adorable. She certainly stands out. And there, at the other end of the group, is Dan, unmistakable with his rakish good looks, his hair still plentiful and dark, his eyes intense as they stare out of the picture as though he knows he looks good in black tie and rather fancies himself as a pin-up.

Olivia studies the faces that stare out of the photograph, so familiar and yet so changed.

What went on between you that night? she wonders. Dan and Cheska stand so separate but by the end of the evening he had his arm around her. And she'd been crying. If Claire remembered it right.

She frowns. *But I know Dan. I know there hasn't been anything between them. I'm sure he would have told me.*

But, she reminds herself, she thought she knew Cheska too, and now she's beginning to doubt that. At once, she wants to scold herself for making the comparison.

Dan is my husband. I know him. I trust him. I know how his brain works.

Or . . .

Do I?

He never told her about Cheska's crush. He never breathed a word until she pushed at it and made him tell her. And then . . . She thinks back to the other thing about him that's always puzzled her, and the time she privately called the Dark Night of the Donor, when they argued and argued and she realised to her horror that he wasn't going to give in. Then, suddenly, he did give in. But she never knew why. What changed?

Olivia leans her head back against the train seat. They are flying along, the afternoon chalky blue sky outside like something from a Regency colour chart, and she is keen to get home. There is still no word from Dan, and she wishes he would get in touch. Another call to his phone brings his voice up on the answer machine but she can't bear to leave another message. He'll see the missed calls and know that she wants to reach him.

She can't understand why he hasn't been in touch all day. That's unusual. But she tries to put it out of her mind as the train brings her closer to home with every minute that passes. Instead, she thinks about the children. Later, when she's home and they're in bed, she will tiptoe into their rooms and kiss their sleeping faces, inhale their soft sweet scent and feel herself restored by the balm of their presence.

That's what she longs for more than anything else.

She urges the train onwards.

Home, home, home . . .

Chapter Twenty-Nine

May Ball, Cambridge, 1995

Francesca is excited. Her ball dress is exactly what she wanted: an emerald-green shantung silk, strapless, with a tiny tight waist and falling gently to her mid-calf. Underneath is a light underskirt and a layer of netting, just enough to swell the skirt out a little bit. The mid-calf length gives it a sixties look, which she has enhanced with a pair of shoes she found in a vintage clothing shop; with bright pink satin, long pointed toes and kitten heels, they are the real thing. Around her neck is a string of pearls – not real but looking very like it. Her hair, which is shoulder-length, has been teased up into an Audrey Hepburn beehive, around which she's tied another string of pearls, and her black cats-flick eyeliner, mascara'd lashes and pale lips complete the look.

She twirls in front of the mirror. She looks elegant, kitten-ish, pretty and sexy. Exactly as she wanted. Standing in front of her reflection, she takes a deep breath. Tonight is the night. She's going to do her level best. After all, she's spent three years watching Dan getting off with other girls. Now their exams are finished, and Cambridge will soon be over too. They'll be leaving in a couple of weeks. There is no saying when she will ever get another chance.

'This is my night,' she tells her reflection firmly. She is certain this is the best she has ever looked, and it feels as though all her years at Cambridge have been leading towards this point. She remembers how she arrived here, with the wrong clothes and the wrong accent, with no friends and no idea of anything except that she desperately longed to fit in with the gilded crowd – the clever, sophisticated ones from their private schools, with their confidence and drawling witticisms.

And now here she is: she knows how to dress and make a joke and smoke a cigarette and pop a champagne cork. She is about to meet her friends – a group of the university's brightest, best looking and funniest – and they will spend the evening drinking and dancing, celebrating the end of their university days and the beginning of the rest of their lives.

Francesca snatches up her wrap, slips her room keys, ball ticket and some money into her evening bag and hurries out to meet the others.

There are drinks first, in a pub near the college. The streets are thronging with ball-goers; the townspeople ignore them but the tourists are enraptured by the spectacle, taking photographs of the students in their finery. There are newspaper photographers out too, looking for the best-looking girls to snap for the tabloids, to show their readers how the posh kids spend an average Saturday night.

Jimmy, who has family money, buys two bottles of champagne and they drink them outside to warm up for the evening ahead, smoking cigarettes and talking.

Claire comes up to Francesca. She looks, Francesca thinks, distinctly ordinary although she's made an effort in a bright red satin dress with a matching jacket, her blonde hair in a kind of messy updo, and lipstick to match the dress, which is a mistake. Claire says admiringly, 'Cheska, you look gorgeous, you really do.'

Francesca smiles modestly but knows she looks polished and put-together next to Claire. 'Thanks. I found the shoes second-hand.' She lifts one to show it. 'Real sixties shoes.'

'Did you? That's clever! I'd never think of second-hand shoes. You can't help imagining verrucas, can you?' Claire wrinkles her nose and laughs. Dan looks over from where he is sitting talking to Stevie, and blows out a stream of cigarette smoke in their direction.

Francesca has the sudden urge to whack Claire across the face, but she restrains it and instead says placidly, 'They're from Harrods, so I don't think it's an issue.'

Jimmy comes over to top up their glasses. 'How's my little scarlet sex kitten?' he says, kissing Claire's cheek as he pours champagne for her. 'You look ravishing.'

Claire giggles and raises her eyes at Francesca as if to say, *What is he like?* But Francesca knows she adores Jimmy. Francesca lets him fill her glass, and compliment her extravagantly too, but the person she is really aware of is Dan. He is coming to the ball single tonight, since he split up with his last girlfriend – a loathsome girl called Emma – on a ticket shared with Stevie, who is habitually single. Stevie works so hard as a medic student that his preferred way of unwinding is with a lot of drink, some drugs and whoever is in the mood for him that night.

That's fine. Francesca has her back to Dan and Stevie as they sit at a table, talking and smoking, but she knows exactly what's going on. *He can keep Dan out of trouble and then, later, he can go off with someone he picks up at the ball.*

She isn't going to talk to Dan yet. Besides, she's going to play hard to get tonight. At first. She knows he expects her to come running whenever he clicks his fingers, so she's going to try ignoring him and see what happens.

In the event, just keeping her back to him at the pub works better than she could have expected. As they make their way along the cobbled streets towards the college, she finds Dan walking beside her.

'Would you like an arm?' he asks gallantly, holding his elbow out towards her. 'These cobbles are tricky in heels, aren't they? Although you're obviously making it look easy. You're gliding along like a duchess at Versailles.'

'Thank you.' She smiles and puts her hand on the rough wool of his dinner jacket. He is even more handsome in his evening clothes, a blue silk bow tie matching his eyes.

'May I say you're looking exquisite this evening.' He casts his gaze down over the shimmering emerald silk of her dress. 'Really lovely.' There's a tone of the very slightest surprise in his voice, but she doesn't mind. This is how it's supposed to go. Tonight he's going to see her differently for the very first time.

'How kind,' she says dreamily, as though barely hearing him. Then she turns and gives him a sweet smile. 'Dan, do you mind if I desert you for a moment? I must have a word with Stevie.' She takes her hand from his arm, gathers up her skirts and runs lightly away along the cobbles to where Stevie is walking alone, smoking, his shoulders hunched and his hand in his pocket.

This is the other part of her plan. She will give the attention she usually gives to Dan to someone else, and see what he makes of it.

At the college, they meet up with Alyssa and some of her crowd from another college. Francesca scans them anxiously looking for competition but no one is dazzling enough to prove too much of a threat. Though there's no telling with Dan, of course. His eye is a very wandering one, and there are so many willing targets. But she has a feeling that she has piqued his interest tonight, and she takes care to keep her distance, all the while maintaining her sparkling, sweet, smiling exterior, accepting all the compliments coming her way with a demure and girlish air.

They go into the ball and begin to explore. The college has been transformed into a funfair, with stalls and rides, a casino and several themed bars. There are tents on the lawns for dining and dancing. Magicians wander around performing tricks, and acrobats stun with their agility on tightropes strung over the quad. Fire-eaters douse flaming torches in their throats and pretty girls ride standing up on white ponies with glittering headdresses.

They go in for their dinner sitting, placed around a table

in the stuffy tent, the ice bucket in the middle crammed with bottles. Francesca makes sure to sit across from Dan, where he can see her but not speak to her without shouting over the bouquet of bottle necks between them. Dinner is perfectly acceptable – the usual college mass catering – but nothing special. They drink with more enthusiasm than they eat, and smoke between courses.

When dinner is finished, it's after ten o'clock and time to start enjoying the real fun of the ball. Francesca has been talking and flirting with Stevie, who seems mildly surprised and rather pleased by the attention he is getting. Now she begs him to take her on the dodgem cars that are set up on the back meadow, and they all go there. She gets into a car with Stevie, tucking her silk skirt under her and squealing as he steers them violently around the floor, a cigarette dangling from his mouth, his bow tie already hanging loose around his neck. Dan is in another car with Alyssa, and Jimmy and Claire in another. The floor is full of metallic shiny cars shooting back and forth, ramming into each other and flying around. Francesca realises with glee that Dan is steering his car after theirs, or cutting a corner to spin round into them and crash head on.

'Fuck off, Felbeck, you bastard!' roars Stevie. 'I'll have you!' and for a while they chase Dan, who seems to enjoy fleeing from them in sharp twists of the steering wheel. He looks so handsome, Francesca's insides go hot and melt a little more every time she sets eyes on him. It is a feeling she enjoys.

When the dodgems are over, she takes Stevie by the hand

and they go to the next ride, the helter-skelter, and after that, the merry-go-round, and then the swingboats. The others seem content to follow where she and Stevie are leading and they are all laughing and enjoying themselves. The last of the big rides is the Ferris wheel, set up so that the little rocking cars will give the ball-goers a splendid view of the college below and the vibrant, fairy-lit proceedings there.

'Come on, Stevie,' Francesca says, running for a seat in the car at the bottom. 'Let's ride up together.'

A voice at her side says, 'Actually, I'll take this one,' and Dan is there, climbing in beside her, while Stevie shrugs and waits for the next car to come along. They move up one shunt, so that they aren't far from the ground. Francesca, alive with excitement, and full of the power of her femininity, says nothing but inside she is revelling. She has Dan alone with her on the Ferris wheel, at his instigation. *Oh, this night is perfect already. It's completely perfect. But I mustn't spoil it.*

Playing it cool has got her this far, so she will carry on.

Without a word, Dan hands her a bottle of white wine he has been carrying and she takes a swig. They move another few feet into the air, the chair rocking gently under them. Soon all the chairs will be refilled with fresh riders and then they will start to turn properly. They have at least twenty minutes together, she reckons. There's no hurry. She passes the bottle back to Dan. They are both pleasantly drunk, uninhibited but perfectly capable of normal conversation. Still she says nothing.

Dan takes the bottle and has another swig himself. The

chair shunts on. Then he leans over to her and says in a low voice, 'What's the idea?'

'What do you mean?' she asks lightly, smoothing her skirt. She gazes out at the Cambridge summer night. 'Isn't this beautiful? Look at the view!'

'Don't change the subject, my dear,' he says strictly. 'What is the big idea?'

He is quite drunk, she realises, from the way he is carefully enunciating his words.

She looks at him over one bare white shoulder. 'You'll have to explain.'

'With Stevie,' he says patiently. 'Are you going to get off with him?'

She doesn't answer at once. Part of her brain is filled with scorn, both for him and for her. Why hadn't she done something like this before? Was it really so easy – all she had to do was play hard to get, flirt with another man and goad him to win her? But mostly she is thrilled and excited at what might be about to happen. He has never expressed any interest in her romantic life before.

'Well?' He passes her the bottle again and she takes another drink, not much this time. She doesn't want to get too drunk. It's still early. The ball goes on until sunrise.

'I'm not sure,' she says. 'Maybe.'

The chair shunts for the last time, and then the ride begins in earnest, the little swings sailing smoothly up into the night air. They will go around twice or three times before they start the process of disembarking in the same order, so that every chair gets the chance to halt at the top and rock there like a little cradle, the occupants enjoying the view spread out below.

They ride in silence, enjoying the peace up here, with the noise of the ball rising and falling in waves as they go round. Then the cars come to a stop again. The first riders start to climb out, letting new ones in.

'So,' Dan says languidly, 'you haven't answered my question, Cheska. What are you going to do tonight? Are you going to snog our friend Stevie?'

'I told you, I haven't decided.' She shrugs lightly. 'Anyway, what does it matter to you?'

He leans towards her, his expression earnest. His nearness is almost too much to bear. 'Because you're my supervision partner and therefore I have a responsibility towards you.'

She laughs. 'Oh, you do, do you?'

'Yes. I do. Ask any supervisor. It's the rule.' He sits back in the chair just as they swing upwards another level, almost at the top now. Once they are there, they will be invisible to everyone.

'Well, it's very sweet of you but I don't need looking after.'

'I'm not sure about that,' he says. 'You don't know what Stevie's like. He's an animal.'

'Whereas you are the perfect gentleman.' She shoots him another coquettish look. 'At least I know I have nothing to fear from you.'

'Oh, really?' He smiles, his eyes narrowed, looking at her in an appraising way she has never seen before, one that makes her skin tingle and sends a fizz of pleasure shooting around her stomach like a pinball in a machine.

'We've been friends all this time,' she says softly, 'and you've never tried anything before now.'

The chair jerks lightly upwards. They are at the top, swinging gently, unseen by everyone. He leans towards her again, his arm resting behind her shoulders.

'Maybe that was my mistake.'

She shuts her eyes, and breathes out slowly. This is her dream, happening now. Actually happening. The next moment, she feels his hand on her jaw, turning her face gently towards him and his lips land on hers, kissing her. It's the most wonderful kiss she's ever known: his soft mouth against hers, then their lips opening to each other, and the meeting of his velvet tongue, the unbearably delicious taste of him, the scent of his skin close to hers. Everything in her wants to yield to him and possess him at the same time. A voice in her head says, *At last. At last he's seen me. He's really seen me. He feels the same way.*

They kiss, deeply, until the car jerks again and they move downwards. Now there are only a few minutes until they reach the bottom and have to disembark. They part slowly, drawing away from one another as their eyes stay locked.

'So, have I dissuaded you from Stevie?' he asks with a grin, stroking her bare shoulder with his fingertip.

'Hmm. I'm not sure.' She wonders if she has any lipstick left now that she has been so wonderfully and completely kissed. Someone seems to have lit a row of sparklers in her belly and they are fizzing and glittering delightfully. She wants to be kissed again as soon as possible.

'Not sure?' He raises his eyebrows. 'I must be losing my touch.'

'You must be,' she returns. They can be seen from the ground now, and she knows there's no question of another kiss. 'May I have another drink, please?'

He passes her the bottle and she takes a deep draught, then sighs. The evening, so far, is bliss.

On the ground, they act as though nothing has happened. She plays a more delicate game now, withdrawing her attentions a little from Stevie, though not completely, and turning them more to Dan, but not so much as to make him think she is a done deal. She intends for him to chase her, and he does. The kiss must have pleased him. When they go to the tent to watch the headline act, a famous band performing their biggest hits, he dances with her although she makes sure to spin away and dance with the others too. But she is triumphant. He wants her still.

Dan is hot and sweaty in his dinner jacket. He heads to the bar at the back of the tent for a drink and she takes her opportunity, following him. He glugs down a glass of water, and buys a bottle of champagne for them all to share. As he goes to leave the bar, she grabs his hand, stands on tiptoe so she can bring her mouth to his ear, and says, 'Why don't we take that outside?'

He looks down at her with a knowing half-smile and nods. They go together through the back door of the marquee and head out into the soft summer darkness.

She already knows where she will take him. It is all

planned. At the side of the college there is a walled garden, closed to ball-goers, but with a little gate that is seldom locked. There in the garden they will have some privacy. She takes him to the big oak tree that grows at the back, and they sit together under its spread of branches, in the semi-dark. Stars glitter high above them in the blue night and a gibbous moon shines its three-quarter light. Dan pops the champagne and hands her a plastic cup he took from the bar. They light cigarettes and smoke them, talking lightly about nothing much, letting the tension between them rise pleasurably.

'So,' he says when he's stubbed out his cigarette, 'did you like our kiss?'

'Of course.' She lies back beside him on the cool grass, her shoulder blades resting against the softness, her arms raised above her head in abandon. 'Did you?'

'Too much,' he says.

'Oh. Good.' She smiles at him, winsome.

'Who are you, Francesca?' he asks, picking a blade of grass and running it down her face and over her nose.

'Who do you want me to be?'

'What kind of answer is that?'

'I want to be the girl you kiss tonight.' *And every night.*

'I think we can arrange that.' He moves towards her and slowly, tantalisingly, he puts his mouth on hers and kisses her. She knows she is lost.

They lie on the grass for a long while afterwards. She pulls her skirts back down and gets him to zip up the back of her dress. The mood has changed since the passion built up between them is spent. She feels luxurious and complete but he seems melancholy and a little distant.

'Are you all right?' she asks, taking a cigarette from him and lighting it. *After all*, she thinks, *what is living if not smoking a cigarette and drinking champagne after making love in a Cambridge garden to the man you adore?* The thought makes her want to laugh.

'Of course.' He lights his own cigarette and they both sigh out smoke on long exhalations.

She hums lightly and reaches for the champagne. The night is not over yet. They smoke for a while, passing the bottle between them.

'Cheska,' he says carefully after a while, when they have stubbed out their cigarettes.

'Yes?'

'You know what just happened . . .'

'Yes.' She giggles throatily. 'Of course.'

'I . . . I shouldn't have done it.'

She freezes. 'What? What do you mean?'

'I don't mean it wasn't lovely,' he says hastily. 'It was. But . . . we got carried away a little. By the night and the way things have been for us, our friendship.' He laughs a little sheepishly. 'I guess this was bound to happen. But it's a kind of goodbye, isn't it?'

She stares at him in shock. In her fantasy, this was the beginning of their life together, not the end. Once they kissed, he would know it was right. He would understand the power of their connection, the inevitability of their being together. He looks away as though he can't take the expression on her face.

'Dan.' She moves towards him on the grass, taking his hand. 'What are you saying?'

'You know this is just a one-off . . . a lovely, sweet happening but only for tonight . . . You understand that, don't you, Cheska?'

Grief wells up in her. All her pleasure drains away as though it has never been there at all. Nothing seems to have any point if she can't have Dan. She lifts his hand and presses it to her face, kissing it, tenderly at first and then with passion. Is this really the last time he will be hers? Can it really have been so brief? It's too much to bear. Tears rise up in her and pour from her eyes, wetting his hands and trickling through his fingers.

'Oh, Cheska, little Cheska,' he says gently, as if moved by her sadness.

'Dan . . .' She looks up at him, her eyes wet. 'I love you. You know that. I always have, since the first day I saw you. I'm not like those other girls, the ones who fall at your feet and fancy you rotten because you're handsome. I love you – *you*. I know you're arrogant and selfish and conceited, but you're also clever and sweet and talented. I know everything about you. My world revolves around you. I can't live without you. I'll do anything, anything.'

She knows she's abasing herself, undoing everything she tried to achieve earlier, but she can't help it. He has to know now, here, in this beautiful garden, because this is her last chance and she knows that her grief is touching his heart.

She bows her head over his hand again, holding it to her heart. His lips touch her head, and then his hand strokes her hair and her neck.

'Cheska,' he whispers.

'I love you,' she says meekly. 'Always.'

He lifts her face to look at her. 'Cheska, I'm half in love with you too, you know that.'

Her soul wells up with hope. 'Really?'

'Yes.'

'Then we can be together?'

'Of course we can. Yes.' He sounds firm, determined. 'We will.' He bends to kiss her again. 'Why the hell not?'

She falls back into his arms, more hungry for him than before.

Chapter Thirty

When Dan drives Olivia to the station first thing in the morning, Francesca feels a sense of calm mixed with a need to prepare for what she feels will be an important occasion. She is looking forward to spending the day without Olivia, relishing the opportunity to experience what it is like for the four of them to be alone together. It will help her understand what must be done.

Dan has had it his way all these years. I did what he wanted. Now he has to do what I want.

She is not entirely sure what that is. She had decided it was sending Olivia away but now she is not so certain. Besides, it would not be easy. Olivia is bound to kick up a fuss about that. So there has to be some other way of establishing her rights over the children, allowing her to share them somehow.

Perhaps I should tell her. Explain. Maybe she wouldn't mind my sharing, once she knows the truth.

While she ponders this, she spends a happy morning with the twins, playing with them in the garden and inside on the play mat. She is expecting Dan at any minute but he doesn't come back for ages and she starts to suspect that he has gone into town to do some shopping or have a coffee somewhere. *Perhaps he's trying to avoid me. I wouldn't be surprised.*

The long-buried feelings of hurt are beginning to rise to the surface. She has spent nearly a lifetime keeping them hidden, but they are bubbling up without her even really wanting them to. Flashes of the past start coming into her head, reminding her of what she gave him and what he took.

I let him forget it. I never punished him for it. And then, when he needed me, I was there for him. I helped him.

She doesn't remind herself that she was the one who made the suggestion, and who pressed her offer on him even when he seemed reluctant, precisely so that she might finally regain some power over him. She doesn't want to think about that, and she won't think about that.

Instead she tells herself again that he has had it all his own way for too long. Then she looks at the children with glee. *But not anymore. Now there are the twins. He can't make me erase them. He can't rub them out. He can't make me pretend they never happened.*

When her phone rings mid-morning, Francesca thinks it must be Dan calling to say where he is but she doesn't recognise the number. Instead, she hears the voice of the builder she has hired to demolish the old pool.

'Mrs Huxtable? It's Terry Ellis here. I just wanted to let you know that we're on site. We're getting ready to start the demolition work. I wondered if you'd like to come round and take a look before we begin.'

'Well . . .' She looks over at the twins, who are playing with the train set she has put together for them. It will do them good to get a little air. 'Yes. Yes. I'll come round. Give me twenty minutes.'

By the time she has the twins dressed and in their jackets, and has given them a snack – she didn't mean to but she can't resist their smiling pleas for biscuits and rice cakes – it is more like forty minutes before they are walking down the broad avenue at the back of the house.

The children get excited as they approach the avenue and start shouting about rabbits and cats and owls but Francesca can't see what they mean, and anyway she is in a hurry to get to the building site and have a look at what Mr Ellis is up to. They finally round the eastern wing, which really is a horrible sixties mess in Francesca's opinion, and can't be gone soon enough. She can see the bulldozers brought on site by large trucks, and men in hard hats walking about, taking measurements and staring up at the building, talking in earnest voices about what needs to be done.

As she nears them, a man leaves the others and walks towards her, holding out his hand. 'Morning, Mrs Huxtable. Glad to see you. As you can see, we're getting ready to make a start.'

'Morning, Mr Ellis.' She smiles politely, and lets go of Stan's hand to take the builder's and shake it. 'How long until you can start knocking it down?'

He turns to observe the brick building that houses the old

pool and gymnasium. 'We've got some surveying to do yet, but it won't be long. The boys are looking forward to it. They always enjoy a bit of demolition. The walls and ceiling will come down pretty quick, and then we're basically carting away debris. As we get on with that, we'll start digging out the old tiles from the pool itself. Then we're ready to start anew at about the same time. I've got the plans if you want to have a look.'

'No, that's all right. I don't want to hold you up,' she says. Bea is straining at her hand, trying to get away. 'What are you doing, Bea? Stop pulling like that.'

'Then we'll get on,' Mr Ellis says. 'Are you stopping around for the knocking down? It won't be too long now.'

'Oh no. I'd like to, but it's a little dangerous with the children.' She looks about for Stan, whose hand she was holding a moment ago. 'Stan?'

'You had two, did you?' Mr Ellis says. He looks about as well. 'Where's he gone?'

A nasty sick fear churns through Francesca. She looks about for the bright pink jacket that Stan wears, but she can't see it. 'He was here a second ago.' She calls out, 'Stan! Stan!' There's no answer and he's nowhere to be seen. 'Stan, where are you?' Panic is rising in her voice. She's suddenly aware of the enormous number of dangers in the immediate vicinity, from the huge bulldozers lumbering slowly but crushingly over the churned-up soil to the piles of tools and the open doors that lead into the abandoned building. If Stan has wandered into the house, he could be lost forever.

'Oh my God,' she says, real fright in her voice now. She is

shaking, her heart pounding so violently it threatens to prevent her from speaking.

'We'd better find the little fellow,' the builder says grimly. 'Hold on to that one, will you?' With a shake of his head, he adds, 'Small kids, the bane of my life on a building site. Why do people bring them?' He strides off, calling to his men, alerting them to Stan's absence.

Francesca picks up Bea and holds her wriggling body close. 'Come on,' she says breathlessly, looking wildly about. 'We have to find Stan.'

The builders are passing on the news of the missing boy to one another and beginning to search the site. But what if he's not there at all? What if he's wandered further off? There are so many places he could be. An image erupts in her mind. *The pond in the rose garden.* She sees the little figure leaning out to touch the surface of the water and toppling in. At once, she starts off along the long walk behind the house, in the direction of the rose garden. Bea jolts in her arms, too surprised by the sudden movement to do more than cling on to Francesca and whimper.

As she races along the walk, past the topiary, she is frantic with panic, nauseous with the thought of having to tell Dan and Olivia that she has lost Stan. She longs to see his little figure with such ferocity that it feels as though she can will him back. But the seconds tick past and there's no sign of him.

How far can he have got? He was only out of my sight for a moment. She sends up a prayer. *Please, please, let me find him . . .* All she knows is that she has to reach the pond as soon as possible. The thought of the little body floating in the dark water drives her on.

I can't lose him . . . not my boy . . . my baby . . . I can't lose my baby . . .

Bea has had enough of the wild run and starts to struggle in Francesca's arms. 'Down, down!' she cries and tips herself over so that she can fall from Francesca's arms.

Francesca tries to hold her firm, forced to slow her pace. 'Stop it, stop it, you'll fall! We have to look for Stan!' She struggles with the child but Bea doesn't care about Stan or about what Francesca wants. She only wants to pursue her own desires, no matter what. She pushes herself further out of Francesca's arms, not seeming to mind that she will plummet to the ground and hurt herself. Francesca is full of anger, frightened and frustrated, desperate to get to the pond. There are only seconds in which to act if Stan has fallen in. But she has to stop, clutching on to the little girl as she twists and writhes, trying to slip free.

'Bea!' she yells. 'Stop it! Don't you understand? Stop doing that!' With her free hand, she strikes the little girl across her cheek. The blow is sharp rather than hard, but Bea gasps and is still, then pulls in a huge breath and begins to cry, her palm over the place where Francesca has hit her. At once, Francesca is mortified, appalled at herself. 'I'm sorry, I'm sorry, Bea.' She tries to kiss the child, who turns away sobbing.

'Mummy, Mummy!' Bea says through her tears. 'I want Mummy.'

'I'm your mummy!' Francesca says, pleading. 'I didn't mean to get angry. I'm scared about Stan.' Her own eyes are full of tears; she's about to start sobbing too. 'I'm your mummy!'

'No, no.' Bea twists to get away from her. 'I want Mummy. I want Mummy!' She starts to howl in earnest, and Francesca begins to cry as well, in fright and despair and remorse.

What am I doing? I don't want to hurt them!

'Put the girl down.' The order comes in a rough, accented voice that's cracked with age but full of command.

Francesca looks up, her vision blurred with tears. The old man, the gardener, is striding towards her. 'I've lost the boy,' she manages to say through Bea's wails.

'That's no excuse,' he answers harshly, 'for hitting a child like that. What were you thinking? Put her down.'

Francesca obeys meekly, letting Bea down gently where, now she has her way, the little girl clings to her legs, her wails subsiding into whimpering sobs. 'I'm sorry, I didn't mean to hurt her, but she was struggling, she was going to fall. I need to find Stan.'

'What would she say? Their mother? If she could see this now, what you're doing with her children?' The old man fixes her with his faded but intense stare. His mouth, wide and surrounded by the deep lines of age, is tight with disapproval. 'Children are precious. Easily hurt. Easily lost.'

Francesca is ashamed that he should see her like this, tearful and afraid, humiliated. But she also needs him. 'Will you help me find Stan?'

William says roughly, 'I'll do it for her, not for you. And on one condition. You keep those little ones away from that pool, do you understand? As far away as you can.'

'Yes, yes, I understand.' She sniffs, her panic still swirling through her body. Without Stan, nothing can be right. 'But please, the pond . . .'

'He's not there.' The old man turns on his heel and heads back along the walk, his old tweed jacket flapping around him. 'I think I know where we'll find him.'

She follows, picking up Bea, who doesn't resist. The little girl has stopped crying, the mark on her cheek has faded and she seems to have forgotten the slap. She holds tight to Francesca, her fingers digging hard into her skin. Francesca is still afraid but she is also grateful that there is someone else to share this awful burden with, and hope springs up that the old man is right and Stan is nowhere near the pond. He leads them back along the walk to the topiary hedge and begins to inspect the hollows within the carefully trimmed figures. He's bent over almost double as he looks under the wall of green to the darkness inside, and then suddenly he darts forward and she sees a flash of pink. The next moment he is guiding Stan out into the open, his jacket bright magenta against the hedge.

'Here he is,' he says, his tone more gentle than she has ever heard. 'I've found him.'

Relief crashes over Francesca in a huge wave. 'Stan! Oh, thank God. Stan . . .' She hurries towards him, Bea still in her arms. Stan has dirty streaks over his face but he gazes up at her with round eyes and says simply, 'Wabbit.'

Francesca laughs and sniffs at the same time. 'What do you mean?' She bends down and picks him up, her arms full of both children but unable to put one down in case she loses them, and kisses his face. 'Oh, Stan, you gave me a fright, such a horrid fright!' Then she turns to the gardener, who's observing her with an unreadable expression. 'Thank you. Thank you so much. Thank you for helping me.'

'I helped the children, not you. And if you ever raise a hand to either of them again, you'll have me to deal with, understand? Just remember what I said. You're not their mother.' He lets his words hang in the air, and this time, she has to accept them. Everything between her and this old man has changed, and she can say nothing in reply. Something in his words chimes in her.

I'm not their mother.

'I'll tell the men the boy's been found. You take them home.' William turns and strides off down the walk.

She gently puts the children down and they trot back to the hedge, clearly fascinated by it. They're both quiet now, docile, prepared to allow her to look after them.

They don't love me the way they love Olivia and they never will.

She has never considered that the twins might not want her to be their mother, or that they might not care that they were grown from her eggs. She thinks about the blow across Bea's face and knows that she never touched Fred or Olympia in such a way. And she knows, too, that if Stan had been lost, Olivia's grief would have been the darker and more desperate.

He's right. I'm not their mother. Nothing can change that.

The realisation seems to break open inside her, spilling out a clear-sightedness that is calm and almost soothing. Her plan to displace Olivia and take the twins for herself appears almost fantastical suddenly, a strange, delirious dream imagined under the influence of something hallucinogenic.

That's not the answer. That's not what I really want. But what is?

Francesca knows she has to take the children home, where they belong. She goes to the twins, takes a pudgy hand in each of hers and starts to lead them back towards the cottage.

When she gets back to the house, Dan has returned and he comes out to greet them with an air of anxiety. 'You're back. Is everything okay?'

'Everything's fine,' she says, outwardly calm now. 'We just went to see the builders, that's all.'

'Really? The builders are here?' He puts his arms out to the children, who come running. With a trace of irony in his voice, he adds, 'So something's finally happening.'

'What do you mean?' she says, unable to resist pouncing on his remark, baited by his tone.

'Come on, children, let's go in for lunch. It's all ready.' The twins, chattering away, obediently take his hands and trot at his side as he says over their babble, 'Well, you've been here for over a month. And absolutely nothing has happened until now. And you don't really need to be here for the demolition either, do you?' He speaks casually, as though he isn't throwing down the gauntlet. Does he want to quarrel with her? She isn't sure, but she needs to decide how to react.

She says nothing as they go inside. Dan washes the children's hands and puts them at the table in front of the plates loaded with their lunchtime sandwiches. Perhaps she imagined that he was setting the scene for a fight. After all, he's in no position to do so. She holds all the cards.

She watches as he goes about the usual task of feeding the twins. Whenever she tries to help, he stands between her and the children, preventing her from doing anything. She would protest if it weren't for the heavy burden of guilt that weighs her down. She nearly lost Stan. Imagine how it could have been if she'd been responsible for harm coming to him . . . Her magical, almost divinely inspired connection to them is not infallible after all. She sits back and watches him bustle about, realising that she is happy to relinquish the children to him. Something in her is beginning to cut them loose and set them free.

They're not mine. I see that now.

But she senses that Dan is spoiling for some kind of confrontation, and she knows that she is ready for it. It isn't about the children at all. Perhaps it never was. It is about them – Francesca and Dan – and the past.

When Dan takes the children up for their nap, she puts out some things for their lunch, trying to calm herself. There is a crackle in the air, like the tension that comes with an approaching storm. As she lays the table, she thinks that this could be their one opportunity. Olivia isn't here after all. They're alone together.

She has a mixture of fear and excitement simmering inside her, like stage fright. But she knows she is ready. He wants to shut her up and make her go away. He wants her to let him get away with it, just as he's got away with everything in the past.

If that's what he wants, he's in for a surprise.

After twenty minutes, Dan returns and wordlessly sits down to eat the soup she has put out for him. She feels something inside her harden at his hostility.

So he is going to take me on. All right then. Let's see what happens.

Dan pushes his empty soup bowl away and takes a breath, his brow furrowed and his mouth unsmiling. He says slowly, 'I think you know that there's a situation here, Cheska. I've given it a few days to settle since we spoke the other night and it comes down to this. Either you leave, or we do. This can't go on.'

'Why not?' she asks lightly but she has a prickle of half-excited apprehension on her palms.

He leans towards her across the table. 'Cheska, you know it can't. That thing you said, about how we're a family. It's not true.'

'Yes it is. You know it is.'

'No.' He speaks slowly, as though this will somehow convince her more thoroughly of his point of view. 'You and Walt and Freddie and Olympia. You're a family. You should be with them, not with us.'

The names echo in her ears. It seems an age since she has thought about them with any kind of intensity. Their images flicker through her mind like the contents of an old photograph album. *Why has it been so long? I miss them.* She feels a sudden yearning for her children.

Dan is watching her, the furrow between his brows growing deeper. 'You know we're not your family, don't you, Chcska?'

Irritation surges through her. She turns to face him. Once she loved that handsome face of his. Now she sees the meanness in his eyes, the selfishness in the turn of his lips. He will give her nothing, even now, after all this time. But, for the first time in their long relationship, she's ready to fight. 'Not a family? How can you say that, Dan? You can't fight biology! You know very well that we are a family, because we're parents. You and I. We are the parents of those children. I am their mother.'

There. It is out. She's said the great unsayable, the thing that has been bubbling up in her for weeks. *Not weeks. Years. Ever since they were born.*

He stares at her, his eyes cold. 'Parentage is more than biology. You might be the genetic half of the babies but that doesn't make you their mother.'

'But it does, Dan, and you can't pretend you don't think so.' Her voice is sharp now. She's glad to be confronting him at last. She's always been so afraid that at any moment he could reject her and toss her out of his life without regret. She knew that she needed him much more than he needed her. She was always at the mercy of her deep longing for his love. But now she has the power. He can't treat her with contempt. He has to listen and accept what she has to say. 'Why was it so important to you that you had a donor you knew? Precisely because you care about the genetic half of the children to such an extent you were prepared to have no children at all rather than risk it. How can you say I'm not their mother, when you yourself value my input so much? You wanted my Cambridge mind and all that intellectual potential.'

'It's different, and you know it is. Olivia gave birth to them. She is raising them. They love her and she loves them.'

Francesca stares at him with all the intensity she can muster. 'I love them too. Because they are part of me. Can't you see it? Bea even looks like me! Don't you think that Olivia is going to guess one day?'

'No, she won't. Why should she? I don't think Bea even looks that much like you, and she's bound to change as she grows up. Are you a carbon copy of your parents?'

Francesca laughs bitterly. 'You want it the other way now, don't you? Now you've got what you want. Beforehand there was nothing so important as the identity of the egg donor. Now it means nothing.' She shakes her head. 'You can't have it both ways, Dan.'

He stands up, and walks over to the countertop, taking his plate. It is something for him to do, to aid a change of tone. When he turns back to her, his expression is softer, puzzled. 'I don't understand, Cheska.' Now his voice is bewildered, hurt. 'What do you hope to achieve? I realise you love the children. They're adorable. I'm not saying you can never see them again. Of course you can. In fact, Olivia and I were discussing whether to make you a godmother – the only one – so that you will have a very special role in their lives.'

Francesca bursts out laughing again. 'Oh, how kind! God-mother!'

'No, listen. We want you to be close to them as they grow up, mentor them, be there for them when they need someone who isn't us. That's a role you could play.'

'I'm sure that would sort everything out for you very nicely indeed,' Francesca retorts. 'As usual, you're trying to work it all out so that you get exactly what you want. But what if I don't want to play ball?'

Dan's mouth tightens and he seems to wince. 'All right,' he says after a moment. 'Tell me what you want. I thought we had an understanding when we went into this. You would donate eggs but that was the limit of your involvement.'

'You'd like that, wouldn't you?' she puts in. 'Keeping me in my box as usual!'

He's exasperated now. 'So tell me what you want, Cheska! How do you see this working? Tell me what it is you want me to do!'

Francesca gets to her feet, shaky but full of passionate strength. 'I want you to acknowledge me,' she says loudly. 'I want to be noticed, and acknowledged. You've rubbed me out. You scrubbed out everything that happened between us and I let you. But I'm not going to be your meek little door-mat anymore. You have to say it out loud.'

'Oh, I see.' Dan nods. He's turning scornful. He knows she can't bear his contempt so he's going to try that on her now. 'It's about that, is it?' He bangs his plate down on the counter. 'All of this pent-up anger and resentment because of one night twenty years ago? All because of that?'

She feels in control but when her voice comes out, it is trembling. 'It wasn't one night. You know that. You know how I felt about you.'

He takes a deep breath and holds it. When he releases it, he says with an air of magnanimity, 'All right, yes, I did know. Of course I did. You had a crush on me, Cheska, we all knew that. I was flattered but perhaps I should have been stronger and more decisive about it. Maybe we shouldn't have been friends, if it was going to cause you so much pain. But I was fond of you, you know that. You meant something to me. I've never pretended otherwise.'

'You always wanted me to be grateful for scraps,' she says bitterly. 'You still do. Throwing me the bone of being god-mother. Telling me that you were fond of me. Thank you so much for that, Dan! Thank you for the dog-ends of your affection. Well, you know what, I'm here to remind you that it wasn't like that. You loved me too! You told me! You know what happened and I won't let you pretend anymore.'

There's a silence, heavy in the room. He is blinking rapidly in the way she knows so well, as he absorbs this piece of truth spoken out loud. Now it is out there, he will be forced to react. That's what makes him uncomfortable.

She can't bear the tension of the silence. She is longing for an answer to what she has said. 'Well?' she demands.

At last he says something. His voice is quiet and low. 'I didn't say that.'

'You did! You did!' she bursts out. 'Don't lie to me.'

'I never said I loved you.'

'All right, you pedant. Let's say you never said those exact words – even though you said you were in love with me—'

'In love?' He jumps on it swiftly. 'That's not the same as love.'

'But what about what happened between us?' She is panting, almost pleading. She is desperate for him to confirm what she has remembered all this time. Sometimes that night in the garden in Cambridge seemed like a fantasy, something she only imagined. If he says it out loud, at least there will be relief in the validation of her memory. 'What about what happened between us, Dan?'

He sighs, and says, 'We got carried away that night. You know how it was. We were young and full of craziness because we were leaving Cambridge, and we got too drunk and acted on impulses that we should have restrained.'

She wants to crumple. So that's how he saw it. Not the romance of it, the joining of twin souls, the great revelation that they loved each other and were meant to be together. 'It wasn't like that,' she says almost in a whisper, her head drooping. 'You know it wasn't.'

'Cheska, darling . . .'

She turns a swift, fierce gaze on him. 'Don't patronise me,' she warns, her voice still trembling. 'Don't do that.'

He shrugs. 'I don't mean to patronise you. I'm sorry. Look, it's a lovely memory for me too. I don't regret the enjoyment of it, but I regret the effect it had on us. The way it interfered with our friendship.'

'Because,' she says, her voice cutting through the air with

resolution, 'you said you were in love with me. You said we would be together. You promised we would be together.'

It hangs there, almost vibrating in the air, the thing that they have never said to one another. Even afterwards, when he destroyed her dream and ruined her life, she never threw his promise in his face. She accepted it, took her pain and went away with it. Then she returned to let him go on, never having to confront the way he had treated her.

Dan looks confused. She has a feeling he hasn't thought about this for many years and that in itself is a source of pain. It was all she could think about for so long, and he was able to brush it aside and dismiss it.

'Did I?' he says, almost wonderingly.

'Yes you did,' she raps out. 'You said we would be together. Have you forgotten? Do I have to remind you?'

He frowns as though things are coming back to him now. 'That night . . . yes. We were close after that. You're right. I'd kind of . . . forgotten.'

His words stab her. She feels physical pain that something that was so important to her meant so little to him.

'And have you forgotten the rest?' she asks in a hollow voice.

His gaze slides over to her. His eyes hold something like guilt within them, and that's when she knows he has not forgotten the rest. He remembered all along.

There is a knock on the door and they both jump as though they have been caught out in something forbidden. Then Dan collects himself, goes to the door and opens it.

'Sorry to disturb you, sir. Is Mrs Huxtable about?'

Francesca recognises the voice. 'Mr Ellis? Is everything all right?'

The builder steps into the kitchen, looking out of place with his high-vis fluorescent jacket and hard hat. 'Well . . . there's been an interesting development. One I think you should see.'

Chapter Thirty-One

1960

In the warmth of the caravan under its blanket of snow, Alice is panting, her expression hopeful. Julia has pulled a blanket over her to keep her warm now that her exertions are over. She has re-emerged from the animal state that possessed her while she was giving birth, though her lips are tinged with blue from the effort.

'Where's the baby?' she asks. 'Can I see it?'

Julia looks down at the little boy in her arms. He is utterly still and silent. They used Donnie's knife to cut the cord and unwrap it gently from the infant's neck, and then they saw that he is a perfect little boy, but he is lifeless, now swaddled in a pillowcase, his eyes closed as though he is sleeping; only the pallor of his face tells them otherwise.

Alice groans with an after-pang. Her body is still contracting, still pushing. Julia wonders why, when the baby is here. When the pain has passed, Alice says, 'Please, I want to see the baby.'

'Oh, Alice.' Julia's voice breaks on the words. Her heart is aching for the dead child and for Alice who, she understands, is gripped by the ancient emotions of motherhood: a longing for her baby, an urgent physical need to nurture her off-spring.

'What's wrong?' Alice says, pushing herself up onto her elbows. 'Something's wrong. What is it?' Her eyes fall on the little bundle in Julia's arms. 'Why isn't it crying, don't they cry?'

Julia cannot find any words. She offers the baby to her. It was warm with Alice's body heat when it came from her womb but now it is cooling. She knows instinctively what the child should be: warm, pinking up, squirming, its mouth eager for milk as it cries for something it does not yet under-stand. It should be helpless but demanding, waiting for its needs to be met by the greater force that it senses is there to protect it, feed it and love it.

What happens, she wonders, *to all the tiny babies who have no one to care for them? What happens to all the mothers who do not have their babies?* She sees suddenly a huge sea of human grief, of wailing and mourning and cry-ing; the devastation of loss and sorrow of the left behind. It's too much. Her eyes are blinded with tears. 'Oh, Alice,' she says with a sob. 'I'm so sorry. I'm so sorry.'

Donnie has retreated to the back of the caravan, staring out of the window at the sparkling snow. He is as still as stone.

Alice closes her eyes and shudders with another after-pang. When it's over she opens her eyes and looks at Julia. 'When will it be over?' she asks plaintively. 'Why hasn't it stopped?'

'I don't know.' Julia sobs again.

Alice lowers herself back to the floor, not looking at the bundle that Julia is holding out to her.

Julia asks, 'Don't you want to see it?'

Alice sighs. 'I know that it's dead.' She turns on her side and stares away into the distance. 'Things would be different if it weren't. You wouldn't be crying for one thing.'

'Yes . . . yes, he's dead. The cord was around his neck. Perhaps he was dead for a while, I don't know, but . . . Alice, he's perfect but for that. So small but perfect and beautiful. Don't you want to see him?'

Alice lies there for a while, blinking into nothingness. When she speaks, her voice is flat and heavy. 'No. He wasn't going to be mine anyway. He was going to be Roy's. His consolation.'

'How did you know about the other baby?' whispers Julia. 'The one his wife lost?'

Alice turns to her, a spark of something in her eyes that quickly dies. 'I didn't know. Perhaps I did – but not from Roy. Maybe I felt it in the universe. But it's all pointless now that my baby is dead too.'

Julia looks down again at the child in her arms. Then she looks up at Donnie, who has turned at the mention of Roy's name. 'What are we going to do?' she asks wonderingly. The reality of the situation is beginning to sink in. Alice is here, still in the aftermath of labour. Julia is holding a dead baby. She cannot begin to understand what must be done.

'What are we going to do?' she asks again, now with an

edge of fear in her voice. All she can think of is that they mustn't be found out.

'You can't stay here,' Donnie says roughly. 'I know it sounds harsh, but there's a lot at stake if you're found. We can't afford to lose our jobs. And if they find out that Roy is the father, he'll be arrested.'

'Arrested?' Julia echoes.

Donnie nods. 'Your girl is under age.'

Alice stirs at this. 'Will they arrest Roy? I won't let that happen. I won't let him and his family suffer because of me.' She starts to push herself up from the floor. 'I'll stop it.'

'Lie down,' Julia soothes, trying to keep calm. 'It'll be all right, you'll see. No one will be arrested.' But she turns frightened eyes on Donnie. 'She's just had a baby. What will we do? How do I get her back to school?'

Donnie looks out to the night beyond. 'It's still early. There's a few hours yet before you'll be missed. Give her a chance to get her strength back and I'll carry her to the school so she doesn't have to walk.'

'What then?' Julia asks, bewildered. 'What do we do after that?'

'You're on your own after that. I'm sorry, but that's the way it is.'

Alice says in her flat tone, 'Don't worry, Julia. I'll be all right. You'll see. I always knew I'd go back without him. I'm ready for that.'

Julia wonders if she is talking about Roy or the baby. *She must mean the baby.* She turns her gaze again to the little body in her arms, wrapped in the flimsy pillowcase. The thought crosses her mind that if she could get a blanket for it instead, perhaps she could warm him back to life. No wonder he's so cold in this piece of cotton. Then she remembers. Nothing will ever warm him.

She lifts her eyes to Donnie. 'What about the baby?'

He gazes down at them. Then he says abruptly, 'Leave him with me. I'll look after him.'

'Will you . . . be kind to him?' she asks, her voice wavering.

'Of course I will. You'll see.'

The hours pass in quietness. The pangs continue until Alice's body delivers a mess of blood and tissue and then they are over. Julia wraps the strange livid wobbliness and the remains of the cord in layers of newspaper for Donnie to bury somewhere. Alice does not say another word but lies staring into space, not wanting to see the tiny body that Julia has placed carefully on a cushion from the bench. It is as though everything has been drained from her and left her a heavy, dull weight that nothing can animate.

Julia cleans up as well as she can, warming water on the hot ring to wash Alice down. Alice lets her do it, neither helping nor hindering, with no sense of shame or embarrassment as Julia tenderly wipes her thighs free of blood.

While Julia does her best to make Alice comfortable, Donnie goes out and comes back with some small planks of thin wood. Julia makes them all tea and he sits at the back of the caravan with a hammer and some tacks, lightly tapping the boards. When he has finished, there is a small box prepared, with an ill-fitting lid.

'There,' he says, putting it down on the floor. 'It's the best I can do.'

Julia understands he has carefully made a coffin for the child. 'It's very nice,' she says, her eyes full of tears again. 'But it's bare. Not very comfortable.'

'Then we'll put in a cushion,' Donnie says. 'You choose one.'

There is some comfort, Julia finds, in preparing the little box for the baby. She selects the softest of the small sofa cushions and wraps it in a clean pillowcase, then lays the little body, swaddled in another pillow case, upon it. It's somehow not enough. Her gaze falls upon a picture on the wall, an arrangement of dried violets and pansies under glass, and she jumps up to get it. They prise the back off and take out the little flowers. Julia scatters them over the baby and on the cushion.

'That's better,' she says. But there is still something missing. She turns to Alice. 'Do you want to give something to the baby?' she asks gently.

Alice has her back to the coffin, though she has been listening carefully to the proceedings and knows what they are doing. 'No,' she says. Then after a second she says, 'Wait. Yes. Do you have any scissors?'

They don't but Donnie has his knife. Alice says, 'Take off some of my hair and put it with the baby.'

'Are you sure?' Julia asks.

'Yes. Please.' She allows Julia to lift one of her long fair tresses and saw slowly through it with the knife blade until the hank comes away in her hand.

Julia places it on top of the little body, curling it round into a golden circle. 'Yes,' she says pensively. 'That's right. That's enough.' She drops her gaze to the floor and feels this is the moment for a ritual of some kind, though she can't think of anything except the Lord's Prayer, so she begins solemnly. 'Our Father, Who art in Heaven, Hallowed be Thy name . . .'

Donnie joins in and they say the prayer together while Alice listens.

When it is finished, Donnie says softly, 'That was very nice.' He bends down and puts the lid over the dead child. Julia bites her lip as he disappears from view, her vision blurring with tears. 'Don't worry,' Donnie says gently when he sees her cry. 'I'll take care of him. He'll be safe with me.' He looks over at Alice. 'Do you reckon she's strong enough to move now?'

Alice shifts under her blanket. 'I'm strong enough,' she says with determination. 'You can take me back now.'

'Come on then,' Donnie says. He stares at Julia. 'Time to go.'

PART FOUR

Chapter Thirty-Two

They all go together back to the east wing of the house. Dan has got the children up from their nap and dressed them, but they are groggy and grumpy, so he puts them into the double buggy and gives each one a beaker of milk. They sit, subdued, as they are pushed back the way they went that morning.

'It's a strange discovery,' Mr Ellis says as they stride along the gravel paths. 'Very unexpected. I'm not entirely sure what's done in such cases but we'll wait for the authorities to tell us.'

'Do you mean you've had to call a halt to the work?' asks Francesca.

'That's about the size of it.' Mr Ellis gives her an apologetic look. 'I hope it won't be a long delay.' As he leads them into the old pool room, he says, 'One of my men discovered this when he started pulling the tiles up off the floor of the pool. It was very close to the surface. Either it wasn't buried deep, or it has floated up over the years. It's all just in bits now, anyway.' He turns to Dan. 'Best leave the kids outside, I think. Rob here will keep an eye on them if they're safe in their pushchair.' He nods at one of the younger workmen loitering nearby.

'All right,' Dan says. 'Just for a minute.'

They go inside the huge chamber, their steps echoing against the tiled surface. The hole in the ground is clearly a swimming pool now that all the debris from the bottom has been moved. The tiles on its base have been broken up and lifted in the centre, revealing a dirt hole, but it's otherwise empty, tools abandoned on the grubby floor.

'Over here,' says Mr Ellis. 'I'm afraid you'd better prepare yourselves for a bit of unpleasantness.'

He leads them to where there is a small pile of what looks like rubbish: some rotted bits of wood and remnants of fabric. Francesca peers down at the pile, trying to make out what she is seeing. Then she notices a coil of long brittle strings. 'Hair?' she says.

'That's right.' Mr Ellis nods. 'But that's not all. Can you see?'

Dan is beside her, staring down. 'Bones,' he says in a wondering tone. 'It's a skeleton.'

At once Francesca sees what he is looking at. The bits of whitish stuff resolve into something recognisable and she realises that he is right – it's a tiny skeleton, a skull, crushed on one side, among the remains of the bones. 'A baby,' she whispers.

'I'm afraid so.' Mr Ellis sighs. 'Dead for some time. Decades, I'd say.'

'What a sad thing,' Francesca says, a strange emotion curling inside her.

Dan points at the skull. 'Look – do you think it was murdered? The skull is broken at the side.'

'Could be.' Mr Ellis crouches down beside the debris. 'But look at this. It's been carefully buried. The wood seems to have been a coffin of some sort. Then there's the hair. You don't put all that kind of stuff in with a murdered baby; you try and get rid of it as simply as possible. No, I reckon it was hidden in here.' He looks about. 'It must be at least fifty years ago, if the style of this building is anything to go by. This was a girls' school then, wasn't it? No. It's no murder. There's a sad story here. Some poor kid's had a child she loved, and put her hair in with it. God only knows how it came to be buried under the pool, or what happened to the girl. There's a mystery there and the only thing we can know for sure is that it's a sorry tale.' He stands up. 'I'll have to call the police, though, Mrs Huxtable. I'm sure you understand that it's unavoidable.'

Francesca hears him but it's as though his voice is very far away, and she has gone somewhere removed from everything around her. All she is aware of is the little skeleton, surrounded by all the marks of a mother's love and grief. A little child, lost at birth. The thought of it is filling her head with confusion and a kind of buzzing sound and a horrible realisation that she is full of a nameless sorrow, pushed down and repressed for years and years. Like the coffin under the pool, it's coming to the surface, moving remorselessly upwards to break free from the carefully cemented layer of tiles that is holding it in.

'Mrs Huxtable? Is that all right?'

'Francesca?' It's Dan's voice. His hand on her arm. 'Are you all right? What is it?'

It's all so muffled and strange. She closes her eyes to stop herself swaying, her breath coming in short hard pants, confusion roaring through her. If only they would be quiet and let her understand what is happening to her. A seismic feeling rumbles in her depths.

Dan's voice sounds from far away. 'Francesca, you'd better sit down. Come this way, let's find you a seat.'

She feels him start to push her and it is the last straw. Her eyes fly open. 'No!' she screams. 'No!' She turns and gives him a mighty shove and he stumbles away from her with an expression of surprise on his face. 'Don't you dare touch me! Don't you dare! After everything you've done!' Her voice is shrill, a true scream. 'Oh my God. I can't bear it!' She turns and starts to run out of the building, out onto the site. The workman she saw earlier is standing by Bea and Stan's pushchair, chatting merrily to them and showing them a spirit level. He looks up as she dashes past but she has no thought to explain herself.

I need to get away. I have to get away from here.

She runs blindly through the gardens, not knowing where she is going. The grief inside is almost too much for her and she is crying as she goes, great heart-wrenching sobs that burst from her. It is a relief to let it out. She wants to turn her face to the sky and scream with all her might, fall to her knees and beat the earth, because of all the bloody sadness that everyone must suffer.

She runs and runs, and when she stops, she is back at the

cottage, in the garden, surrounded by all the normality of life there. Washing flaps in the breeze. Toys are scattered by the back door. Olivia's gardening things lie on the path where she was weeding yesterday. This is the antidote to the sadness, isn't it? The small pleasures of existence, the patterns of the garden, the seasons. Life going on despite the tragedies and the suffering, and people coming through it after all.

But have I come through it? Am I all right?

She kneels on the ground, crying, tears running down her face, streams of water and mucous all over. *I'm not all right. I haven't been all right for ages.*

The knowledge bursts in on her like a firework exploding in her head. Suddenly she understands. It only makes the tears flow faster and a moaning sound spring from somewhere inside.

'Francesca, what's wrong?' Dan is beside her, his arms around her. She collapses into him, letting him take the weight of her grief, and cries against him, allowing it to spill out at last.

They are inside, back at the kitchen table. She is calmer now. The workman pushed the twins back to the house and they are in front of the television, happy with their cartoons and building bricks.

Dan has made her a cup of tea, which cools in front of her. Actually she would like whiskey but there's no point in that right now. It would only make things more confused, with the state she is in.

'You remember, don't you?' she says to Dan, her voice flat. 'I don't mean the night of the ball. We both remember that. I mean the other thing. You know how we left the ball. You said we would be together.'

Dan sits across the table from her, gazing at the pale polka dots of the oilcloth. He seems to have come through some important process by means of Francesca's grief. It appears that, at last, he is able to admit what happened between them all that time ago. He nods. 'I know. I did say that.' He looks up at her. 'I shouldn't have said that. I knew it was a mistake. I didn't really mean it. But your tears, the way you said you loved me . . . it all moved me. I thought, just for an instant, that we could make it work, because I did love you, in a way. Just not in the right way. I tried, though. I did try.'

She nods. 'I know you did.'

The heady days that followed the ball come back to her. They passed in an ecstatic blur of being with Dan, but secretly. They agreed that no one must know of the great change that had taken place between them. So during the brief time before term ended and everyone went their separate ways, they hid away, in Dan's room, or by riding out of town on bicycles to have lazy picnics in a shady meadow. They made love often.

But Francesca felt something was missing. There was a strange lack, as though Dan wasn't entirely there. He was acting a part, somehow – doing it very well, but still playing a role. When they went to bed, it was intense and vigorous, but as if Dan had the teeth-clenched determination to see the act through. There was a sort of tenderness afterwards, when they lay with their fingers laced together and their limbs entwined, but she sensed he was rallying himself to do what was expected and his tenderness was partly born of relief that it was over. She was afraid that he was slipping away from her. She had this chance, this golden moment when she was living her dearest dream and he was her heart's companion, and she could feel it disappearing no matter how hard she tried to hold on to it.

'I don't want to lose you,' she said to him, filled with yearning.

'You won't,' he said with a smile.

She wanted so badly to believe him. But she knew deep down that he was lying.

'When will we tell the others?' she asked. She tried to convince herself of a future where she and Dan and Jimmy and Claire were a pair of couples, venturing out into their lives beyond Cambridge together. They would all have fun and go travelling, then there would be marriage and children, and family holidays on windswept beaches, with kids running and playing on the sand while they laid out picnics and laughed. Why shouldn't it happen?

But every day, she felt him slip further away.

The end of term split them up. He went home to his parents and then off on a holiday to Greece with his family, and she went down to London to work for a contact her supervisor had given her, to earn money before she started at law school in September. She thought she might look for a flat for her and Dan to live in. He would come to London too, in due course, he said. He'd get some temporary work while he looked for his proper job.

When he returned from his holiday, he phoned her. She had sent letters to his home to await his return, full of chat and the expectation that they would soon be together, telling him her new address and all the ways he could reach her. She had missed him so much. Time had dragged without him, with only her dreams and fantasies to fill the void of his absence. By now, she was already familiar with the rush-hour tides, the heat of the Underground and the slapping of her sandalled feet on the pavement of Tottenham Court Road as she trudged to her job.

'I need to see you,' he said.

'That's good.' She sat in the hallway of the flat she was staying in, another favour from a contact of her tutor who was away in America. 'I want to see you too. I've missed you.'

An infinitesimal pause. 'I've missed you too. I'm coming to London tomorrow. Shall I meet you after work?'

'Yes, please!' She was excited at the thought, hungry for the sight of him, the feel of his body and the taste of his mouth. 'You can stay here.'

'Okay. Tell me the address of your work. I'll meet you afterwards.'

The next day passed in a fever of anticipation. At lunch-time she went out and spent some money on a new top that she hoped he would like. When the day was over at last, she hurried to the ladies to put on make-up and smarten her hair. In the mirror her reflection was anxious despite her smile, and she wondered what she was afraid of. He was waiting downstairs, handsome as ever in shorts, a T-shirt and some flip-flops, and she felt overdressed in her work clothes and the new smart top. He was cheerful but muted and she overcompensated, chattering away as she held his hand. She felt proud as they walked along the streets together, obviously girlfriend and boyfriend. Other girls eyed Dan as they went by, and she felt the thrill of possession.

They found a restaurant, took a table and looked at the menus. When their orders were taken and glasses of wine sat in front of them, she looked across at Dan and her heart turned over. She loved him so much, every inch of him. He made her happy. And yet the expression in his dark blue eyes was chilling her to the core.

'Cheska,' he said softly, the same way he had after they first had sex in the garden that night. 'I've got to talk to you.'

She tried to divert him, babbling away about her work, but he wouldn't be distracted.

'Cheska.' He took her hand over the table. 'Please. Let me say it.'

She was still. 'No, Dan,' she said, her voice quavering. 'Don't, please don't say it. Please. Not tonight. Let's have dinner and go back to my place. You can say it tomorrow.'

He shook his head slowly and sadly. 'I'm not staying tonight. I'm going back to Jimmy's.'

'Please,' she whispered, something sinking inside her, pulling her down towards a dark pit she couldn't bear to look at. *Let me stay in the light just a little longer.* 'Don't say it.'

'I've got to.' He took a deep breath. 'Cheska, you'll always be my friend, you'll always be dear to me but—'

Her eyes were afloat in hot tears. Her breath jerked into her lungs in little painful hops. 'Stop it,' she whispered. 'No.'

'Don't cry, Cheska.' His eyes were full of pity. She didn't want pity, or favours. She just wanted to be loved, naturally and truthfully, and if she lost Dan, what else did she have? 'Please don't cry.'

She closed her eyes. Her shoulders jumped with a stifled sob.

'I can't be with you, Cheska, I'm sorry.'

'You said you love me.' It came out as a whisper.

'I do love you, in my own way. But we can only be friends.' His hand closed over hers. She couldn't open her eyes. 'Can we be friends, please?' There was a pause and he said in a lighter tone, 'Look, I'm not good enough for you. You'll find someone else, I promise. You'll be glad in the end. One day you'll come to me and tell me I did you a favour.'

She was crying now, not able to bear the humiliation of it. People on the neighbouring tables were nudging and looking over, sympathetic and amused in equal measure. 'Look at the poor girl, he's dumping her.' She couldn't see them but she knew. And his pity was too much to take.

She scrambled to her feet, reaching for her bag, and stumbled out of the restaurant onto the hot pavement. All she wanted now was to get away. Behind her, Dan called her name, dropped a fiver on the table for their drinks and came after her. She ran down the road, and he ran too, reaching her at the corner where she had to stop.

'Cheska,' he panted, turning her round to look at him.

'Go away!' she screamed, furious with the pain. 'Go away and leave me alone!'

The lights changed and she ran across the road. He stood and watched her go, then turned and walked off in the other direction.

That summer is acute in her memory because of the pain. It ambushed her all the time: on the Underground; at the desk in her office; at lunch; and, worst of all, alone in her flat at night. Tears would appear unbidden on her face. Sometimes she sat crying for an hour before she realised it was happening. The grief was a physical burden that bent her under its weight and felt as if it would crush her. She longed for him but she knew it was over. He was gone. He'd never wanted her the way she did him. Even though she'd offered herself to him without reservation and even though he'd tried to love her, he couldn't.

It's my fault, she told herself. *I'm not loveable.*

When September came and term began, she started at law school and moved to a new flat with some other law students. By then she knew.

Dan had moved to London, sharing Jimmy's flat, so it was easy enough to write him a letter.

Dear Dan

You should know that I'm pregnant. I think it was probably the night of the ball, when we didn't use anything, because all the other times we did. I can't have a baby on my own, not with my law course to do. So

I've arranged an appointment at a clinic to have an abortion. I'm going to be outside an hour beforehand and I'll wait for you. The address and time are on the appointment card with this letter.

Perhaps I'll see you there.

All my love,

Cheska x

On the appointed day, she waited, walking back and forth in front of the railings outside the clinic, looking for him. Occasionally she put a protective hand on her stomach, as though wanting to shield the tiny thing within from harm. But he never came, and when it was time, she went inside as she had planned.

She tried to be brave and strong, and manage alone. She tried to forget it and not to care. What more was the baby, after all, than a little bundle of cells, a small pale tadpole built on a tiny spine, with a miniature pulsing heart and the start of a brain? It was not a person, not really. But it had been hers, and Dan's, and she had killed it. Where was it now? Sluiced away down the drain? Tossed in a rubbish bin with all the other unwanted waste?

She tried to cope, but the guilt and pain were too much. She couldn't tell anyone what she was suffering. Her law work was impossible to complete: words swam in front of her eyes, blurry in the constant tears she angrily tried to brush away. Facts couldn't stick in a brain that pounded with thoughts of rage and despair. She started to fail and there was nothing she could do about it.

The school warned her. She was told to pull her socks up. But she lay on her bed in her shared flat, away from the other girls, night after night in the dark, tormented by her grief. Then she did them all a favour and left without being formally asked to go. She got a job as a temporary secretary in a_big corporation and then, her bosses impressed by her ability to spell words like 'satellite' and 'supersede', she was made a permanent PA to one of the executives.

A few months later she met Walt, and he began, slowly, to heal her. She put all the pain behind her. She erased the memory. Or so she thought. And when she came back into Dan's orbit, she let him pretend nothing had happened. She never mentioned the letter or that awful hour in the clinic, when they'd sucked out the little living symbol of Dan's fleeting love.

She let him go on lying and pretending, and treating her as though she had never really mattered.

Francesca looks at Dan across the table. 'Why didn't you come to the clinic that day, when I had the abortion?' she asks.

That's the pain. I understand now. She thinks of the little skeleton with its tokens of love, and the careful burial, even if it was under a swimming pool. *What happened to my baby? No funeral, no acknowledgement. Thrown away, ignored and forgotten.*

Dan says nothing. He frowns, as though wracking his brain to remember.

'You got my letter, didn't you?' A flame of hope sparks to

life – that he never got the letter, and it was a misunderstanding. Then, perhaps, she could forgive him.

'Yes.' He says it slowly, his voice heavy with regret as he stares at the tabletop. 'I got it. I was a coward. I didn't come to you.' He looks up at her again. 'I let you go through with it, and I let you allow me to forget it. Because you never once reproached me for it. You never said a word. You stayed true and loved me just the same.'

'I loved you,' she says, her voice wobbly again. 'But I couldn't forget it, even though I tried.'

Dan stands up. 'It was wrong to let you donate your eggs. I see that now. In a weird way, when you made your offer, I felt as though I was making it up to you somehow. Letting you have the chance to meet the baby we never had. But as soon as Olivia was pregnant, I knew it was a mistake. I hadn't thought it through. I should have let her choose an anonymous donor like she wanted. I suppose you let me get away with things, Cheska. I thought I could get away with this too.'

He looks at her, his gaze candid. For a moment, he is her Dan again – the one from the garden, the one who made love to her for a few heady weeks one summer, and then broke her heart. He says, 'I'm sorry. For all the pain I caused you. I never wanted to hurt you but somehow I did. I'm sorry about the baby and how callous I was. I never spoke about it to you and I should have. I let you marry Walt without ever telling you that I was sad about the baby too.'

'Really?' She is amazed. It never occurred to her that he might have mourned the child as well.

Dan nods his head. 'Yes. I mean it.' He smiles weakly. 'I did care about you, Cheska. I just couldn't love you in the way you wanted.'

She gives a little half-laugh. 'What a mess.' She shakes her head. 'And now we have two actual children together. What are we going to do about that?'

Dan walks over to her, pulls her up from her seat and takes her in his arms. She sighs as he wraps her in his embrace, and rests her head against him. Not so long ago, she yearned for this kind of contact with Dan. Now it feels like a resolution. The truth is out. He has acknowledged everything. She feels validated.

Dan presses his mouth down towards her ear and says softly, 'You won't tell Olivia, will you? It will stay our secret. Won't it?'

She pulls away from him, looking up into his face, and sees the look there that she knows so well. It's complacency. Complete belief in his power over her.

He thinks I'll do what he wants. Nothing has changed.

'Oh no,' she says. 'You have to tell Olivia. She has to know.'

His expression changes. First it's incredulous, then panic sets into his eyes. 'What? I can't tell her, you know that.'

'You have to tell her everything. She needs to know what happened between us, and about the baby. And about the eggs. You can't let her go on believing a lie.'

This is his test, she knows that. It's all very well to say the right things, to acknowledge the past and apologise, but it's

423

worth nothing if it's merely a ruse to keep everything just the way it was.

Dan pulls away from her, outrage on his face. 'What are you talking about, Cheska? You know I can't do that! Are you fucking crazy? You know very well she'll never forgive me. I did a terrible thing, I know that, and I should never have done it. It was idiotic. It was stupid. In all sorts of ways. But I can't tell her. It's bad enough that I never told her we were lovers. But it's a thousand times worse than that. You know it would destroy her.'

'Not knowing the truth could destroy her too. Don't you know how easy it is to ruin a life when someone loves you? Look what you did to me. And it nearly happened to me all over again with the twins.' She shakes her head. She's sorry for him, but it's clear what the right thing is. 'You can't let lies poison your life. If you tell her, explain why you did it, she might forgive you. It will be much worse if she finds out from someone else.'

Dan's expression changes again. Now it's hard, the blue eyes icy, the mouth twisted. He stares at her with menace. 'And who might tell her? Who else knows?' He takes a step towards her. 'Only you, Cheska. You're the only one. Would you tell her?'

She sees that he has clenched his fists. 'Are you threatening me, Dan?' she asks, wonder in her voice. She has always suspected he is capable of more than she ever wanted to acknowledge. Is he about to show her exactly what? 'You can't get away with it, you must know that. I'm not your underling, to be ordered about or punished.'

'Just tell me.' His knuckles are white, his teeth clenched. 'Because if that's what you intend to do, I'm going to fucking stop you, understand?'

A rush of courage goes through her. So it's come to this. He's tried every other form of manipulation and now he is going to resort to threats or worse. She stares at him with scorn. 'What did I ever see in you? Why did I waste my life dreaming about you? I must have been a fool. I'm sorry, Dan, but you can't change facts, even by force. Olivia needs to know that I donated those eggs. She needs to know that those children are ours – yours and mine – and if you don't tell her, I will.'

The back door swings open suddenly and standing there is Olivia, her face a picture of pain and fury.

'Oh my God,' she whispers in a broken voice. 'Oh my God.'

Chapter Thirty-Three

Francesca and Dan stare at her, guilt all over their faces. Olivia can tell that they are trying to work out how much she has heard.

I've heard enough.

Sick horror courses through her. On the train home, she was anxious and worried, unable to understand why. Well, now she knows. There was nobody to meet her at the station, and she was afraid that something was seriously wrong. The taxi driver brought her back, evidently aware of her agitation and desire to be home as soon as possible. But as she came through the gate, she heard the voices floating through the open window, and caught the sharp exclamation, 'Are you fucking crazy?'

She stopped short as though an invisible wall had appeared in her path, her breath frozen in her chest. As she stood there on the path, she heard them talking: Dan saying that he and Cheska had been lovers. Cheska saying she, Olivia, needed to know; Dan resisting. She walked silently towards the door, hardly realising she was moving. Then came words that made the bottom drop out of her world.

Olivia needs to know that I donated those eggs. She needs to know that those children are ours – yours and mine – and if you don't tell her, I will.

A sick feeling in her stomach makes her want to throw up, and for a moment she thinks she's going to fall to her knees and puke by the back door, but outrage and fury are stronger. She throws open the door. 'Oh my God.' Her voice is full of a treacherous wobble. 'Oh my God.'

She stares at them, the guilty two with their dirty, monstrous secret. She is shaking now as the implications start to sink in. Are they really saying that Bea and Stan, her darlings, are . . . Francesca's children?

She looks at Dan. She doesn't care about Francesca now – she is dead to her. That is over, she knows that for certain. All she wants is to be out of her poisonous, evil presence. *Claire was right all along.* But Dan. Her Dan.

The lies.

The evil fucking plot he cooked up.

She shakes her head and says in a voice of almost preternatural calm, 'Why? Why did you do it?'

His face is full of horror and she can read the despair in his eyes. 'Please, Olivia, I'm sorry.'

'Sorry?' It comes out in a wondering tone, as though she's never heard this strange word 'sorry' before and has no idea what it means. 'Sorry?' she repeats through gritted teeth, her voice rising. By the way he flinches when she looks at him, she knows her anger must be awful to behold. 'You're fucking sorry?' She picks up the bag she is carrying that contains the socks she bought and throws it at him. It's not heavy enough to travel far and drops at his feet. 'What the hell have you done, Dan? What have you done?' She points in the direction of the television room from where the sound of cartoon mania floats. 'Are you honestly telling me that our babies are from eggs donated by Francesca?' Her gaze flicks on Francesca, who hasn't moved but stands frozen by the table. A horrible realisation comes over her. She remembers again the Dark Night of the Donor and then Dan's volte-face, and it all makes sense. 'Oh, I see. You went crying to Cheska, and she offered you her eggs so you'd know what to expect when I pushed your fucking children out of my body!' She shudders. 'How did you swing it? No, wait, let me guess. She went out to the clinic first, to donate her eggs, and then you took me out to receive them. Or was she there the whole time we were? Was she in the next room, having them harvested while I waited next door with my legs apart?' She laughs brutally. 'Oh, that's a good one! That's really good.'

The other two watch her, Francesca's expression growing grief-stricken, and Dan's still frozen with horror as he hears her unravel all the plots and schemes he has concealed from her.

'Well?' she demands. 'Are you going to tell me?'

'It's not what you think,' Dan says weakly.

'You can do better than that!' she jeers. 'Aren't you supposed to be a playwright? I'm expecting some good dialogue now. A speech explaining to me exactly why this isn't the most appalling mess. Why you thought it was a good idea to deceive me in the most fundamental way possible. Dan . . .' She walks towards him and he cowers a little as she nears him. 'And you two used to sleep together, did you? You let me bear your ex-lover's children?' She gestures towards Francesca. 'You lied to me about you and her. You never told me what happened between you. Do you think I would have let her into my life, into my home if I'd known? Do you think I'd ever have left her alone with my children? Are you mad?' She's close to him now, shouting. 'You've ruined everything, you stupid bastard! It didn't have to be like this! And now we're living in her fucking house!' A manic energy possesses her. 'Well, that's over right now.'

She turns and runs out of the kitchen, heading upstairs to the children's room. She grabs a bag from Stan's wardrobe and starts stuffing it with his things, mentally racing through what they need: *clothes, pyjamas, nappies, coats, shoes, hats, blankets, toys* . . .

Dan is there in the doorway. 'What are you doing?'

She casts him a glance. He is pale and trembling. She has never seen him like this before. He's afraid. He's powerless. 'I'm packing up. We're leaving.'

'Where are we going?' He sounds meek and docile. Not like the strong, commanding Dan she has always known, with his confidence and his good looks and his charm.

'*We?* I don't know where you're going, but the children and I are leaving.'

'What?' He looks baffled. 'Without me?'

'Yes, without you!' She stops packing the bag and stares at him, feeling the first ache of the avalanche of pain she knows is coming. Anger is easier right now. 'What do you expect? Can't you see what you've done? How can we come back from these lies? You've deceived me. I'm your *wife*.' She is speechless suddenly, a bitter blockage in her throat. She turns back to the bag.

'Are you leaving me?' he asks miserably.

'Of course I am,' she says briefly. 'You can stay here with your darling Cheska for all I care.'

'She's going,' he says. 'I called Walt yesterday. He's coming to get her.'

'Then you'll be here all on your fucking own, won't you?' she snaps. 'Plenty of quiet to get that bloody play written!'

She thinks suddenly of the children, downstairs in the television room on their own, with just Francesca there, and gasps. Dropping the bag, she pushes Dan out of the way and runs past him, down the stairs and along the hall. She bursts into the sitting room, and there they are: Stan and Bea, each nestled under one of Francesca's arms.

'Let them go!' cries Olivia in a terrible voice, full of strength and fury. She feels able to lift Francesca up and toss her against the wall. She feels she could crush her with her fingertips, she is so strong and fierce.

Francesca looks afraid but she tightens her arms around the children. 'Please . . . let me say goodbye. I only want to say goodbye.'

'Don't touch them.' In a flash she is there, wrenching Bea from Francesca's grip. Bea is saying, 'Mummy, Mummy,' but as she senses the aggression in the air, she starts to cry. Stan wails too in sympathy. Olivia reaches for him.

'Don't upset them,' pleads Francesca. 'Here – take them. They're yours.'

Olivia nestles both children to her chest, their bodies awkward against hers. They press into her, crying loudly. 'Never, never touch these children again. They *are* mine, do you understand?' Her eyes are flashing and she is mighty, a mighty goddess who will destroy anyone who threatens her children. 'They're mine and you can't have them!'

Francesca drops her gaze to the floor, then says, 'I'm so sorry, Olivia. I wanted him to tell you. I feel . . . more terrible than you can know.' She covers her face with her hands.

Olivia has no pity for her. *She was part of this lie. This filthy scheme. They both were.* She turns and pushes back past Dan, who is now in the doorway, and takes the children upstairs back to their room. She puts them in their cots, where they howl until they forget why they were upset and start to play with their toys. Olivia continues to pack their things, until she has two bags stuffed with necessaries.

She looks at them, satisfied. For now, she is only going to think about the practicalities of getting herself and the children away from this place. She'll think about the rest later, when there's time. Dan stands, a pale shadow of himself, in the hall outside, unable to be far from her. She bumps into him as she comes out. She closes the nursery door behind her and says warningly, 'You're not to go in. You can't touch them. Understand? You've forfeited your rights for the time being. We'll sort out what they are later.'

'I can't lose you and them!' he cries in a broken voice. 'I can't take it.'

'You should have thought of that before you decided to perpetrate your fraud. Because, make no mistake, that's what it is. Fraud.' She strides past him to their room to pack her own things, leaving the bedroom door open so that she can hear if he attempts to go in to the twins. As she packs, she is able to think dispassionately about the shift in power, and the way she is now the one in charge, and Dan, so often dominant, can only obey her.

Or perhaps he is even now downstairs with Francesca, cooking up some other plot.

Let him. Olivia's love for him feels dead and cold. *He's killed it.* She finishes her packing, although she's bound to have forgotten something, and heads back towards the nursery.

I have the children. That's what is good in all of this. I still have them.

When they are all ready, she brings the twins downstairs. Dan is there alone. She puts the twins on the play mat. 'You can say goodbye to them now,' she says coolly, 'while I pack the car.'

'Where are you going?' he asks. His voice is thick with tears and his eyes are red-rimmed and bloodshot.

'I'll tell you when I get there.' She leaves them with Dan. The massive sadness that is pooling inside her threatens for a moment to break free, but she manages to keep it contained. If she can just stay icy and calm until they are somewhere safe, she'll be all right.

When the bags are stowed in the boot, she heads back to

the house then stops with a gasp. A form emerges from the twilight of the garden and she realises it's the gardener, William.

'It's you,' she says, with a puff of relief.

'Are you going?' he asks, looking past her to the car.

'Yes, that's right. It's all rather sudden. My husband will be here, though. I don't know for how long.'

'And the children, going with you?'

'Yes.' She goes to pass him. 'So now, if you don't mind . . .'

'It's for the best,' he says. 'The children. It's no place for them. Not here. Too many ghosts. Too much empty space. Take them somewhere else.'

'I'm going to. Well, goodbye. And thank you.' She smiles.

'Goodbye.' He melts back into the shadows and is gone.

In the kitchen, Dan has his head in his hands as he watches the children, tears streaming down his face. He looks up as she starts to gather up things for the journey: bags of rice cakes, cartons of juice, beakers, raisins, and all the rest. *Another bag. How will I manage it all on my own?*

'Please don't go, Olivia. I told you, Cheska is leaving.'

'Cheska's whereabouts don't concern me any longer. I don't give a shit where she is.'

'What about me?' he asks. 'Don't you care how I feel?'

'How you feel?' she shouts, enraged. 'No, at this moment, I don't care a bit. I only care that you've destroyed our life together. You've poisoned our family with your lies. Did you really think you could go through life concealing this from me? Or maybe I've misjudged you. Maybe you can go through your whole life refusing to see what you don't want to see!

But I can't. I can't understand why you've done this, or how you thought we could have a marriage with this secret in it. It's over, Dan. I can't bear to look at you.'

She hoists the bag over her shoulder, lifts up the children and carries them all to the car. Dan comes to watch as she buckles them in, then climbs into the driver's seat and fires up the engine.

As she reverses away, she doesn't look at the figure of her husband on the driveway. And as she turns the car down the lane and heads off, she doesn't look at the magnificent front-age of Renniston Hall. She can only think of the passports in her handbag, hers and the children's, and the warm sunshine and peace of the villa in Argentina.

Chapter Thirty-Four

Francesca lies on the bed in the guest room, utterly drained. She feels as though she has lived a life today; or relived the most crucial moments in her past, the ones that set her on the path to where she is now.

Now she understands so much more. But she is also flabbergasted by things that she never questioned till now.

What impulse of mischief made her offer her eggs like that? Why did she inveigle Dan to accept her offer in the way she did? It was surely obvious that it could only end badly.

But she knows that the urge came from long before, because of what had happened between her and Dan, and the lost baby that kept a ghostly existence between them over the years.

So is it Dan's fault?

She is eaten up with grief for them all, and the stupid things that have happened. She loved him all those years ago but it was the passion of a teenager. Why didn't she grow out of it? She's never been satisfied with what she's got in her real life; she's always hankered after a fantasy that didn't exist. She let her desire for him scupper her chances of a brilliant degree. Her despair at the end of their affair and the loss of the baby ruined her dream of a great career. She accepted a life that could never fulfil her in the same way, and clung on stubbornly to a pointless fantasy. She persuaded herself that Dan was somehow worth it. But now she sees him for what he really is, and understands her own terrible mistakes. Here is the result.

The noises in the cottage tell her that Olivia has taken the children and the sound of car tyres on gravel signals her departure with them. A while later, there is a knock on her door. It opens and Dan is there, tearful. His malevolence has drained away.

'Cheska?'

She lifts her head to look at him. He's bowed and broken. Where is the romantic hero in the dinner jacket who seduced her under an oak tree one night? He never was a hero, or a god, or the man of her dreams. He was just an ordinary guy, a little better looking than most, but just a man all the same. Maybe not even as decent as the majority of men. 'Yes?'

'They've gone. She's taken the children.'

'I know.'

He leans against the door jamb. 'I don't know if I'll ever see them again.'

'You will. You're their father. Give her time. She's angry. Write to her and explain. Tell her how sorry you are and what a ghastly mistake you made.'

He looks at her hopefully. 'Would you write to her as well, Cheska? You could tell her that you wanted to do it.

You could tell her that I regretted it from the start and it was all your idea.'

She gazes at him, not sure whether to laugh or scream. 'I don't think more lies are the way ahead.'

'She'll never trust me again,' he says, bleak once more.

'You can hardly blame her for that. And that's exactly why you have to start telling the truth. Why don't you stop that stupid play and start writing something that might achieve something? You could tell her the whole story. Everything. Honestly.'

He stands there, thoughtful. They look at each other, old friends once young and confident, now middle-aged and full of regret for their mistakes. She knows that she's lived with a dream all these years, and that the buried grief in her heart has infected her life. That's all gone now, blown away like ashes on the wind.

It's time to move on. At last.

She has a sudden yearning for her old life: for the comfort of home and the presence of her children. She gets up off the bed. 'I'm going now, Dan. I can't stay any longer.'

'You're going to leave me alone?' he says plaintively.

'Yes, I'm afraid so.' She has a new energy. There's nothing more she can do here. She needs to get back to the people who love and rely on her. *I have to go home*. She scoops up her phone and sees a text message there from Walt.

I've arrived in London. Leaving for Renniston soon. I'm coming to take you back.
We miss you. Wx

Her heart swells with unexpected happiness. She remembers the last time that Walt swooped into her life and made her whole again. When she saw only darkness ahead of her, he brought life and hope and love back into her world. That mattered then, and it matters now. Why did she chase the illusion of Dan, when she had the solid, reliable, loving reality of Walt all along? Why did she scorn him when he is worth a hundred devious Dans? She taps out a message.

Don't come here. I'll come to you. I'm on my way. See you at the flat. Fx

She looks up at Dan. 'I need a taxi. I'm going back to London.'

'I could drive you,' he offers.

'No thanks.' She picks up her bag and starts to pack it. 'You can stay here as long as you like. But Dan . . .' She stops and fixes him with a stare. 'If you want Olivia back, you'll have to work for it.'

'Do you think I have a chance?' he asks mournfully, and she can hear the self-pity in his voice.

'I don't know,' she says frankly. 'But you have to try. That's all we can do. Keep on trying.'

Francesca sleeps for some of the taxi ride, exhausted by the events of the day. The rest of the time, she gazes out of the window at the motorway as they drive into the gathering night. She wonders where Olivia is and how she is feeling. The devastation she witnessed on her face is something

Francesca will never forget and she feels wretched for her part in it.

I have to make amends somehow. I don't know how yet. But she has to know how sorry I am.

She thinks of Dan and whether Olivia will ever forgive him. But she knows that the greatest struggle will be with herself. She, Francesca, can hardly believe she spent so long obsessed with something that never existed and never could. What will Olivia be thinking about her own failure to see through Dan's lies? She will blame herself. She will want to punish herself for being so stupid.

But she's got the children. She'll stay strong for them.

Francesca thinks about the beautiful babies. She feels the same core-deep love for them, and the need to be with them, but her lust for ownership has faded. Perhaps it was because they were partly a means to bring her to Dan, and that's over now. Or perhaps it was because today she knew the truth: they are Olivia's children and nothing can change that.

Will I ever see them again?

She can't bear the thought that she might not. But that isn't a question for now. It must wait. Now, she has to get back to her old life and make sure that everything in life she really values is still there. And to her surprise, she longs most of all for her husband.

When she gets to the flat, Walt greets her with a huge hug.

'Frankie, you're back.' He stands back and smiles at her. 'I thought that house had cast some sort of spell on you. I was beginning to regret ever buying it, if it meant I was going to lose my wife!'

She hugs him again, drawing strength from his solidness. She can rely on him. He's not a dream; he is real and he loves her. 'You haven't lost me, I promise.'

'Is all this madness over?' he asks. 'You're ready to come home?'

'It's over,' she says with a sigh. 'I'm ready to come home.'

'Good. Then let's go out for dinner and you can tell me all about it.'

He takes her to their local brasserie, where the staff know them well and bring Walt's favourite wine over immediately. Francesca begins to feel her tiredness lift. It's a relief to be out of the emotional turmoil that's been her life for the last month.

Walt looks at her over the bread basket and lifts an eyebrow. 'Now, Frankie. I get the feeling that something's been going on. Is there anything you want to tell me?'

She hesitates. Once, she would have said airily, 'No, nothing. Everything is fine,' and she would have kept all her anger and sadness and secrets to herself. Her legendary self-control. But now she sees how pernicious it's been, leading her into a fantasy world, making her do foolish things, and feel false emotions.

And look at what the lies and silence have done to Dan. His world is shattered. The pieces may never be put back together.

'Well?' Walt asks. 'You're awfully quiet.'

'Yes,' she says. 'I've got a lot to tell you. But it all starts a very long time ago. Twenty years ago, in fact.'

'Sounds like a long story,' he says and smiles at her. 'But we've got all the time you need.'

Chapter Thirty-Five

1960

In the lushness of spring, Julia sometimes wonders if the events of that winter's night were all a dream. There is certainly a dreamlike quality to the way Alice simply vanished. The night the baby was born was the last time she saw her. They went back to the school, Donnie carrying Alice in his arms to the door, and when they made it back to the dorm, they crept into their beds, Julia wondering if they could ever really conceal the fact that Alice had given birth, then she slept soundly for the remaining few hours of the night. When she woke, Alice's bed was empty and Miss Allen said she had been taken ill and was in the san. It had snowed too hard for any cars to get through to them immediately but a few days later, she heard that Alice's mother and stepfather had come and taken her away.

She has not told anyone of the events of the night, but she is haunted by the memory of the birth and the dead baby. She becomes introverted and quiet, concentrating on her work and staying away from the other girls in case they ever ask her what she knows about Alice. All she wants is to get to the end of the year, and back to her parents in Cairo, where she intends to beg to be taken away from Renniston forever.

Before then, though, there are the holidays to get through, and when everyone else leaves the school, she is sent to stay in a cottage on the grounds with a retired schoolmistress who looks after girls not sent home. Julia is the only one this holiday, and she finds, to her surprise, that she treasures the peace and respite of the cottage. Miss Pelham is almost deaf and requires very little of her. There are regular mealtimes and bed is strictly at eight thirty, but the rest of the time is her own.

She spends long hours wandering through the woods at the side of the school, or lying next to hedgerows reading and thinking, but she stays well away from the east side of the school. The builders are still there. The pool is finished now and the gym in its last stages of construction. They will soon be gone, and then she can finally forget what happened.

But there is a reason why she wants them to stay.

She is lying on the soft green grass and staring up at the sky, watching clouds move slowly overhead, their titanic billows shifting and changing as the wind urges them on. Birds dart across her vision, riding the air currents, swooping and diving. Are they swallows or swifts? Or neither?

'Hello.' The soft lilting voice comes gently into her consciousness, and a body lies down nearby.

She turns to him, her sight adjusting from the bright

expanse above to the face close to hers. 'Hello, Donnie.' She smiles. 'You came.'

She wondered if he would get away today. So far he's managed most days, now that the work is winding down and a lot of the men have already returned to Ireland. But he's been able to wangle another week or two, clearing up.

He takes her face in his hands, gazing at her gently. 'I didn't want to miss you. You're all I live for. You know that.'

She closes her eyes as his lips meet hers. It's the most wonderful feeling in the world: his soft, tender kiss, her mouth opening to his, the hot feelings that start in her depths and then engulf her whole body. From the first moment he kissed her, she knew she was lost. It isn't like Alice and Roy, though. It isn't dirty and wrong. It's beautiful and feels like the most natural, the most right thing in the world.

He stumbled on her by mistake right at the start of the holidays, when she was lying on her stomach in her favourite place, lost in a book, and he was out looking for rabbits. At first it was awkward and uncomfortable. When they looked into each other's eyes, they saw the memory of that night, the dead child and the box Donnie made for him. But it also brought them together. They could only speak about it with each other.

'So what happened to your girl?' Donnie asked. 'Is she all right? I haven't seen her since.'

'Nor have I. They took her away.' Julia bit her lip. 'I don't know how to reach her and no one will tell me anything.'

'Poor wee lass. I hope she gets better.'

Without ever agreeing it, they began to meet at the same

time every day, talking idly about anything that crossed their minds. It took a while before she dared to ask about the baby and what had happened to him.

'He's safe enough,' Donnie said. 'I made sure of that. I didn't want him dug up by foxes or anything, so I put him somewhere very safe where he'll never be disturbed. Better if you don't know where.'

Julia's eyes filled with tears. 'Oh, Donnie. It was so sad. So terrible.' She choked on a sob.

'Hey! There, there, it is sad. Children are easily lost. But don't cry, Julia.' He put his hand out to her face.

She gazed up at him. He had never called her Julia before. When their eyes met, clear and half afraid, she knew that he was going to kiss her and she started to shake. He was trembling too, but he moved towards her until, with small advances and retreats, his lips touched hers for that first, amazing time.

'Donnie,' she sighs as they lie together in the warm grass now, insects buzzing above them. 'Oh, Donnie.' His hands caress her, moving under her clothes, his kisses driving her wild for him. Every day, they get a little more adventurous, a little braver in the sating of their mutual need.

If Miss Pelham knew what her charge got up to in the warm meadow with the thin Irish boy, she would have twenty screaming blue fits. But no one knows. It is their secret, this trembling exploration and lush enjoyment of one another.

'Julia,' he whispers in her ear, as her fingers touch him lightly, making him draw in a sharp breath. 'Oh, Julia.'

Chapter Thirty-Six

Olivia knows that nothing will ever make her love her children any less.

The first months away from Dan were a challenge as she came to terms with the knowledge that Bea and Stan were not the result of an anonymous donor, but of the worst confidence trick she can imagine. Her husband fooled her. He allowed her to be implanted with Cheska's fertilised eggs. He let her raise Cheska's children and never told her. She knew that was a fact, but her heart could not accept it.

At first she was scared. In the early hours of her departure, as they headed for the airport, she was deeply afraid of only one thing: that she would stop loving the children. She was terrified that they'd been somehow infected with the disgusting poison of Dan's lies, and she would never be able to look at them in the same way again. She feared that she would only ever see Cheska in them and that would be too much to overcome.

They reached Heathrow, but there was no room on a flight for twenty-four hours so she booked them into an airport hotel and sent the car keys back to Dan in an envelope with nothing else enclosed but the parking ticket and a note of where the car was to be found. He would guess from that where she had gone, if he hadn't already.

The hours in the hotel were spent in their room, Olivia dazed and distracted, playing over and over the events of the last few days, making connections, working things out. She was alternately grief-stricken and furious, stabbed by the betrayal, humiliated, and then energised and released by her intense, almost elemental fury.

But the thing that she most feared never happened. Never for a moment did she see Cheska in the children, even when she stared at them, searching for something that might make her feel that these were no longer her babies.

She sent a silent message to Dan and Cheska: *You can't take them away from me. They'll always be mine.*

When at last they were able to board the flight and she strapped them into their seats, preparing for the long journey across the Atlantic, she felt more than ever what she had first sensed when the babies were born: they didn't belong to anyone. They were themselves. Dan's attempts to control the creation of his children had failed because they couldn't be defined as only their genetic inheritance.

They are who they are.

They all slept on the flight, as they left their old life behind. When the twins woke and asked for Daddy, she told them he was at home. She couldn't bring herself to say they would see him soon, but she knew that if they asked, she would lie, to keep them happy.

Does that make me as bad as he is?

When the twins were safely asleep again, she wept silently as she began to feel the pain that so far had been blessedly numb.

Dan . . . Dan . . . I loved you. We had everything. Why did you destroy it all?

Part of her understood that he must have regretted what he'd done. She remembered how he became colder towards Cheska, how much he didn't want her to visit them. He must have realised that he'd made a massive mistake allowing her into their lives like that. What possessed him to let her donate the eggs? Couldn't he see what a hostage to fortune that was?

But Dan was the arch controller, the man who had to make things go the way he wanted. He must have thought he could keep Cheska quiet. But she wouldn't stay in the background. She moved in.

Olivia saw it all: the reason why Cheska wouldn't leave. Why she couldn't keep her hands off the children. Her desire to join the family.

Perhaps she even hoped that I'd just piss off and leave her to it, with Dan and the twins. Can she really have been that unhinged? Maybe it was her plan to break the news to me all along and see if I scarpered.

She didn't want to think about Cheska, not at all. She shut her resolutely from her mind. Her focus was on Dan and what he had done, and what it meant for all of them. She would work that out before too long. Until then, she had to concentrate on the twins and on getting through every painful hour until the suffering grew easier to bear.

Her mother and sister welcomed her back with open arms, and it was a huge relief to be back in the safety and comfort of the villa. She was able to pass the twins over for a while and begin to recover from her bone-deep exhaustion. And here she was surrounded by sympathy, by people who listened as she rattled off her feelings, venting her sorrow and anger. Her mother hugged her as she wept and sobbed, and wiped her eyes, and held her hand while she spat invective about Dan and Cheska and vowed she would never see either of them again. When her mother reminded her that Dan was the babies' father and he would eventually need to see them, she could rail against the idea even while she knew that it would have to happen in the end.

Her comfort was the twins. Their love was the only thing that could heal the hurt in her heart, and their soft warm bodies soothed and helped her in her grief. They soon forgot to ask for Daddy very much at all, and she began to think that perhaps she could just stay here, nesting in the family home, bringing up her children far from the people who had hurt her.

But there was no escape. The letters from Dan began arriving soon after they did, each one sent registered mail, pages of carefully composed script which she knew had been laboriously crafted and copied. There were emails too, but she filtered them out so she didn't see them. The letters, by turns pleading and threatening, made her feel bludgeoned when she read them. He wouldn't just shut up and let her absorb what had happened, and make her own choices about how to deal with their situation. He demanded that she put an end to his misery of not knowing what was going to happen. He wanted her to jump to his orders, do what he wanted when he wanted it. His apologies were heartfelt but having made them, he evidently felt that the onus was now on her to accept, forgive and move on. If she failed to do so, then he became the wounded party and she was now the wrongdoer.

She read the letters, then put them away, wishing he would be quiet and bide his time. Every letter put off the time when she could bring herself to communicate with him again. Each one made her feel more that he wanted to control her.

But that was what he was always like. I can't believe I didn't see it.

When she tries to imagine a life with Dan, she cannot. Apologies are not enough, promises to be good are not enough. She meant what she said: he has taken their love and killed it stone dead. Although she is still deeply hurt, angry and betrayed, and in mourning for the marriage she thought she had, she feels very little for him on a personal level except for a firm conviction that she can't have him in her life anymore. There is no place for him. She doesn't want to let men like him within a country mile of her. She needs honesty, generosity and emotional truth. When she tries to imagine going back to Dan, she feels physically sick.

No more lies, she tells herself. *I might learn to trust again – but it won't be Dan.*

Olivia is gardening, her back baking in the heat even though it's now early evening. The children are in the kitchen having supper with their cousins, looked after by Olivia's sister. She enjoys taking the odd evening to herself, finding peace in digging and tending the flower beds. There is always plenty to do in a garden and while it might not look like much at first, the work gradually has its effect as the plants flourish, the weeds subside and order comes out of the chaos.

She doesn't hear any footsteps approaching over the lawn so the voice, when it comes, makes her jump and gasp. 'Olivia?'

She turns around, already knowing who it is. 'What the hell are you doing here?' she asks in a freezing voice. 'How did you find us?'

Cheska has her hands out in a gesture of supplication. 'Please, don't be angry. I need to talk to you. This was the only way. I'm sorry to spring out of the blue like this, but really . . . it was the only way.'

'I suppose Dan told you.' Olivia stands up. She is taller than Cheska and at once she feels her dignity return. She strips off her gardening gloves. 'You've got a nerve showing up here. Don't you understand that I never want to see you again? And if you think you're getting your hands on my children, you can forget it. All your money won't buy them, I can promise you that.'

'I don't want that,' Cheska says quickly. She looks older,

451

Olivia notices. Her legendary polish is still there, but a little rougher round the edges as though life has been a bumpier ride lately. 'I just want to apologise. And explain a little.'

'And you've come all this way to do that?' Olivia laughs mirthlessly. 'You must really want to have your say. Why not send an email?'

'I wanted to make sure you understand the spirit I'm talking to you in.'

'How kind. So thoughtful and considerate. You're such a good friend.' Olivia begins to walk towards the villa, wishing the biting sarcasm could help relieve her anger at Cheska, but it doesn't seem to. Her voice grows icier. 'I'm afraid I have no desire to hear what you've got to say. Now will you please leave? You can talk to me via my lawyers.' She heads back towards the white house as though it's her sanctuary from attack.

'Please, Olivia.' Cheska is following her, her voice beseeching. 'I would just like to explain. Just a little. I want you to know that it was nothing to do with you.'

Olivia spins round, her eyes flashing. 'Well, I guess I got that message. Because if you'd thought about me for a moment, perhaps you wouldn't have done it.'

'It was wrong,' Cheska says humbly, dropping her gaze. 'But there were reasons. I suffered too. I lost so much as well. I wish you'd let me tell you.'

Olivia stares at her, and she recalls something she overheard that awful day. Cheska said something that stuck in her mind. What was it? She hears it again in her head. *Don't you know how easy it is to ruin a life when someone loves you? Look what you did to me.* She thinks of Claire's description of Cheska at university, treated like a joke by Dan, ordered to do his bidding. Her agony when he ignored her. She always knew, somewhere deep down, that there was a story like that at the heart of Cheska and Dan's relationship. She has been wondering what happened between them, when they became lovers and how it ended. She knows it must have been before she and Dan met. *Did he really ruin her life? But how?* She feels a tiny buzz of pity for Cheska, and something in her relents. And besides, she wants to know. She senses that Cheska is here to tell the truth.

'All right,' she says slowly. 'We'll walk around the garden and you can explain.'

'Thank you,' Cheska says gratefully. 'Thank you for the chance.'

'Come on then.' She walks off towards the gravel path that will take them around the perimeter of the garden.

Cheska follows, and as they go, she begins her story.

Olivia doesn't know how many times they go around the garden as Cheska tells her what happened right from the start. She loses count after the first half dozen. It is almost dark when Cheska stops. By now they have left the garden and are sitting on the veranda, looking out over the lawn with its riotously coloured flower beds.

There is a silence and then Olivia turns to her and says softly, 'It doesn't excuse it, you know. It doesn't mean you did nothing wrong.'

'I know that, really I do. But you should have known it all

a long time ago. I shouldn't have buried everything away as I did. If I hadn't, perhaps this wouldn't have happened.' Cheska looks more peaceful now that she has shared her story.

Olivia thinks for a moment and then says, 'I'm sorry. About the baby. That was very cruel.'

Cheska says slowly, 'I think that under any circumstances I would probably have had an abortion. We were far too young. Well . . .' She laughs with a touch of sorrow. 'If Dan had wanted to marry me it might have been different. As it was . . . the damage was caused because he pretended none of it had ever happened. And because I couldn't let go of a piece of fantasy. Even when Walt came along, I always thought I'd ended up with second best.'

Olivia is surprised. 'Didn't you love Walt?'

'Oh yes, I did love him. But I couldn't help clinging on to my romantic notions about Dan. I didn't realise how much I need Walt, or what a good man he is, until all of this.'

'Then something good has come out of it,' Olivia says ruefully. 'I suppose we should be glad about that.'

'Well, it was a terrible and traumatic way for things to right themselves,' Cheska says drily, 'but yes, some good things have come out of it. I'm going to restart my career, for one thing. Walt is encouraging me to get back to work. No more charity balls. Proper human rights work, although it won't be as a lawyer, unless I go back to law school. I'm afraid my legal career was another casualty of my stupid infatuation.' She shakes her head. 'I'm going to tell Olympia – and you must tell Bea – never to let herself be derailed by romantic dreams. Sometimes I think they're half the reason why women don't make it to the top as often as men. We let ourselves get distracted by fantasies.'

'Maybe.' Olivia likes the way Cheska talks as though Bea is not her daughter, but entirely Olivia's. 'I think it's a good thing that you're reclaiming your work. Good for you. I'm going to do the same. My work will have to support us a lot more than it has. I've got all sorts of ideas on the go.'

'Well, while we're all waiting for Dan to finish that bloody play . . .' says Cheska jokily.

Olivia laughs. 'What was he doing all that time?'

'I think I might know.' Cheska smiles conspiratorially. 'I went into that study of his one day and the spider solitaire was open on his computer in the middle of a game. So I went to the statistics. He'd played seven thousand games in the last two years.'

'What?' Olivia is disbelieving. 'He spent all that time playing solitaire?'

'Maybe not all the time,' Cheska rejoins. 'I think sometimes he might have played fantasy cricket.'

They both laugh.

Cheska regards her in the twilight, her expression hard to read as the light fades. Then she asks, 'Do you think you'll take him back?'

Olivia slides a glance towards her, wondering if Cheska has in fact been sent by Dan and all this is to be reported back. But then she realises it doesn't much matter either way. 'No,' she says at last. 'I don't think so.'

'No.' Cheska nods. 'I can see why you wouldn't. The trust is gone.'

'Utterly gone. Utterly.' There's a long pause and then Olivia says, 'But you and Walt are fine?'

'Yes. He knows everything. He knew some of it anyway, in a vague way. But not about the baby. He didn't know that.'

'So he knows about . . . the twins?' It's hard for her to say it out loud. A nasty pain stabs her in the gut, and she feels a return of her fury towards Cheska for doing what she did. She breathes slowly and lets it drift away from her.

'Well . . .' Cheska colours slightly. 'I said that I'd allowed myself to get too close to the twins; that I had emotional reasons for feeling connected to them. I don't feel any longer that I'm their mother, and I don't want that to be lodged in Walt's mind. I know I'm not being entirely straight with him. I will be, one day. But there's a lot for him to absorb at the moment, so we're taking it slowly. He knows there's more to the story. He's willing to give me time to tell him. So far, he still seems to want me to stick around so . . .' Cheska smiles again, although this time her lips are a little twisted as though she might be on the brink of tears.

'I'm glad,' Olivia says simply. 'I wouldn't have wanted Dan to spoil any more of your life for you. You deserve to be happy now.' She is surprised to realise that she means it.

'There's lots of lost time to make up,' agrees Cheska. 'But I want you to know how deeply . . . deeply sorry I am about—'

Olivia cuts her off. 'Don't. Let's not talk about it. I have my children and that's all that matters.'

'I know you'll be a wonderful mother,' Cheska says softly. After a moment she says, 'I do love them too. I want you to know that. If you ever need help or anything at all, please come to me. I mean it.'

'I know. But I hope it never comes to that.'

There's another silence as they sit in the deepening blue of the night. Insects flit around them, drawn to the lighted windows behind them. Someone has looked out to see if Olivia is there, and discreetly withdrawn. Cheska says tentatively, 'May I . . . can I see them?'

Olivia turns to her. The hatred she felt for Cheska, all the cold contempt, has gone, but while she has sympathy for her and what she suffered at Dan's hands, there is still the fact of the pain she has caused and the deception she practised. It can't be wiped out just like that. 'No. I'm sorry, Cheska, but no. Not yet. Maybe one day. I'm still working up to letting Dan see them again. I know he'll have to one day. We'll need to start hammering out a divorce and custody and all of that. Maybe after that, you can see them. But not now. I hope you understand.'

She can just make out the sadness in Cheska's eyes. 'Of course,' she says humbly. 'I understand.' She stands up. 'And now I'll be going. Thank you for listening.'

'Thank you for coming.' Olivia realises she means it. She feels a deeper peace than she has for a while. One of the sources of churning despair has been quieted. 'It took guts. Thank you, Cheska.'

She puts out her hand and Cheska takes it with a sorrowful smile. 'I hope we meet again,' she says. 'And . . . will you please kiss the children for me?'

'Yes.' Olivia returns the smile. 'I will.'

Epilogue

Julia Adams gets out of the taxi and walks up to the front gate of Renniston Hall. She stares through the bars at the old place. It's so familiar to her and yet it's been years since she set eyes on it. It's empty now, but she remember the huge door open, with girls running in and out, staff carrying bags and trunks, teachers greeting parents, the Headmistress regally descending the staircase as though she were Queen Elizabeth the First herself.

The taxi driver calls from the car. 'Do you want me to wait, missus?'

'Yes please. I won't be too long. Please wait.' She expects he's wondering what a white-haired old lady is doing visiting this empty old ruin on her own. 'I'm just going to take a look around, but I'll be back.'

The gate is locked, so she starts to walk around the side of the house. She wanders along the eastern side. Out where the playing fields used to be there is a smart housing estate, concealed from the house by a large row of trees. The school must have sold them off before it closed down. Of course it never recovered from the scandal. Julia remembers all the terrible fuss, though it was all so long ago now. A schoolgirl, pregnant by an Irish builder. A precious middle-class English girl, defiled by a working-class Irish navvie! It got into the papers, goodness only knew how, and caused the most awful outcry. The school tried to ride out the storm but the parents took their daughters away in droves. It couldn't survive.

The path towards the back of the house is there, though, slightly muddy, as though there hasn't been much rain, but even so, it hasn't dried out completely. Julia walks down it, a little hesitant in her smart, gold-buckled leather shoes. Ahead of her she sees the empty bulldozers and the abandoned cement mixers of a building site.

'Nothing's changed,' she says out loud, and laughs wryly. *They must be knocking down the old gym and pool. Amazing it lasted so long, really.*

She walks around the empty, half-demolished building, remembering nights when she stood shivering, waiting to let Alice in after her trysts with the builder. For the thousandth time, she wonders what happened to Alice. Even though she asked many times, she never found out. Later in life, when she thought of tracking her down, she found no trace, partly because she had no record of Alice's mother's married name, and the school was long since shut down, its files lost.

She has not been back for many years, not since her parents withdrew her from Renniston and took her to Cairo, where she was taught by a governess for the rest of her education. They said it was for the best, and they were probably right. What, after all, was the alternative? But Renniston Hall cast its influence over her whole life.

She walks around the rear of the Hall, to the broad avenue there. There she takes in the magnificent back of the house, not as showy as the front but still beautiful, even more so in its plain symmetry. It is a Georgian addition to the main house, looking out over what would have once been parkland, and one winter was a caravan park, and is now fields with more housing a mile or so off. She turns to walk along the avenue and notices at once that the hedges have been trimmed into the shapes of animals.

Continuing her walk, she keeps her eyes open for the sight of the old gardener. This journey is because of him. She was watching the television late one night in her flat in London when a documentary about Renniston Hall came on, a late repeat on some secondary channel, but she was gripped at once. Her old school, left to moulder away, and only one man looking after the whole thing. He was interviewed on screen and as soon as he spoke, she knew him, though his accent was softer now than ever after all these years in England.

The sight of him made her old heart pound just as it did all those decades ago.

Julia sees him before he sees her. He is bent over his spade, digging up a border. She stops and stares, her memory replacing his white hair with a dark, oily quiff and the rounded, stooped frame with a skinny rocker's body.

'Donnie?' she calls.

He freezes. Slowly he turns his head to look at her. She

waves and walks towards him. His eyes are faded now and he squints at her. He doesn't recognise her.

Why should he? It's been years. And I'm not a fifteen-year-old schoolgirl anymore. I'm an old woman.

And yet, his face clears as she comes closer, astonishment taking the place of suspicion. 'Is it you?' he asks, his voice trembly as she nears. 'After all this time, is it you?'

'It is. Julia.' She holds out her hand, smiling. It feels more natural than kissing him. After all, they are virtual strangers now. 'Donnie. I knew it was you when I saw you on the television. But they called you William.'

'My first name.' He takes her hand and shakes it, as stunned as if he is shaking hands with the Queen. 'William O'Donnell. They always called me Donnie on the site. What are you doing here?'

'I came to see this old place.' She looks around. 'So many memories. And to see you, of course. I had no idea you were here. I thought you left years ago after . . .' She colours slightly. It isn't easy to talk about what happened.

Donnie digs his spade into the soil. 'I left for a while,' he says brusquely. 'But I came back. I got a job helping the caretaker and stayed on when he left. I couldn't bring myself to leave, you see. Not when I was the only one who knew about the wee lad.'

She nods. She knew too. Not everything, but enough. She nods back towards the topiary animals. 'And you did those?'

'Just my bit of fun. To make it a bit more of a joyful place. More fit for a child.' He frowns at her, shaking his white head. 'I still can't believe it. Will you have a cup of tea?'

'Yes,' she says. 'I would like that very much.'

He takes her to a small cottage on the edge of a patch of woods. 'I used to live in a cottage attached to the house,' he explains, as they go in, 'but it was taken over when the place was bought.'

'Who are the new owners?' she enquires as she follows him in and takes a seat at his small kitchen table while he makes tea.

'Oh, a rich couple, American with an English wife. But they've never lived here. They started all the renovations and then it all just stopped when they found . . .' Donnie stops and stares her right in the eye. 'They found the little chap. I thought he'd never be disturbed. I thought about the forest and the garden but I couldn't stand the idea he'd be dug up by foxes or discovered later. So I thought . . . well, the ground under the swimming pool is safe enough. But once they'd finished it, filled it with water . . . I found I couldn't leave the lad there with no one knowing he was underneath it all. And now they've found him after all.'

'And did you explain?' she asks gently.

'I'm not saying anything!' he says stoutly. 'It's all too long ago. No point now. Let 'em wonder. We did our bit for him. What more could we do?'

She nods. 'Yes. I couldn't forget him either.'

Donnie fixes her with his fierce gaze, his white brows beetling, and brings over two mugs of tea. Then says shortly,

'There's another reason why I came back here. So you'd be able to find me if you needed to.'

She blushes again, harder this time. 'I tried to find you,' she says quickly. 'Many times. But I didn't know your whole name. And I was looking in Ireland.'

'When I was here all the time.' He sits down opposite her. 'So. Are you going to tell me what happened?'

'Well . . .' She knew this was coming. How could it not? It was why she had come here to find him. He deserves the truth as much as anyone. 'Yes. Of course. You know that once the school found out, there was uproar. And somehow it got into the papers. They forced me to tell them who it was. So I gave them a name.' She drops her gaze.

'Roy's,' Donnie supplies.

She nods. 'It was wrong. But I had to protect you. I couldn't let them know that you were the father.' She looks up a little shamefaced. 'What happened to Roy? I never saw his name in the papers.'

'He was back in Ireland by the time it all came out. He was already a sick man – drinking himself to death, he was. He died not much later. They never went after him.'

'Oh.' She takes a sip of her tea. 'I'm sorry for him, in a way. But he did wrong, we both know that.'

'Aye.' William gazes over at her. 'But I did the same.'

'Oh no, it was never the same!' she protests quickly. 'What we had . . . It was never like Roy and Alice, you know that. The poor girl was ill, I think, and he was an exploitative, violent alcoholic. We weren't like that. We were pure and innocent and . . . we loved each other.'

There's a long silence as they both remember the far-off days in the sun-warmed fields and meadows, the afternoons of bliss together when all the world was just the two of them.

At last William speaks, his voice gruff. 'You need to tell me what happened, Julia. I've never known all these years and it's been hard to live with. I've been here alone for so long, just me and the little dead fellow, wondering where my own child is and if they're alive or dead.'

'Oh, Donnie.' She leans across the table and puts her hand on his. She recalls when his hands were smooth and strong. Now they are craggy, veined and spotted. But they are still his hands. 'He's alive. My parents came and took me away, and my mother and I travelled to Switzerland where I had him. They wanted me to give him up, but I wouldn't. He was so beautiful, Donnie, and he looked like you with your black hair and your eyes. I couldn't give him up. And my mother could see that I wouldn't. So . . . we went back to Cairo and she pretended the baby was hers. My parents brought him up as my little brother until he was four years old. I was nearly twenty by then, and my father's posting in Egypt came to an end. We returned to England and Donald became mine again. We said I'd been married and quickly widowed, left with a child.' She shrugs. 'So many lies. We even said that my dead husband was also called Adams, by coincidence. I suppose it's not that uncommon a surname. No one questioned it – at least, not to our faces.'

'Donald?' he whispers.

'As close to Donnie as I could get.' She laughs.

Donnie looks bewildered but moved. 'Donald. It's good. But he's . . . how old is he now?'

'He's in his fifties! He's a married man with children of his own. A good man, Donnie. You'll be proud of him.' She squeezes the hand that still lies beneath hers. 'He knows about you. He wants to meet you. I never married, you see. He never had a father.'

'I've got a son,' whispers Donnie. His faded eyes moisten. 'And grandchildren!'

'Yes. You'll meet them all, if you want to. I wasn't sure if you would.'

'Of course I do,' he says, choked. 'Of course.'

'I'm so pleased,' she answers simply. 'Very, very pleased.'

They are quiet for a moment as they both absorb the joyful gravity of the moment. Then Julia lets go of his hand, drinks her tea and says brightly, 'So tell me, Donnie, is there anyone here now or are you on your own?'

'There's a man on his own who's in my old cottage. He had a wife and children here but they left a few months ago and I haven't seen them since. It's a shame. I miss the little things wandering about, and the wife was a breath of fresh air. But he must have done something to send them on their way. Ever since then, he's moped about on his own, shutting himself up most of the day. He'll be gone soon enough. The place is for sale again.'

'For sale?' echoes Julia. 'Really?'

Donnie nods. 'Someone'll buy it. Some other nuisance who wants me gone, I suppose.'

'I suppose so.' She sits back, resting against the chair. She's a little tired after the journey.

'You never married, you say?' he asks, taking another sip of tea.

'That's right.' She smiles at him. 'When we returned to England, I took up social work, specifically for young and unmarried mothers. Alice . . . her experience . . . everything about that night, it stayed with me. I was lucky – my parents loved me and let me keep the baby. But Alice wasn't. Goodness only knows what happened to her. What you said always stayed with me too – about it taking two to make the baby, but only one being blamed for it. I felt the injustice of it so strongly. It was Alice who was punished, no doubt, but she was just a child. And I thought of all those girls who want their babies but have them taken away. I couldn't bear the pain they suffered, and the hypocrisy of everyone involved. I remembered how right it felt to us when we . . . we made Donald. Why should people and babies be punished for something so natural? In the end I used a legacy from my parents to buy a house as a home for unmarried mothers, or any women who needed help and support in their pregnancy and a place to live afterwards. It's been my life's work. My charity is a large one now. We're still needed, even with the change in attitudes to unmarried mothers. There are still women, abandoned and alone, who need our help.'

'Well, well.' They sit in silence, bound by the lifelong repercussion of that night.

Julia says slowly, 'This is a big place, isn't it? Too big for one family.'

'Too big,' Donnie agrees. 'It needs people.'

'Lots of people. And children. Some babies, perhaps. Some mothers and babies.' She smiles at him. 'Perhaps I should buy it.'

He turns slowly to look at her, a smile creeping over his own face as he understands. 'Yes,' he says, 'mothers and babies. It's a good idea.'

'It's a place where children could be happy, isn't it? There are plenty of children in the cities who might appreciate a place like this to stay in.'

'Yes. There are lots of possibilities.'

'Then I'll think about it.' She smiles again. 'There's no reason why you should stay here alone anymore. Not now we've found each other. So. Now. Tell me about yourself since we last met. I want to hear everything.'

Donnie looks across at her, a smile hovering on his lips, as if he still can't believe she is real. 'Yes. Let's go back and we'll start from then.'

Olivia sits on the veranda gazing out at the bright gardens. The twins are sleeping inside, keeping cool in the afternoon heat underneath the whirring fan in their bedroom. The house is quiet in the hottest part of the day, and Olivia sits alone, a glass of lemonade on the table beside her. She is staring straight ahead but she sees nothing. On her lap is a letter that arrived this morning. It's taken a long time to get to her. Over two years. It was sent to the London flat, where the tenants are not particularly assiduous at sending on post. From there, it went at last to Renniston, where Dan opened it and read it. Then he resealed it and posted it on to Argentina. Now it is, finally, in her hands.

She sits and stares for a long time. Then, at last, she smiles. It is neither joyful nor sarcastic, but a wry twist of the lips that speaks of amusement at life's ironies, and all the human squabbling and fuss that amounts to so little in the end.

After a while she gets up and goes inside, leaving the letter on the bench on the veranda where anyone might read it if they choose. A light breeze wafts it up and across the decking where it catches against the railing and flaps there, the text blurring as it moves.

Dear Mr and Mrs Felbeck

It is with regret that we must inform you of a mix-up in the application of your donated eggs. Your preferred donor was not able to supply us with viable eggs but through administrative error, her label was applied to those of your other specified donor, candidate number 121. Therefore, although you were told that your preferred donor, supplied by you, was the donor of your eggs, it was in fact the other donor whose eggs were implanted.

We apologise sincerely for this mix-up which has only just come to light, but we understand that you have carried a healthy pregnancy to term and therefore we are sure you are currently happy with your circumstances

Please contact us with any queries and we reattach the details of your donor for your information.

Candidate number:	121
Donor type:	Frozen eggs
Race:	Caucasian
Ethnic origin:	French
Eye colour:	Green/brown
Hair colour:	Brown, dark
Skin tone:	Light/fair
Height (cm):	168
Weight (kg):	64
Highest qualification:	MSc Biological Sciences

We remain at your service.
Yours sincerely,

The signature is illegible.

Acknowledgements

With all my grateful thanks to Wayne, Louise, Eloise, Katie, Becky and the marvellous team at Macmillan. They are all wonderful. Special thanks to Gill Paul for her help and advice. Thank you to Lorraine Green for another splendid copy-edit, and my grateful thanks to Nicole Foster for proof-reading. As always, my endless gratitude to my agent Lizzy Kremer and to Harriet Moore.

Thank you to my friends and family for all their help and support, especially to James, Barney and Tabby.